BLACK TAJ

Also by Mohini Kent

The Noon Book of Authentic Indian Cooking (co-author)
Chief Longhooknose and Trader Jim

BLACK TAJ

Mohini Kent

hoperoad : London

HopeRoad Publishing Ltd

P O Box 55544
Exhibition Road
London SW7 2DB

www.hoperoadpublishing.com
First published in 2016 by HopeRoad

ISBN 978-1-908446-45-9
e-ISBN: 978-1-908446-51-0
Printed and bound by T J International Ltd, Padstow, Cornwall, UK

CHAPTER 1

Thoughts crossed Simi's mind like scorpions scuttling across desert sands. Rummaging through her drawers for her bejewelled dragonfly hairpins, she turned the contents out on her bed. She was convinced a goblin lived in her room and tormented her by hiding her things. The items always turned up again but the goblin had a definite shape and size in her head, down to his orange polka-dot shoes. She found the pins hidden under a pile of panties and put them away with her dress in a case. Had she forgotten anything? At the last minute she threw in a pashmina shawl. Not that she planned to use it; it was a balmy February evening, a spring breeze playing among the sweet peas which grew like scented sonnets.

Simi paused at the wall mirror on her way out. Green eyes like gooseberries looked back at her. She had gone a long way back in the genetic chain for those eyes. They were lustrous and thickly lashed with narrow arched brows that gave her a permanent look of surprise. Her thick black hair hung down to her elbows. The rest of her – thin body and narrow hands – had been pegged on almost as an afterthought. Turning away, she ran lightly down the stairs, leaving an untidy heap of clothing on the bed and sandals scattered across the rug. Simi was untidy, but Marriam would soon have the room looking neat as a pin. Her old ayah fussed so!

'I'm leaving!' she called out to her parents in their bedroom. Simi was on her way to the family farmhouse, where her first cousin, Anjora, was getting married that night. Pinky Aunty, the mother of the prospective bride, had chosen the twenty-first of February, 1993, for the wedding because it had been her guru's birth date. Fortuitously, it also happened to be a Sunday, so it suited everyone.

Simi, however, didn't approve of Anjora's bridegroom, or the way her cousin had said 'yes' under pressure from their families after meeting only three times. But what to do? Punjabi families were like that. Still, how could Anjora share her life and bed with a stranger? A few hours from now she would become the freshly-minted Mrs Anand.

Simi stepped on the gas, driving past the dark government secretariat buildings that housed miles of dusty files; she had often heard her father complain about how much it cost in bribes to have files moved from department to department. Elvis Presley's voice filled the car, a sound that she first heard in the womb. Devi, Simi's mother, was an Indian classical singer who belonged to the Elvis Presley generation.

It had been a difficult time for Simi. In the years since she had turned seventeen, her grandmother had become obsessed with marrying her off. Anjora's engagement had made it worse. The old lady would introduce the subject into every conversation. Only last month, on a bitter January morning when the fog had swirled like thick cream and brown owls cried in the gloom, her grandmother had harangued her when they were at the breakfast table.

'You should have gone first!' she said.

'Gone where?' Simi responded, deliberately misunderstanding.

'By now you should be the mother of two children. You're almost twenty-five. Look at Anjora. She's a year younger.' The old lady was proud of Anjora's engagement.

Simi bit sharply into her toast. She knew what was coming next and often made her mother laugh by mimicking the old lady: *'That Simi, she won't let a fly sit on her nose but soon there won't be a boy left to marry.'*

Part two of the standard complaint was: *'And how your mother can sleep with a grown girl in the house unmarried, I don't know!'*

Her grandmother held Simi's mother responsible for everything from burnt food to the state of the nation. The old lady and her daughter – Pinky – would sometimes huddle together and whisper, excluding Devi.

With a child's sensitivity, Simi had been hurt by that, 'Do you really blame Mama?' she asked.

Old Mrs Bhandari raised her eyebrows, which she had lost long ago to the heat of a faulty lamp. They had been replaced by black pencil lines, which the family had learned to use as a barometer of her mood. On bad days they were drawn short and low, like flags at half-mast; on good days they soared like kites in the heavens.

Simi's grandmother continued: 'Listen Miss Hoity-Toity, the Sharma boy's here from England for the wedding. They're good people, Brahmins, and the girl who marries him will be a *kismet-walli*. Good job he's got in England, earns well, I hear he even owns an apartment. What more do you want? Do wear something decent, child!'

Child! 'If he's such a big Brahmin, why should he look at a low-caste girl like me?'

'*Tchh, tchh!* Low-caste? Aren't you ashamed to talk like that? Why, my family were Kshatriyas. Warriors and kings! Your mother's people are Kshatriya too.'

'I hate the caste system,' Simi retorted. Brahmins had a lot to answer for, keeping the low castes under their collective thumb for centuries. 'When I marry it will be to a man, Dadi, not the whole caste, or family!'

'Wrong! One marries a family.'

'So you want me to marry any old pyjama?' Simi sparred with her grandmother out of habit.

'Young Sharma earns lakhs of rupees in London. And these Brahmin-*log* are very clever – sharp brains, generations of learning. You dress like a *mahi*-boy. Look at your jeans!'

'Even the Prime Minister of England wears jeans,' Simi responded.

'*Hunf!* In his own home he can do whatsoever he likes but in *my* home I like to keep up standards.'

To the old lady, managing a family was like the art of war – it was best to subdue the enemy without fighting. Although arthritis had slowed her down, she retained her haughty bearing and left the room before Simi could think of a rejoinder.

The White House belonged to the old lady, widow of Judge Bhandari. Simi had lived there since she was four days old. Her grandfather had bought the house from a white colonial in 1943 when the British Empire was fighting for its life. Justice Bhandari, distinguished, urbane, the first Indian judge to be appointed to Atmapuri's High Court, was a *pucca* chap so the Englishman had sold him the house in a white enclave. The judge then promptly razed and rebuilt it. He had been a good man; the family joke was that hardened criminals would rather face him than his feisty wife. But when she began calling herself *Mrs* Justice Bhandari, her husband soon put a stop to it.

Later that same morning in January, after arguing with her grandmother, Simi was up in her room reading a Marquez novel when suddenly her cousin burst in. Since her engagement, Anjora had been running and jumping a lot – it seemed she could no longer just walk.

'Hullo Simms!' Anjora leapt onto Simi's bed and sat cross-legged on the green velvet quilt. She was a pretty girl who liked to dress in carefully coordinated colours. 'Guess what? Today, I'll choose my wedding suite.'

'No you won't!' said Simi, 'Dadi will choose the jewellery, she always does. And "wedding suite" sounds like a hotel.'

Anjora refused to be put down. 'You should get married, Simms.'

'I'll wait to see the jewellery first!'

'I wish you were coming on honeymoon with me – I mean us. London, Paris, New York. Just imagine! First class too! Isn't it magic?' Anjora sighed contentedly.

A sharp pang of envy shot through Simi. The great European capitals! She had never been outside of India, barring two short family holidays to Hong Kong and Bangkok, which hardly counted. She would have given her right arm to visit the museums and bookshops of London and New York. 'Tony' Anand, Anjora's fiancé, came from a wealthy family but Simi thought him pompous, especially for a twenty-six-year old.

'Why marry him?' she asked abruptly. 'Only hairdressers are called Tony!'

Anjora hesitated. 'What's wrong, Simms? You've been … angry ever since I got engaged.'

Simi loved her cousin and was very concerned that Anjora had made a hasty decision. Was money everything? The two of them had run wild as little girls on Pinky Aunty's farm, sharing dolls and childish secrets. The family farm was large and Pinky Aunty treated it like her personal kingdom. She was immensely proud that her daughter would soon be wed there.

'Nothing, nothing! As long as you're happy. Are you? Anj! You could have had anyone you wanted. You could've married for love.'

'Love? What does that mean? Besides, I didn't have anyone in mind. And neither do you. Or do you? You're very bright, Simms, and pretty – if only you'd go to the beauty parlour and use lipstick or do *something*.'

That was another one of Simi's mutinies against her grandmother. Old Mrs Bhandari wore a strong red shade of lipstick that she applied first thing in the morning, even before bed-tea, leaving a bloody trail on cups all day long. Simi refused to follow her example.

While they were still talking, the jeweller arrived and the girls were called downstairs. In the sitting room, Old Mrs Bhandari huddled with Pinky Aunty as Anjora modelled the pieces. Simi and her mother watched too. Simi distractedly picked up a box containing a set of rubies, a cascade of Burmese gems, and earrings shaped like chandeliers. She put them on, picked up a hand mirror and admired herself.

Turning to her mother, she whispered, 'Do you think this a good price for Tony Anand?'

Her mother bit her lip but her eyes sparkled. The Burmese rubies were magnificent. Simi coveted them, consoling herself with the thought that the red clashed with her green eyes. She secretly desired to fall in love, to find someone to laugh and joke with, to travel and set up home with. But where would she meet such a man? She didn't have a job, so not in the workplace. She lived at home and the family decided most things. She was beginning to despair.

The jeweller next opened a long blue velvet box. Simi gasped. Inside lay a necklace of unsurpassed beauty. Two long rows of large uncut diamonds set in enamel were strung together with ropes of gold. Simi reached for it involuntarily.

The jeweller turned to her. 'Ah! You have an eye,' he exclaimed. 'That's the Jaipur Queen! A necklace fit for a maharani.'

It even had a name! Somehow Simi was not surprised. The necklace was matchless. They watched in silence as Anjora placed it around her neck, lifting her long hair so her mother could fasten the clasp. Anjora wore a beatific expression on her face. Simi knew that Dadi would buy it – it was a matter of family prestige – and couldn't help feeling jealous. When Anjora removed the necklace, Simi put it on and preened. Her mother looked on over her shoulder. Devi was tall, unlike Simi, and broader, like her army general ancestors. An attractive woman with a chiselled Punjabi nose and large brown eyes, she loved her daughter with the passion of a tigress.

'Having second thoughts, Sam? Just think, you could have had this,' Devi murmured. Simi flushed and hastily removed the necklace.

CHAPTER 2

Simi eventually arrived at Pinky Aunty's farm after successfully negotiating Atmapuri's heavy traffic, with cars, cycle-rickshaws, horse-buggies, stray cows and buses all jostling for space on the roads. In 1947, Atmapuri had been a town with a strong cultural tradition, renowned for its musicians, dancers, writers, doctors and courtesans. All that changed with the sudden influx of Hindu refugees from the newly formed state of Pakistan after the partition of India. New colonies mushroomed and now it was a bustling metropolis with Hindus, Muslims and Christians living cheek-by-jowl.

As was traditional, Anjora's wedding had been preceded by week-long celebrations. It had been perfect so far, a typically Punjabi affair with dozens of relatives sated and soused to the gills. On the day of the ceremony, Simi ignored the revelry and immediately sought out her cousin to help her prepare. Anjora had oscillated between smiles and tears all week long, which continued even while Simi massaged her with the turmeric and mustard oil paste used to make brides glow.

'I'm scared. Simms, I just can't do it!' Anjora blurted.

Simi's own misgivings about Anjora's choice of husband now resurfaced. Would it be enough to live in a big house surrounded by lalique and capo-di-monte flowers? Anjora had compromised to please her family. Simi suddenly realised how different they were emotionally, making her even more determined to marry a man she loved with every heartbeat.

She escaped from Anjora's room as soon as she had calmed her cousin and went looking for her mother in the marquee of a thousand guests, large enough to satisfy even Pinky Aunty's vanity. Women wore their husbands' wealth around their necks, while men quaffed fine wine and whisky. Simi spotted her mother in the crowd easily. Majestic in a plum and gold sari, Devi sat on the carpet with her legs folded and sang suggestive Punjabi folk songs. Everyone joined in. Young girls rose to dance like colourful butterflies. Her husband, Gogu, watched proudly, whisky glass in hand. Only two years into their marriage, Devi had stunned Gogu by announcing that she would be singing professionally on radio.

'My father will be apoplectic when he hears,' he had responded after a pause.

'So don't tell him,' Devi had replied. Gogu had spluttered and protested, but Devi calmly explained that she needed a creative outlet. Her only concession to family honour was to adopt the pseudonym Saraswati Devi, a name borrowed from the goddess of the arts. Gogu's parents never discovered the truth, or never mentioned it if they did. To Simi, her mother's voice sounded like the chorus of a thousand song-birds.

Old Mrs Bhandari was watching her daughter-in-law perform with reluctant pride. But when Devi switched from Punjabi folk songs to a *qawwali*, she frowned.

Turning to her old friend, Mrs Puri, who lived next door to the White House, the old woman asked, 'Aren't there enough Hindu songs for her to sing? Why should she sing a *qawwali* of the Ms?' Mrs Puri couldn't bring herself to say 'Muslim.'

Her grandmother's querulous tone carried to Simi, who glared at old Mrs Bhandari, only to be ignored. Simi hated her grandmother's prejudice against Muslims, which was so bad that she couldn't even bring herself to utter the word. On one level she could understand it; the old lady's father had lost much of his wealth when the old country was partitioned, including four sprawling bungalows in Lahore, bank accounts in Peshwar, and his many businesses. Old Mrs Bhandari blamed Mohammad Ali Jinnah for creating a separate state for Muslims. She also blamed Muslims for the millions who died in the massacres of 1947.

In fact, both Hindus and Muslims had killed during the bloody days of the partition, so Simi knew that her grandmother's version of events was not wholly accurate. But Dadi never let facts stand in the way of her convictions.

Simi waited for her mother to finish singing before approaching. 'Anjora's freaking out. I left her sucking lemon drops for her stomach ache,' she said.

Devi sighed. 'I'll go and see her'. But before Devi could leave, Mrs Bhandari waved to them across the marquee.

'Oof! She wants me to meet the Sharma boy,' Simi moaned, mimicking her grandmother's quasi-British accent.

'You must marry *someone*, Sam! Why not meet the Sharma boy?' her mother said encouragingly.

Devi had given her daughter the boyish sobriquet of 'Sam' when she was a toddler in shorts. Later, when a son failed to arrive, the nickname had stuck. But her mother-in-law had never forgiven Devi for not producing a boy to continue the Bhandari name.

Simi rolled her eyes. 'And Micky Malhotra too. She told me he's *America-returned!* God! I hate the American twang!'

Yet her grandmother beckoned her with a crooked finger, impossible to ignore.

Sharma was an earnest young man with an aloof manner and thick glasses that magnified his eyes. He earned a great deal working as a fund manager in London but Simi found him insufferably pretentious. Her grandmother's eyes burned holes into her back as she made an excuse and escaped, so she braced herself for a reckoning later. She would have to think of a good reason to reject Sharma, as well as Malhotra, whom her grandmother had been unable to locate in the crowd.

Waiters thrust trays of food at her but she waved them away and hurried outside to wait with her aunt for the groom's party to arrive.

Pinky Aunty shifted uncomfortably in her high heels. Dressed in her favourite shade of pale pink, from which she derived her nickname, she was freely perspiring. Her husband sported a large turban in pink silk, his bushy eyebrows peeping out like nesting birds.

'How's my baby?' Pinky asked, leaning heavily on Simi's arm to take the weight off her feet.

Simi hesitated. Pinky Aunty would panic if she knew how nervous Anjora was.

'She looks beautiful!' she replied. The bride's mother beamed.

Simi too looked beautiful, a garden sprite in emerald green silk, but she had stubbornly refused to wear jewellery. She felt she deserved the best or nothing at all – and the best jewellery belonged to the bride. Instead Simi wore flowers, like a Kashmiri bride, wrapping strings of braided jasmine around her neck, arms and waist, with more threaded through her hair and piled on top of her head, adding inches to her height. But her love of gemstones made it impossible to resist wearing a pair of diamond solitaire earrings borrowed from her mother.

The groom's party finally appeared at the end of the lane with a fanfare of drums and a blaze of gaslight, led by a brass band of thin men in red uniforms with golden epaulettes, giving them the air of military dictators. The groom rode a white

steed and his friends danced *bhangra* around him. A curtain of
rosebuds hung from Tony's turban – *no bad thing*, Simi thought
spitefully, *because he's not handsome.* But Pinky Aunty thought him
the perfect son-in-law.

As guests gathered to watch the groom's approach, it started
to feel like a spirit was haunting the wedding, filling minds
with vague romantic longings and causing saris to slip from
women's shoulders as they danced. An old crow, roused from
his slumbers in a nearby lychee tree, cackled to see humans flap
their arms like birds.

Suddenly Pinky Aunty gripped Simi's arm and whispered,
'*Hai Ram*, I completely forgot! The necklace, it's still in the safe
in my room! Quick!'

The two women hurried back into the house. Simi was glad
to get away from the noise because a week of pre-wedding
merriment had left her weary. They went to Pinky Aunty's
bedroom, opposite Anjora's, to retrieve the Jaipur Queen. Simi
and Pinky Aunty then went into Anjora's room and placed the
necklace around her neck. An audience of around a dozen
young girls, an assortment of Anjora's cousins and friends, *ooh-
ed* and *aah-ed* with envious delight.

Anjora forgot her fears as her mother offered unnecessary
instructions to chivvy them along, 'They're almost at the
door! Anjoo must be ready – my darling girl, such a beautiful
bride!'

Pinky continued to fuss over her daughter, placing a black
spot behind Anjora's ear to ward off the evil eye. But then
they heard a commotion outside and three masked men ran in
waving guns, eyes glittering through the narrow slits of their
balaclavas. Everyone froze. One of the men pointed a pistol
at Simi's stomach. She panicked and felt a strong urge to pee,
but remained quiet. Simi found out later that they had entered

unseen through the back door, avoiding the party on the front lawn.

The leader was built like an ox. Simi shivered at the sight of his massive shoulders, rippling muscles and arms like hewn tree trunks, which seemed vaguely familiar. She unconsciously dug her nails into Pinky Aunty's flesh. The eerie silence was broken by Pinky Aunty's terrified scream, after which the other girls screeched hysterically too.

'Silence!' a dacoit snarled. It felt unreal, as though they were in a movie. 'Don't move.'

Simi, Pinky Aunty, Anjora and the other girls stood still as statues, though their frantic eyes darted in every direction. Nothing in life had prepared them for dacoits.

One of the bandits stepped into the centre of the room, whipped out a gunny sack and shouted, 'Your jewellery. In here. Quick!'

The guttural command panicked Simi further. She wanted to run, to hide, to be safe ... but where? The bandit built like an ox had blocked the door. The other exit was bolted. Instinct made her furtively remove the pins from her hair, which tumbled down around her cheeks and concealed her earrings. She was partially hidden by Pinky Aunty, so nobody noticed. If only she could turn back the clock and hide Anjora's necklace too. If only it was still in the safe ...

Pinky Aunty slumped against her, her head rolling from side to side. She was moaning: *'No! No! No! Govinda, protect us! Om namo bhagvate ... '*

Simi heard the dacoit with the gunny swear above her aunt's prayer: *'Om namo bhagvate.'* Still no one moved.

'Madar!' A second man rushed forward and stuck his gun under a girl's neckpiece. Snivelling with terror, she removed it. One necklace in the sack, he moved on to the next girl, jabbing

his gun into her waist. She jumped at the cold touch of metal and collapsed to the floor. The other girls hastily removed their jewellery with shaking hands, throwing their gold into the sack as though it burnt their fingers. Rupa, only eighteen, was hysterical and the panicking teen hurled her jewellery at the wall instead of dropping it into the sack. The dacoit gave her a hard slap and sent her reeling.

Simi gritted her teeth. *How dare he! How dare he rob us and beat us!* Pinky Aunty had by now put her entire weight on Simi and kept muttering: *'Om namo bhagvate Vaasudevaya; Om namo bhagvate ... '*

What should I do? Simi asked herself. Her mind was full of wild fantasies about being rescued by her father, by the police or the army. Perhaps *she* could rescue everyone! Brave thoughts whirled around her head but she had never been so terrified in her life. Her legs felt wobbly and it required a Herculean effort just to keep Pinky Aunty from falling.

The Ox, who had remained motionless at the door, now walked up to the bride. Anjora stared at him with terrified eyes. He was looking at her necklace as he stretched out his hand. Anjora screamed. Pinky Aunty stumbled forward but Simi held her back.

'Shhh!' The Ox placed a finger to his lips to quiet Anjora, a childish gesture that suddenly seemed menacing. Anjora's voice died in her throat. The man reached out and removed her necklace. Holding it in the palm of his hand, he examined it before stuffing it into his pocket. They watched him in silence. Turning on his heel, he uttered a rasping command and his henchmen ran out behind him. It was all over in minutes. Nobody stirred. The men were gone, *but suppose they waited outside the door?*

Pinky Aunty kept praying under her breath: *'Om namo bhagvate ... '*

'*Mummeee!*' Anjora screamed, breaking the spell.

Mother and daughter clung to one another, sobbing. Simi thought, irrelevantly, *Anj's make-up will be ruined*. She caught her own reflection in the mirror and was mildly surprised. Somehow she expected to look different after the trauma, but nothing had changed. She went to Rupa, who had not yet recovered from the slap. She had an ugly bruise on her left cheek.

Then Simi noticed Marriam, heaped against the wall. *Marriam?* She hadn't been in the room earlier. Or had she? It was all a confused blur. Simi could no longer tell what was what. She ran to Marriam and tried to lift her, but the maid cried out in pain.

'What's wrong?' Simi asked.

'It's here, Simi*baby*. Oh Allah!' Marriam grimaced in pain, indicating her left arm.

Simi made her comfortable against the wall. 'I'll get help,' she said. She approached the exit tentatively, poking her head round the door to ensure the bandits had gone.

The gaiety of the wedding party grated on Simi's nerves when she returned to the marquee. It too seemed unreal, as unreal as the burglary. She unscrewed her mother's diamond solitaires with shaking hands and clenched them tightly in her sweaty right palm. She spotted her mother and gestured to her.

Alarmed by her daughter's distraught countenance, Devi hurried forward. 'What is it, Sam?'

Without a word, Simi pulled her mother out of the marquee and thrust the diamond earrings into her hand.

'What's this?' Devi asked in surprise, looking down. 'What's *happened?*'

'We've been robbed,' Simi said, her voice wobbling before she burst into tears. Devi looked nonplussed.

Simi swallowed hard and wiped her nose with the back of her hand.

'We've been robbed, Mama. Of everything. Even Anj's lovely ... ' but she could not bring herself to say the words. Instead she implored her mother to hurry, saying she would find her father.

With a worried frown, Devi turned and bustled into the house. Simi covered her wet cheeks with a curtain of hair, then went looking for Gogu. The party was a blur of noise and colour through her unshed tears, but she managed to spot her father, a tubby, genial man with a big mole on his left cheek, in the midst of a circle of friends. Gogu was the life and soul of the party wherever he went. She waved to him and he excused himself. She then explained the situation as best as she could and urged him to help, starting to feel a little better. Being close to her father always calmed Simi down.

'The bounders! Attacking little girls! That's not on,' Gogu fumed. 'I'd give them a run for their money by George – if I'd only been there. Dash it all, Sam, are you hurt?'

She assured him that she was not but he took some convincing before he would leave. She wished he wouldn't say things like 'by George!' and (his favourite) 'by Jove!' Archaic expressions like those made him sound like something the British left lying forgotten in the club when they marched out of India in 1947.

Alone now, Simi looked around at the party, then ran towards the rear exit of the marquee. But her path was barred by a young man. He was very tall. His hair glowed red in the overhead light and his teeth were white against his lips.

'Hi! Great party, isn't it?' he said. She instantly hated the American edge to his accent. 'I missed that in New York,' he continued, 'the music, the colour, families. That's how weddings should be, don't you agree?'

She shook her head and looked longingly at the exit a couple of yards away. She suddenly couldn't stand these people, who had no idea of the trauma she had just endured. She could feel her self-control slipping. *Who's this presumptuous guy? Micky Malhotra?* Had to be. Her grandmother must have sent him looking for her.

'Excuse me,' she muttered, pushing past him. She could no longer rein in her tears. She blundered into the quiet garden, making her way to a stout tamarind tree which she and Anjora had climbed as children. The lizards, chameleons and snakes that hid like secrets in the dark fled at her approach. The wispy fronds of the tamarind tree brushed her face as she threw herself down on the grass.

He had followed her. Kneeling beside her, he raised her up but she turned away. Nevertheless, he helped her to a wrought iron bench, spreading out his hanky for her to sit on.

'What's wrong?' he asked, sitting down beside her. 'I'm a doctor. You can tell me.'

Doctor? No one had told her that Micky Malhotra was a doctor.

'What sort of doctor are you?' she snivelled.

He chuckled. 'Hmmm ... I mainly treat beautiful girls in distress. So tell me, what's wrong?'

Beautiful? Despite herself, she was pleased with his compliment.

'What's *wrong*?' she repeated with a bitter laugh. 'Oh nothing, nothing! Only, Anj is hysterical, the Jaipur Queen's gone and Pinky Aunty ... '

The whole story tumbled out. It was a relief to talk, but that brought the nightmare flooding back and she broke down. He put an arm around her and she buried her head on his shoulder, shivering and sobbing. She could smell his masculine scent as he stroked her head. Eventually she stopped and looked up at the spring moon, which dissolved in silver ribbons in her tears. He waited quietly as she rose and wandered over to the flowerbed.

She felt drained and mortified. 'You don't know what this means for my family,' she said sadly, shredding her jasmine bracelet with nervous fingers.

He had initially marked her down as a pampered girl suffering hysterics, but realised now he had misjudged. 'You poor thing!' he replied, trying to comfort her. 'And the bride? Your sister?'

'My cousin – she's *like* a sister. And I did nothing. I wanted to stop them but didn't … they even took Anjora's necklace.' Simi paused. *I should go back inside*, she thought, *Anj might need me.*

The doctor gave her a searching look. 'It's been a nasty experience. Don't underestimate the fright you've suffered – take care of yourself, won't you?'

Talking to him had helped, but Simi was embarrassed at revealing all to a stranger. She walked away quickly. He watched her go, trailing her long dupatta on the grass, but stayed outside to smoke.

Inside, Old Mrs Bhandari had instructed her family that no one was to be told anything. Anjora had to be married at the auspicious hour or it would bode ill. She was stern with Pinky, telling her to be strong for her daughter's sake. Sympathy could come later. Following her lead, they rallied and prepared to face the guests.

Anjora leaned heavily on her cousin's arm as Simi led her to the wedding mandap. The bride's face was veiled, concealing her swollen eyes. The wedding procession of glum girls, minus their jewellery, made the guests curious. But it was only when they saw Pinky Aunty's puffy, unsmiling face that the whispers began. The family did their best to conceal the theft, but that was impossible in Atmapuri's tight-knit Punjabi community.

And Simi's father couldn't dissemble for the life of him. When confronted by a friend about the sombre bridal procession, Gogu confessed. The news electrified the party. Mrs Anand, the groom's mother, was offended that she had not been personally informed by the Bhandaris, forever prejudicing her against Anjora.

The Vedic marriage rites were long, the sacred fire smoky. Anjora clung desperately to Simi's arm, her other hand resting limply in the palm of a groom she scarcely knew. The priest ended with an excruciatingly long lecture on how to be a good Hindu wife. It was impossible to stem his tide; some of his most influential clients were present and moralising was good for business.

Pinky Aunty's carefully selected menu was a success. The delicious aroma of lamb seekh kebabs cooking over charcoal fires and fresh tandoori paratha wafted over tables laden with Murg Mumtaz chicken in almond gravy, venison in spicy sauce, Goan fish curry and vegetarian kebabs, amongst a dozen other dishes. But Pinky Aunty no longer cared whether or not the food was served hot and Simi felt that she would choke if she ate anything. She stuck by her cousin's side the entire evening and only once saw the doctor across the room. It didn't matter. Right now, nothing mattered.

At the end of the evening, Anjora left in her wedding dress with her new husband, whose Mercedes had been covered with strings of fragrant white jasmine and red Indian roses. She wept as she said goodbye to her family and friends. All brides weep, but not like this. The shock of the robbery had been too much. They drove off soon after midnight, leaving behind the sad remains of the party.

CHAPTER 3

Dr Imran Khan Chaudhry was jogging in Sultan Gardens, his breath condensing in the crisp morning air and hanging like speech bubbles in cartoons. He liked the park because it reminded him of New York's Central Park.

After nine years in Manhattan he had returned home, drawn back by a compulsion he couldn't explain to his Indian friends in New York. *Professional suicide*, they cried. His American girlfriend, Jenny, had been unforgiving and it ended bitterly. Yet another ending. There had been too many in his thirty years. But Jenny was now just a fading memory which he occasionally called upon, perhaps because no girl had replaced her.

In Atmapuri it was difficult to even meet girls, let alone get a date. That was one of the things he had forgotten about India. That and the September heat that had cornered him like a bailiff when his flight touched down in Delhi. Even today, at the end of February, at seven in the morning, he was perspiring as he jogged down the grassy verge. He wiped his temples with his wrist-band but the sweat continued to trickle into his clipped moustache. His colourful T-shirt and Bermuda shorts suited his tall, lithe figure and long limbs.

He passed a couple he knew but merely raised his hand and ran on, his mind dwelling on the difficult meeting ahead, scheduled for ten at the Atmapuri Municipal Corporation. It was time to return home and prepare.

'Hudson!' he yelled and whistled.

The bushes nearby shook and parted to reveal a hefty Alsatian, who looked at him with one ear cocked.

'Heel!' Imran commanded. The dog emerged reluctantly and they trotted off together to the car. Hudson leapt into the back and settled down on his blanket with a contented sigh. Imran got into the driver's seat and they set off home.

Imran had loved the house the minute he saw it; a colonial-style bungalow with spacious rooms and a deep verandah, located in the unfashionable South side of the city. It had taken Imran's old school friend, Tony Anand, over a year to renovate it. Now, with new wooden floors, uncluttered spaces and three layers of Roman blinds on every window, it had the feel of Imran's old Manhattan apartment.

While growing up, Imran had lived with his adoptive parents, Dr Chaudhry Snr and Mrs Kamala Chaudhry. As a little boy, Imran had sensed that Mrs Chaudhry, a devout Hindu woman, had been uncomfortable with the Muslim child her husband had brought home. But she was a maternal sort and had never attempted to convert him. Currently on pilgrimage to Vaishno Devi, they had their own house, but Imran had moved into the bungalow after his return from America.

Imran emerged from the shower with drops of water glistening on his red-flecked brown hair, dressed quickly, left his home and climbed into his car. A glance at the back seat confirmed that his Nepalese servant, Bahadur, hadn't forgotten his medical bag, despite the dour Nepalese cook ignoring most of his instructions. Hudson gazed longingly as Imran drove off, but didn't budge from the verandah.

BLACK TAJ

The mandarins Imran was going to meet were masters of all they surveyed, though notionally they were public servants. He wore one of his sharpest suits for the occasion, along with a pair of heavy black-rimmed spectacles to lend him gravitas. He had brought a Public Interest Litigation against the municipality when he got back from America, seeing Atmapuri's shanties as though for the first time. *Had there been so many when he left?*

Encountering them again, his professional eye noted the open sewers, the flies and mosquitoes, and the hard dry shit by the roadside that crumbled into dust and blew into his face. The poorest people still cooked on buffalo dung pats, the acrid smell of their fires lingering in his nostrils. And when the monsoon lashed Atmapuri with high winds things just got worse. Last year, the streets had been transformed into muddy streams; the wealthy were safe but the poor could never get dry.

Dr Chaudhry had battled typhus and dysentery before, but a new peril had been posed by rat piss contaminating water and causing paralysis. Hundreds had died and the city was gripped by hysteria until the rain stopped, when everyone conveniently forgot about the problem. Perhaps that's why he'd returned from America – to remind them. It was Dr Chaudhry's dream to inoculate the entire population against typhoid and cholera. But that was only possible if the Atmapuri Municipal Corporation cooperated.

The growing lawlessness of the city also concerned him. He knew that people scoffed behind his back when he raised the issue, jeering that he should stick to his 'doctoring'. But it was he, not they, who had to treat traumatised teenage rape victims and watch tears roll down the leathery cheeks of mothers whose boys had died of meningitis. And the theft at Tony Anand's wedding was still fresh in his mind. He wondered how the green-eyed girl who had cried on his shoulder now fared.

Would the thieves ever be caught? Not likely, if precedent was anything to go by.

His lawyer, who had helped file the Public Interest Litigation petition, met him outside the municipality's dusty gothic building, built by the British. Spectators filled the big hall inside. Mr Arora, the head of the municipality, sat with his fellow officials behind a long table. Government employees were unused to this kind of scrutiny and Imran smiled to note a nervous tic in Mr Arora's right eye.

'Gentlemen we are sitting on a time bomb!' Dr Imran Chaudhry began when invited to speak. 'Question is – what will we do about it? Wait for it to explode? Or defuse it? Untreated sewage is like a cancer growing in the belly of our city. And the monsoon floods will spread it even further.'

The Atmauri Municiple Corporation (AMC) should take responsibility, he argued. Unscrupulous businessmen used an arcane law to bury industrial effluent underground and it was seeping into the water supply. In shanty towns, where they shared communal taps, people stored polluted water in cooking pans and clay pots that grew moss and became nurseries for mosquito larvae. He had come armed with a report on soil samples collected from four points along the riverbank. All clearly showed signs of contamination.

'Not true! Not true! These claims are false!' Mr Arora roared back.

'Sir! Dozens died last year. It's still cold but the summer rains will bring catastrophe! Why not check the industrialists? Fine them, put them in jail, do something!'

Imran knew that money had changed hands – the industrialists believed in finding a man's price and paying it. Atmapuri's bureaucrats were rumoured to own strings of properties and their children often studied abroad at expensive universities.

The former head of the AMC now lived in a six hundred acre dairy farm, boasting that his herds of Jersey cows were a gift from the Queen of England.

Mr Arora gave him a bland smile. 'Sir! You ask me to harass respectable men doing lawful business?'

'No! It's their *unlawful* acts that worry me!' Imran replied. Turning to the public in the hall, he waved the papers in his hand. 'You want proof? Here's the proof! Water. Clean drinking water is a basic human right but our taps deliver death. Don't think you're safe because you can afford expensive filter systems. If an epidemic hits us – and it will! – it'll sweep right through our city. Death can't tell the difference between rich and poor.' Turning back to Mr Arora, he cried, 'And you think you're secure sitting in this temple of yours?'

'And you think you're the one to save this city?' Mr Arora sneered.

'No. *You* are. And you *will* save this city. You want the truth? Here it is!' Furious, Imran flung the papers at him. They landed with a thud on the desk.

'How dare you, sir!' Mr Arora spluttered, jumping up.

'No, sir, it's you who dares to play with peoples' lives. What'll it take? How many more must die before we act?' Imran shouted.

He handed a copy of the report to an attending journalist, telling him, 'By printing this you'll do a great service to your city.'

There was uproar, with people shouting, gesticulating and crowding around Imran. He leaned across the table, his face inches away from Arora. 'People will burn your effigy if the worst happens.' Mr Arora sank back into his chair.

Afterwards, in his car, Imran did a deep breathing exercise – learnt from a mindfulness course he had attended in Manhattan – to calm himself before facing the patients at his surgery.

Khuda! He felt sure he had won that round – Mr Arora would be unable to deny the contents of the report once it had been made public – but he was also acquiring an unsavoury reputation as a meddler. Sometimes, when a dark mood descended upon him, he wondered if they were right. But what else could he do in the face of injustice?

The poet Mevlana Rumi had once written: *Start a big foolish project, like Noah!* Imran clung to this idea. Thinking of Rumi reminded Imran of his father, who read him Sufi poetry in Farsi when he was a child. In America, Imran had re-discovered Jalaluddin Rumi in English translation. *Start a big foolish project, like Noah!* If only he were not so alone. He had no parents or siblings. And Atmapuri's more traditional Hindu families would not invite him, a Muslim, to their homes. The irony was that the Muslim priest was also suspicious of him because he never attended mosque and worked with a Hindu doctor. He even kept a dog, an unclean animal! Imran loved Hudson the faithful, who was more loyal to him than the priest had ever been.

CHAPTER 4

Simi only spoke to Anjora once during her month-long European honeymoon, while her cousin was in London. Simi sensed Anjora was not happy, but the distance made it impossible to tell, especially since she suspected that Tony had been in the room. Anjora had left her relatives with bittersweet memories of the wedding. Pinky Aunty ached with fright and loneliness; every inch of her farmhouse reminded her of Anjora, while the thieves haunted her dreams and made her days a trial. She could often be found brewing tea in the middle of the night, wandering through her rooms in an embroidered pink nightie.

Simi too suffered from nightmares. As she slept, three bloated, red men chased her with giant knives and forks, wanting to eat her up. Waking up in a sweat, she would switch on the bedside lamp and rub her stomach where it hurt. She'd had a stomach ache ever since that day. The weather had changed abruptly on the eighth of March, when the colourful festival of Holi is celebrated as the sun starts moving into the equinox. One day it was spring, the next it was summer. The growing heat made it even harder to sleep.

Simi's mind relived the past over and over, bleeding with regret that she had not been brave enough to foil the robbers. But her constant stomach cramps reminded her of the fear she had experienced. Life after the wedding had become fraught. Her grandmother was deeply upset, both by the financial loss and by Pinky Aunty's anguish. They had neglected to insure Anjora's new necklace because they never imagined it would be stolen before the wedding. Anjora's father had jumped through the hoops of lodging a report with the police, but the family placed little faith in law enforcement. The loss made Old Mrs Bhandari's arthritis flare up and the pain made her tetchy. She criticised Devi for Simi's refusal to accept a suitable groom even more than usual.

'What about Damyanti's son?' she asked. 'She mentioned Ashok the other day. Reliable family and they're our neighbours – there's nothing we don't know about them.'

'And nothing *they* don't know about *us!*' Simi commented tartly when her mother relayed the conversation.

That irritated Devi. 'Is nobody good enough for you, Sam? Why can't you settle down like other girls?'

'Marry the boy next door? Mrs Puri's darling!' *And live right next to her grandmother for the rest of her days?* 'You make me feel like a stale cake.'

'You're the giddy limit, Sam!'

'Don't be mad, Mama. What does Ashok Puri do except play golf?'

Devi smiled, despite herself. 'You should have been a lawyer like your grandfather.'

Simi changed the subject. 'It's Marriam we should worry about.'

The maid had been the worst casualty of the theft. Her left arm was fractured in two places and the plaster cast was uncomfortable, but that was nothing compared to Old Mrs Bhandari all but accusing her of being complicit in the theft. Marriam protested that she had opened the door when she heard a knock, expecting it to be a servant who had been locked out. She was shocked when the thieves burst in and propelled her into Anjora's room ahead of them. Old Mrs Bhandari, in her self-appointed role of nasty magistrate, asked what she was doing there in the first place, implying that she was there to guide the thieves to Anjora's room. Intimidated, Marriam failed to point out that Anjora's room was hard to miss because of the voices emanating from within.

Simi was accustomed to her grandmother's prejudice against Muslims, because of which Marriam was barred from entering her room or handling her things. Initially, Dadi had even prohibited the maid from setting foot in the kitchen, but that had changed some years back. Marriam had been with them for twenty-three years and Simi could not bear to watch her receive such a drubbing. So when Dadi threatened to sack Marriam, Simi cried, 'If she goes, I go!' That, at least, proved a temporary solution.

Simi attempted to make it up to Marriam in other ways too, one day insisting upon giving the maid a lift home. It was only when she asked for directions she realised she had no idea how Marriam lived when she wasn't at work. Ashamed at this oversight, she resolved to take more interest in her old ayah.

Guided by Marriam, Simi drove to Nawabganj, a shanty town about two miles from the White House. The roads got narrower as they approached. Eventually, she had to park the car a short distance from their destination, since it was impossible to drive into the slum.

'How about some tea, Marriam?' she asked the maid as they walked down the higgledy-piggledy lanes of the sprawling settlement. Through open doors Simi saw women squatting on the ground, cooking dinner over smoky fires and staring back at her. Marriam introduced her so proudly that Simi felt like royalty.

The interior of Marriam's home was just like her – neat and spare. Highly polished steel utensils shone like mirrors. Simi passed through the low doorway into a room with a barred window, a single bed and a cooking stove in the corner, with a wall cupboard above. Through a makeshift curtain made from an old sari, she glimpsed a second room. The place dismayed her but she perched on the bed, forcing herself to be cheerful. It was so tiny and threadbare. What did Marriam feel, working in a rich, elegant home, then returning to this dump at night? Was she jealous? She looked at the maid's wrinkled face, three green dots tattooed on her chin, her ear lobes pierced with a series of silver earrings, and wondered whether she resented the Bhandaris. Simi wouldn't blame her if she did.

Simi pointed to a black-and-white photograph hanging on the wall in an old-fashioned frame with a garland of paper flowers. It was a picture of an unsmiling young man.

'Who's that?' she asked.

Marriam said it was her son's father, who died years ago. Convention forbade her from taking his name.

Simi knew Marriam's son, Ahmed, but had not seen him recently. When he was small, Ahmed had sometimes accompanied his mother to work. Simi remembered him as a sullen boy. She felt guilty again that she'd taken no interest in the maid's life. *But that will change, it'll be different now.*

With one hand, Marriam brewed strong milky tea with a knot of ginger in it. Simi poured it into a thick white china cup for herself and a steel tumbler for Marriam. Even at the White House, the maid used a steel tumbler, cradling it in her dupatta. Marriam sat down on a wooden stool, the only other furniture in the room. It was growing dark outside and the aroma of meals being cooked wafted in through the open door. A yelping puppy ran by as they talked, chased by two grubby cherubs with tousled hair.

'When Simi*baby* you marry, I'll take care of your babies as I took care of you,' Marriam beamed.

Simi chortled. Marriam persisted in calling her 'baby' even though she was now in her mid-twenties. Before she could reply, a man appeared, hesitating with his hand on the door jamb. He looked like a mountain idol, a figure to be worshipped in a smoky Himalayan hut. His skin was like oiled teak, while his large black eyes glowed like burning coal. His shoulders filled the doorway. Rigorous workouts at the wrestling ground had given him the physique of a bull. Simi noted the rakish red and white polka dot kerchief around his neck. He also wore a cheap leopard-skin print jacket and tight jeans, the sort worn by young loafers who whistled at girls on the streets.

Marriam noticed Simi's startled look. 'My Ahmudi,' she explained, turning to the man. 'Come, son. It's only Simi*baby* from the big house'.

Simi and Ahmed stared at one another for an instant before he dropped his gaze. His guttural 'Salaam!' – spoken with his right hand against his heart – was addressed to the floor and he entered reluctantly.

'Tea, Ahmudi?' Marriam jumped up from her stool but he shook his head. Muttering something, he beat a hasty retreat.

Simi sipped her tea silently. Why should Ahmed run away from her, bolting like a wary animal?

'What does he do, Marriam?' she asked.

Marriam sighed with a world of motherly concern. 'It's been very hard, Simi*baby*. He never had his father's hand on his head …'

'What exactly happened to— ?' Simi was almost sure that Marriam's husband had been called Behram but could not risk a name.

Marriam stared unseeingly at her husband's photo. He failed to return one night, she explained. The next morning they carried him home dripping wet. She took one look and knew he was dead. They found him floating face down in the river. Some said that he was murdered by the Don's men over a debt; others said he fell into the water, drunk. Marriam had screamed when she heard the rumours. Behram never drank. Never. It was against Islam. And she didn't know of any overwhelming debts. They had buried him in the Muslim graveyard before sundown, leaving her alone with the boy.

Father and son had barely known each other. They sent Ahmed to live with his grandparents when he was about five, unable to handle their jobs and raising a child at the same time. When he came to live with them again at eleven years old he was a stranger. Two years later his father was dead. And Marriam was left with the responsibility of raising a moody teenager, unable to apply a firm hand.

'Not a single day passes, Simi*baby*, that I don't remember him,' she concluded. 'When we first married, he talked poetry like a ... a poet at *Badshah Akbar's durbar!* His father was the village teacher. He taught him – and my Ahmudi too. My Ahmudi's clever – see his books.' She pointed proudly to a small pile of books stacked in the alcove.

Marriam smiled at the memory of her late husband, but it faded quickly.

'Later he forgot poetry-shoetry,' she said. 'And I'm not a reader-writer. In this city, poor people like us know our place.'

Simi left feeling depressed and angry with herself. Why had she neglected Marriam for so long? She had never seen the woman behind the maid.

At least six people accompanied her back to the car, women who had helped Marriam with the shopping and cooking while her arm was in a sling. Marriam's friends idolised Simi because of what she meant to Marriam. Simi waved to them as she switched on the car headlights, before driving back into the city.

Her mind soon returned to Ahmed. A coarse young man who read books. She knew that her parents had paid for some of his schooling, but had taken no interest until now. Something about his massive frame niggled her but she shrugged it off and concentrated on the heavy traffic.

Ahmed was waiting at home when Marriam returned from seeing off Simi. His mother shrank back when he scowled at her. What she really wanted was to place her hand on his brow and smooth away the tension etched across his forehead, as she had done when he was little. But Ahmed was a grown man. His hands were weapons honed by years of body-building in the *akhadas*.

She cast her mind back a dozen years to his first childish tantrum. Soon after his return from the village, he had smashed some marigold pots and laughed when Marriam had scolded him. His father never knew this side of their son. She had concealed it from him. Even when Ahmed threw a knife at his mother after being served lentils instead of chicken curry, Marriam had kept it to herself. The blade had missed her by some distance and she convinced herself that he never meant to harm her.

'*Beta*, that was Simi*baby* and you didn't even talk. They're good people, like family,' she chided him gently.

'*Family?* Not *my* family. Living in big houses, driving big big cars, every day eating meat, chicken … *and* we..?' he glanced contemptuously around the room. He was intensely jealous of the rich.

'After your *abba* became beloved of Allah, it was Devi*bibi* who helped us. Paying your school bills. Allah doesn't like ingratitude, *beta.*'

He turned on her with blazing eyes. 'Allah? Ammi, Allah's on *my* side. He doesn't belong to the rich. And those people are mere *kaffirs*. The doors of paradise will never open to them.'

Marriam pulled her white cotton dupatta tighter around her hunched shoulders. She no longer understood him. His rage had intensified after his father's death. Ahmed had broken her tooth one day when he was about fifteen, striking her with the back of his arm. It was like being hit by an iron bar. The pain was excruciating, though not worse than the anguish of being beaten by her son. But he always repented afterwards, so she made excuses for him. She hid her bruises and didn't tell a soul – except for the holy man, the baba. She loved Ahmed – and knew that he loved her.

But Ahmed scorned her loyalty and gratitude to the family, saying that she was old-fashioned and only money talked these days. She was afraid that, in his hurry to get rich quick, he would end up in jail. She'd heard that the police beat poor men to within an inch of their lives in prison. She silently prayed every day: *Allah! Keep Ahmudi safe!*

If only he would take up a decent job so that she could find a bride for him. Marriam had been married at twelve; Behram had been fourteen. That's how it was in the village. She had remained with her parents until she was sixteen, when her father took her to her husband's village by bullock cart and left her. Now her parents were dead and she could not forgive her brother for ill-treating their widowed mother. They hadn't spoken in years. Ahmed was almost the only family she had left.

Marriam looked again at her son. 'Ahmudi, I can talk to *saab* about a job. A driver earns more. A company job's even better, with pension and everything.'

'Ammi!' he howled at her. 'You want that I become their servant? No, Ammi, no. I will start my own business, you wait and see. Soon I will have the best mechanic's garage in Agra. Big big cars, Mercedes, Jaguars, BMWs and Rolls Royce. Even Ferraris. They'll all come to me because I'll be the best!'

The car names meant nothing to her but the green tattoos on her chin wobbled with anxiety. 'A business will cost. We don't have money.'

'Money will come! Don't worry about that.'

'From where?' She knew he had stashed bundles of notes behind two loose bricks. She'd discovered them by accident when dusting. She also wondered about the odd hours he kept. Unable to sleep until he was home, Marriam would lie awake before rising at six to go to work.

She reached out a brown hand, tentatively stroking his shoulder. '*Beta*, be careful … you were born after many prayers, if something was to happen to you … ' He was doubly precious, having been born after five years and four miscarriages.

'Ammi, don't worry yourself,' he snorted, pulling out a thick wad of notes from an inner pocket. 'Here, let's eat chicken curry, like *our family!*' He laughed. Then, glancing at her arm in the sling, he said, 'I'll get it.'

Marriam rose with a sigh to prepare masalas for the curry.

Later, after a satisfying dinner, Ahmed swaggered through the shanty town, fantasising about a Ferrari he had seen in an imported magazine. *What it must feel like to own such a car!* He was not content to exist in the malodorous colony that his mother called home. He hated the half-naked children, the sad-eyed mothers in cheap cotton saris, and the fathers who scraped their way obediently through life. Look at his mother, old before her time, with calloused hands and her lined face. Ahmed adored her, even if he got angry sometimes, and wanted to honour her with silk and jewels.

As a child he had occasionally accompanied his mother to the Big House. They'd been kind enough to him, giving him a banana to eat or a cup of milk, sometimes even a piece of cake, while he waited for her to go off-duty. But he hated them for their largesse.

Money was what he needed; with it he would be *somebody*. And the only way to make a quick buck was by joining the Don. The underworld boss had a terrifying reputation. Ahmed had met him only once, prudently fixing his gaze on the man's stubby fingers, which glittered with rings of coral, pearl, topaz and emerald. The Don was a man who listened to his astrologer and chose his jewellery accordingly.

Ahmed had profited from two years working for the Don, gaining a reputation for his strength. He was known by his nickname: The Bull.

Mostly they traded in white gold, the street name for cocaine. His team disseminated it across the city. He liked to think of it as a shimmering white net covering Atmapuri, with him at its centre. Another year and he would have enough for a motor garage in Agra. But supply had declined due to regional tensions disrupting supply channels from central Asia. Add to that the soaring price of corruption and Ahmed feared profits would sink so low that it wouldn't be worth being in the business.

He was wondering how to diversify when his mother inadvertently gave him an idea on a frosty January night by describing the expensive jewellery purchased for Anjora's wedding. At first he had been angry they could afford it, but he had listened intently and started to formulate a plan. The heist had gone smoothly, except that one of his accomplices hurt Marriam.

Ahmed did not realise the extent of his mother's injury until later. Seeing her arm in plaster left him guilt-stricken and he had been gentler with her since. Even though the theft had been his idea, it was the Don who had taken the necklace. Ahmed was unhappy with his pay-off but could do nothing about it. He stewed on this as he walked through Nawabganj, thumping a wooden post in passing, splintering it under his fist.

CHAPTER 5

Devi was out walking with her husband in the early morning. The Sultan Gardens had helped her and Gogu become closer over the years and she savoured every dew-scented moment there, like a yogi seeking God in the gap between two breaths. They passed other joggers and walkers, including the young Dr Chaudhry, whom Gogu vaguely recognised.

It was reassuringly peaceful, but Devi had something on her mind and eventually gave voice to her troubles.

'You must talk to Sam,' she said to her husband. 'Girls her age are mothers by now.'

'Me? Dash it, Dee, she'll find it bally odd if I steer her into a corner and start yapping about birds and bees.'

'You *are* her father!'

'And Sam's my girl! Any man would be proud to have her, by golly he would! She's got plenty of time.'

Devi had a sudden vision of her baby girl with wispy black hair and perfectly-formed fingers, laying on her stomach after the delivery, so tiny that she fitted into her mother's cupped hands. It was obvious from the start that Simi would not be tall

'She'll be twenty-five soon,' she reminded her husband.

'Bless my soul! Still, where's the fire?'

'Explain that to your mother,' Devi commented drily. 'Don't forget I was only seventeen when I married you.'

Her formidable in-laws had made marriage difficult at first. The Judge was a possessive father and Devi often wept alone in her bedroom, until she learned to sing again. Pain had leant a depth to her voice that it lacked before, turning her into one of the foremost singers of soulful love *ghazals*. The words of Mirza Ghalib, her favourite poet, came to mind: *Love demands patience but desire will not wait; What hues will my heart reflect as it bleeds to death?* Lost in reflection, Devi paused to pluck an Indian wild rose.

'I'm afraid Sam could be left unmarried,' she sighed.

Gogu grinned. '*Sam?!* Perish the thought! Her prince will come for her.'

'Her *prince?* Don't go filling her head with such nonsense! She won't even meet boys we suggest. She just makes some idiotic remark. You should have taken your belt to her when she was little!'

He cocked a brow at her. 'Beltings, eh? That's rich, coming from you, Dee! Mother hen! Ring any bells, darling?!'

'And you, *darling*, are afraid to bell the cat. Shame on you!' she said with a withering look.

'I say, that's below the belt! It's a woman-to-woman thing. By George, who better to discuss marriage than a mother?'

Devi gave up and surrendered herself to the garden. Red canna lilies grew like soldiers in rows and she spotted a kingfisher flying across from the river. Slowly, as time passed, she had reached a plateau of love with her husband; not the heady, tumultuous love of passion, but a steady flame that had survived the difficulties.

Back home, Gogu picked up an armload of newspapers and went to wrestle with his stubborn Bhandari bowels. Devi decided to talk to Simi, who was out on the verandah. In typically direct fashion, Devi pointed out to Simi that couples were the social norm, emphasising this by rubbing her forefingers together, palms face down. For some reason the gesture made Simi think of migrating wildebeest and she chuckled.

'Do be serious, Sam! Life's not a joke!' Devi snapped.

'What did I do? What did I do?'

'You're not serious about *anything!* What *are* you doing with your life?'

Simi's mother rarely lost her temper, but when she did it was best to get out of the way. *Jesus!* Continuing the African theme in her head, Simi imagined her empty stomach growling like a lion. She fantasised about having an omelette for breakfast, stuffed with onion, tomato and green chillies, along with toast so crisp that it snapped.

'You're lucky we've given you *so much* freedom. I married the boy my parents chose. I had no choice. But if you find a nice young man on your own I'll say yes, *provided* he's decent and from a good family.'

Simi shook her head, casting about in her mind for a man who had stirred her pulse. *It might boil down to Ashok Puri from next door, after all! Blast!*

Then Devi gave her an ultimatum. 'I give you till the year end. You must be married by then, or engaged. Or else let me find you a suitable boy. The system works — why not try it? Anjora's done the right thing.'

Simi longed to fall in love — but now she had to fall in love to a time-table?

'Anj compromised,' she muttered.

'And what do you think marriage is? My mother's old astrologer used to say that marriage is a fruit regretted by those who eat it and those who don't. Didn't *I* compromise?'

'A bitter fruit? That's not very encouraging, Mama!' Simi said, rolling her eyes.

Devi put her cup down with an angry little click and stood up. 'Well, one year ... and as long as he's not Christian or a Muslim.'

Simi couldn't believe her ears. Her parents had many Muslim friends. She had grown up with the children of Reziya Aunty, and the Siddiquis. They played badminton and swam together at the Gymkhana Club. They had gone to the same Catholic convent schools, learnt the Lord's Prayer and sang hymns at Christmas. They even enjoyed the same movies and had the same heroes. They were, in fact, exactly like her. Muslim families came to the Hindu Bhandaris for Diwali and, in turn, they visited Muslim families during the Eid festival. Not her grandmother, of course. The old lady had no Muslim friends, would never share bread with one of *them*, and never ate halal meat.

'What *do* you mean, Mama?' Simi asked.

Devi shook her head. 'We're not ready for mixed marriages,' she said, before going upstairs to bathe.

Surely her mother was wrong! Atmapuri, city of the soul, was a bustling metropolis with traffic jams and high-rise buildings where the lifts didn't always work. Muslims had lived here for as long as anyone could remember. They had even ruled Atmapuri until the Muslim nawab was deposed by the East India Company.

Simi read the newspapers and watched television like everyone else. Hindu-Muslim conflicts had left fifty dead when Hindu militants had demolished the Babri Mosque the previous year. The riots that followed raged in Atmapuri too, with knifings, burnings and looting making the streets unsafe for a whole week. It was always the poor who suffered most, people like Marriam. Simi had been shocked by how quickly a civilised city could descend into communal hatred.

The talk with her mother had disturbed her more than she let on, so Simi skipped breakfast and left the house after a cup of tea. Her best friend Pia was due to arrive from Nainital after spending two months with her widowed mother, who found it difficult to manage the family provisions stores alone. Simi was going to fetch her friend from the station, but she had an hour to wait and decided to visit the baba first.

After driving to the mausoleum of the Thirteen-Yards saint, beneath which the baba lived, Simi found the baba's blue door shut. So instead she approached the tomb of the Sufi saint, whose exaggerated name was derived from his grave being thirteen feet long. In reality he had probably been a slight man. Men of God never seem to eat much. Simi walked around the deserted mausoleum, looking wistfully at the thousands of black thread knots tied to the stone latticework. Each knot represented a wish. This is where Marriam had come to pray for a son two decades ago. Simi imagined that one particularly discoloured piece of thread might have been Marriam's knot.

It was Marriam who had first brought Simi to the baba, six years ago, after telling her the story of how her prayers had been answered. Half of Atmapuri came to him, Hindu and Muslim. No one knew which religion the baba followed – he neither feasted nor fasted during the Hindu Diwali or the Muslim Ramadan. If asked, he said: 'I'm a servant of the Master.'

Few made such enquiries of him anyway, being wholly preoccupied with their own desires. When the sick were healed and barren women bore children, they brought gifts of clocks to the shrine. Hundreds of them, going *tic-toc tic-toc*, measuring life in hours, *tic-toc tic-toc*. The baba had looked so ordinary when Simi first met him, a dark wiry man dressed in white cotton kurta-pyjama, but she soon discovered how extraordinary he was.

She went and sat outside his door, idly watching the river flow past and a monkey picking lice off her baby. Suddenly he appeared, like a grand actor making an entrance. She scrambled to her feet but he walked by with unseeing eyes and squatted by the river. There was not an ounce of extra flesh on him; his black hair, dramatically streaked with white, fell to his shoulders. Though in his seventies, he could be taken for thirty-five at a glance. Having washed his face, he walked back briskly and sat opposite her on a smooth stone, tucking his legs beneath him.

'The fish were singing last night,' the baba spoke in Hindustani and had a deep voice which surprised many people. 'Did you hear them?' he asked.

Singing trout? Hidden worlds lurked behind his every word and Simi waited for him to explain. His eyes, shining like black glass, were only half-open, as if part of him dwelt forever in some remote inner world.

'You didn't know that fish sing?' He chuckled as he saw her confusion, laughter rising from his belly. 'The fish sing when the breath of the Master is upon the waters of the Earth. The ocean currents carry their song to the heights and the depths. You too can hear them if you're silent.'

Simi was enchanted.

He continued, 'He gives us the Earth with everything in it, but what do we give Him in return?'

His eyelids dropped as though someone inside had pulled down the shutters. A hundred elephant herds were pacified by his meditation, a thousand fires doused. Simi experienced a great sense of peace. The terror of the theft, her nightmares, her mother's anxieties, everything receded as she followed the baba on invisible sunlit paths. He spoke to himself, and she listened quietly.

> *O Baba, what will you sacrifice*
> *To the Master of your life?*
> *A body of dust, a mind of fire*
> *A life of toil, then the death of desire*
> *Gather it, lay it all at His Feet*
> *So that you may emerge on silver shores*
> *To stand as a pure thought of the Master*

The words hung in the air long after he had fallen silent. She had no idea how much time had elapsed when she opened her eyes, feeling as though waking from a long sleep. The baba said that sacrifice, an old fashioned virtue, was an invitation to the Divine, and that He would always leave gifts in His wake, as the ocean strews shells upon the beach. The baba always knew what ailed Simi and this time was no different. 'Fear,' he said, 'is as real as you or I sitting here. It comes from outside and you should leave it there, else it will take up permanent residence.'

He asked her to fetch a fruit knife from inside to cut one of the apples she had brought and they shared it.

'The Divine lays a feast before you. Enjoy! The universal energies have combined to create this apple for you.'

She told him of Anjora's wedding and glamorous honeymoon. He mulled over the word *honeymoon* like a child examining a dragonfly. Suddenly, he said, shaking his head comically, 'You'll be married this year.' He laughed at her surprise, adding, 'The wise one allows himself to drift like a leaf on the current of life. Anxiety is the mother of all ills.'

BLACK TAJ

That was the baba's way, to plant a seed but to wait for her to understand it herself. Simi thanked him and took her leave. Just before rounding the corner, she turned for a last look. She loved the old man. And she loved the idea of him even more.

CHAPTER 6

Simi arrived at the station shortly after leaving the baba, only to discover that Pia's train was late. With signals and sidings getting in the way, there was no guarantee when it would arrive. Atmapuri's gothic railway station was a relic of the British Raj, with giant pillars and a high vaulted dome that hosted innumerable pigeons and spiders. It was a gusty April day, the wind tugging at trees like a petulant child at its mother's petticoats. Dust, smoke and coal particles blew into Simi's eyes as she waited impatiently for Pia. They had become best friends on the first day of their undergraduate philosophy course at Lady Mountbatten College seven years ago and still shared their deepest secrets, laughed at the same jokes and enjoyed the same books. Pia had stayed on at university to work for a doctorate, but Simi had quit after completing a Master's Degree in Literature.

While she waited, Simi drank four sweet milky teas from little clay pots, amusing herself by smashing them on the railway tracks. Eventually her bladder was near bursting with tea but there was no question of using the smelly platform loos, so it was a relief when the Victorian steam engine chugged into view wearing a top hat of white smoke. Simi was swept aside as the platform sprang to life and a family of five ran past her to squeeze their bedrolls and cases through the door of the second class compartment without allowing the passengers off first.

She searched for her friend but it was difficult in the crush. Then she heard Pia's voice call out, '*Simms!* Here, Simms, here.'

Pia was waving to her and they ran to hug each other before clattering up the iron staircase to the exit, ensuring that Coolie No. 420 followed with the luggage. Pia paid him off at the car and rebuked him when he grumbled at the amount, holding out the rupees accusingly. Simi would have given more but kept quiet. Pia was prickly about money and never accepted favours, preferring to scrape by on a small allowance from her mother.

'God! I couldn't wait to get away from Mother! I hate her sometimes,' Pia cried as they drove away from the station. Fumbling in her tapestry bag, she pulled out a pack of 555 cigarettes and lit one, rolling down the car window to blow a smoke ring. She wore a cheap calico gypsy skirt of the sort worn by women who labour on building sites. Her black hair was cut short like a skull-cap and she had a habit of pulling the short curls on the nape of her neck.

'Tell me about Anj's wedding,' Pia said between puffs on her cigarette, 'I'm gutted to have missed it. Was it fabulous?' No detail was too small for her. 'Honeymooning in London, Paris, New York? Lucky girl! So Anj married money and won't have to lift a finger again. Just as well, because she's not clever.'

Simi was inclined to defend her cousin but she let it pass. Pia was just jealous. Bright though she was, with a razor wit and mind, she was deeply envious of rich and happy families. Instead, Simi invited Pia for lunch at the White House.

'Drop off my bags first?' replied Pia. 'And I have to see Sanjay.'

Sanjay Sethi was a leader of the Students' Union. Pia had talked about him before but Simi had never met him. She obediently turned the car towards the university, which was some distance out of town, beyond the south side of the city.

'Take deep breaths, Mother kept saying. Take in the clean mountain air of Naini! But, Simms, I swear I missed the pollution of Atmapuri! I wish my brother would do more for her. It's sons who should take responsibility for parents,' Pia sighed, flinging her cigarette butt out of the window.

Simi had never understood how her friend could dislike her own mother. Pia was about fifteen when her adored father, an army colonel, had died unexpectedly.

After passing through tracts of open land dotted with trees, like paperweights holding down a brown sheet, they arrived at the redbrick university buildings. Simi drove straight to the residential block. Pia got out of the car and gave a sharp wolf-whistle, causing an urchin to materialise in front of them. She promised him twenty-five rupees to carry her luggage inside and clean her room, after which they paid the boy and went looking for Sanjay Sethi. He was not in the Union office and Pia's crestfallen expression spoke volumes. Instead, they found a young history student packing bundles of posters.

'Sanjay sir will come in the afternoon only,' he informed them, adding that Sanjay had organised a rally the next day to protest against the municipality's plan to clear the shanty towns. It was to be held at the large *maidan* adjoining the Boat House on the river. Hundreds of people were expected to attend. Simi remembered seeing in the newspapers that the residents of the posher enclaves had petitioned the court to move the slums to distant Govindpuri, an uninhabited stretch of land beyond the airport. The matter would come up for hearing in September.

'God! This country! Sahibs and serfs. When will it change?' Pia cried, lighting another cigarette. 'Trust Sunju to be on the ball! He's awesome! I'll be there. You'll come too, Simms, won't you? Don't just stay in your ivory house!'

'White House,' Simi corrected automatically. Dadi disapproved of girls 'exhibiting' themselves at gatherings of the 'riff-raff' and there had been past trouble at the Boat House.

'Whatever,' Pia shrugged.

Simi knew that Marriam needed to be near the White House for her job and had no idea what the maid would do if she was moved out to Govindpuri.

'Of course I'll come!' she said, though decided not to tell Dadi.

Sanjay Sethi was on his way to the Boat House with his childhood friend, Dr Imran Chaudhry. They had gone to school together, along with Ajay 'Tony' Anand. After school, Imran had gone to medical college and became a successful doctor, while Tony had joined his father's flourishing construction business. But Sanjay remained a student, contriving to spin out his doctorate degree for seven years. When Imran ribbed him about this, Sanjay remained unabashed.

'Listen, *yaar*, I'm waiting to win the election. Once I'm President of the Students' Union, I can use that to join the Swaraj Party and *proper* politics. For now, the PhD keeps my family off my back!'

Sanjay chose to live on campus instead of in his family's luxurious home. He was a tall, broad-shouldered man with a high forehead, large eyes, quick temper and booming voice. His impetuous nature and natural ability to lead made him an irresistible force of nature.

Sanjay drove his army-surplus Jeep hard over the rutted road and Imran cursed as he bounced on the seat.

'You're a lousy driver, Sanjay! We should have gone in my car.'

'Imagine arriving in a Mercedes!' Sanjay understood the importance of image and knew that his ramshackle Jeep was more appropriate if he wanted to make the right impression.

'Do you think the papers will carry my picture tomorrow?' Sanjay asked.

Imran threw his head back and laughed. The two of them were like chalk and cheese. He had encouraged Sanjay to organise the rally but not for the sake of his friend's political career.

Imran's biggest challenge as a doctor lay in the slums; that's where the battle against typhoid, cholera, dysentery, malaria and dengue fever had to be won. After returning from the States and setting up a private practice, Imran's clinic had been largely empty until he saved the State Chief Minister from almost certain death. Since then his surgery had always been full and new patients had to be turned away. This meant he could now afford to engage with the poorer half of Atmapuri. He had cancelled his afternoon appointments today to face another old enemy, the Atmapuri Municipal Corporation officials, who would undoubtedly come to spy on the rally. The April sun felt warm on his neck, so Imran removed his jacket and rolled up his shirtsleeves. Atmapuri's noise and dust poured in from all sides of the open Jeep, making him miss the cool of his air-conditioned car.

'*Sala! Haramzada!* Want to die under my wheel?' Sanjay swore at a passing cyclist, jamming his thumb on the horn. The startled rider turned to look and ran into a jackfruit tree. Sanjay saluted him with a triumphant toot of the Jeep's horn.

Imran scolded his friend. Sanjay was always late, always in a rush and always on the verge of killing someone on the road.

Sanjay shrugged. 'Don't blame me – blame the traffic. I know! Let's take a short-cut through the old city.'

Imran protested but it was too late. Sanjay had turned the wheel and turned into a side street.

The old city was the most congested part of Atmapuri. Cramped shops lined both sides of the road, selling everything from tinsel garlands and colourful calendars to hair oil that promised fertility as well as healthy tresses. Every inch of the footpath was taken by itinerant vendors and pedestrians fought for space on the road with cars, cycle-rickshaws, mongrels and cows. A large bullock had stalled traffic, refusing to pull his cart, ignoring the curses and pleas of his master.

Imran leant back resignedly and thought of the people awaiting them at the Boat House. He had promised Sanjay to speak at the rally. What should he say? That *life is unfair?* They already knew that. Their families had lived without water, education or electricity for generations. Past run-ins with the AMC had taught him how difficult it would be to save them. *Promise justice?* He was not even sure that justice existed. Imran suddenly imagined his father, as vividly as if he was stood beside him. A tall man with gentle eyes and a scholarly stoop, he would dress in a cashmere coat from London's Savile Row. His father – Nawab Hyder Ali Khan of Akbarabad – had been a man of expensive tastes. Their family's kingdom, Akbarabad, originally carved out by the Great Moghul Emperor Akbar, had flourished for four hundred years before vanishing almost overnight.

What was his father trying to tell him? Imran woke from his reverie to find they were at a standstill outside the old clock-tower. It took him a minute to realise they were going in the wrong direction.

'Hunh? Can't be! We must be near now!' Sanjay cried, sticking his head out of the Jeep.

'What kind of idiot takes a short-cut through the old city!?' Imran scolded. 'Next time, I'll drive. I'd better go see what's holding us up.'

He hopped out of the Jeep and disappeared. The crowd swirled around him, dense even by the standards of the old city. Luckily, Imran had a trick for handling crowds.

'I'm a doctor!' he announced. The sea of men parted to let him through.

About four hundred yards ahead, a fight raged, the sound of heavy blows audible even before Imran reached the scene.

'What's happened, brother?' he asked someone in the crowd. The man explained that a young woman had been meeting her lover in the bazaar, dallying over aubergines and other vegetables to exchange coy glances. This gossamer romance had been discovered by her family and now her two brothers were teaching the young man a lesson. It was the sort of hooliganism that Imran despised.

'What madness!' he roared. 'Stop it, stop it!'

But the crowd bayed in encouragement. The excited faces all around made Imran even angrier. He yelled, 'Fools! Fighting each other! Don't you have problems—'

The rest of his words were drowned out by the din of bystanders cheering the pugilism. Imran lost his cool and waded in to separate the fighters, receiving a bloody nose for his troubles. The pain was excruciating. Momentarily blinded, he would have fallen if a man in the crowd had not stepped forward to catch him. When the world swam back into focus Imran saw the powerful young man who had come to his aid, thanking him as he regained his balance.

'I'll do it for you,' the young man spat.

Ahmed had been with his cousin Farid, who lived in the old city, when the fight broke out. Now he stepped forward and grabbed the two assailants by the scruffs of their necks, lifting them onto their toes. Their expressions were comical. Their victim, unexpectedly finding himself rescued, disappeared quickly into the crowd.

'What should I do with them?' Ahmed asked Imran.

Imran motioned him to set them down and asked their names.

'I'll pass your names to the police commissioner,' he scolded. 'Leave your poor sister alone or you'll go to jail! Is she your prisoner?'

Ahmed then slapped them hard. They howled with pain and ran off. The crowd too slipped away faster than money through a gambler's fingers, leaving the road clear. Imran stomped back to the Jeep.

Turning to Ahmed, who had followed him, he asked, 'Where did you get a body like that?'

Ahmed beamed at the compliment.

They found Sanjay peering into the open bonnet of his Jeep, muttering: '*Haramzada!* You had to pack up now! One of these damned wires should be wiped – but which one?' He kicked the Jeep.

Ahmed approached, 'Let me.'

'Are you a mechanic?' Sanjay asked suspiciously.

'One day I'll own a garage,' Ahmed boasted. He ducked in under the bonnet and busied himself for a few minutes, after which he asked Sanjay to start the engine. It came to life on the second try. Ahmed surprised Sanjay by refusing the money he offered.

'No,' Ahmed shook his head, wiping the grease off his hands on a rag that Sanjay handed him. 'You're rich and I'm not – but a poor man can also help people.' There was a dignity about him, despite his cheap clothes.

Sanjay saluted flamboyantly. 'Your name?'

'Ahmed Behram Hussain.'

Muslim! Sanjay made a quick mental note of that.

'*Shukriya!*' Imran thanked Ahmed and extended his right hand. Ahmed looked surprised and hesitated before shaking it. His grip was normal, not the bone-cruncher Imran had expected.

'Can we give you a lift?' he asked. Ahmed nodded and climbed into the back of the Jeep. He too was going to the rally.

Imran glanced at his watch as they drove off again. Three o'clock. They might miss the rally if there were more hold-ups. As if to spite him, he heard the distant sound of voices chanting, drawing nearer. He turned to ask Sanjay about this but the driver was busy trying to squeeze between a cartful of caged chickens and a cycle-rickshaw. From the hum of a single bumblebee, the chanting swelled into a torrent.

Imran slapped his forehead in despair. 'Another bloody religious procession!'

Rows of saffron-clad men walked past the Jeep, beating small drums and metal triangles to keep rhythm. Their synchronised chanting was hypnotic. They didn't even glance at the traffic they were holding up while they passed.

Imran practised his yogic breathing to help him calm down. At least they were on the move again.

'What was *that*, Sanjay?' he asked.

'From the temples' Sanjay replied, indicating the road ahead with his chin. Across the river lay a group of five small Hindu temples, and the pilgrims were headed there.

'Religion, religion, religion!' Imran fumed. 'It's got more blood on its hands than empires!'

Sanjay gave him a distracted look. 'Calm down, *yaar*. You know this country breathes religion! Lives for it.'

'And dies for it!' Imran replied. As a doctor he had encountered much suffering after the riots that followed the Babri Mosque's demolition – Muslims with first-degree burns from being doused with petrol and set alight by Hindus; Hindus with stab wounds or eyes gouged out. Whatever vestige of religion had clung to him from childhood had evaporated over the years.

'We need a Mao Tse Tung – or Kemal Ataturk. Just for fifty years – that's all. That should sort things out and get us healthcare, education, housing and lights that work'.

'*Yaar*, Imran, what did they do to you in America? Changed your bloody DNA! Now you don't like anything here,' Sanjay said.

'Aw, c'mon. You can see it too, even if you don't admit it!'

Ahmed, who had been silent in the back, now chipped in. 'It's true. They give us nothing.'

Imran was intrigued by the rough youth, but by then they had arrived at the Boat House.

CHAPTER 7

Simi had arrived early at the rally, chivvied along by Pia. A rudimentary bamboo platform had been erected at one end of the open ground. They cadged two folding chairs from Sanjay's men and sat in the shade of an old mango tree. Marriam then joined them with some friends from her *basti* and her cousin, Jaddan Bai, who lived in the old city with her son, Farid, and his children. Marriam, whose arm was healing but remained sore, proudly introduced her companions to Simi.

Simi was surprised to see how animated Marriam was in the company of her friends as they squatted in the dust, talking spiritedly. They complained bitterly about the plan to relocate them 'twelve stones' away, as one of them quaintly remarked, using the medieval system of measuring miles. Another woman, the wife of a vegetable vendor, lamented that nobody would buy his produce out in the wilderness. The unpopulated wasteland beyond the airport would be their ruin.

Simi wondered what she could do. By now the ground was packed with men gossiping and smoking *beedis*, along with women whose children played with cycle wheels and marbles.

'Sisters! Nobody can touch you. Sanjay*babu* says so,' Pia declared.

'But where is he?' Simi asked, glancing at her watch. They drank sweet tea from plastic cups while they waited. Another half hour lapsed. The crowd was restless and the women wondered if it was time to return home and start the evening meal.

Suddenly, the Students' Union volunteers, who had been drowsing in the warm afternoon sun, perked up and shouted, 'Long live Sanjay *babu!*'

The crowd took up the cry. Sanjay had appeared and ran up to the platform. Simi studied him curiously. Black hair sprang straight up from his high forehead and he wore the politician's uniform of inexpensive white *khadi* cotton kurta-pyjama, once a symbol of humility but now associated with power and wealth. Turning her attention to his companion, she was surprised to see he looked familiar. He was even taller than Sanjay, a lean man with red flecks in his hair.

'Who's that?' she nudged Pia.

'Sunju, of course.'

'Tchh! The other one.'

'Oh! Dr Imran Chaudhry.'

'And that's my son,' Marriam pointed out with satisfaction. Ahmed now stood at the base of the platform, having accompanied Sanjay and Imran. Simi was again surprised by Ahmed's rugged physique.

'Brothers and sisters! You're welcome!' Sanjay's voice boomed across the ground. No need for a mike there. 'Do you know what the letters AMC stand for? All-Mighty Conqueror!' Waves of laughter greeted his quip. 'Now we must appeal to them – for how will you live so far away? How will you earn?'

He made a stirring speech, entirely without notes. Simi felt his magnetism. He addressed them in a colloquial dialect, using his hands to emphasise and illustrate his points. He rocked imaginary babies in his arms, spooned invisible food into his mouth, sketched a roof by joining the tips of his fingers.

The man was a dancer! He outlined a political programme of leafleting, street protests and sit-ins outside the high court.

'He sounds like the Home Minister,' Simi whispered to Pia, but got a disapproving look in return.

Sanjay continued, '*Mein jo huin* with you ... your home is my home, your wife is my-' he paused and grinned. 'What did you think I would say? That your wife is my wife? *Chee, chee.* Dirty minds! No, your wife's my sister!' The crowd laughed and clapped. 'And now I invite my old friend, Dr Chaudhry, to speak. He's a very big doctor – he went to America to train but didn't stay there. Why? Because his heart is Indian!'

Simi suddenly recognised Imran as the doctor who had comforted her after the theft at Anjora's wedding. How could she have forgotten him? She leaned forward.

'Friends! With Sanjay*babu* as your champion, how can you lose? I've known him since he was that high' – he reached down and hovered his hand close to the ground – 'and now he's a giant, a great leader!' Thunderous applause.

Imran continued: 'Justice is on our side; you have rights, just like everyone else. My father used to say that all a man really needs is a roof over his head, the love of his family and a piece of land to be buried.' He did not mention that his father, once the master of domed palaces, had lost his own roof by the end.

Dr Chaudhry went on to talk about clean drinking water, good schools and good health. He said that malaria, typhoid, dysentery and dengue were diseases that should have been eradicated by now.

'Sanjay*babu* gave you one definition of the AMC, I have another one. I call it "The Anthrax, Malaria and Cholera Council." And now you know why they don't like me!'

'Lucky they aren't your in-laws!' Sanjay interjected. The audience tittered, relishing the reference to loathed in-laws.

Simi wondered whether the doctor was married, receiving her answer when Imran responded to his friend's joke: 'Hey Sanjay, don't give me in-laws without giving me a wife!'

Simi felt a sense of relief. There was something special about the doctor. He sounded so genuine.

Dr Chaudhry continued: 'I pledge to you, here and now, that from next month I'll come to your homes with Dr Gupta, my friend and partner, and we'll get rid of these diseases.'

That came out so spontaneously that he surprised even himself. Perhaps that's what his father had been trying to tell him. A mobile medical unit, an outreach programme for the slums! He was elated.

Simi felt as though he had articulated her own hazy notions about doing something for Marriam. She excitedly explained to her ayah what he had meant, as though it was all her idea. She barely heard the other speeches, distracted as she was by her desire to talk to the doctor. She waited for him as he climbed down from the platform. He was even more handsome up close, with amused hazel eyes and a cleft chin.

He recognised her, saying, 'I know you!' She was thrilled, even though she had forgotten him until today.

Imran continued, 'I've often wondered how you were after that dacoity. I thought I might see you at Tony's place.'

She was flattered he had looked for her. But one of the Union volunteers approached Imran for medical advice, so he turned away to talk to the interloper. Pia came across to join Simi, followed by Sanjay, who had finished talking to the crowd that had surrounded him upon leaving the stage.

He gestured to Pia. 'Pi! What did you think of my speech? And who's your friend?'

Pia gushed over his speech. When she introduced Simi, Sanjay asked, 'Are you going to be in the play too?'

Simi knew nothing about a play.

'Do say yes!' Sanjay continued without pause. 'Pi will be in it, won't you Pi? It's *The Importance of Being Earnest.* Oscar Wilde. I wanted one of our home-grown writers but the director insisted. As long as we've got songs in it, it's okay by me.' *Songs?* Simi knew the play, having read all of Wilde's works, but it had no songs!

Pia promised to take Simi to meet the director, as they would be holding an audition soon.

Dr Chaudhry finished conferring with his patient and turned back to Simi. Marriam had joined them, so Simi introduced her old ayah, who promptly informed the doctor that the young man with him was her son. Ahmed offered a hasty greeting, but otherwise ignored his mother and Simi.

Simi said, 'Marriam lives in—'

'Nawabganj, sahib,' Marriam interrupted eagerly.

'I'd like to volunteer for your medical camp,' Simi concluded.

'Great! Then we'll start at ... what's the name of the place?'

'Nawabganj.'

'Nawabganj then. I'll fix the date and let you know – where can I get in touch?' Simi told him. He already knew her name, having got it from Ajay. 'Cool,' he said with a dazzling smile, his teeth a vibrant white under his brown moustache. She noticed his habit of raking his hair with his fingers.

Time had passed swiftly while they talked. Most people had left the *maidan* and the stars were out. It was time to go home.

Simi offered to drive Marriam back to Nawabganj, but the old maid refused and took the bus with her son. Ahmed was deep in thought. The doctor was unlike anyone else he knew. He talked in a language that Ahmed appreciated, especially when he spoke about their rights. Here, at last, was someone who had articulated what he felt. Poverty was not a disease, just an adversity to be overcome. Ahmed believed he was just as good as anyone rich. It was just that he owned less. Much, much less. But he *deserved* no less. It was true that Devi and Gogu had paid for his education, but he resented that almost as much as being poor. Why should he accept charity for his birth right?

Dr Chaudhry had spoken about *rights*. His words rang in Ahmed's head: 'we've never given you anything.'

True. *And* he was Muslim! After his father's death, Ahmed had gravitated to the mosque. At first he went to eat dinner there with his friends, only gradually becoming interested in what the preacher had to say. The priest pointed out that they were oppressed by the Hindu majority. Ahmed had not believed him initially because he had grown up with Hindu friends in the shanties, but after his father's death he began to rage against the heartlessness of society. Hindu society. Confused by guilt and grief, he had found a father-figure in the priest. He was glad that Dr Chaudhry wasn't Hindu, as it made it easier for Ahmed to admire him.

CHAPTER 8

A few weeks later, on a stifling early May morning, Simi finished breakfast and left the White House for Marriam's home. A blast of heat hit her as she stepped outside and her thin cotton kurta clung damply to her back, while cars baked in the sun. She dreaded the hot weather, but Dr Chaudhry's first medical camp was in just under a week and Simi had promised to help them prepare by identifying the main health issues in Nawabganj. Her relationship with Marriam meant that the other women there were forthcoming with information. Simi was surprised by how much she enjoyed being around them. Under their subdued facade these women were lively and outspoken. They had stories to tell of child-brides living with buffaloes in remote villages, fascinating stuff. But for now there was the medical camp, so Simi focused on collecting information for the doctor.

Two days before the camp, Old Mrs Bhandari found out about it when she overheard Simi talking to her mother. She demanded to know what was going on, so Simi thrust her chin out and told her.

Old Mrs Bhandari wrinkled her nose disdainfully. 'Roaming among sweepers and scavengers!'

'Dadi! I'm doing something that matters! It'll make a difference to someone's life!'

'Nonsense! Everyone lives their own karma. Don't fancy you're changing things.'

'Of course things can change, otherwise what's the use? I might as well stay in bed the whole time,' Simi retorted.

Dadi shook her head. 'Each one of us has to pay for our karma. They're where they're supposed to be.'

'So we do nothing to help? That's not fair. Marriam could lose her home.'

'Good! Let her go! Marriam should go back to Pakistan. Why we have to have an M in the house ... ' she trailed off bitterly.

That took Simi's breath away. She was furious. 'Go back? Marriam's not from Pakistan! Her village is in U.P. She's Indian, just like us!'

'Then why the partition if we still have to live with Ms?' Dadi demanded. '*They* should have left us in peace. My father lost everything!'

'For Chrissake! Can't you forget the partition?'

'*Forget?* How can I forget? We lost our home!'

'Then you'll understand how Marriam feels about losing her home!' Something had shifted in Simi while working with the slum women and watching their struggles.

'Since when did you get twenty tongues in your head?!' Dadi scolded. 'You are not to go to the slums. And in the sun! You'll only get darker ... '

... *and who'll marry you then?* Simi winced at the unspoken words. The Sunday papers carried pages of matrimonial advertisements. Bachelors with BAs and LLBs all seeking 'fair brides'. Simi, who resembled a peanut more than a milky cashew, rejected the fair skin prized by Punjabi families.

Dadi continued, 'Let's have no more of this nonsense.' Old Mrs Bhandari finished on this and left the room.

Simi let out a long breath and turned to Devi, who had watched the dispute in silence.

'She makes me so mad, Mama!'

'What's the use of fighting her? She won't change,' her mother replied.

Her father too had something to say the next morning. 'Dash it, Sam, hope you know what you're doing. That doctor chappie's ruffled a few feathers. He's become the AMC's bête noir – it's in the papers.' Gogu held out the *Atmapuri Times* for her to see. 'Should you be mixed up in this?'

'Papa, you too? Dadi's already had a go at me.'

They were sitting in Gogu and Devi's bedroom. After returning from their walk, Gogu was now reading the papers. Devi sat before her old-fashioned dressing table, stocked with neat columns of lipsticks, imported perfumes and other cosmetics. Rows of brightly coloured glass bangles hung on wooden rods. Simi had loved playing with them as a child.

'You go ahead, Sam,' Devi said, turning round. 'Just don't get carried away. Politics is dirty business.' She sprayed on her French perfume and stood up, straight as a cedar in her green cotton sari.

On the day of the camp, Simi got up two hours early, had tea and toast, then slipped away quietly to avoid encountering Dadi. Arriving at Nawabganj, she found a carnival atmosphere, despite it being a chilli-hot day. Mirages rose like genies from the tarmac. Marriam and her friends had also turned up early, despite Simi's strictures not to crowd the doctor. Sick or not, they wished to register their names on the list. No one had ever paid them attention before and now they clamoured for it. They adored the doctor without even having met him. She made them squat in orderly rows to await his arrival.

Dr Chaudhry arrived in a Jeep he used for home visits, with his colleague, Dr Gupta, in the passenger seat. Simi re-introduced Marriam and her cousin Jaddan Bai, who wouldn't have missed the excitement for anything. Ahmed was there too, while Jaddan Bai had brought her grandson, Munna, who followed Ahmed everywhere he went. Simi wondered why Ahmed was there. He didn't seem to need medical help.

As well as Dr Gupta, an attractive young woman accompanied Dr Chaudhry. It was little consolation to Simi that the woman was also a doctor.

'Meet Nina – Dr Nina Singh,' said Imran, making introductions. 'She's an amazing gynaecologist! It's great that she sacrificed her day off to come.' He smiled, lightly patting Dr Singh's wrist. She beamed radiantly in return.

Simi's heart sank and the din around them suddenly grated on her nerves. She realised with a start that she was jealous. *Jealous? Not me! Why should I be jealous? He's not my boyfriend!*

'Sure, sure,' Simi responded when Imran said something to her, not really paying attention. She took her place at a table under a *neem* tree and began noting the personal details of patients. The bare-legged men in *dhotis* and women with children straddling their hips knew their names, but not how old they were. There were no birth certificates in remote villages, so it fell upon Simi to guess their ages instead. An old woman, her face lined like a walnut, said she was born the year that locusts destroyed the crops in her village. Locust plagues were a thing of the past, almost biblical, so Simi put her age down as eighty.

Time flew and she was surprised when Imran called a halt for lunch. The four of them – Dr Gupta, Dr Singh, Dr Chaudhry and Simi – got into Imran's Jeep, with Simi next to the fragrant Dr Nina. Her grooming was impeccable, almost on a par with Anjora. How did a busy doctor find time to put bronze highlights in her hair? Simi's own black mane suddenly appeared dull by comparison and she tried to conceal her short unvarnished nails.

Lunch was at a roadside café with a fixed menu. The soporific waiter brought them piping-hot tadka dal and goat curry, with a side of naan bread and yoghurt. The two men ate with gusto, while Nina Singh delicately spooned food into her mouth. Simi lost her appetite. She had felt useful, needed and important while they were preparing for the camp. But now Dr Nina Singh would take over. All she could manage was some tea.

After he finished his meal, Imran yawned, stretched and lit a cigarette. 'That was surprisingly good! I've had little time to eat the meals my servant cooks. Or get much sleep, thanks to amoebic dysentery.'

'What's the problem?' Simi asked.

Nina Singh replied. 'Don't you know? Amoebic dysentery is *raging* in the old quarters and Imran's been fire-fighting. He's quite a hero!' She bestowed another radiant smile upon him.

Simi felt excluded and tried to think of a smart reply, but none jumped to mind. It would come to her later and she would kick herself!

Dr Ravi Gupta chuckled. 'So, it's Saint Imran now?'

'Hero? Or zero?' Imran laughed.

'Hero, Imran! Hero,' Nina smiled archly. 'And you shouldn't be smoking. What have I heard you telling your patients?'

'You're right, you're right,' he said, making no effort to stub out his Marlboro. Turning to Simi he said, 'A saint? Hah! You should hear me abuse the AMC and patients who ring me at five am when I know they could have waited. I know more swear words than any truck driver in Peshawar! And for what? Half my patients don't even want to pay! I've got a woman in my office working round the clock sending out reminders!'

They all laughed. But Nina said, 'That's why it's so important for a doctor to have the right wife. Doctors should marry doctors because only they truly understand.'

The pious statement made Simi feel sick. She had all but married them off by the time they finished lunch. The rest of the afternoon was less busy, and the lunch and heat made Simi drowsy, her thoughts dwelling on Dr Nina Singh's comments. She turned her mind to Anjora instead, who she was going to meet the next day.

Her cousin had returned from her honeymoon in late March but Simi had seen little of her. Dadi had declared that she must be left alone to adjust to her new family and become an Anand. But Simi protested to Dadi about not seeing Anjora often enough.

'It's like you've packed her off to boarding school *and* quarantined her at the same time!'

'What d'you know of these things? In the old days, a girl was expected forget her past. Her in-laws even re-named her!' Old Mrs Bhandari explained. 'My mother-in-law, your father's dadi, was called Shakuntala but her in-laws changed her name to Lilavati. No one ever called her Shakuntala again.'

'Jesus!'

'And I wish you'd stop sounding like a Christian! That's not why we sent you to a convent.'

Simi tossed her head. 'Nobody would dare change my name to anything!'

Nevertheless, the day after the medical camp, Simi went to spend a lazy afternoon alone with Anjora. The Anand men were at work and Mrs Anand Senior was at a kitty party, so the two of them could talk undisturbed.

'So you're happy, Anj?' Simi asked.

Anjora's agitated fingers tortured the silk tassels of her bedspread. 'You know, Simms, I imagined my mother-in-law would be just like Mummy but ... she's got this bee in her bonnet about the robbery. She doesn't seem to trust me.' The older woman thought the theft had been a bad omen.

'Funny, she doesn't look the superstitious type,' replied Simi. 'Not with her diamonds and kitty parties. Still, as long as you're happy with Tony, that's all that matters.'

Simi looked up and was surprised to see Anjora's brown eyes brimming with tears. She rose to comfort her cousin, upsetting the cold coffee at her elbow. Grabbing the nearest thing to hand, she mopped up the brown puddle from the marble floor. Anjora was blubbering.

Simi put her arms around her cousin. 'Shhh Anj! Stop! Tell me what's wrong.'

Anjora dashed the tears off her cheeks with the back of her hand. 'I'm okay,' she sobbed. 'But you've wiped up the coffee with my new jumper.'

Simi looked down and saw she was holding an expensive-looking white cardigan, now stained brown.

'I'm so sorry!' she exclaimed, but couldn't resist teasing her cousin. 'Don't tell me you're crying for the sweater!' Anjora giggled weakly.

Over the rest of the afternoon, Simi slowly elicited the truth from her cousin. Anjora was feeling humiliated at having to beg her husband for tiny amounts of cash, even to buy something as modest as a bag of oranges.

'On our honeymoon, Simms, we stayed at swanky hotels, but if I wanted to buy something, he didn't let me. And I had no money.'

'Such as? Diamonds at Tiffany's?!' She knew Anjora's penchant for pricey baubles.

'Don't be silly! I saw a black pant-suit in Paris in a showroom window, but he pulled me away. And he promised to buy me a good watch. We went to a shop but when I chose one he said it was too expensive,' Anjora cried.

Simi burned with anger on behalf of her cousin. She tried to reassure her.

'Once the babies come, it'll be a cakewalk! Meanwhile, just rub along, Anj, rub along! At least he doesn't snore in bed. Or does he?'

But Anjora was following her own train of thought. 'And his mother treats me like an outsider.'

The old mother-in-law syndrome. The one to which Devi had fallen victim.

'A pox on murders-in-law!' Simi announced dramatically. 'Shall we make an effigy of yours and stick pins in it?'

This, at least, prompted another giggle from Anjora. But her cousin begged Simi not to breathe a word to the family so as not to upset Pinky Aunty. She left Anjora feeling disturbed, but what could she do? It was just another thing to worry about, along with the plight of Marriam's friends and the play.

CHAPTER 9

The audition for the play had been held in late April, a fortnight after Pia and Simi had attended the meeting at the Boat House. Simi was not surprised that Sanjay, with his brimming vitality and strident voice, dominated the day. He demanded that Pappoo, the director, cast her and Pia and received immediate agreement. Sanjay was the producer after all, responsible for raising the funds to stage the play. Simi was astonished to be handed the role of the lovely Miss Fairfax. She had little stage experience apart from school plays, but after a brief moment of panic, excitement took over. Pia was less happy at being cast as the plain governess, Miss Prism.

'A governess?' she complained. 'She's just a bloody ayah.'

Simi suggested that she talk to the director, but the cast was complete and it would have been difficult to switch roles without a brouhaha.

Rehearsals began the next day. The sizzling afternoon slipped in through the open windows of the university hall where Sanjay had arranged to meet. Two inadequate ceiling fans did little to counter the heat. Sanjay was not in the play, but popped in regularly to suggest changes. He did this throughout rehearsals, the play eventually evolving into something Wilde would not have recognised.

'We must have music,' he said one day, breaking into song. He then dropped to one knee with his left hand over his ear, warbling about lovers under the moon. He had them in stitches with his clowning. The director agreed to have music. Simi protested but no one was listening. Pia couldn't take her eyes off Sanjay and was certainly not going to oppose him.

Sanjay continued, 'The old movies are the best! Meena Kumari, Madhubala, we'll never see their like again! Those songs had melody.'

'How about *Casablanca*?' the director countered. '*Play it again, Sam*. Bogie and Bergman! *The Graduate* is another great. How about *Mrs Robinson*?'

Sanjay gave him a disapproving look. 'Not in Atmapuri! I was thinking more of Raj Kapoor. Nargis. Or Madhubala in *Mughal-e-Azam*.'

'But Sanjay, we're doing an *English* play!'

'Correct, but where are we doing it? In Atmapuri! I want to give them a night to remember.'

Of course, Sanjay had his way, adding four song and dance routines. Simi began to regret being in the play, though not enough to quit. She kept track of Dr Chaudhry's subsequent medical camps during the weeks of rehearsals, but since they were held in other parts of the city, Simi was not involved.

The premiere of *The Importance of Being Earnest* was held at the Banke Bihari Centre on the twenty-seventh of May. Simi feared the worst. Posters advertising the play had screamed from the city's walls for weeks: *Unmissable! Original! Music & Dance!* She wondered how the Bollywood version that Sanjay had created would go down in a city largely indifferent to the theatre.

On the opening night, Simi was ironing her heavy brocade costume in the green room she shared with Pia. Brocade in

Atmapuri in the summer! She would be lucky if she didn't faint in the heat of the footlights. She prayed that Atmapuri's Electricity Board wouldn't cut off their supply during the play, killing the air-conditioning. Power cuts were a regular feature of Atmapuri life, especially in the summer, when the northern grid tripped every other day, plunging entire colonies into darkness.

'Nervous?' Simi asked Pia, who sat blowing smoke rings over an overflowing ashtray.

Pia shook her head, 'easy-peasy. Nothing to it!'

Simi shrugged and got dressed. The director stuck his head round the door, calling out airily, 'Best of luck, girls!'

He disappeared after giving them a thumbs up. Pia snorted and shook her fist at the closed door.

'Relax, it's just a play for Gods sake!' Simi said.

'It's alright for you, *Miss Fairfax!* Why couldn't I have been Miss Worthing?'

Simi clicked her tongue. 'Why does it matter now? It'll be over soon.'

'It matters! It matters!' Pia hurled a wire hanger at the door. 'Sanjay … ' She wanted Sanjay to see her as a desirable woman, not an ayah.

Simi could no longer ignore her friend's infatuation with the mercurial Sanjay. Nor could she shake the feeling that he was the wrong man for Pia. Simi saw Sanjay as charming but selfish, someone who could electrify a gathering with his presence but who was driven primarily by ambition.

Simi again regretted her impulse to join the play. Even her reason for doing so had not worked out far from having fun with Pia, her friend had become moody, ogling Sanjay like a lovesick *chakor* bird staring at the moon when she thought no one was looking. Simi was anxious for her vulnerable friend.

'Are you serious about him?' Simi couldn't help asking.

Pia swivelled round. 'Meaning?'

'Well, he's clever … '

'He's very special, no?'

' … but, Pia, he's also selfish, interested only in Sanjay Sethi.' She stopped, noting her friend's reaction.

Pia's tightly pursed lips formed a thin bloodless line. 'Not true!' she cried. She added that Sanjay cared about people and their struggles. 'Sanjay cares about *issues*. Do you know *anyone* else who's bothered about the state of the country? You should hear him!'

'Where have you heard him speak?' asked Simi, 'Other than the Boat House?'

'*Everywhere!* At the university, the cricket stadium … you should know what's going on in the world, Simms, not just stay holed up in your castle.'

The comment left Simi speechless. Her friend knew little of what she had been doing in Nawabganj, but did that give her the right to insult her?

Pia continued. 'He's going to change things, mark my words.'

Simi had been more impressed with Dr Imran Chaudhry's quiet convictions than Sanjay's rhetoric when they'd seen them speak at the Boat House, but she held her tongue.

'He's dynamic! The most exciting man I've ever met. Reminds me a little of my father.' Pia believed her father would have become a full-blown general had he not died a mere colonel.

Simi stayed quiet. Her friend had fallen in love and did not want her advice. If she offered any, it would only antagonise her. So she turned back to the mirror, distractedly applying make-up, puffs of powder flying around her face like mini-doves. Pia was insecure, but stubborn as a blood stain. And now she was in love. If Simi was honest, she almost envied her friend that. But with fifteen minutes to curtain up and butterflies waltzing in her stomach, this was not the time for such thoughts.

'I wish you wouldn't smoke so much!' Simi snapped, fanning away the cigarette smog.

'Oh just get off my case, Simms! If you had my life, you'd smoke too!'

Simi bit her lip. Her parents were in the audience. Even her grandmother had agreed to come, although only after grumbling about *Judgesaab's granddaughter prancing about on stage like a low-caste girl.* Surely the age of Kali was upon them. Old Mrs Bhandari had a habit of attributing her own likes and dislikes to the late Judge, who was in no position to deny anything.

Sanjay, meanwhile, waited with Imran in the theatre foyer for an MP who had promised to attend the premiere. Even the Member of the State Legislative Assembly would be there. His eye was on his future and the Students' Union elections in September; being photographed with the MP in the local press would help seal his victory. He had rehearsed his speech in front of the mirror and planned to deliver it before the play started, because audiences in Atmapuri were notorious for scrambling over each other in their haste to leave at the end of any performance. While he waited, Sanjay was at his charming best, talking with girls and their mothers, all of whom were potential supporters, if not today then tomorrow.

Imran, who had watched his friend effusively greet two pencil-thin girls, muttered, 'They can't be more than thirteen. Too young to vote for you!'

Sanjay laughed uproariously, as though he'd said something witty. At that moment, Dr Nina Singh arrived. Imran had invited her because she said she loved the theatre, and it felt good to have company. Most of his nights were spent with only Hudson for company.

Imran and Nina left Sanjay and took their seats as the lights dimmed. The chatter around the auditorium slowly subsided, leaving only the whisper of tongues licking ice-cream. Nina's strong perfume was like a breeze wafting through a spring garden. She was a nice girl, attractive and sophisticated, and an excellent doctor. On Imran's left was an empty seat for Sanjay, who was now galloping up to the stage to flatter the two politicians in attendance. There was little mention of the play in his speech.

The curtain opened with a Hindi song. 'What the hell?' Imran muttered.

'*Mughal-e-Azam*,' Nina supplied helpfully. 'My mother's favourite. Madhubala sings it at the emperor's court.'

Imran recognised a second song as one that Sanjay sang compulsively when at the wheel of his car. But he sat up when Simi appeared on stage, watching her intently.

'*Oh myyy God!* What's she *wearing*?' Nina twittered.

'Looks OK to me,' Imran said. The warm colour of her costume suited Simi well.

'She looks ten months pregnant!'

He shrugged. Suddenly, Simi did a little jig. She danced with her petticoats raised to display small feet shod in golden shoes. Nina's shoulders heaved and she giggled aloud.

'Shh!' Imran whispered.

'But she's got two left feet!' Nina chortled, tapping the back of Imran's hand with her fingertips.

He quietly removed his hand. 'She's an actress, not a dancer,' he rebuked.

She leant closer to him. 'Did you know that *I* played Gwendolen Fairfax at the Gymkhana Club in 1990? Now *that* was a *proper* play. Wish you'd seen it, but we didn't know each other then. *My* Gwendolen was not some basket case. *Myyy God*, you must be so bored, after Manhattan, I mean.'

People started shushing from behind, which curbed Nina not a moment too soon for Imran. He concentrated on the stage again. Miss Prism appeared *with a cigarette* in her hand and took a few defiant puffs. He heard the sharp gasps this provoked from Atmapuri's matrons. Nina tut-tutted but refrained from comment.

'Who's that?' he asked Sanjay, who had finally joined them.

Sanjay laughed. 'That's Pia! She's something, isn't she? So is Simi.'

At the interval, Sanjay spread his arms out wide and asked, 'Great, huh? I chose the songs myself!'

Imran raised his eyebrows in surprise. 'It's a soap opera, Sanjay!'

Sanjay grinned and slapped him on the back. 'They love it! Trust me.' He rushed off.

After the play, Simi felt drained. The heat and the heavy costume had made her legs ache. She had been taken aback by the whistles and applause at the end, which showed how little she had understood the audience. Sanjay obviously had his finger on the pulse. She still approached her family with trepidation but they were very kind, even if Dadi was at her haughty best.

The after party was held in an old villa with a circular lily pond that had once belonged to a Muslim nobleman. Unable to maintain it, the nobleman had sold it to an entrepreneur. The new avatar of the old haveli was now a boutique hotel. The cast took the circular staircase up to the second floor, finding the terrace bedecked with bamboo chairs, plants, candles and low lamps. Simi picked up a glass of cold lime juice soda and wandered off to the parapet to snatch a few moments alone. The heady scent of Queen-of-the-Night creeper was strong. In the distance she could see a small mosque. Typically for

Atmapuri, there was an old Hanuman temple adjacent to it. Hindu and Muslim, side by side.

During the play, Simi had seen in the audience that Dr Nina was Imran's companion for the evening. She wondered whether they would marry. *Good! They can discuss diseases over dinner. And name their children Thermometer and Syrup.* The spiteful thought cheered her up.

Her reverie was interrupted by a loud 'Hi!' and she turned to find Imran at her elbow.

'Hullo!' she replied, looking for Nina Singh. But he was alone.

'Stunning view,' he said, with a sweep of his right hand, in which he held a full glass of beer. She nodded. They were quiet for a while, but it was a comfortable silence.

'So, how do you feel?' he asked. 'Relieved that it went well? Everyone seems to have enjoyed the play.'

She remained quiet. He continued, 'Typical of Sanjay, really. He adored the circus when we were boys. Some things never change!' They exchanged a knowing glance and burst out laughing.

'And you were wonderful, Simi,' he added.

Her mood soared and she let out a self-deprecating giggle, 'Oh come off it! I don't know how many lines we fluffed. At least my mother enjoyed the songs. She sings, you know. But *Madhubala* in Oscar Wilde?'

'Your mother sings? Talented family.'

'You must have heard her at Anjora's wedding. She was the tall lady in maroon who sang most of the songs.'

'I *remember*. She's your mother? You must be so proud.'

She turned to look him in the face. 'And you? What are you when you're not being a doctor?'

He looked intently at her and smiled. 'Where *did* you get those eyes?' he asked.

Confused, she lowered her gaze and blushed. The noise of the party had receded for Simi. She was very conscious of Imran standing next to her, of being at eye level with his open-collared blue shirt, his short chest hairs curling like question marks.

Imran spoke softly, in Urdu, '*I recall those tearful eyes, and my sore heart is brimming again.*'

Tearful eyes! He meant the night of Anjora's wedding, when she had cried on his shoulder. Her blush deepened.

He continued, '*A hundred crocodiles lie coiled in the heart of every wave; see how a grain of sand suffers to become a pearl.*'

She looked up again and asked, 'Are you a poet?'

He shook his head. 'Borrowed words, from Ghalib. My father's favourite poet – or one of them. He had so many.'

'My mother loves poetry too.' Devi would love him for quoting Ghalib. 'Your father was a poet?'

He shook his head, looking down at the beer foam in his glass. 'No, not a poet.' He changed the subject. 'Can I get you a drink?' he asked.

Nina Singh joined them, her eyes raking Simi from head to toe. '*Congratulations!*' she said. 'That was ... *most* enjoyable. Tell me, how did you figure out how to play Miss Fairfax in that *particular* way? *Most* interesting. We have a lot in common – I played Miss Fairfax at the Club three years ago.'

Simi gritted her teeth. 'I remember that! *Most* enjoyable!'

'As I said to Imran, he's seen the best of Broadway – and now has only our homespun shows.' Nina smiled and touched his wrist. 'And those *songs!* Your idea?'

So they had discussed her! The doc was so hypocritical – complimenting her to her face, then bitching about her with his girlfriend in private.

'And have you seen many shows on Broadway?' Simi asked.

She was glad when Anjora and Ajay joined them, followed by Sanjay. But where was Pia? Simi looked round and saw her friend standing alone near a tall plant. Pia had refused to mingle with the audience after the play, preferring to stay alone in the dressing room. Simi wondered why Pia had decided to smoke on stage. In Atmapuri, women rarely smoked openly. They smoked in toilets and at private dinner parties, but never in front of elderly parents or their in-laws. Those were the rules. Some women tried to get around this by farcically puffing away behind an open newspaper held up as a screen; others wasted quantities of expensive French perfume to mask the smell.

Simi was about to approach Pia to ask, but the music changed to a pulsating *bhangra* beat and her friend glided forward as smoothly as a ghost. Pia began to dance with flailing arms, gyrating wildly until sweat poured down her face. Other dancers stopped and formed a semi-circle around her, clapping to the beat.

Sanjay leapt in to join Pia. He danced with the same energy as he poured into everything else he did, but he was clumsy. Pia, by comparison, moved like liquid mercury, like a goddess on the turn of the wheel. When the music ended, she stumbled, dazed and breathless. Sanjay placed a protective arm around her shoulders and guided her to a chair. He snapped his fingers and a waiter brought them cold lime juice. He leant forward to whisper in her ear. Simi was riveted. Her apprehensions for her friend persisted, but there was little she could do.

Later that night, Simi tossed and turned. She saw Pia in her dreams. First, she was seated on a wildly swinging chandelier and daring Simi to catch her; then Sanjay was building a green pyramid in a desolate landscape; then Pia cowered before a giant cat. She woke up in the morning feeling tired, her sheets like the waves of a storm-tossed sea.

CHAPTER 10

The day after the play, Simi decided to visit Marriam again. It was another sizzling morning and sweat licked her back like a lizard's tongue as she drove to Nawabganj. She wiggled against the seat to make herself comfortable and took a sip from the water bottle she kept in the car. Dr Chaudhry's medical camp had brought her up close to another world, which existed right on her doorstep. Now she wanted to do more to help Marriam and women like her, so she'd asked to meet the maid's friends in the slum.

When she arrived, Simi left her car on the high bank above Nawabganj and walked down carrying two bags of food. The slum children spotted her and followed her down the lanes, shouting 'Didi! Didi!'

Through open doorways, she spied clothes hanging on wall nails and grubby quilts that doubled as mattresses. Most homes had aerials on their roofs, sticking up like chicken feet. The television brought exotic images of a different world, yet the people of Nawabganj accepted their fate, blaming karma for their circumstances. But the baba had told Simi that karma was a mysterious thing and that the cycle of justice is not visible to men.

Simi had now visited Nawabganj often enough to recognise some of the brown children surrounding her: Mamta, Suman,

Shabana, Rehana, Farzana and the hopefully-named Rajkumari, meaning princess. They followed her in search of handouts, but the sweets Simi carried, and the bread and pickles, were for Marriam.

Thirteen women had crowded into Marriam's home, gathered at her request, including Marriam's cousin, Jaddan Bai, who had come from the old city with her daughter-in-law. Simi greeted them and opened the sweets, laying out milk cake squares on a steel plate. The women squatted on the floor or leant against walls, cooling themselves with straw fans. They had left the *charpoy* for Simi, who sat on it alone, rather self-consciously. Then women stared up at her, waiting to see what she would say.

'So, where shall we start?' Simi began uncertainly.

Jaddan Bai's round face split into wide smile. '*Aree*, but you're brave, Simi*baby*.'

Simi couldn't recall anything remotely brave she'd done. 'How so?'

'Sister Marriam told us about how you protect her, and your grandmother doesn't even like mussalman!'

Simi was mortified. Why did Marriam have to babble about Dadi? She was not responsible for the way her grandmother behaved.

She tried to explain, 'It's like this, you see, she doesn't mean it but she's old and it's hard to change.'

'No, no, it's good! That means you're on our side!' Jaddan Bai exclaimed.

When Jaddan Bai said it, Simi knew it to be true. She *was* on the side of these vulnerable women in their tidy but poor homes, not just the Muslims. She couldn't help noticing the grimy rag Marriam used for handling hot tea, stiff with old, dried liquid.

'Yes, we're friends, good girl-friends, aren't we?' They smiled and nodded. 'Now tell me what can I do for you?' Simi expected a stream of complaints about their children's health or lack of drinking water, or the hundred and one practical problems they faced daily.

Instead, Jaddan Bai said, 'When you get married, we'll come and sing for you, old wedding songs from our village! You'll invite us, *na*? I was twelve when my father got me married. How old you?'

Simi's years suddenly weighed heavy. 'Older than twelve!' she said and they laughed. 'Where were you born Jaddan Bai?'

Me? No one had ever taken an interest in her before. She leant forward with relish, adjusting the widow's white muslin scarf on her head before beginning.

'It was the bright night of the moon when I was born. My mother told me. A good time to come into this world, she said.' Her mother had loved the little Jaddan and wept when she left for her husband's home at fifteen, a couple of years after the onset of menstruation. At sixteen Jaddan gave birth to a son, Farid's older brother, assuring her position in the family. Hers was a tale of life in a dark village without electricity or running water, where women relieved themselves behind bushes in the early dawn and bathed with brackish well water. Buffalo slumbered inside the house with the rest of the family on frosty winter nights, while in the stifling heat of summer they all slept out in the open. Snakes were a menace in the summer, especially cobras.

Jaddan Bai continued for some time. Simi paid particular attention when the old woman started discussing her husband.

'He went to Moradabad looking for work. There was plenty for masons. He was the best mason!' she explained.

Being traditional, Jaddan Bai never took her husband's name. He was *He,* like God. The mason found lucrative work in the city, saved up and sent money home. Once a year he returned for a month and a child would be born in due course. Jaddan Bai had five children, two sons and three daughters, but the middle daughter had died of *bokhar* – 'fever' – which Simi knew could mean anything from cancer to kidney failure out in the villages. The mason had built a pucca home for his family with his own hands, but died young after falling from the bamboo scaffold on a construction site in Moradabad. Jaddan Bai discovered she was a widow when a yellow postcard arrived, written by a friend of her husband's in Moradabad, informing her that the mason had become *dear to God.*

'It was Allah's will,' Jaddan Bai said resignedly.

It had not been easy for her to raise four children alone. After hearing the news of her husband's death she couldn't eat for days. And even before her tears had dried, her brother-in-law tried to usurp her house. That got her up on her feet again. Land mattered. People thought that land belonged to them but really *they* belonged to the land. It gave them an anchor, a sense of worth.

'What did you do?' Simi asked.

'What did I do? I took my brother-in-law to court!' Jaddan Bai chortled, slapping her knees with glee.

Taking her fourteen-year old son with her, who had studied at the village school so could read and write, Jaddan Bai had boarded a bus for Moradabad. First, she sought out the friend who had written to tell her about her husband's death. From there, she went straight to court and filed a complaint against her brother-in-law.

'The police came to the village – never before had the police visited our family, we never did anything wrong. He lost face!' she explained.

The other villagers had mocked him and Jaddan Bai won her case. Through the years she had cultivated the land with the help of her children and made enough to pay for everything, including her children's marriages. Now her eldest son tended the land while she lived in Atmapuri with Farid.

'She showed him!' Marriam hooted. 'He wasn't fit to show his face in the village again. She's a tigress!'

'*Arre*, Simi*baby*, Allah sees everything,' Jaddan Bai explained. 'In Allah's house there may be delays but there is always justice.'

Simi loved the stout-hearted woman, but the only stout thing about Jaddan Bai was her spirit. She was thin with a worryingly persistent cough.

'You must let doctor*saab* look at your chest,' Simi said.

Jaddan Bai glanced down at her sagging breasts, then looked up and grinned at Simi, who laughed. It was all so unexpected, the earthiness of these women, their sense of fun. She had come prepared to uncover tragic lives, but she was enjoying herself. The mention of Dr Chaudhry brought a shower of blessings.

'He's a *farishta*. Allah loves the merciful,' Marriam said.

'Lucky girl, whoever he marries,' Jaddan Bai added.

Simi felt the conversation was getting off track. 'The doctor*saab* can help us,' she promised. 'I'll talk to him.'

Later that same day, once home, Simi rang Dr Chaudhry at his surgery, arranging to meet him the next evening. Their exchange was brief, but friendly. She smiled at the thought of seeing him.

They greeted each other in his consulting room at the appointed time, Dr Chaudhry courteously drawing out a chair for Simi before taking a seat on the other side of the desk. His old fashioned manners struck her as unusual. He had suggested she come late when all of the patients had gone. Eventually, the receptionist left too, popping her head round the door to announce her exit. Before leaving, she stopped to study Simi, hastily departing when she caught the doctor's eye. His clinic was rather chic for a surgery, with contemporary furniture and lighting. She looked for personal touches – photos of his family, paintings, bric-a-brac, anything – but there were none.

'So, what did you want to talk about?' he asked. He fidgeted with a pack of cigarettes on his desk, extracting one then pushing it back, stymied by his own rule forbidding smoking in the surgery. Simi noticed his long, bony fingers, rounded nails and half-moon cuticles.

She told him about her visit to Nawabganj. 'They're calling you a *farishta.*'

'*An angel?* God forbid! If only I was half as good as that.' He reflected for a moment, adding, 'And only *half* as bad as the municipal commissioners think I am!'

It was easy to talk to him and she liked his sardonic humour. Her father was fond of jokes and had enjoyed tripping her up with clever word games when she was little. They returned to the subject of Nawabganj.

'What do you want to do there?' he asked.

'Me?' Simi replied.

'Who else?'

She had arrived with half-formed notions of helping the women, thinking God-knows-what. Perhaps she expected him to tell her what to do? In her confusion, she got up and walked to the large window. The clinic was on the sixth floor of a modern building. Simi gazed at the lights of Atmapuri below. She recognised a couple of landmarks, including the squat, bulky buildings of the Muslim Imambaras, where the faithful congregated. In the foreground lay the imposing Oberoi hotel, the first in the city.

'Nice view,' she commented.

'Let me give you a guided tour,' he said. Taking her by the elbow, he steered her to a second window where he pointed out the brightly lit State Governor's house on the hill. From a third window, she saw the long red sandstone buildings of the State parliament, with their domed cupolas, constructed not long after partition.

Imran stood close to her, pointing out the sights. She could feel his bodily warmth and caught a faint whiff of patchouli. He was a good head taller than her. She noticed how his dark eyes, the colour of honey, crinkled at the corners when he smiled. She felt herself flush and moved away with a nervous laugh.

'What panoramic views! You could never get bored here.'

'Not that I have time to look!' he said. 'My father would have done better. He would have known some poem about it. He was a scholar of Farsi and Urdu. Rumi, Ghalib, Hafiz, Saadi, Attar, he studied them all. I regret never learning Farsi.'

He then declaimed something in Urdu. It was familiar to her, having heard it from her mother. His voice changed, assuming a rhythm and tempo not apparent in his everyday speech.

'Do you like poetry?' he asked.

'A little. English, I'm afraid.' She wished that she knew a little Urdu. Just then, it seemed terribly important.

'I learnt Urdu from Dr Tammana, my tutor,' he said, as though reading her mind. 'Poetry was his pet passion. That and the Quran. Poor man, he never understood how useless Urdu poetry is for modern life.' Dr Tammana had equipped his pupil to become a 19th century prince, not a twenty-first century doctor.

She wondered with a start whether he was a devout Muslim. He had cast little chinks of light on his background but never elaborated. Meanwhile, the question of what she planned to do in Nawabganj was still gnawing at her. A surreptitious glance at her watch told her that it was almost time for dinner and she should start making tracks.

Turning to face him, she said, 'I couldn't help noticing, when I was with Marriam yesterday, their basic lack of hygiene. I studied hygiene at school, so I could start there maybe?'

She could remember little of what she had learnt at school but felt it was enough to teach the women the basics.

'That's good,' he said, raking his hair with his fingers. 'It would make a huge difference, especially during the hot months and the rains. Yep! Washing hands, being careful about cooking and storing food, that sort of thing. That would help.'

His enthusiasm was infectious and she felt a surge of energy, until his next words dashed her spirits.

'I'll ask Nina to help you. She could structure it and even visit sometimes. I'm sure the women would prefer a woman doctor to me and she's very nice.'

Simi swallowed her protest and they fixed a time for her to meet Dr Nina Singh.

He glanced at his watch and exclaimed, 'Wow! Look at the time – have we really been here that long? How about some dinner? Shall we grab a bite somewhere?'

She declined reluctantly. 'Sorry, got to get back. My family will be waiting.'

He shrugged. 'OK, some other time then.'

Simi returned to the Nawabganj settlement some days later, with wall-charts acquired from Dr Nina Singh during an uncomfortable-but-informative briefing session. Dr Singh had been cool and condescending, but at least Simi had learnt something. However, the women of Nawabganj sniggered when Simi talked of germs.

Jaddan Bai asked, 'Why should we be afraid of something we can't even see?'

Simi was taken aback. She had not realised how difficult it would be to reach minds unaccustomed to abstractions. They understood drunken husbands and sick children, but microscopic germs were another matter entirely. A chart that Simi had put up on Marriam's wall showed how pathogens and diseases, such as malaria, were spread by the anopheles mosquito. The other two charts she had brought, one depicting the human skeleton and another bearing a graphic drawing of the womb during pregnancy, were laid rolled up on the bed.

Simi decided to change tack, since the direct approach had failed. An idea was taking shape in her head: why shouldn't she write down these women's stories? Their tales were alive with the sounds and smells of buffalos and calves, goatherds who took their flocks to graze at the edge of the jungle, and mothers who toiled from dawn till nightfall, winnowing wheat and carrying pots of water on their heads. Simi would start with her beloved maid.

'Marriam! Tell us about your wedding day,' she said.

Even Marriam's wrinkles appeared to smile at the suggestion. She was happy to recall the distant day when her mother had oiled and braided her hair in preparation for her nuptials. Her mother had always favoured her, putting an extra meatball or handful of rice on her plate. Her groom and his family had arrived in bullock carts from a village five *kos* away.

'Only the men came, no women,' she explained.

The bullocks were slow, the roads rutted and a stream they had to ford was swollen with rainwater, so the party arrived well past midnight. By which point the young bride-to-be had fallen asleep. But her father, uncles and village elders greeted the groom's party respectfully with folded hands, recognising them as honoured guests. After a few years, of course, they would find themselves barely on speaking terms, but for now they were to be treated like gods.

The bullocks which had pulled the carts had to be fed and watered. Afterwards, they washed their guests' feet and served a meal prepared by the women, with a rice pulao of basmati, lentils, three types of vegetables and goat curry. The goat had been killed that morning, so the halal meat was very fresh. They also served hot *chappatis* dripping with ghee and raw onions, smashed by a heavy fist and sprinkled with salt and red chillies. To finish off there were two sweet dishes – a milky carrot pudding and semolina halwa. Once the guests could eat no more, it was the turn of Marriam's father and his side of the family. By the time the pots and pans had been washed, it was already dawn. Throughout, Marriam waited in an inner room with her cousins, too excited to sleep.

Later that day, at noon, her *nikaah* was performed in the traditional way: Marriam in one room with her mother, female cousins and friends, and the groom in a separate room with the males. The priest was the go-between. Marriam had little idea of what was happening at the time, but when someone congratulated her mother, who cried, Marriam knew she was married. She had no idea what marriage meant, but was happy to have received new red clothes with glittering gold braids, silver bangles for her wrists, silver anklets and tiny gold hoops for her ears. She had never before received so many gifts and was ready to get married every day if that's what it meant.

Marriam, like Jaddan Bai, stayed with her parents until her first menstruation, after which they performed the ceremony for her departure. Her father then escorted her to her in-laws' village.

When Marriam had finished her tale, they had another round of tea. Out of the blue, Simi asked the women, 'Can you see death?'

They tittered with laughter. Simi smiled and added, 'But we all die, don't we? Just because you can't see death, that doesn't mean you're not afraid of it, *hain?*'

They fell silent. Hindu, Muslim, rich or poor, all feared death. Being Hindu, Simi had grown up with the image of Yamraj, the God of Death, who rode a buffalo. Or was it an ox? She couldn't remember. Of all the gods, she had least interest in him. But how did Muslim women think of death? She asked Marriam.

Marriam responded sombrely, 'The Angel of Death took him away in January.' She referred to her husband. 'It was very cold, the wind was like a knife. *Malkul Maut* took his soul away.' Death, to Marriam, was inseparable from thoughts of her husband. She explained that on Judgment Day he would rise. Then the Angels Munkir and Nakir, the account-keepers, would make a tally of his deeds on Earth.

Who wasn't afraid of death? Each of them thought of their unfinished business in life. One of the women had a daughter to be married off, another a sick child to be nursed, another still a daughter-in-law waiting to deliver a baby.

Simi also realised that many of the women were illiterate. How could she discuss hygiene, anatomy or biology if they could not read and write? Her heart quailed at the scale of her task. She slowly rolled up the medical charts and resolved to bring one with the Hindi alphabet first, the shiny calendar-like ones that depicted green parrots, white cauliflowers and Mahatma Gandhi.

CHAPTER 11

The morning after the play, while Simi was getting ready for her trip to Nawabganj, Pia lay in bed with a smile on her face. She was euphoric. The evening before, Sanjay had been solicitous of her every need, snapping his fingers at waiters to bring her food and drink, treating her like a queen! *Sunju! Sunju! Sunju!* She rolled over in bed, kicking off the top sheet to cool her legs and hugging her pillow. It was the one she had brought with her from Nainital, made in Delhi especially for her father and stuffed with feathers: goose or chicken, she wasn't sure which.

Sanjay had dropped Pia off at the hostel at one in the morning. The hostel doors were normally locked at eleven, but she had special permission to stay out late because of the play. Boys – men – were not permitted to enter the 'Girls Only' establishment and the matron raised hell if she caught one, so Sanjay had parked outside, near the scented creeper, under the dark shadow of the gulmohar tree. The tension between them had been palpable before he kissed her. It had been so sudden, so spontaneous, so *natural,* as though they did it every day. After that, of course, sleep evaded her in her virginal room.

The memory of their passionate kiss was more real to her in the morning than the cheap mat on her cement floor or her square scratched and tea stained table, over which she had spent so many hours with her books. Even the dispiriting sight of the corridor outside her room, with its film of dust and wilting money-plants in cracked terracotta pots, failed to dismay her. This morning everything vibrated with love.

So when the blow fell it was crueller for being unexpected. Collecting her post from the mail room, Pia noticed there were two letters from her mother. *Why two?* That irritated her. Hadn't she just spent two months in Nainital, doing her duty? She stuffed the unopened blue letter-forms, addressed in her mother's spidery handwriting, into her tapestry shoulder bag and pulled out a cigarette instead. *The look on their faces when she walked on stage with a smouldering 555 in her hand!* She laughed aloud, hugging herself. Sanjay had admired her daring and that's all that mattered. The play had been a success and she loved Sanjay even more for that.

The letters remained unread until after lunch, when she was alone in her room. She carelessly split them both open, tearing off some of the text and wondering what desultory details they contained of provincial life. Her mother was preoccupied with meals and her letters often included the previous day's menu and complaints about how the cook over-salted the dal. One letter was postmarked the twenty-first of May and the other the 15th. She picked up the later one. It contained little more than a paragraph.

21st May

Dear daughter Pia,

I am still with Urmi. Ten lifetimes will not be enough for me to repay what she's done for me. Ramesh too has been like a son to me. His contractor's men carried our roof up from the valley and with Mahadeva's blessings it was still in one piece. Can you imagine that? Tiles are missing but they'll fix that. So you need not come. In case you've already left, then that's okay, otherwise don't leave. Urmi's going to take care of me until it's all done. Mahadeva is great and I rest at His Feet but the bill for the repairs is very big and I worry about other bills because the damage is great. Water is everywhere! And you know what water's like when it gets in. So I won't be able to send you money for a while. I am sure you've saved something from the money orders I've been sending you and will manage through this difficult time come to test us. I don't know what God wants of me. First he left me alone and now this. I pray to Mahadeva to protect us.

With love and blessings,
Mummy

Pia tugged at the short hair on her nape, worried. Urmila and her husband Ramesh were their neighbours in Nainital. She grabbed the earlier letter to try and make sense of it all.

15ᵗʰ May
Dear daughter Pia,

What a storm there was, as if the demons of our hills got together to blow us off the Earth, that's how bad it was. I thought that our house would come down. With Mahadeva's blessings it didn't but the roof blew off. I could see it, a patch of blue down-down in the valley below. Hey Bhagwan! Why did I have to live to see this day? I was sleeping when the noise woke me up and thought thieves were entering the house. I nearly died of fright. But Urmi rang immediately and said Aunty, don't be afraid, it's only a bad storm. But then I heard the most frightening sound that I can't even describe and our roof disappeared. My heart almost stopped and my eyes were red with crying. Urmi ran across at once in that howling wind and rain such as I've never seen before. I didn't think I'd live through the night but Urmi took me to her house and with Mahadeva's blessings I am still here. I don't know what I would have done without her. So considerate, so loving she is, making sure I eat before she eats. She cooks dal and at least two vegetables. I told her one vegetable would be enough – but no! She even puts me before Mahesh. I told her she mustn't do that, for what is a woman alone without a husband? Why am I being punished like this? First your father was taken and now it's raining as though the holy Ganga's falling on our heads. Many things in the house have been ruined, even the picture of your father hanging in the drawing room that you like so much although I tried my best to dry it. The shop is safe by the grace of God and everything in it.

Come quickly, Pia. Whatsoever it is, a friend is a friend and flesh-and-blood is flesh-and-blood. Your last letter took almost two weeks to reach, the post is really getting very bad these days. Send a telegram telling me of your arrival.

Love and blessings,
Mummy

Pia felt as though her head was exploding. Did her mother imagine that the pittance she sent each month would allow her to save up? Pia pinched and scraped, never splurging on taxis or good clothes, but everything cost three times more in Atmapuri than Nainital. Short of starving, she didn't see how she could spend any less. Even the greasy omelette she'd eaten at the college canteen for lunch cost money.

She was also devastated about the damage to the house. The blue tiled roof had been laid by her father, becoming a symbol of his enduring protection. She recalled the spring day when he died. Cold and crisp, the air had been crystal clear, as if you could reach out and touch the distant snowy peaks beyond the valleys. The servant had fetched her from school, dispatched by her mother with a chit, the contents of which prompted her teacher to let her go without a word. She had skipped along, wondering when the wild strawberries would ripen. Back home Pia found her face pressed into her mother's silk sari, her mother clasping the schoolgirl to her wet bosom. When she heard the tragic news, Pia was too stunned to cry. Confused, she had turned against her mother, as though breaking the news made her responsible. She spent days curled up on the sofa with a silent scream trapped inside her.

How will I manage without money? At first, Pia had intended to return home as 'Dr Pandey' and teach at the Sherwood, Nainital's premiere school, perhaps even becoming its headmistress in time – but not now. She had decided to stay on in Atmapuri. As for living with her mother again – not now, not ever. Should she try and borrow money from Simi? Too humiliating. And Sanjay? She felt sick at the thought. A man who paid a woman's bills had bought her.

Restless, she threw off her cotton skirt and splashed water on her bare legs, but the ceiling fan merely stirred the warm air without cooling her. She opened her window but the desolate landscape under the scorching sun outside intensified her loneliness, so she shut it again. She tried the shower instead, but when she stood under it the head belched, sprinkled her with rusty water and dried up. *Hell!* She picked up a tin of talcum powder and flung it across the room, where it hit the toilet with a clang before rolling away. Ignoring the little shrine she kept in a corner that her mother had given it to her, with a small image of Mahadeva, Lord Shiva, and a brass bell that she had never rung, Pia threw herself down on her bed, naked, staring up. A lizard crawled across the white plaster ceiling, grabbing spiders and insects with its darting tongue.

Two weeks later, Pia felt that she had plumbed the depths. She had written a brief letter to her mother telling her not to worry and had resolved to work part-time until she completed her studies. She scrutinised job advertisements in the newspapers and on the university notice boards, but finding employment became a task for the gods she no longer believed in. A small publisher in a poky office on the fourth floor of a shabby building needed a full-time secretary but she couldn't put in the hours; the beauty parlour required a trained hair stylist, not a receptionist; the printer tried to proposition her. She even applied to become a researcher for a renowned cookbook author. The woman seemed interested, but when they talked about money she offered only lunch and travel expenses. As a consolation, she sent Pia off with a copy of her first cookbook. The succulent dishes pictured therein only made her more ravenous.

The harsh sun burnt her to the colour of a walnut as she trudged from interview to interview. *It was that dread law again.* Pia's Law said that, if something could go wrong, it would. It had first struck her at fifteen, when her father died. Her brother returned to his boarding school after the cremation, so she was left alone to bear the burden of her mother's fears. Mrs Pandey had worried so much about money that the little girl imagined they might have to become street beggars. That sense of insecurity had stayed with her. Of course, her mother had gone on to make a success of the shop. Pia conveniently forgot that.

She had at least managed to clear her canteen bill for May, which meant her credit was good until the end of June, but she had cut down on food. Anxious, unable to concentrate, she avoided the library. If she got a job she could continue with her studies, even if she had less time. Now she had the time but couldn't focus.

She spent the evenings with Sanjay but told him nothing. She had her pride, after all. She masked her anxiety with love. They discussed politics, shared plates of kebabs and naan bread, and she listened avidly to his ambitions of becoming a member of parliament and moving to Delhi. She came to know every millimetre of his craggy face, with its high forehead, sensuous mouth and the 'cow's lick' in his hair. His teeth were stained, perhaps from too much tea. She quietly decided to take him to her dentist when she knew him better.

'Will you be my lover?' he asked boldly on their second evening together, as they sat in an air conditioned coffee shop with marble tables and soft cushioned seats.

She almost choked on her cold coffee with ice-cream. '*Sanjay!* I'm not *that* sort of a girl,' she replied primly.

Later, in the car, she slapped away his wandering hand. He merely laughed and ran his fingers through her short hair, muttering under his breath, 'It's like petting a sheep!'

'What? What did you say?' she drew back to glare at him.

'Nothing, sweetie. Only, you have beautiful hair – why don't you grow it?'

'What *is it* with men and hair? If you're looking for a dolly-bird with long tresses, I'm not the one. Cavemen dragged their females around by their long hair.' *She* was not about to become a slave to any man.

'Relax, darling, only a thought. I *love* your birdy ostrich look!' he roared, pulling her back into his arms. He understood her defiance and enjoyed the challenge. She had a good mind and had surprised him with her grasp political nuances. His kisses were impetuous, just like him.

As time went by, it became harder to bid him goodnight at the hostel gate, especially when he pleaded with her to stay longer. But she tore herself away, muttering about 'The Matron … ' and returned to her lonely room.

Some luckless days later, depression overcame her. She considered the desperate measure of working in a large dairy with a hundred cows, but the stench of cow-flesh-and-sweat mixed with dung and bovine urine made her nauseous.

There was a job for her though, now that she was at the end of her tether. Not much of a job, but it would do. She hesitated outside Mr Lall's shop, watching him pick his nose. Mr Lall was not fit to spend ten minutes with her, let alone ten months, but ...

She steeled herself and went in. His forehead was daubed with religious markings after his morning prayers and his eyes studied her through pink-rimmed spectacles as she mounted the steps from the street. *Lall's General Merchants* was just outside the university, within easy reach of students and local housewives, so she could easily walk to work. It had an old-fashioned interior, its wood-and-glass cabinets piled high with Lux soap, packets of peanuts, pencils and various other sundries.

'Yes, sar?' he enquired, picking up a brown paper bag to fill it with her order. He addressed all customers as 'sar' regardless of gender.

She stammered slightly as she explained that she wasn't here as a customer. He examined her doubtfully. Pia's heart quailed but she brazened it out.

'Look, Mr Lall, I can make your business grow. I'll make you an inventory so that we're never over-stocked. I'll also make it more attractive to students to draw them in. Not like now!' she sniffed.

'What's wrong with my shop?' he said, defensively.

She waved dismissively. 'It's not trendy – but I can show you how. That will be good for business. Will you hire me?'

She managed to cow him, but got stuck on the point of wages. They compromised by agreeing that Pia would only work in the afternoons, five times a week. That would leave her with plenty of time to work on her thesis, which she would now try and finish early.

She started work immediately, re-arranging the counter, removing the collapsed pyramids of soap and generally sorting the jumble of produce in the shop. Foodstuffs went into the counter, neatly laid out in rows on the glass shelf inside. The oil, washing powder and other household cleaning materials went on the wooden shelves lining the walls. She neatly stacked the brooms in an old umbrella stand and lit sandalwood joss sticks to drive away the odour that lingered like an unwashed ghost. Next, she would attack the small dark storeroom, which was a total mess.

For five days, she avoided encountering anyone she knew, adroitly ducking into the store at awkward moments. This was hard to explain to Mr Lall, but he was a passive, intensely religious man and she managed to keep him sweet. But her luck ran out on the sixth day, when Sanjay drew up outside.

Pia froze when she saw his car and disappeared into the storeroom before he managed to park under the shade of a flowering gulmohar tree. Inside, she gasped for breath and inhaled the spice. With a muffled curse she pinched her nose to arrest a sneeze, listening intently to Sanjay and Mr Lall in the next room. They exchanged greetings, then Sanjay cracked a joke and she heard Mr Lall respond with a slow, heavy laugh. *He was so good with people, her Sanjay! A born politician!* She heard him reel off a list of things he needed and shut her eyes, dreading the summons that soon came.

'Miss Pia, Sanjay sar is here. Don't you know who he is? Don't keep him waiting!'

She had been praying that Mr Lall would just give him the things he needed and send him away. But now she dragged herself to the door, paused for breath and plunged into the shop, her chin glued to her chest. She darted one quick look at

Sanjay's face and saw him staring in disbelief. Without risking a second glance, she sidled along the counter to the farthest end of the shop. He turned and strode after her.

'What're you doing here?' he demanded. Her face was flaming red and she stood with her head bowed, conscious that Mr Lall was watching them. Small gusts of warm air propelled little crimson gulmohar petals into the shop. She looked at them, thinking that she'd have to clear them away later, after Sanjay had gone.

'C'mon, let's get out of here,' he said.

'I don't finish till six,' she replied miserably. 'What did you come for? Just gimme your order.'

'Six-wix nothing! You're coming now.' Turning his head, he called across, 'Lall! Miss Pia is needed back at the university. Urgent business. She's taking the afternoon off.' He knew that Mr Lall would not resist him. It would take more than a mere fifty years of independence to destroy the servility of the Lalls of this world.

Pia quietly picked up her handbag and followed Sanjay out to his car, forgetting to bid Mr Lall goodbye. They drove in silence until they were in the university grounds, which were deserted in the afternoon heat. He parked under a leafy tree and climbed out. She went and stood beside him but averted her face, acutely embarrassed.

'Why?' he cried. 'What *were* you doing there?'

She ignored him, doodling in the dust on the car's bonnet with her finger until he grasped her shoulders and turned her round to face him. 'Pia! Talk to me!'

She stuck out her lower lip and replied, 'OK. I need the money. My mother can't support me – maybe never again. What do you expect me to do? There's my studies, my room rent and … I took a job. That's all.'

'With *Lall?*

'Yes, with Lall!' she shouted, her pent-up frustration breaking through. 'Nobody in this wretched place wants a part-time anything! I tried, but no publisher, printer or office wanted me!'

He turned, kicking a pebble that struck the tree trunk with a dull thud. She half-turned to stare at the redbrick university buildings, dishevelled and dusty, yet so vital to her. She felt like running off, howling, moaning and lamenting. Instead, she stood paralysed as the minutes ticked away.

Suddenly, Sanjay struck the car roof violently with the flat of his hand. 'That's it! This is the end.'

'What? What're you saying?' she asked in a small voice.

'*Sweetheart!*' he said sarcastically, 'If you think so little of me that that you won't come to me when you're in trouble – my God! All those evenings we spent together and you never breathed a word! Tight as an ant's bum.'

'Please Sunju, try and understand. How could I ask you for money?'

He threw up his hands. 'No, you'd rather go to that *Lall!* I understand.' He told her how he felt. She saw that his pride was hurt. Did he love her? The word had not been spoken. She wanted to believe it but her fear taunted her.

'What would you have thought of me?' she asked.

'That you trusted me. But go on, ride your high horse and slave for that donkey Lall!'

She shivered, feeling empty, as though all the colour and noise had suddenly been drained away from the world.

'Do you love me?' she prompted, holding her breath.

'Of course I love you! Why else would I waste my time with you?' His loud, booming laugh fell like rain on her parched being. Intense relief flooded through her and she faced him, two young bodies brimming with life. 'Listen Pi, you're the cleverest girl I know. You've got a quick mind and you're beautiful and I love you. I thought you'd have understood that.'

It had been said. The temperature was almost 40°C and he was sweating profusely when they got back in the car. She reached out to wipe his forehead with a hanky, an old-fashioned habit inherited from her mother. She had reached a decision.

'Perhaps you can make me a loan. A loan, understand? Just to tide me over.'

'All this loan-shoan business! Why don't you just let me help you?'

'No, Sunju, no. A loan, not a gift. That's my condition.'

He reached out for her hand, resting his cheek against her palm. 'Yes, my queen.' Their silence now had a new quality, like the embrace of a family member.

It was time for Sanjay to attend a meeting, so he dropped Pia off a short distance from her hostel, swivelling round to say, 'And no more Lall?'

'Good riddance!' she answered with an impudent grin.

Pia's life had transformed and she went home walking on air. They arranged to meet later for dinner, which left her with four hours to burn. She turned her fan on full speed and flung open the window. Without thinking, she went to crouch before the small shrine in the corner of her room. Who had delivered her? Her mother's God? She was not quite ready to believe that. She shut the window, locked her room again and made her way to an expensive beauty parlour in an auto-rickshaw.

CHAPTER 12

Simi had arranged to see Marriam's friends again a fortnight after their last meeting. On the morning in question, word came of trouble in the streets of Old Atmapuri. It was a crowded part of the city and Hindu pilgrims on their way to the ancient Shiva temples had added to the congestion. Having so many people of different faiths crammed into the narrow lanes had created a tinderbox. Any small incident could spark off communal trouble, as the police knew from past experience, so they now patrolled the streets day and night.

Simi never visited the old city, nor had any reason to, but the unrest meant she could not leave home that morning. Marriam had not shown up either. Television reports showed empty streets and the smoking remains of an auto-rickshaw. Simi occupied herself by thinking about the book of the women's stories she wanted to write, tentatively titled *Baby Brides* or *The Marriam Mothers*. She thought about the cover too – a photograph of Marriam and Jaddan Bai? And Sangita, who was Hindu, *because* she was Hindu?

Her India, as her parents had raised her to think of it, was a place that ignored a person's religion, but outside the house Atmapuri seemed to be altogether different. Hindus and Muslims did not mix well. Then there were the Christians, who ate both beef and pork, not to mention those Sandras in short skirts, flashing their bare legs. Simi had abandoned skirts when she was about fifteen, perhaps because of her grandmother, who mocked her for wearing them, saying, 'You look like a Chutney Mary!'

By midday, the city seemed to have returned to normal and Simi was restless, so after lunch she told her mother she was going out, then set off into the hottest part of the afternoon. It was the middle of June and dust clouds whirled like dervishes in the burning breeze, the sun beating down fiercely on Simi's car as she drove to Nawabganj. When she got there she parked under the shade of a laburnum tree, its yellow flowers falling gently like gold flakes.

Marriam was astonished to see her.

'*Arre* Simi*baby?* Allah! On a day like this!' she pulled her in and shut the door behind her. Worry lines ran like gorges across her forehead and cheeks.

'I know there was some trouble this morning,' Simi said, 'but things are quiet now.'

Marriam shook her head. 'No, Simi*baby*. There are many, many strange men in Atmapuri. Who are they? Where they come from? I don't know. My mother told me that when she was little, locusts ate up all the crops. No food, so people die. They'd eat anything to live, even dead baby.'

Locusts? 'No one's seen a locust in sixty years, Marriam!' Simi countered her old ayah. 'Why are you talking about locusts? These must be pilgrims or something, or maybe scholars.' The Nawab's library was one of the finest in North India. Scholars came from all over the world to study the manuscripts within. But Marriam shook her head dolefully.

Simi decided to take control of the conversation. 'Let's think of what we're going to discuss today,' she said. 'Where are the others?'

'At home. Jaddan Bai's in Old Atmapuri. I'm so worried. No news. No bus,' Marriam explained. None of them had phones.

'Let's go get Sangita then,' suggested Simi. Sangita lived just across the main road, in the Hindu half of Nawabganj.

'Allah! You want me to go *there* today?'

Simi nodded and went out, so Marriam was forced to follow. The Hindu half of Nawabganj looked identical to the Muslim half, except for the tree shrine to Hanuman the Monkey-Faced God. The tree was daubed with vermilion and saffron markings, a marigold garland hanging from a nail in its trunk. Marriam dragged her feet but they finally arrived at Sangita's door. Like Marriam, Sangita, a fresh-faced woman of about twenty, was shocked to see Simi. Simi smiled, gestured that she wanted to enter and walked right in. Marriam hesitated by the door. Inside, Sangita's baby lay in a wicker basket, howling. His mother picked him up and cradled him, crooning softly. Another shrine to Lord Hanuman was nailed on a wall bracket in a dark corner.

'Did you forget our meeting, Sangita?' Simi asked.

'But ... but ...' Sangita looked past her at Marriam, who stood squinting in the sun. Her voice dropped, '*Didi*, haven't you heard of the trouble in the old city?'

It was stifling in the small clammy room and Simi was thirsty, but she had left her water bottle with her papers and charts at Marriam's place.

'Listen, Sangita, you're doing so well in our classes – we must carry on. Come on, let's go.'

Sangita paused before speaking, worry in her voice. 'What will Hanuman say,' she asked, referring to her husband, not the God, 'if I go to *that side* ... ?' Sangita had been to Marriam's home umpteen times before, but today it was different.

'*Your Hanuman* will know you're safe with me,' Simi declared, drawing herself up to her full five-foot-two inches.

Sangita shook her head doubtfully, but followed Simi obediently, baby Mahesh on her hip. Simi noted sorrowfully the strained silence between her and Marriam. On the way out they collected Rajkumari. Neither of them had refused to come, but Simi was deeply dismayed nonetheless. Things had been so different last time.

Back at Marriam's home, Simi served the women the biscuits she had brought, then settled down with her pen and notebook, coaxing Sangita to tell her story. Sangita spoke bashfully, covering her mouth with her *pallav*.

'*Didi*, I was so high when they married me off,' she said, indicating a spot about two feet above the ground. Simi estimated that she couldn't have been much more than five years old at the time.

'Hanuman was the same age as me. I was happy playing with my wooden toys, what did I know about marriage?'

Simi could just imagine the two children togged up, she in red with gold bells stitched to the hem of her tiny skirt. She would have been like a doll. Child marriage was forbidden by law, but this country stuck doggedly to custom.

'I sat in my father's lap and the holy smoke from the fire hurt my eyes, so I closed them and fell asleep. Then father shook me. Hanuman, for some reason, jumped up and tried to run away, but then his pyjama fell down!'

Marriam chortled. Simi laughed. She wanted to encourage the women.

'Women are great, Sangita, just remember that. They're mothers to kings and saints.'

'*Didi*, *Bhagwan* gave you everything. You're rich but we're poor. It is hard without money.'

Simi reflected ruefully that they looked up to her. In her view, her twenty-five years didn't amount to much. She had lived in the White House her entire life. Sure, she'd been to university and read a few books, but that was not a lot compared to the stories these women had to tell.

'If you were me,' Simi asked, 'what would you do?'

'Learn English. And do git-mit just like you!' Sangita replied promptly.

'OK, OK, English next, but Hindi first. And counting. You must learn some maths.'

Simi had also brought a box of milk cake with her and shared it with everyone as they talked, but the Hindu women unapologetically refused Marriam's tea. Everyone knew the score and nobody resented it. Simi was beginning to discover the true meaning of food and drink – one could tell a lot from who could accept water from whom. That simple act was like a microcosm of the complex caste system. Hindus did not accept water from Muslims; upper caste Hindus didn't accept it from low caste ones. Hindus didn't eat *halal* meat and Muslims didn't eat *jhatka* meat.

The women were restless, though not only because of the morning's commotion. They were more worried about their homes. Simi had forgotten about the court case and the threat to Nawabganj, but the women thought of nothing else. *It would be dreadful if they were moved just when they were coming to grips with the alphabet*, Simi thought to herself. She did her best to reassure them, but could not guarantee anything.

The sun was setting fast when Simi left, Marriam walking her to her car. Preparing to drive away, she switched on the car's headlamps, but was arrested by the sight of a man running towards them. Marriam recognised him at once as Jaddan Bai's son and started forward, crying, 'Farid! All well, Farid?'

Reaching Farid, Marriam grabbed him by the arm, peering anxiously into his face. 'Is it my Ahmudi? What's wrong?'

Farid shook his head. 'I haven't seen Ahmed all day,' he explained breathlessly, 'It's Ammi! There's been trouble at the bazaar. Ammi's hurt!'

A stone flung by a miscreant had struck Jaddan Bai on her left temple. His mother had been caught in the crossfire when she went to the bazaar to buy eggs.

'Ammi fell down, she was unconscious. Had our neighbour not seen ... she's home now but coughing, coughing. It's difficult for her to breathe.'

'I'll come now!' Marriam exclaimed, running to lock her door. But it was already dark, which put Simi in a quandary. She knew the bus service was still patchy and Farid had hitched a ride on a two-wheeler scooter, so she wondered how Marriam would reach Jaddan Bai. Should she take her, despite not knowing the old city?

'Marriam, I'll drive you,' Simi announced.

Marriam objected. '*You*, Simi*baby*? But ... you must go home.'

'No, I'm coming with you. Hop in.' Simi stopped at a tea stall and asked to use their phone. Luckily, they had one. She rang her mother to say she would be late, hanging up without giving her time to protest. She also rang Imran and explained that Marriam's cousin, who lived in the old city, needed a doctor. And that she was on her way there.

'No, don't come here,' warned Imran, 'I'm at the Shastri Hospital in the old city. It's dangerous.'

Simi hesitated, but made up her mind. 'Marriam's in the car,' she said over the phone, 'I'll find some way to call you when I get there.' She hung up.

Was he angry with her? She squared her shoulders, paid for the calls and went back to the car. Marriam sat in front with her, while Farid fidgeted anxiously in the back. It was hot, dark and crowded on the road to the old city, with horns *phoennnn-toooont-*

toont-ing and cyclists suddenly appearing from nowhere. Black and yellow auto-rickshaws fought for space like angry wasps. It was impossible to drive fast and the car's air-conditioning didn't work at this speed, so Simi rolled down the windows to cool herself. Marriam was praying next to her, under her breath.

Imran's warning echoed in Simi's head as she glanced at the rear-view mirror for signs of trouble. She had left behind the bright street lamps of modern Atmapuri and entered a maze of unfamiliar lanes, blindly following Farid's directions. Gritting her teeth, Simi negotiated the narrow lanes. They turned a corner and three figures emerged from the dark, forcing the car to stop. A fist thumped the car bonnet.

'Hey, you! Out!' A face appeared at the window. Simi was petrified.

'Asif! Is that you?' Farid called out from the back, showing himself. 'It's Farid. That's my aunt in there. Ammi's ill.' Asif bent down to peer at Simi and Marriam before waving them on. 'Thanks, *yaar*,' called Farid, as he settled back into his seat.

They drove off. Simi exhaled noisily. 'Who *were* they?' she asked.

'Friends – sort of,' Farid replied laconically.

It was a relief when they reached their destination, the journey having taken almost an hour. The front door of Farid's house, like most here, was made of thick wood with iron nails and bolts. Farid's wife opened it almost before he had time to knock. They rushed through the tiny front courtyard, past pails of washing and scraggly cactus plants, into the front room, where an exhausted Jaddan Bai lay in bed. The dim yellow light of a zero-watt bulb cast a jaundiced pallor over her skin. A bandage covered her head like a turban.

'Sister! We're here – Simi*baby* too,' Marriam patted her cousin's hand. 'Everything will be alright.' Jaddan Bai greeted them with a wan smile.

Simi held her other hand, stroking it gently. 'Any pain? Doctor*saab* wants to know.'

Jaddan Bai's voice was feeble. Simi made a quick mental note of what she said then went out again in the car, with Farid, to find a phone and tell Imran where she was. The Shastri Hospital was not far away and Farid gave Imran directions to a nearby petrol pump, where they waited for him.

The evening had acquired a dreamlike quality for Simi and she was immensely grateful when Imran arrived in his Jeep. She jumped out to meet him.

'Are you alright?' he asked, grasping her elbow. '*Khuda!* You're either very brave or–'

'Or very foolish?' Simi was perilously close to tears.

'Or an angel, I was going to say!'

An hour later, Jaddan Bai lay in a room in the Shastri Hospital. Her wound was deep and she had lost a fair amount of blood, but her eye had been saved. She looked cadaverous in the big white bed with the drip in her arm. By now the other visitors had left and the duty doctor had returned to his room. Farid and Marriam sat quietly at the foot of the bed.

Imran drew Simi outside and shut the door behind them. 'A nasty blow – plus there's the shock. She needs to stay in hospital for a couple of days.'

'And the cost?' she asked anxiously.

Imran removed the stethoscope from around his neck and stuffed it into his pocket.

'She may have TB the way she's coughing. I'll get the tests done. I won't charge my fee, of course, and I'll get a discount for the room but-' he stopped. 'Hey, are you OK? You look like *you* need a doctor!'

Simi was shivering. 'It was horrible, horrible! I was so frightened … it reminded me of Anjora's wedding … '

He was about to place his arm around her, but hastily checked himself.

'Shhh, shh. It's all over. You're safe.' She had cried on his shoulder once before and he suddenly chuckled at the memory.

She stiffened and frowned at him. He held up his hands, palms out. 'Sorry! Sorry! It's just that you're such an innocent – I've seen *too* many thieves and scoundrels! Forgive me.'

She sniffed irritably. 'But what *happened*? Another riot? We never heard anything more after this morning.'

He gestured with his hand. 'No, no, but there were some ugly incidents and poor Jaddan Bai got caught up in them.' It had started with stones, then knives were flicked open. 'Forget it. Life will be normal again tomorrow.'

She shuddered. 'How can they live like that?'

He gave her a compassionate look. 'You need some fun. Tell you what; I'm visiting a friend soon. A lovely woman. Will you come? You'll enjoy it, I promise you.'

A lovely woman? She didn't like the sound of that. 'Who is she?'

He grinned. 'A mystery woman! And if you don't come, you'll never find out!'

She nodded. 'But only if you promise to come to my birthday.' She would turn twenty-five in three days.

'A party? Great.'

'I know what you're thinking – that only children have birthday parties!'

'Twenty-one?' Imran smiled as he said this.

Simi wasn't about to correct him. 'Let's just say it's a special one. Friday the 25th at the White House.'

'It's a date!' he said, adding to himself, *or as close as I'll get to one in Atmapuri.*

They went back inside and Simi soon left with Marriam. Once they had found their way back to a familiar part of the city, Marriam insisted that Simi drop her off at a bus stop.

When Simi finally arrived home, she felt gutted. Her mother rose from the sofa as she entered.

'Sam! Where *were* you? Do you know what time it is?'

'Emergency!' Simi called out without pausing. 'Mama, I'll quickly shower and come down in two ticks.' She wept in the shower, wiped her face and put on a fresh cotton salwar-kameez. Over a late meal in the air-conditioned dining room, she narrated the evening's events as blandly as possible.

'Sam, what possessed you?' Devi cried. 'Gogu, you let her go out and look what happens. The old city!'

'She can take care of herself, darling,' he murmured, ladling mutton curry onto his rice *pulao.*

Devi frowned at him before turning back to her daughter. 'You've gone too far, Sam. I encouraged you to work with the slum women, you were so excited about it – but not like this. Now you're putting yourself in danger! In the old city! At night!'

'I'm famished! I didn't have any lunch,' Simi said, spooning yogurt *raita* into her mouth and trying to ignore her mother's admonition. They ate in silence until Simi pushed her plate away with a contented little burp, eliciting a frown from Devi. For dessert, Simi ate a golden *dussehri* mango, which tasted like saffron honey.

Then she ate another. And another. She only stopped after the fifth. 'I could *live* on mangoes!' she declared.

'You already do!' her mother replied, scrutinising her daughter's cheeks, 'I'm surprised you don't have pimples.'

Still at the supper table, Simi determined to get the money for Jaddan Bai's treatment from her parents. She toyed with the slice of lemon in her finger bowl before wiping her hands dry, plucking up the courage to ask for their help.

'Mama, Papa, there's something else. Jaddan Bai's room in the hospital will cost and she can't pay.' Drawing in a deep breath, she added, 'Can you – will you? She's probably got TB.'

Devi chewed on a piece of *amla* in syrup. She ate one every night for her voice.

'How much?' Gogu asked.

'Ten thousand rupees?' suggested Simi. 'For now anyway. Dr Chaudhry's not charging and he'll get a discount from the hospital, but the tests and … '

Devi shook her head.

'Please, Mama, we can't let her *die!*' Turning to her father, she cried, 'It's the price of a life, Papa.'

'Don't be melodramatic!' Devi chided her.

Gogu glanced sideways at his wife, as if seeking her consent. Drawing a deep breath, he said, 'Alright, Sam, if it matters so much to you. Marriam's lucky to have you.'

Simi clapped her hands. 'I knew you'd do it! I knew it! I'll take it across first thing tomorrow morning.'

'Let that be your birthday present,' her father said, but his mouth twitched.

That night, Simi lay sleepless, unable to put the day's events out of her mind. Imran seemed to take it all in his stride and obviously thought her naïve!

Meanwhile, in their bedroom, Devi scolded her husband.

'You've always spoilt Sam. Look what you've gone and done
– taken on the responsibility of someone we've never even met.
And a Muslim too – what will your mother say?'

'All because of you, Dee,' he replied drowsily.

'Me?'

'I saw your face and, by George, I knew we would pay! Turn
off the light and settle down like a good girl.' He shut his eyes,
pulled the thick cover up to his chin and was soon snoring
gently.

CHAPTER 13

Simi had been born in the midst of a June storm, with racing winds and lashing rain. That was why, perhaps, she had loved storms ever since. When she woke up to squally weather on her birthday, she laughed and ran out onto the terrace to dance joyously with raised arms. The water dripped down her long hair and swirled around her bare feet. She stuck out her tongue to catch the raindrops and within minutes her nightie was soaked. The ferocity of the shower had silenced even the raucous crows, who cowered in the depths of a mango tree.

'*Sam!*' her mother called out from the doorway. Simi ran to hug her, leaving a damp patch on her sari. 'Just *look* at you. Behaving like a kid!' Devi laughingly pushed her away. She held out a narrow, gift wrapped box. 'Happy birthday, darling!'

Simi thanked her mother and tore through the wrapper with eager hands. Inside was a bracelet with the dull sheen of age. Five gold chains inset with tiny rubies were linked by gold clasps studded with small emeralds. It had once belonged to her maternal grandmother.

'Wow!' Simi placed it on her wrist, holding it out for her mother to close the clasp. She then hugged Devi again, kissed her on the cheek, and scampered off to bathe. She wore the bracelet at breakfast that day.

'Oh, I say!' her father exclaimed, feigning surprise when he saw the jewellery. He also handed her an envelope stuffed with cash. She gave him a big smile and tight hug.

Her grandmother gave her both a gift and a lecture, an enamelled image of Lord Krishna and the words: 'Aren't you ever going to get married? *Twenty-five!* I'll die before I see my grandchildren.'

'I'll do my best,' Simi replied, determined not to let anything spoil her mood. She refrained from pointing out that *she was* the old lady's grandchild, because she spotted Pia swinging down the driveway. It was a point of honour with both girls to greet each other early on birthdays. Simi ran out and hustled her friend upstairs before they were waylaid by family. She threw open her bedroom windows and saw the raindrops sparkling like diamonds on leaves. The shower had rinsed the air of dust.

'I have so much to tell you!' Pia cried. She sprawled confidently on the bed instead of sitting scrunched up on the chair, as she usually did. 'But first, here's something for your birthday, dearest Simms. Here's wishing you a wonderful year!'

She gave Simi three books wrapped in purple crepe paper – one novel, the Penguin Classics edition of the *Bhagavad Gita*, and a book of crossword puzzles. She also gave Simi a silver necklace from her native hills, a piece of tribal jewellery that Simi immediately placed around her neck, saying, 'It's beautiful! Gosh, thanks, Pia. But it's too much!'

'Nonsense! It's your quarter-century after all.'

Simi grimaced. 'And yours too, soon.' Pia's twenty-fifth was in October. 'We're fifty-years-old between us!' They laughed. 'What were you going to tell me?' asked Simi.

Pia drew in a deep breath. 'It's just that – I've moved in to live with Sanjay.'

'Sanjay Sethi?'

Pia clicked her tongue. 'How many Sanjays do you know?'

Simi was stunned. Pia looked at her face and laughed. She pulled out a cigarette, pushed it back, then pulled it out again, saying, 'What the hell! It's a special occasion, and surely I can have *one* cigarette in your room.'

Simi nodded absently, even though she hated the smell of smoke. 'How? When? Tell me what happened?' She listened in wonder as Pia told her story.

'He's wonderful, Simms! And I love him!' She looked besotted.

'Why didn't you come to me when you got your mother's letter? I could have helped you.'

Pia shook her head. 'I was too ashamed. And if I could have worked and earned, then why not? Except it didn't work out that way – but something more amazing happened. Destiny, that's what it is.'

Shacking up with a man in Atmapuri! Simi gazed admiringly at her. 'Wish I had your guts.'

'This isn't the Dark Ages, for heaven's sake! It's 1993.'

'Tell my family that! Will you marry him?'

'Marriage-sharriage, who cares? We're having a great time together.'

'And your mother? What'll she say?'

Pia shrugged. 'My mother has lived her life. I want to live mine.'

Simi noticed that Pia had started dressing differently. Gone were the shapeless skirt and oversized man's shirt. Now she wore a red-and-black cotton salwar-kameez that suited her dark skin.

'He makes me feel beautiful, loved ... like a proper *woman*! You can't be a woman, Simms, until you have a man of your own.'

A man of her own! Simi wondered where she would find one and what would happen if she did, considering her family's attitudes. Pia left after promising to return early that evening for Simi's party, adding that Sanjay would arrive late since he had to attend a political meeting. Simi's life suddenly seemed so dull compared to Pia's. She envied her friend, who had got what she wanted – perhaps because she knew what she wanted. Did Simi? She decided to visit the baba.

She arrived at the baba's door armed with questions about life and love, and found him in deep meditation. His door was ajar and he was sat against the far wall, so she quietly removed her sandals and entered. Outside, the river steamed gently under the hot sun. The baba's silence was never empty – it vibrated, it was golden, it was hypnotic. She closed her eyes and let the peace envelope her. Time lost its sting in his presence. When she opened her eyes, she found him peering at her curiously.

'It's my birthday,' she said. He smiled and nodded. She offered him a bag of mangoes, which he accepted before setting it aside.

'Baba ... I am confused. Speak to me about family, about marriage. And love.'

Pia had followed her heart, but Atmapuri was a conservative city and sharp tongues could cut like scissors. Pia had dismissed her mother's reaction, but Simi cringed when she thought of the shame and pain it would cause Devi if *she* did anything like that. So she quelled her heart when it beat faster at the thought of the doctor.

'Love?' he queried. 'When you understand the Divine, then you'll understand love. Only He *loves*. *We* barter. First learn to give, give all you have, all you are. *Arre*, first become *human*, an *insaan*. Do you understand?'

She was not sure she did.

BLACK TAJ

'Love, *mohabbat*! An ancient quest. Everyone wants it but who wants to give it?' he scoffed. His next words were spoken so softly that she had to strain to hear.

> *What is this pain You gave me?*
> *Days of darkness, nights of unrest*
> *Searching for what once I had*
> *But mislaid in this busy world*
>
> *Life's a furnace and I cried in pain*
> *But You came and You whispered*
> *Tenderly, like a mother to a sleepy child*
> *'Never was there a time I was not with you*
> *Pain too is My gift: Divine gold*
> *To be traded in for Divine grace*
> *Sent to smite you, limb by limb*
> *Consciousness by consciousness*
> *Until you are you no more*
> *And there remains only That'*
>
> *Then I understood*
> *And cried no more*

But cry he did. His brown cheeks glistened and he said nothing. Simi sat with him in silence for the next half hour, quietly leaving after touching his feet. He had retreated deep into contemplation and gave no sign that he noticed. As usual, he left her to figure out his cryptic words by herself.

Back home, the White House buzzed with the excitement of preparing for her birthday party. The guests were not expected until seven-thirty, but the family was dressed and downstairs already. Old Mrs Bhandari wore pale blue French chiffon, French of course, with a rope of fat black pearls around her neck.

Simi asked, 'Are those real?'

'Worth a king's ransom if real!' the old lady teased, refusing to divulge any more.

Simi hid a smile, knowing these little games gratified her grandmother. As if the old lady would wear artificial jewellery, especially on an evening like this! Many Bhandari relatives were coming to the party. There was Uncle Hari, *Dirty Harry*, who was well into his sixties but never missed a chance to pinch Simi's bottom. And the two po-faced daughters of Uncle Lal, with their sad eyes. If Uncle Lal's family was invited, then great Uncle Harbans's could not be excluded. Uncle Harbans himself was dead, as was his wife, but his genes swilled round in two daughters and five grandchildren. Simi sighed at the thought of those overfed boys running round the house, breaking things. It was impossible to pinpoint exactly when the guest list had got out of control. Simi had wanted to invite only her friends, but now it seemed every surviving blood relative was coming. Then her father had added some of his golfing cronies: a prominent politician and the Vice Chancellor of the university, who was his old college mate.

'*Mama!*' Simi had moaned to her mother the day before. 'It's no longer *my* party. It's turned into a Bhandari clan summit! Can't we just cancel it?'

Her mother was horrified. '*What?*! Darling, they'll have ironed their saris and sharpened their teeth for the feast.' Family was family. And that was that.

While Simi waited for guests to start arriving she wondered what the baba had meant. She asked about love but he had talked about pain. Two sides of the same coin? She shuddered. Was life so dreadful? Earlier that afternoon, while showering, she had reflected on her mother's life with Old Mrs Bhandari – the snubs, slights and compromises. *Well, I won't compromise*, Simi thought to herself, as Marriam blow-dried her hair.

Pia was the first guest to arrive, wearing a yellow crepe-de-chine sari with a paisley print, along with a sexy sleeveless blouse.

Simi was stunned. 'I've never seen you look like that, Pia! New? You look gorgeous!'

Pia nodded and twirled happily, the loose *pallav* of her sari floating like a canary's wing. 'A present from you-know-who!' she said. 'We shopped for it together.' A tiny gold *bindi* winked at Simi from the centre of Pia's forehead.

A sense of longing swept through Simi and she trembled a little. She too wanted to be happy, to be in love.

Soon relatives started turning up. They each pressed gay red envelopes of crisp bank notes into Simi's hands, then settled around Old Mrs Bhandari like beasts coming to heel, gossiping while tucking into lamb kebabs and chicken *tikkas*.

As more guests arrived, the party split up. The old lady held court with the blood relatives in the drawing room, while the other guests crowded into the marquee that Gogu had hired for the garden. He was in his element, chivvying guests with cries of 'Tally-ho!', 'Bottoms up!' and 'Chin-chin!'

Eventually, everyone had arrived except Imran. Simi's eyes flew to the door each time it opened, hoping to see the doctor. But Sanjay Sethi was urging Simi to introduce him to the politician, Raja Babu, so she gave up looking and didn't notice when he entered. Then, suddenly, there he was: Dr Chaudhry.

Simi saw him and stopped in mid-sentence, until Pia nudged her, muttering, 'You fancy him, don't you?'

'Don't be silly!' Simi protested, but couldn't control the blush that scorched her cheeks.

'Go on, introduce me to Raja Baba,' Sanjay enjoined again, oblivious to the exchange between Simi and Pia. Simi obliged and led him to where the minister stood with Gogu.

'Minister ... meet Sanjay Sethi, an important Student's Union leader. And this is Pia, my good friend,' she murmured. Imran sauntered over to join them and she introduced him too, adding 'one of our leading doctors. He does a *huge* amount for the poor.'

While Sanjay was ingratiating himself with the politician, Simi turned to Imran and said softly, 'I thought you weren't coming.'

'Sorry, I am *so* sorry for being horrendously late,' he said, spreading out his hands. 'Worse, I came empty-handed. I really meant to bring you something, even just a bunch of roses, but patients fall ill at the most awkward times! There should be a ban on illness between eight at night and nine in the morning!' He ran his fingers through his hair while he spoke.

'You're not late,' she fibbed. 'The party's just warming up. Meet my father.' Gogu smiled affably and shook hands. He was aware of the unsavoury reputation the doctor had garnered from his run-ins with the AMC. But then, Gogu was no admirer of the municipality.

'I say, you've given those chaps in Town Hall a bollocking! Jolly good! Servants of the people, my foot! Little Napoleons, more like it! What'll you drink? What's your poison?' he asked drolly.

Imran asked for a cold beer and Gogu snapped his fingers at a nearby waiter, who went off to fetch it. 'And have you talked to our VIP?' Gogu aimed a meaningful glance at the minister, who turned to nod at them.

'*Aah* Bhandari*saab*,' the minister said, 'I was just telling this bright young man he must join the party. We need youngsters like him in politics to serve the people. Forty-six years of independence and there's still much to be done,' the minister said.

'Another *servant* of the people!' Imran murmured to Simi behind his glass. She grinned.

'And you, Dr Chaudhry? Tell me about yourself,' the minister said. He had heard about the doctor and the controversies surrounding his work.

Imran shrugged. 'Me, sir? I am just a doctor. I tend to the sick. Politics I leave to my old friend Sanjay.'

The minister snorted disdainfully. '*Hnpf!* But politics is *life*. The price of onions is politics and pigeons shitting on Mahatma Gandhi's statue is politics! Come, come, Dr Chaudhry. You can't pretend to divorce politics from medicine.'

'No, you're right,' Imran responded. 'So let's talk about Nawabganj.'

The minister frowned, trying to recall the name. Simi jumped in to say: '*Nawabganj!* I wish you could just see them, see the difference Im … Dr Chaudhry's made. The women are learning about hygiene and their children don't fall sick. They feel *good* about themselves. They're finally becoming part of Atmapuri!'

'Nawabganj, Nawabganj, of course, of course,' the minister said. 'Very dear to my heart, as is every inch of Atmapuri. I may have become a minister in Lucknow but I'll never, never forget my Native.'

'Then why not stop the people who are trying to clear them out, sir?' Imran asked. 'It would ruin their lives if they're removed to some Godforsaken wasteland on the edge of town!'

'*Me?* If I had my way those men and women—'

'And their votes!'

'-would stay put!' The minister frowned at Imran's interruption.

'But you're the minister! If you ask, the municipality can't refuse,' Imran mocked.

The minister silently cursed the doctor for putting him on the spot then thumped his open palm with his fist. 'For my brothers in the slum, for my mothers there, I'll fight. I'll stage a sit-down. Let them send in the bulldozers. Let them put me in jail! My father was jailed by the British. He was a freedom fighter and I am not afraid.'

Sanjay gazed adoringly at the minister.

'Amen,' Imran replied. 'If that's your promise, Nawabganj is safe. But if something goes wrong, we'll come to you. The people can come to you, right?' His soft tones belied a hint of menace.

Gogu, fearing the conversation was getting out of hand, steered the minister away to the dinner table.

Left alone, Imran turned to Simi and muttered, '*Khuda!* That guy should be in Bollywood. I was afraid he'd start crying and I'd have to give him my hanky.'

'Why?' she asked, confused. 'He sounded very committed.'

He laughed. 'Brave words! But we need action, not words. Jail! What good will jail do to anything except his own career? Jail is the short-cut to political glory in our country.' He shot a moody look at the politician's retreating back, with Sanjay in attendance. Pia had tagged along too.

With a dismissive gesture, Imran said, 'Aw, let's just forget it. What will be, will be. *Que sera sera!* My mother sang it sometimes.' He remembered seeing her – his birth mother – seated at her dressing table when he had been a young child, watching her apply pale pink lipstick and singing the song sadly.

Simi saw a haunted look flicker across his face, but then it was gone and he grinned at her, enquiring with cocked brow, 'So, will you come to visit my lady friend? I've promised to go on Saturday week. You won't regret it!'

She nodded and smiled. 'Love to.'

'Great! Elevenish? Let me know where to pick you up from. But right now I'm starving. I didn't have time to stop for lunch.'

Simi kicked herself for being a careless hostess. On the way to the dining table, they passed her grandmother, who called out to them to join her.

Simi reluctantly introduced Imran. 'Dadi, this is Dr Chaudhry.' Imran greeted her with folded hands and a courtly bow.

Old Mrs Bhandari looked up at him. 'Dr Chaudhry? A Dr Chaudhry was our family doctor long ago. Do you know Dr Manu Chaudhry?'

Imran nodded. 'He's ... my father.'

'*Your father!*' she grasped his hand. 'Welcome, son. How is he? Haven't seen him in years, you know how it is. We lost touch. Sad. He must be retired?'

'Yes, but he still works. Part-time. For charity.'

She nodded. 'He was always a good man. And you're a doctor too?' The old lady liked young doctors because they kept abreast of the latest medical advances. She smiled. 'I must consult you some time. It'll be nice to have the family link again. What's your name, son?'

'Imran.'

'Imran?'

Simi cringed. Her grandmother's voice, incredulous, conveyed a world of meaning. The old lady let go of his hand and rubbed her palm on her chiffon-clad knee.

'But Dr Manu Chaudhry's Hindu, isn't he?' the old woman asked incredulously.

'He's my *adopted* father,' Imran replied. He seemed calm, but Simi noticed him clench his fist before quickly releasing it and flexing his fingers. Hastily muttering an excuse to her grandmother, she hurried him off to the dining room.

'I am sorry,' she apologised without glancing at him.

He shrugged. 'She obviously doesn't like Muslims,' he observed. 'Perhaps you want to reconsider going to my friend's place with me?'

'How can you say that?' she said, dismayed. 'I'm not like *her*. And my parents aren't like her either. She's ... she's a dinosaur.'

'If she's a dinosaur, this city is teeming with them. There's enough prejudice here to fill an ocean.'

Surely he was wrong! But for now they concentrated on the food. Devi had laid on a feast and they tucked in happily. Simi arranged for Imran to fetch her from the university next Saturday in order to avoid her family's scrutiny.

On the appointed day, she went early to spend time with Pia. She met her in Sanjay's office, finding her friend busy wrapping brown paper bundles of election posters. They depicted a laughing Sanjay with Mahatma Gandhi's face floating above his left shoulder.

'I wonder what the Mahatma would have made of our Hindu-Muslim conflicts. The partition was meant to put a stop to that,' Simi observed.

'India should have become a Hindu nation at the time of Partition, Simms.'

Simi couldn't believe her ears. A year ago, Pia had no strong views on religion. But now they hotly disputed the role of Muslim stone-masons, weavers, tailors and artists in Atmapuri, descendants of craftsmen who had built the Taj Mahal. Simi could feel her temper rising and instead asked if her friend was happy with Sanjay.

Pia beamed. 'I've found my man!' She hesitated before adding, 'And I think I'm pregnant.'

Simi was astonished. 'How do you know? Have you seen the doctor?'

Pia shook her head. 'But my monthly cycle is regular as clockwork and I missed this month. Oh Simms, I'm so excited. You don't know what it's like to love a man, to want his baby.'

Simi couldn't see anything but trouble ahead. 'But your mother? And his family? What did Sanjay say?'

'I haven't told him yet, not until the doctor confirms it. You're the only one who knows.'

Simi felt as though she had never really understood Pia. They finished bundling up the posters and went to the university café for a herbal decoction.

When Simi told Pia she was meeting Dr Imran Chaudhry later, her friend stared at her.

'Oh *Simms!* You still have a *thing* for him?'

Simi deflected the question. 'We're only going to visit someone. We're friends.'

'Being friends is fine – but you can't marry a Muslim!' Pia was insistent.

'Who's *marrying* him? What's wrong with you Pia?'

'Nothing, it's fine.' Pia pulled out a cigarette. 'Still, remember he's Muslim.'

Simi was too shocked for words. Just a few weeks ago they had been doing a play together.

'He's Sanjay's oldest friend. You told me that!' It was ironic that Pia had spurned society to shack up with Sanjay and now dreamt of becoming an unwed mother, but disapproved of her spending an afternoon with Imran. 'Honestly Pia, you're the limit.'

'Think about it,' Pia answered.

Simi wanted to defend herself. But it was time to meet Imran.

CHAPTER 14

On the Friday after the party, Imran arrived home late. His evening surgery had been crammed with patients and it was almost nine when he pulled up in his Jeep. He felt smothered by the warm, still night, pressing down upon him like a hot wet towel. The last thing he wanted was to hear his cook complain about monkeys ravaging his garden that afternoon. The simians had pelted Bahadur with raw green guavas and threatened him with bared teeth when he tried to shoo them off.

'What do you expect *me* to do?' Imran snapped.

'They're not mere monkeys, *sahib*. They're *jinns*! *Shaitans* in monkey skin. There is only one answer – shoot them with your gun.'

'*Shoot them?*' If there was room in his reputation for further notoriety, this was it: the monkey-killing doctor. Imran gave Bahadur a filthy look, but it was lost on him. He decided a jog along the river would revive him.

'I am going out. I'll eat later,' Imran muttered irritably to his servant, before heading off to get changed.

Imran sweated profusely as he jogged through the tepid night, Hudson following at his heels. The River Boomi lapped gently against its banks, sounding like a giant tongue slurping ice-cream. It was a dark night, the ground dry and unyielding under his feet. He hoped it would be a good monsoon this year.

He was to meet Simi the next day, fetching her from the university at twelve. *Why not from her home? Is she ashamed of being seen with me?* The poisonous thought nibbled at him like a piranha. He pushed it away and conjured up the image of her face. And her eyes, those shining green globes, the memory of which made his heart race. He really had misjudged Simi when he first met her. She'd seemed like just another spoilt rich girl having hysterics at the wedding. But since then he had watched her slog in the slums. He also admired the way she had cared for that poor woman, Jaddan Bai, during her illness. *There can't be many girls like her*, he thought.

'Hey Hudson! Time to go!' he yelled and whistled for the dog. The Alsatian had been cooling off in the shallows and emerged to shake himself dry, spraying Imran with muddy water.

'It would serve you right if I made you run home!' he scolded the unrepentant dog, before ordering him into the car.

Back home in his bathroom, Imran stripped and showered, but it was like bathing in warm beer. The overhead water tank had become hot during the day. He wondered if he could shield it from the sun in some way – perhaps erect an awning above it? Afterwards he put on a crisp white kurta-pyjama and went to the living room, where he ate a light dinner before dismissing Bahadur.

Alone, he watched the CNN news and restlessly flicked through channels, his mind already on Simi and their outing the next day. He loved Simi. He knew it now, even if he had refused to acknowledge it at first. He found himself pining for her, talking to her when she was not there. She was small and fragile, but she had the spirit of a tigress. She was *real*, unlike the other affluent young women in Atmapuri, who drifted from tailors to hairdressers in lives of pure leisure.

What *could* he offer her? He was an orphan, a Muslim. A doctor, granted. He came from a good family – but where were they now? Once upon a time he would have been the most eligible bachelor in the kingdom, but the time of kings was gone. And why would her family permit her to marry him, even if she wanted to? When she could take her pick of Hindu bachelors? Hindus like her.

He reached out for a photograph on a sofa table, a softly lit black-and-white shot taken in the 1960s. It was in an old-fashioned silver frame bearing the family coat of arms. A tall, impeccably dressed man stood behind a smiling woman draped in yards of pale chiffon. He had high cheekbones and a patrician nose. She had had a soft face and her fair-skin looked luminous in the photograph. His mother had died within a few months of his father. Such loneliness was like being lost in space. He had watered her grave with his tears, until Dr Chaudhry had picked him up and carried him home.

'Wish me luck, Ammi,' Imran murmured, running a gentle finger across the glass in the frame.

After two hours, his ashtray overflowing with cigarette stubs, Imran went to bed. He had made up his mind: he would propose and if she accepted … But suppose she rejected him? He shut the thought down before it could swamp him with misery.

The next day, Imran was up and dressed early. The traffic on the way to the university was light, it being a Saturday morning. Simi was waiting when he arrived and Imran spotted her from afar, sat in the shade of a lychee tree. He noticed that Pia was with her and groaned, wondering if she intended to tag along.

To his relief, however, after some chit-chat they left Pia behind and drove off.

The cool air conditioning caressed their faces. 'Where are we headed?' Simi asked.

'The old city. That's where my friend lives,' he explained. 'Not long now. You'll know her when you see her.'

'Someone I know? *Who?*'

He wouldn't tell her. Instead, he related the history of the old city and the medieval nobleman who had designed it.

Simi already knew the story. 'I love Atmapuri,' she said. 'I can't see myself living anywhere else.'

'Not even when you marry? I mean, you might fall in love with a guy from some distant place.'

'Oh, I couldn't leave Atmapuri. I love it in winter and the monsoon – the rain makes me want to dance like a peacock!'

It was now early afternoon and the traffic had begun to build up, with handcarts and cycle-rickshaws clogging up the roads. Simi and Imran found themselves moving at a snail's pace as they passed through a massive stone arch set in thick stone walls, but eventually emerged into a leafy green suburb. Simi had not known that anyone lived beyond the old city.

Imran came to a stop before a two-storey house and parked under a tall bottlebrush tree. 'This is it!' he announced.

It was an old redbrick building next to the river. Simi liked it. They approached the big wooden front door, which opened almost immediately. An old servant, his beard dyed bright orange with henna, greeted them with a low bow, saying '*Janab!*' as he did so.

The servant then stepped aside and they entered into a large room, its wooden shutters closed against the piercing sun. It was an old-fashioned place with commodious divans covered with silk carpets, brocade bolsters and miniature pillows encased in white muslin. Simi was amused by the sight of two deep, typically Bengali *babu* armchairs, the sort once seen in clubs.

A woman came forward to greet them, the oily scent of patchouli following her like a pet. She bowed with exaggerated courtesy and said, '*Chotte sarkar*, welcome to the home of this *kaneez*. My house is your house.'

Simi was struck by the grand way in which she held herself, with her back straight and chin held high. Her long black hair was like a raven's wing and she wore a blue *chikan-work* salwar-kameez. One detail stuck out in particular though: the woman was wearing the earrings stolen from Anjora at the wedding! Simi recognised them instantly and froze.

Who was this woman? Her face was familiar. An old actress? No. Then it came to her – she was Meena Kumari, the famous classical Kathak dancer! Simi and her mother had watched her dance on stage several times. But what was Meena Kumari doing with Anjora's earrings?

Imran introduced them. 'Meet Sunehri Begum. And this is Simi.'

The begum's lively eyes passed over Simi, her arched eyebrows dramatically enhanced with black pencil. She sat down on a divan and started talking to Imran. Her voice was deep and warm, though slightly nasal, like a mountain breeze rustling through Himalayan pines. Simi noted the lines etched on her face and put her down as fifty. A strange woman in an old-fashioned room.

Sunehri Begum? But she was Meena Kumari. Or was she? And how did she get hold of Anjora's earrings? Simi greeted her mutely.

Sunehri Begum cooled herself languidly with silk fan, which she also used to cover her laughing face as she talked and joked. Simi primly took a seat in one of the *Bengali Babu* armchairs.

Imran was sprawled on a divan looking relaxed, even boyish. Why he was so familiar with the begum? Simi felt very jealous.

The begum turned to her servant, scolding him, '*Arre* Kader. Don't you know that Imran Nawab*saab* has come a long way? Bring water, bring tea!'

The servant disappeared silently and soon returned with a tray crowded with hot *samosas*, milk cake, cardamom tea and tumblers of water with ice cubes.

Simi was fascinated by the begum. Her red and green glass bangles tinkled tunefully as she served them, all but putting the food into Imran's mouth. He tucked in with gusto.

'Did they eat like this all the time in the old days, *khalajaan*?' he asked the begum between morsels. 'If Dada*saab* had lived, I think I'd have been a very fat man!'

He had called the begum 'aunt'! And his reference to Dada*saab* – had the begum known his grandfather? And why did she call Imran 'Nawab*saab*'? *Nothing* made sense to Simi.

'Those earrings are beautiful,' Simi said, unable to wait any longer for an explanation.

The begum smiled, fondling her ears.

'Do you like jewellery? I love it! These are new. I've got a very good jeweller if you ever want anything, *bibi*.' She addressed Simi formally.

The begum had acquired them recently. Now Simi was convinced they *were* Anjora's earrings. Did the begum know she had received stolen goods? Simi munched a *samosa* and wondered whether to tell Imran.

'Your Dada*saab*,' the begum sighed. 'I remember the first time I saw the old Nawab*saab*. I was only twelve and he was visiting my … my aunt … my mentor … I peeped at him from behind the curtain.'

'The Nawab*saab*? The Nawab of … ?' Simi asked.

The begum gave her a startled look before turning to Imran, 'Doesn't she know?'

Imran shook his head imperceptibly. The begum's mouth flew open and her eyes widened in such a theatrical gesture of surprise that Simi had to suppress a smile.

The begum said, speaking in chaste, classical Urdu. *'Bibi*, yonesu should be told. He was His Highness Janab Mir Haidar Ali Khan, the Nawab*saab* of Akbarabad. A hundred pigeons flew over his head to shade him from the sun when he walked! He was the royal grandfather of Janab Imran Haidar Ali Khan here … who would be His Highness of Akbarabad, but for Indira Gandhi, who stripped the true royals. And now political dynasties are growing faster than the population of India.'

Royal? Imran was *royalty*?! Simi turned to him in amazement, but he just shrugged. There was no trace of the harried doctor in the way he lounged, like a – a nawab! There was no other word for it. Simi had heard of the old Nawab, a legendary patron of artists, from her mother. He had used his immense wealth and position to create a legacy of song and dance, including a particular style of singing named after him, The Nawab*saab* gharana.

'Tell me about it, Begum*saab*,' Simi whispered.

The begum, a consummate story-teller, conjured up a bygone world of banquets and beautiful dancing girls. The begum was very amusing, poking fun at the absurdities and pretensions of an age where keeping up appearances meant everything. Every man was an aspiring poet and the royal court was full of fops and dandies. As a girl, the begum had even witnessed an elephant fight!

'The ground shook as if it was an earthquake! They screamed at each other and attacked with their ears spread out like wings. Terrifying! Very cruel it was, too. There was lots of blood.'

'What a thing to do – and to enjoy it too!' Simi cried, but the begum shook her head.

'It's not half as cruel as some of the things people do to each other. As for the Nawab*saab*, the first time I saw him I wanted to burst out from behind the curtain and stun everyone with my genius.'

She shook with laughter at the memory of her twelve-year old self, and only halfway through her classical dance training.

'And did you?' Simi asked.

'*Toba! Toba!* Impossible. The Nawab*saab* was our king, our patron, our *Sarkar*, our *Qibla*, *Huzur-e-Ali*. Respect, respect and respect was drummed into me. But enough talk! You must be hungry. Imran*saab* I'll send for your favourite kebabs. *Arre* Kader!'

The begum called out to her servant and opened a silver betel-leaf box in front of her. It contained – betel leaf! She stared blankly at it then tried another box. The money was in the fourth one she opened.

She winked at Simi, saying, 'That's my poor housekeeping!'

She then handed a small wad of notes to the servant with the instruction to fetch fresh kebabs from Mian Dabir's café.

When alone with the begum, while Imran went to the toilet, she asked, 'Do you miss the old days?'

The begum sighed. 'Many people were good to me – but I was never free. What's the use of living in a cage, even one made of gold?'

Imran returned to the room and Sunehri Begum fell silent. Taking her cue, Simi too was quiet. Curiously, Sunehri Begum reminded her of Marriam's friends. Her story was like their stories, tales of women negotiating their way in a man's world.

After eating, the begum insisted they accompany her to her terrace. It had just been sluiced down with water and steam rose from the warm bricks. She sang a plaintive Persian love-song and danced on the bare floor.

Eventually, it was time to leave. Simi turned back for a last look before descending the staircase. The begum was feeding her pet parrot, Tansen, named after the legendary singer. There was a faraway look in her eyes.

CHAPTER 15

Simi and Imran drove off into the dusk. The smell of wood smoke from domestic fires floated across the gloaming. Birds settled down to sleep after a final burst of cheeping and cawing. The sun, having mellowed from a ball of fire into an old gold plate, cast a halo around saints and sinners alike. It was Simi's favourite time of day and she settled back into the seat of the Mercedes with a contented sigh.

'Tired?' Imran asked. Leaning over to insert a cassette in the car stereo, he lightly caressed Simi's arm. She felt a tingle. Nina Simone's cappuccino voice sang to them.

'I've never met anyone like her!' Simi said. 'But, isn't she Meena Kumari, the famous dancer? Why did you call her Sunehri Begum? And how come she knew your grandfather? And she was wearing Anjora's earrings! The ones stolen at the wedding! And who *are* you?'

He laughed. 'Whoa! Whoa! So many questions! I'll tell you over dinner, OK?'

She nodded. 'OK, but I can't be out too late. You don't know how my grandmother fusses. Wait until my mother hears that I met Meena Kumari and she danced for me – for us! Wow! My mother never misses her performances. Isn't she lonely, living on the edge of the world?'

'Aren't we all? Lonely, I mean. Yes, that is Meena Kumari. And your mother, she's nice. I like your father too. Decent folk.' She was glad. There was no need to ask what he thought of her grandmother.

He added, 'What did you say about the earrings?'

She explained. They discussed it, but there was little they could do about it without proof. Simi wondered whether to tell Anjora, or her own mother, before deciding to keep quiet.

Night descended as they plunged through the old city. He took her to a small restaurant by the river, a family enterprise where the chef and the maître d' were brothers and the food was good. Simi realised that Imran was something of a gourmet. He ate the meat with relish.

'I'm surprised you're so trim if you eat like this every day!' she exclaimed, pecking at her own food.

He grinned, shaking his head. 'Only on holidays. Mostly, I don't get time to eat, so if I'm trim it's because on weekdays I usually only have coffee for breakfast. Lunch is some fruit on the run, if at all. Dinner's my only proper meal.'

'Do you live alone?' She knew so little about him.

'Afraid so,' he said, rinsing his fingers in the bowl provided. She noted how meticulously he used the slice of lemon to clean under his fingernails.

'There is my dog,' he added after a moment, 'you'll like him, and my cook, who you won't like. Even I don't like him! And the sweeper and washer man. But they come during the day so I never meet them. Oh yes – and three monkeys who visit regularly to wreck my garden. Let's see, have I forgotten anyone? No, that's all.'

She laughed. 'Don't tease! Tell me all about your grandfather and Begum Whatever-Her-Name-Really-Is.' She declined a dessert but he ordered *kulfi* ice cream.

'It's true, my grandfather was His Highness the Nawab of Akbarabad. My father was an HH too.'

'I've heard of your grandfather' replied Simi. 'My mother talks about him as a patron of musicians and dancers. And the begum? How did she know him?'

'Haven't you guessed?' he asked with a strange look. She spread out her hands in silent appeal.

'Tchh! You're too innocent,' he mocked gently. '*Jaan* Sunehri Begum was his … his mistress.'

'*His Mistress?* She's too young! With your *grandfather?* She can't be more than fifty *now.*'

'Didn't they teach you anything at that boarding school of yours? Yes, if he was alive he'd be – about hundred! She was fifteen and he about fifty when they … *Kichi-cooed* together!' He suppressed his laughter.

'Who told you that?' she demanded.

'She did.' In his second year at medical college in Atmapuri he had been approached by the begum's red-haired manservant with a note asking him to visit. Not having heard of her, he refused. A couple of weeks later, the servant reappeared with another note that mentioned his grandfather and stated that the begum had information for him. It was an irresistible offer.

'By the time I was ten they were all dead – my mother, father and grandfather. I was hungry to learn all I could. What were they *really* like? My grandfather was a demi-god to his subjects, but what was he like as a man? Kind? Or cruel? Patient? Angry? I had no idea. And my grandmother died before him, so I don't remember her at all. You've no idea what it's like not to know your family.'

Simi listened intently, her face cupped in her hands, elbows on the table.

At first, the begum had given the impression of being distantly acquainted with the old Nawab, but just before Imran had left to pursue medicine in America she disclosed all.

'That house we went to, my grandfather bought it for her. She wants to leave it to me in her will. She has no one else. Sweet of her to consider me her heir, but I dread to think I might inherit that red-haired Kader too!'

When things had changed, Imran explained, the begum used her classical training to reinvent herself as a stage dancer.

'Good for her!' Simi cried. 'My God, the things she's seen and done. It's like a movie. I'd love to talk to her sometime.'

'Does that mean you like her?'

'Very much.'

'Hooray! My two favourite women like each other. Phew!' He wiped his forehead in mock relief, but watched her closely. She blushed as she understood what he meant. Then he settled the bill and they left.

'Where to?' he enquired, switching on the engine when they were back in the car. Simi was intensely aware of the tension between them. She nervously cleared her throat, glancing at her watch. Almost nine. She should go home but didn't want to.

'Let me show you Victoria Park before I drop you home. It's nearby,' he suggested.

'In the dark?'

'Best seen by moonlight!' he grinned. 'It looks awful in the sun – almost a junkyard. All those grumpy white men!'

She knew of the park but had never visited. After gaining independence from the British in 1947, the municipality had removed all the statues of exalted Englishmen, consigning them to Victoria Park. This included a larger-than-life stone statue of Queen Victoria, after whom the park was named.

When they reached the park they got out to stroll past the sleeping flower beds. A single red rose stood out like a bride in the moonbeams.

Suddenly Imran stopped, grasped Simi by the elbows, turned her to face him and said, 'You know why I took you there today, don't you?'

Simi shook her head. He put a finger under her chin and lifted her face. She was glad he couldn't see her flushed cheeks in the dark.

'I love you, Simi,' he said. 'And I want to marry you.'

Simi was stunned but her heart leapt with joy. She wanted to hug him and say how happy she was. Then her family crowded into her head, wagging their fingers. *Jesus!* Her grandmother would kill her. She turned her head away.

'What's wrong?' he asked, crestfallen.

Without thinking, she plucked the bridal rose and slowly shredded it with her fingers. 'No one's ever proposed to me before,' she said.

Relieved, he laughed. 'Is that all? For a bit there I thought I'd offended you, *jaan*. It's alright to call you *jaan* isn't it?' She nodded then shook her head in confusion.

'So what do you say?' he asked.

She couldn't look him in the eyes. 'I ... my ... Oh, what's the use? You know what sort of world we live in, all narrow-minded, gossipy and bitchy.'

'What *are* you saying?'

'My family ... my grandmother is something else.' She felt him stiffen and looked up. 'I ... I like you very much. But marriage? That's different.'

He moved away. 'You mean because I'm Muslim?'

Her heart wept when she heard him so hurt. 'Oh please don't misunderstand! I admire you ... a lot.'

'Admire? Is that all?'

She had to be honest. 'More. Much more but ... '

'Hey! It's you I want to marry, not your grandmother!'

How could she explain that it was impossible to cut her grandmother out of the picture? Or her mother. What would Devi say? It would come as a shock for them.

He was so tall and self-assured. She could feel his warmth through his thin cotton shirt and smell the faint aroma of aftershave mixed with his personal scent. She reached out to comfort him and the next thing she knew she was in his arms and he was kissing her passionately, like a drowning man.

'*Jaan*,' he murmured, stroking her cheek with a gentle finger. He told her how much he loved her, how he admired her grit in working in the slum on hot and dusty afternoons.

She laughed. 'Tosh! It's nothing compared to what you do.'

'I'm a doctor, that's my Hippocratic Oath, but you ... you could take it easy. Instead you put yourself out, day in and day out.'

'Stop it.' Simi wasn't comfortable with the praise. 'Tell me, in the old days would you really have been a nawab?'

He shrugged. 'History saved me from being idle. Instead, I'm a struggling doctor working for a crust! My family lost everything.'

'Everything?'

'Everything.'

She had so much to ask but it was growing late. They walked back to the car. He helped her in so tenderly that it brought a lump to her throat. He held her right hand in his left while he drove, keeping only one hand on the steering wheel. He dropped her some distance from her home at her insistence and drove away reluctantly. At least she had not said 'no'.

CHAPTER 16

Simi spent the next day pining for Imran. Pinky Aunty and her husband had come round for the family's traditional Sunday lunch, but Simi was lost in imagined conversations and recollections of the night before. The rice pulao and fish curry came and went between scenes that flashed through Simi's head like glimpses of paradise. She glanced across the table at her grandmother. *How happy we could be, the two of us, if left to ourselves*, she thought. Imran would return home after a hard day's work and they would spend the evenings together. *What about children?* If it was a boy, Simi wanted to name him *Siddhartha*, after the Buddha. But it was a Hindu name. And *Rukmani* for their daughter. She had been the wife of Lord Krishna – but did Imran's children have to have Arab names? Dadi *would be furious*.

'The Ms should have given *us* the mosque,' Old Mrs Bhandari said suddenly.

Simi grabbed her glass of water and drank hastily. *It's almost as if she can read my thoughts.*

Her grandmother continued, 'Provocative! What else do you call it, huh? An empty building, no prayers offered, no priest to light a lamp, not for FIFTY years! And they call that a mosque!'

She was referring to the demolished Babri Mosque in Ayodhya again. 'And then there's those smelly M tanneries in Atmapuri, under our very noses.'

'Do you mean that we should demolish the tanneries?' Simi asked.

'You always like to argue!' her grandmother retorted, ignoring the question. 'If the Ms had handed over the mosque quietly like decent people, none of this would have happened. After all, that's where Sri Ram Bhagwan was born.'

'Dadi, *who knows* where Ram was born? If he was born at all. Are gods actually born?'

'Hai Ram, this child! *Everyone* knows where Sri Ram was born. *Arre*, Babar, that *junglee*, came only five hundred years ago. There was an old Ram temple there before and Babar destroyed it. Why should we put up with the mosque he built there?'

Only five hundred years ago! *Jesus!* Couldn't the past be left alone? Too much past and too little future, that's the problem with ancient civilisations.

'Five hundred, five thousand years – how far back do we go, Dadi? I'm sick of it.'

Gogu cleared his throat loudly. 'Sam's right, Ma. Can't just go round pulling down historic buildings. We've got a constitution and judiciary to deal with that sort of thing. By George, if every Tom, Dick and Harry got away with breaking the law, things would come to a pretty pass. What's the use of law, dammit, if every passing dog pisses on it?'

His mother grimaced and pushed her plate away. 'Gogu!'

'Sorry, Ma, but I stand by what I said. Life's jolly decent until politico types stick their oars in. Yes sirree!'

'Law-phaw! I've seen the law – the law can't even find Anjora's necklace. The law molly-coddles minorities. Pampers them! If I had my way, all Ms would be shipped off back home to Pakistan.'

Simi jumped up. 'Dadi! Go *home* to Pakistan? They never came from there – they're Indian.'

'*Lo! Arre*, this is Hindustan. Hinduism is our state religion, and why shouldn't it be? Pakistan is Islamic. But you won't understand, Simi, because you didn't suffer through the partition.'

'Partition! Partition! I hate that word,' Simi cried.

'For Pete's sake, Ma! The old trouble should have ended when the country was split up in 1947,' Gogu said.

'I think Mummy's right,' Pinky intervened.

'You too, Pinks? By Jove! The mob could march into your garden tomorrow – or claim that farm you're so proud of – claiming some important chappie was born there three thousand years ago. Crap! Such talk will make thugs of us all.'

Gogu threw his napkin down on the table and stalked out of the room. Pinky Aunty's husband followed him, the two men retreating to the study to drink beer. Devi left quietly and Simi got up too, trailing behind her silvery fragments of broken dreams. But she overheard her grandmother as she spoke to Pinky.

'By Bhagwan's grace, Anjora is safely married. This is dark *Kaliyug*. Women have lost all propriety. All this mixed marriage nonsense, diluting bloodlines, where will it all end? Hai Ram!' Another poison nail twisted in Simi's heart.

With nowhere else to go, Simi whiled away the day in her room. She was no longer sure of anything. She loved Imran, but she loved her family too. The novel she was reading failed to grip her; her own life was far more dramatic. She missed Pia but her friend was busy until the weekend.

At that moment, Pia was engaged in complex political analysis with Sanjay. Voters could be broadly categorised into three groups and she counselled him to play the numbers game. The important thing was to ensure that the largest group turned out for him and the smallest block remained neutral.

'The undecided will see which way the wind blows and vote for you,' she concluded.

The plan's simplicity appealed to Sanjay. 'You're a genius! My Pi, sweetheart, what would I do without you?' He planted kisses on her head, neck, shoulders and ankles.

'Stop it!' she laughed, tousling his hair, thrilled by his exuberance. They were friends, lovers and political colleagues. She cooked for him when there was time, using recipe books, though not always successfully. It hardly mattered because Sanjay barely tasted his food, devouring it in hasty gulps.

Pia had so far shrugged off the disrepute attracted by her living openly with a man to whom she wasn't married. She told herself that, being an outsider, a hill girl from Nainital, she cared nothing for society. She had found her soul mate and was deeply in love. They never stopped talking and she astonished Sanjay with her astute grasp of politics. Although her own political instincts were liberal, Pia had swiftly embraced his more right-wing beliefs. With her quicksilver mind and voracious intellect, she had fast become Sanjay's chief adviser. Without either of them being aware of it, she was managing his life. She spent hours in Sanjay's office answering phones and dispatching publicity material. She struggled to find time for her studies, but rose early to shut herself away in the university library for a minimum of four hours a day.

Sanjay fired on all cylinders. He could be rude sometimes. Just yesterday he had roared at a volunteer, a lad named Arvind, for losing a bundle of posters. Without giving him a chance to explain, Sanjay had berated him and walked out. Arvind was furious and threatened to quit. It was Pia who persuaded him to stay on. She resolved to make Sanjay apologise to Arvind the next day, but meanwhile *she* apologised profusely and Arvind finally relented.

'He's lucky to have you. I hope he appreciates you,' Arvind said, heavily implying that she was too good for Sanjay.

Sanjay clocked up many miles in his Jeep while out campaigning. He had to manage his own election as well as help out his mentor, Rajababu Mahajan. 'Fear is the key,' Rajababu had said. 'Fear drives our actions. People are afraid of losing what they have and we offer them protection. Make them feel safe and they are yours.'

Rajababu also had a motto: *Find a man's price and pay it, otherwise it'll take a hundred years to get anywhere.*

A scheme was beginning to take shape in Sanjay's mind. Atmapuri was a complex mosaic of religions, castes and communities. The question was how he could use that? A twinge of conscience assailed him but he shrugged it off. Yes, the plan might work, but it called for an accomplice or two. Someone unknown who would remain in the background.

A week later, Simi went looking for Pia on the day they'd agreed to meet. She found her in Sanjay's office. Her friend was preparing bundles of posters for dispatch and had a pinched look.

Puzzled, Simi asked about the posters. They were the same ones she had seen before, depicting a smiling Sanjay and the face of Mahatma Gandhi.

Pia explained, 'Oh that! It links him with the golden age of Indian politics. But Gandhiji gave too much to Muslims and Harijans.' She blew a perfect smoke-ring.

'Stop it! You're beginning to sound like Dadi!' Simi said, irritated.

Pia shrugged. 'Why should we turn the other cheek when they come here to take over our land? The Parsees, the Arabs, the Brits, even the Dalai Lama.'

'The *Dalai Lama?* He's … I've heard him in Delhi, with my aunt. He's so joyful. My mother says he's a Divine Being.'

Pia waved dismissively. 'OK, forget the Dalai Lama.' Suddenly she sat down. 'I went to the doctor the other day. He confirmed that I'm pregnant. What am I to do, Simms?'

Simi stared. 'What are you going to tell Sanjay? Didn't you take precautions?'

Pia shook her head. 'At first, there was no time. Then it didn't seem to matter.'

Life was so untidy. There was Anjora longing for a baby, and here was Pia …

'Will you marry him?' asked Simi.

Pia sighed. 'I don't want him to feel trapped.'

'So … ?' An abortion? Simi didn't say the word out loud but it had to be considered. Who did abortions in Atmapuri? How could they find out?

'I want to keep the baby,' Pia announced, as if divining her thoughts. 'I love Sunju.'

'Should you be smoking?'

Pia angrily stubbed out her cigarette. 'So, what's new with you?'

Simi was glad to change the subject. 'You'll never guess who I met on Saturday. Meena Kumari, the famous dancer, but she's called Sunehri Begum.' Unwittingly, she gave away too much as she talked about Imran.

'Oh *Simms*, are you still seeing him? But he's Muslim.'

Simi did not tell Pia any more. She stayed for a while, then made her excuses and left. She had come to share everything with Pia, her excitement, her doubts … but the gap between them had grown.

CHAPTER 17

Simi had taken to speaking on the phone with Imran whenever possible. At first this was to discuss her work in Nawabganj, visiting Marriam and the other women. But now it became their love line. He phoned her between patients and she pretended to sound casual, but poured her heart down the handset. He suggested dinner one evening. She longed to say 'yes' but couldn't.

'Why?' he asked. She could hear the pain in his voice down the phone.

'I wish you could have heard my grandmother the other day,' she said dejectedly. She wanted to add 'ditto Pia' but bit her tongue. That would hurt him more.

'And what's that got to do with the price of tea? *Khuda*, Simi, I only want to have dinner with you!'

But it wouldn't be just dinner; she knew she would forget everything else in his presence and right now she was trying very hard to retain her grip on reality.

Imran sighed. 'At least come to the surgery – we'll *only* talk about the slums.'

She went early the same evening. Inhibited by the presence of his receptionist, they confined themselves to talking about Nawabganj. But he did make Simi promise to accompany him on another trip at the weekend, assuring her it was 'as a friend, only as a friend.' His dancing eyes belied those words.

'Where to?' asked Simi. 'To meet Meena … Sunehri Begum again?'

He shook his head. 'No. A different pilgrimage this time. Will you come?'

Simi had been a curious child and the urge to see everything for herself remained. So she agreed to his suggestion, then said she really must go. He didn't attempt to detain her. Just before she left, he held her close, breathing in her scent.

'I can't bear to see you go, *jaan*,' he murmured, nuzzling her cheek.

The receptionist gave her a funny look as she went out. He stood watching until she was gone.

The week dragged by and nothing Simi did made her feel any better. Marriam's group was making progress with the alphabet, but that failed to excite Simi as it would have once done. Even their health was holding up, so there was no excuse to ring Imran on that count. He rang her at every opportunity though, forcing Simi to pretend she was speaking with one of her girlfriends when her family was around. On the Saturday she met him outside the university as agreed, leaving her car parked not far from Pia's dormitory. Imran was already there when she arrived, waiting for her.

It was an oppressive day of windless heat, but it was cool inside his air-conditioned four-wheel drive. He caught her right hand, raised it to his mouth and lightly kissed its back, his moustache a tender brush. Then they were off. It was a long drive and the familiar landmarks soon began to fall away.

'Where are we headed?' Simi asked.

'To my kingdom.'

She frowned. 'But … ?'

He flashed a smile but refused to elaborate. Leaving the city behind, they drove past open stretches of wasteland with trees dotted about like green paperweights on a dusty sheet. When they finally came to a halt, he announced, 'Here it is! My kingdom on wheels! Welcome!'

Simi saw nothing until he pointed out a railway saloon hidden behind some trees. She stepped out and he followed. The carriage looked like it had been caught in the spell from *Sleeping Beauty*, its green paint flaking and sparrows nesting in its roof. In the nearest mango tree a *koel* sang her silvery song from behind a curtain of leaves. Imran produced a key but the lock was stiff and he had to heave the door open with his shoulder.

'Come in,' he said. 'Or shall I carry you over the threshold?'

Simi laughed and stepped nimbly past him into the carriage. They were instantly assailed by a musty mixture of camphor and old carpet. It was dark inside, but once their eyes adjusted the outlines of furniture began to emerge. Imran strode across to the windows and threw open the shutters to admit fresh air.

'What *is* this?' she asked.

'My childhood home.'

'I don't understand,' she said, looking round at faded tapestries and wooden panelling that bore testimony to younger, better days.

'Don't blame you. It's a little confusing. But I did grow up on this train.'

He had been about seven when his father had whisked him and his mother away in the family's saloon coach, after which they had travelled incessantly until his father's death three years later.

'By the time he had lost his palaces, land, servants and jewels, his horses and carriages … all he had left was the saloon. The rest was locked up in court cases – still is.'

He could almost see his father standing there in the middle of the carriage, as he had done so often. Living on charity, subsisting on the pity of his friends, was unthinkable, so the saloon it had to be. The boy Imran had become so accustomed to the rolling motion of the train that it took him a long time to adjust to terra firma later.

'*And?* Tell me more!' Simi cried.

He led her by the hand and showed her the room where his tutor had lived, just past the kitchen but before the servants' compartment. There were no utensils in the kitchen, or vats or jars in the pantry. The adjoining two rooms were equally empty.

'The kitchen is where I liked hanging out most. No one makes roly-poly puddings the way the old *khansamer* did. He always bought fresh fruit and veg from the stations we passed, oranges from Nagpur and rice and sweets – there's not much you can't buy on Indian railway platforms!'

'Growing up on a train? It's magic!' Simi exclaimed. He gave a grin and stroked her arm.

He steered her back through to the family wing, with three bedrooms leading off a corridor and a bathroom at the end. The smallest bedroom had been his mother's dressing room, where her maid had slept. It was lined with expensive rosewood cupboards bearing the family crest of an elephant and a tiger surmounted by a coronet. The ghost of a perfume lingered there; jasmine. Even a tiny whiff evoked his mother. It was the only scent she had worn.

'Don't you think … ?' Simi spoke tentatively as she looked around. 'Don't you think the past should stay in the past?'

He took her back to the sitting-room and pulled her down on the sofa beside him. The fans didn't work and the heat was stifling.

'You think it's a … sort of memorial to my parents? No, it's just that I don't know what to do with it.'

'It's very beautiful,' she sighed, revelling in the ornate ceiling, exquisitely painted in gold and green.

'At first it was merely parked here, then the railway changed route and it was forgotten,' he explained. 'I own the saloon, not the line, so it has been here ever since.'

'How about the Rail Museum in Delhi? They would love it.'

'Or we could live in it when we marry,' he teased. When she turned her face away, he whispered, 'What's wrong?'

She gave a nervous little cough. 'It's just so *impossible!* You've *no idea* of how nasty people can be, what they'll say.'

He recalled the scorn and the snubs he had faced in a city that could not reject him because of his profession. He *knew* far more than she could imagine.

'I understand, *jaan*, trust me. But I love you. I want a home with you … I … '

He got up and walked down the corridor, returning to stand tall before her. He had brought her to this place because it he found it easy to bare his soul here.

'Look!' he sat down to face her, cradling her hands in his. 'At ten, I had lost both my parents. What did I have to fear after that? When you're little you think everyone will live to a thousand. But suddenly, they were gone.'

'You must have been so lonely,' Simi reached up to stroke his right temple. His wavy brown hair was thick under her fingers.

'*Khuda*,' he gripped her wrist and held her hand to his chest. 'My point is this: marry me with your whole heart or not at all. But don't turn me down for the wrong reasons.'

He had walked alone for so long. If she would not have him, he had decided to free them both from the half-light of *maybe*. His eyes hid the difficult years in their deep shadows: *many have loved you, many still to come, but none as I do in the throb of eternity which is ours.*

Simi freed her hand and cupped his face. She leant forward and kissed him; there was something sacred about the fleeting touch of her lips, light as the breath of God upon his soul. He looked at her with questioning eyes and she nodded, laying her head on his chest, bashful and peaceful all at once. He gathered her in his arms and they sat quietly. The years seemed to roll away from him until he was ten again. He had come home.

Simi and Imran forgot the world, wrapped up in a thousand happy thoughts. Over the following weeks they met at his home, his surgery, or in quiet cafés away from curious eyes. His dog had accepted her after a good sniff but his dour cook did not, worried that a new mistress would turn the kitchen inside out. Every time he served them he would bang the tea tray down in front of her, spilling brown liquid.

He did this with particular vehemence one warm evening in early August, when Simi and Imran had settled down in Imran's living room. Simi stared at the small pool of spilt tea in front of her, but Imran held her hand, whispering, 'Don't worry, darling, Bahadur doesn't like *me* either. Now, don't move. I've got something to show you.'

He disappeared into his study. Hudson was sprawled on the carpet and she wanted to reach out and stroke his thick fur. But instead she got up to look at Imran's framed certificates on the wall. The dog raised his head, watching her. She caught herself mentally rearranging the furniture in the room and laughed, which brought Hudson to her side in one bound.

Imran returned and placed something in her right palm, closing her fingers over it. 'There! Now you hold the treasury of my kingdom.'

It was a large silk handkerchief, discoloured and carrying the whiff of an old-fashioned perfume. The letter 'N' was embroidered in one corner, with a coronet above it.

'N for Nargis. My mother,' he said, glancing at the old photo.

Simi slowly unwrapped it. The white silk was flecked with brown, like age spots, but inside there was an enormous emerald ring. Imran held it up against Simi's eyes.

'Perfect match!' he said, reaching out for her hand.

She pushed him away before he could slip it on her finger. 'No, not here. You'll have to do it properly, in front of my whole family.'

He dropped it back into her hand.

'And that's all that's left of your kingdom?' she asked, stroking the smooth gemstone with her fingertip. He explained that his mother and grandmother had adored jewellery and commissioned it from the world's best. During summers spent in London and Paris in the '30s and '40s, they had bought many pieces from Cartier and Asprey's.

'*Jaan*, they had so much expensive stuff that a special strong room was built for it in the palace.' Simi fantasised about a room with shelves labelled 'Diamonds' and 'Emeralds', subdivided by colour and origin.

'And all that's left … ' He playfully ticked off the items on his fingertips. '*Abba's* ruby *achkan* buttons, his signet ring, half a dozen English snuff boxes, the gold chain that he always wore. And Ammi's diamond solitaires, diamond ring and some jewellery she kept for rough use. And this ring.'

Jewellery for *rough use*? Had his mother said to the maid: *Bring me the rough rubies?*

Looping a tress of her hair around his finger, Imran said softly: 'Had I the kingdom of my ancestors, I'd spread it under your feet; but I, being poor, have only my dreams. Tread softly because you tread on my dreams.'

She recognised Yeats' poem. 'Ah, that's lovely – but I want to hear *your* poetry, darling, not another man's words. Something written by you.'

'*Mine?* But I've not written anything.'

'Maybe you should then! You'll be a fine poet, Imi, I know it.'

'For you, *jaan*, I will.'

Later, she asked, 'Do you want children?' She had thought about it so much since their first kiss. 'If we had children, that's if we can ever marry, they would be … what? Hindu? Muslim?'

'*Khuda!* Just like a woman! We haven't done *bismillah* yet and you're worrying about children. But, now that you ask *jaan*, how about naming our first son Moses? Moses son of Imran. Has ring to it, don't you think?'

He was laughing at her but she loved the way his eyes crinkled at the corners.

'Oh, be serious!' she said, elbowing him in the ribs.

'OK darling. As you say. I'd like to name my children after my parents if you agree. Perhaps their middle names? If it's all so complicated here, why don't we live in New York?'

Leave Atmapuri? She couldn't! Leave behind the scent of mangoes, water-melons, the whisper of starched cotton saris, even the blazing sun? She loved Atmapuri's open markets too, with its bananas, chillies and pomegranates the colour of sin. And New York didn't have snake-charmers with poison cobras in wicker baskets!

'But how can I be happy far away from everything I love?' she murmured.

'Relax, *jaan*,' he reassured her. 'It'll work out, I'm sure.'

BLACK TAJ

The hours they spent together flew, ending in love. She looked into his passion-bright eyes and saw her own reflection. He played with her thick long hair. He was her healer-poet, she his salvation. Simi forgot everything, even her family, but her grandmother was about to remind her.

CHAPTER 18

Old Mrs Bhandari was in pensive mood as she waited at the Club for her bridge partners. She had first come here as a young bride in 1941, when the highly polished silver reflected white faces and the brass sparkled like gold. Back then the dance floor, now a dusty thoroughfare for careless waiters, was freshly waxed and they had danced to Cole Porter records. Her husband, the anglophile judge, had no objection to her waltzing with the Englishmen. On the contrary, he was proud: she was the only Indian wife in town to socialise on an equal footing with the Empire. Other Indians left their wives at home. In any case, their wives did not know the waltz, or any of the old dances.

The old lady could even recall what she had worn on that first night – a beautiful china-blue chiffon sari with gold sequins that twinkled when she moved. Within a year, she had taken up smoking Dunhills in a long, stylish holder. She had worn daring sleeveless blouses and high heels at a time when Indian women were either freedom fighters – dressed in drab *khadi* homespun cotton saris – or else remained cloistered in their homes. *What elegant days!* she sighed to herself. Today, nobody dressed up except for special occasions.

Even the Club looked tired and shabby now, as though exhausted by all that had taken place under its roof. She wondered where the others had got to. Her friend, Mrs Bhatia, often made wrong calls at bridge because of her poor eyesight. But at least she and the colonel turned up reliably every night to make up a foursome.

Eventually the others all arrived together: Colonel and Mrs Bhatia, and Mrs Puri, who bustled in with an air of suppressed excitement. They went straight into the card room and settled down at the same table as always. The waiter brought their usual drinks without having to ask: whisky for Old Mrs Bhandari, gin-and-tonic for the Bhatias and tea for Mrs Puri. They began playing in earnest.

Two hours later they packed up contentedly, tallied their scores and prepared to leave.

'Want a lift, Damyanti? Or have you got your car?' Old Mrs Bhandari asked Mrs Puri.

'Yes. No. I mean, Tillotamaji, that I came straight from my sister Kamala's daughter's child's birthday and their driver dropped me at the Club. You remember Dolly, my niece? What excellent eats she had. Very, very good arrangements! Her husband is with Deutsche Bank you know and their little Arjun is one. How time flies!'

'Come along then,' Old Mrs Bhandari nodded, sailing out imperiously. Joseph, her driver, opened the door of her car and the two women settled into the back. He drove off carefully.

They had barely gone a few yards when Mrs Puri leaned forward to whisper: '*Bhenji!* I met Vimla Lal at Dolly's house today and you'll never believe what she said!' She spoke loud enough for the driver to hear.

Old Mrs Bhandari was fond of Mrs Puri but she was an incorrigible gossip. Mrs Puri went on, 'Vimla Lal said to me *that young Dr Chaudhry's a clever doctor, why even my husband goes to him, but not suitable for our girls.*' She paused to observe the effect of her words.

Old Mrs Bhandari frowned. *Dr Chaudhry?* Who was he? Then she recalled him, dimly, from Simi's birthday. She shifted uneasily in her seat, wondering what was to come.

Mrs Puri's voice dropped a few notches. '*Bhenji*, Vimla Lal said our Simi's been seen with him. I didn't know which way to look, naturally. I was so embarrassed! Of course I denied it – why, she's like my own daughter! Not her, I said, not Mrs Bhandari's granddaughter, not with a *mussalman!*'

Old Mrs Bhandari's throat suddenly felt as dry as last year's bread but she rallied quickly. 'Rubbish! Simi works in those slums – I've tried to stop her but you know what girls are like these days! I believe the doctor also does some work there. Strange notions young people have now – in my time no decent girl would risk her complexion in the sun.'

'The slums?!' Mrs Puri hastily suppressed a chortle. 'No, no, Tillotamaji, they've been spotted in restaurants. And at his surgery. People have seen her there.'

Old Mrs Bhandari shifted away from Mrs Puri. 'I *told* you it's all that nonsense with the slums! And Simi's not a doctor, is she? Of *course* she needs to talk to doctors for her work.'

She could feel Mrs Puri's beady eyes on her but remained tight-lipped. Mrs Puri dared not say any more and Joseph soon dropped her off. Old Mrs Bhandari was fuming by the time she reached home. All her anger at the loss of the past, the vanished world she had enjoyed with her husband, of what the partition had cost her father, and the new social mores she did not understand, it had all coalesced in her hatred of the community she blamed for it.

The rest of the family was gathered for dinner when the old woman entered, her knuckles standing out sharp as spikes on her tightly clenched hands. She told them to shut the door in a vain attempt to keep it from the servants.

'Ruined! I am ruined. I'll never be able to show my face in decent society again!' she cried, throwing herself heavily into a sofa-chair.

'What on earth's the matter, Ma?' Gogu asked in alarm.

She pointed at Simi. 'Ask her, don't ask me. Ask her where's she been going all these days and who she's been doing it with!'

They remained silent. She continued, 'The Bhandari name is on everyone's lips. Why? Simi, did you not spare a thought for our family? The family of Rai Bahadur Bhandari.' She had added the honorific after her husband's death, despite the Judge not receiving it in his lifetime.

Gogu turned to his daughter. 'What does she mean, Sam?'

'*Mean?* I'll tell you!' the old lady lamented. 'Simi here's been meeting that doctor, the M doctor. *Hai Ram*! Why did I live to see this day? Didn't *they* do enough harm in the partition? Dishonoured our girls, cut their throats, murdered and looted.'

'Whoa, whoa! I say, Ma, you've lost me,' Gogu cried. 'Which doctor? What's he done?'

'The trouble with you, Gogu, is that you don't see what's under your nose! Must I repeat it? Simi here's been seeing that M! The doctor. She'll ruin herself and who will marry her then? It's your fault, Gogu. And Devi too. What do you expect when you make friends with Ms? They'll carry off our daughters!'

'Dash it, is this true, Sam?' her father asked.

'Papa! Dr Chaudhry and I work together,' Simi protested, blushing.

Old Mrs Bhandari harrumphed. 'You, Simi, you'll not step out of the house from today, not until you're safely married. All this slums-chums business must stop, you hear me?'

'Dadi, I am not going to quit my work just because some old witches have nothing better to do than gossip.'

'Devi!' the old lady bawled, turning on Simi's mother. 'Don't think I've forgotten Jehangir. Is it any surprise that Simi should turn out like this? Even though your own family wasn't so ... distinguished ... still we accepted you. And Gogu was getting excellent marriage offers from other families!'

Devi looked mortified, Simi mystified. Gogu protested.

'I say, Ma, that's a bit thick! Dee's the best, dash it! The best wife a man could have, the best mother. She's been damn near perfect.' But Devi had left the room.

His mother's angry glare said: *Perfect?! A millions miles away from perfect!* It riled her that her son should defend his wife.

But before she could speak, Simi cried, 'Dadi, you're always blaming Mama for everything! But I'm grown up now and it's my life!'

'My life, my life!' the old lady mimicked. 'You're wasting your life, Simi.'

Simi ran out of the room in tears, following her mother.

Upstairs in her bedroom, Devi held her daughter in her arms and stroked her hair the way she had done when Simi was little.

'Shhh, she's terrible I know – but she's like a dog's curly tail, so curly that not even twelve years in a clamp will straighten it out.'

Simi sat up and disconsolately wiped her eyes. 'Mama, what did Dadi mean about Jehangir? Who's he?'

Devi went to switch on the table lamp. With her back to Simi, she looked out of the window at the front street.

'Jehangir, Jehangir. God, she never lets go, she's wicked, that old Dadi of yours. It never ends – people die, but the story never ends.'

She turned to face Simi across the dimly lit room.

'You're grown up now Sam so you might as well know. Jehangir – Jeh – was a lovely man who came into our lives long ago, before you were born.'

A bachelor friend of a friend, Jehangir had been quick-witted and charming. Devi was floundering in the early unhappy years of her marriage and he made her laugh. They shared a passion for music too.

'There was nothing improper in our friendship – oh no, nothing of that sort. I was too young, too sheltered for any hanky-panky. We were friends, nothing more. He made me happy. But of course *she*, your Dadi, said some terrible things. I almost died of shame! But your father, Sam, he stood up for me and put a stop to her nonsense.'

Simi felt a great rush of love for her father.

'Wow! Dadi must have been boiling.'

'You saw what she was doing, didn't you Sam? Jeh was Muslim too. As if to say I've corrupted you! She's gone too damn far this time!' Her mother never swore.

Simi jumped up and hugged her, nuzzling her shoulder and breathing her scent.

'What would you do with your life, Mama, if you could do it all over again?'

'Hmmm,' Devi mused. 'I would marry your Papa all over again. He's decent to the core but no pushover. We're well suited. But it took us years to discover that. As for your Dadi – would I trade her in? In a jiffy!' They laughed together. 'And you, Sam? I'm glad you're not involved with the doctor. A Muslim. Not a good match for you, not in Atmapuri.'

'Mama! What's wrong with being Muslim? They're the same as us, that's what you've taught me.'

'Yes, darling. Exactly the same. But society is cruel. Too much conflict can tear a couple apart.'

Simi's heart sank. What would her mother do if she knew that she was engaged to Imran? For they *were* engaged, in their hearts and minds.

Her mother said softly, 'Sam, why not go away for a few days? A change will do you good. Let the ruckus die down.'

Simi longed to confide in her mother but silently swallowed her secret back into her heart.

CHAPTER 19

A few days later, Ahmed was at home stretched out on his charpoy, dreaming of his garage in Agra, when four men walked in through the open door. He quickly sized them up through a chink in his eyelids while pretending to sleep. They didn't seem to be armed. One of them shook him and he sat up, rubbing his eyes with feigned casualness.

'Kalludada asked for you,' the man said. Ahmed had no choice but to follow them.

Kalludada was the Don's right-hand man and his home was the biggest, most ostentatious place in the whole shanty town. Everything there had been free – TV, fridge, bed and all. No one dared refuse him anything. A naked light bulb dangled from the ceiling and cast harsh shadows on Kalludada's pockmarked cheeks, a legacy of childhood smallpox.

'Karimbhai wants the tempest!' he said, referring to the Don. 'There's a Hindu fest soon … Which one is it?'

'The birthday of Krishna. Janamashtami,' one of his men vouchsafed, 'A week Wednesday, the eleventh of August.'

'Janamashtami!' Kalludada repeated to Ahmed. 'And Bhai wants the tempest. We must be ready.'

The tempest! 'What does Bhai want us to do?' Ahmed asked.

'They'll be having a procession and we must be ready for it.'

As far as Ahmed knew, the Janamashtami festival was celebrated indoors, in people's homes at night. Kalludada, however, had done his homework. He informed Ahmed that this year the Krishna Temple had organised a street procession at midday in their large wooden chariot. Ahmed had seen the chariot before, with wheels as tall as a man and a canopy which reached to twice that height.

'But why?' Ahmed asked.

'*Lo!* Look at this idiot, questioning the Bhai! *Arre,* isn't it enough for you that Bhai wants it? And have you forgotten what they did to us on the tenth of Mohurram?'

Ahmed had not forgotten. Hindu fundamentalists had disrupted their Mohurram street procession, pelting their floats with stones and firecrackers. He was also aware that two annual festivals in the lunar calendar, one Muslim, one Hindu, were coming round again soon: the Prophet's Birthday on Monday August thirtieth and the Hindu Ganesh Chaturthi on Sunday the nineteenth of September.

Ahmed was deeply dismayed. Of course Kalludada wanted him by his side, for he was the bull. But he felt cheated by the Don. Anjora's wedding necklace was a royal piece – even *he* could see that – but what had the Don given him for it? Loose change. *He'd* taken all the risk but the Don had taken the cream. He owed the Don nothing. *Allah, is there no justice in this world?*

Yet he kept this to himself and listened quietly as Kalludada talked. He stayed for a cup of tea then left without arousing suspicion. Kicking a stray dog on his way out, he walked restlessly until finding himself near the River Boomi.

The tempest! Talk of it had freed the jinns in Ahmed's mind. In '91 his best friend had died in another tempest. Abu Hakim, his friend, his brother. They had been cornered in one of the old city's narrow lanes and ran for their lives. Ahmed managed to throw off their pursuers, but when he looked over his shoulder Abu was nowhere to be seen.

Later, after things had quietened down, they found his body covered with charred grass. His bones had been broken to stop him escaping while the grass burned him to death. Ahmed was consumed by guilt. If only he had not lost sight of Abu, if only he had turned to face the Hindu gang ... he was haunted by the thought that Abu might have cried out for help. He couldn't erase from his mind the image of the charred and mangled body.

Following Abu's death, guilt and horror had gnawed at Ahmed's guts and he became thin and gaunt. But after a few weeks, he started training again. Now he was the Bull.

Ahmed reached Scandal Point on the riverbank and sat down, idly throwing pebbles into the water. There was no money in it for him either – not even a forged tenner. He now had only one goal: to save enough to start his own garage in Agra with his cousin. The disappointing sum he had received for Anjora's necklace meant he was still short by almost fifty thousand rupees. He cursed the Don and his henchman. He cursed himself for being born poor. Could he just disappear? But Agra was not far and he couldn't just leave his mother. He shouted angrily into the wind and thrashed the foliage with his arms, as if fighting against invisible bonds.

Turning away from the river, Ahmed caught a glimpse of a light through the trees. The rising wind screeched like a banshee as Ahmed walked towards the light, which he knew came from the mausoleum of the Thirteen-Yards Saint.

The baba sat outside, defying the wind with a hurricane lantern. The sight of the holy man annoyed Ahmed. As a child he had accompanied his mother here, but later he began to question whether the baba was a true Muslim. So what if his mother had prayed to him? He resented the man who, he felt, had deflected Marriam from the true faith. His rage, never far from the surface, welled up. In that instant he could have killed the baba. It wouldn't take much to squeeze the life out of the lean ascetic. His hands tightened into fists.

But then the baba turned his head and looked towards him. Ahmed was at least two hundred yards away and the wind was shaking the trees as if they were pencils, so the baba couldn't possibly have heard him or seen him, but what if … Ahmed stood still. He returned home, discouraged and angry, only after the baba had turned away.

On the morning of the eleventh of August, Ahmed was out on the streets early. Janamashtami was a big day in the Krishna Temple's calendar and he watched as they wheeled out the great chariot of the gods. About fourteen feet tall, it had ample room for half a dozen priests. Volunteers drove to the wholesale flower market at four in the morning for masses of carnations, jasmine, marigolds, lotus and lilies. A group of thirty women, sitting on white sheets in the temple courtyard, worked with nimble fingers to make dozens of garlands and posies.

By nine everything was ready. The chariot was festooned with blooms and draped with silk, a large silver image of baby Lord Krishna on a swing at its heart. Some foreigners from the Hare Rama-Hare Krishna temple in nearby Mathura had brought sweets and were due to lead the procession, singing and dancing. The local administration and police had been informed and made arrangements for the huge crowd that would accompany them on foot through the main streets of Atmapuri. But Ahmed and his companions had their orders from the Don.

At the White House, after lunch, Simi was with her parents when Gogu switched on the small radio he kept on the sideboard. Since her last argument with her grandmother, Simi had managed to avoid the subject of religion around her family, only talking to Imran on the phone when she was alone. When she heard that the Janamashtami procession from the Krishna Temple had run into trouble, her heart sank. Miscreants had thrown stones and set off fireworks in the vicinity, scattering the crowd. Simi knew that Dadi would blame 'the Ms' for everything.

'Damned nuisance!' Gogu muttered. 'Mummy's at the club – better phone her Dee. Say to stay there until it's safe.'

Devi called the club and waited while the secretary sent someone to find Old Mrs Bhandari, who was irritated at being summoned to the phone when lunching with her friends. She reluctantly agreed to stay at the club for the time being. Gogu felt reassured by this and instructed the day watchman to lock the White House gates.

Just then Imran rang. He was on his way to the hospital. She was afraid for him, but he laughed.

'*Jaan*, if the police chief's wife begged him to stay at home, what would happen? I'll be alright.'

At least he had promised to be careful, whatever that meant.

She hung up, feeling low. She was desperately worried about him – what if hooligans started throwing stones? Would the green medical cross on his car be enough to protect him? She feverishly hoped that Muslims had not been responsible for the violence. What happiness could they have, she and Imran, in such an ugly climate?

It was about four before her grandmother arrived home, almost frothing at the mouth at being cooped up at the club and missing her afternoon nap. Reports had not confirmed whether the people who disrupted the procession had been Muslim and politicians were denying that the clash was religiously motivated. But Old Mrs Bhandari had made up her mind.

'What a day I've had! What a day! Ganga! Where's she gone?' The maid came running. 'Help me with a sponge bath, I'm so sticky. And you, Simi, don't go anywhere alone. *Lock up your daughters*, that's what people said during the partition. Those days are here again.'

Unable to sleep, Devi rose early the next morning and made herself a cup of tea. She took it out onto the verandah abutting the garden. Since yesterday she had been thinking about the partition of 1947, a date her mother-in-law never let them forget. Devi had been nine-months-old at the time and didn't remember anything. Her family had suffered, but they never spoke about it. However, they did hire a Hindu ayah for the young Devi, who fed her gory tales about rivers of blood and bloated corpses to go with her nightly glass of Ovaltine. The maid had fled from her native Multan, now in Pakistan, one of millions of people who tried to cross the border without knowing where exactly it was. Muslims went west, Hindus east, on foot, by bullock-cart, by train. Inevitably, they clashed. Trains arrived at stations carrying corpses; wells were choked with bodies. A million died. Devi's ayah lost her entire family and wished she had died too. Her bedtime stories left a searing impression on the child's mind. Now she found herself listening to Old Mrs Bhandari's tales of 1947.

Later that same morning, Simi was combing her freshly shampooed hair when her mother walked in with a vase of flowers. Devi placed the blue vase against the mirror to reflect the sun-like yellow calendula and white gypsophila, standing back to admire it. Then she sat down on Simi's bed and cast a critical eye around the room.

'Did Marriam sweep under the bed today?' she asked, bending down to peer.

Simi rolled her eyes at the mirror. Her mother was a stickler for cleanliness, even washing her own toilet bowl each day with an imported brush that stood in a shiny stand.

Simi, on the other hand, was untidy. Books teetered in higgledy-piggledy piles next to and under her bed. Several more were stacked up in the recess of her bathroom window.

'How's Pia?' her mother asked, abandoning her previous line of inquiry.

'Pia?' Simi responded in surprise.

Between her work and Imran, she had neglected Pia, whereas before not a day passed without them phoning each other.

'She's fine,' she muttered vaguely before adding, 'Today I'm going to talk to Marriam's friends about nutrition.'

She rushed about collecting books and stuffing them in her handbag, then bending down to strap white sandals to her brown feet.

'Must you go today, Sam? After yesterday, I'll worry about you out on the streets.'

Devi idly picked up a book on Italian cooking from a pile Simi had collected to take with her.

'Don't tell me you're giving them cooking lessons as well. You can't cook!'

Simi smiled. 'I just want to show them the pictures. Whet their appetite so to speak. Then I'll talk about nutrition. And nothing *happened* yesterday, Mama. There was no riot, nothing like that.'

Devi looked doubtful but continued to flick idly through a cookbook.

'Wonder what they'll make of this?' she asked wryly. The book contained pictures of al-fresco dining on the edge of the turquoise Mediterranean. It might as well be on another planet, as far as the slum women were concerned.

Simi laughed. 'At least they'll enjoy the pictures! Balanced diet. That's my theme. Proteins. Carbs. Sugars. Fats. The lot.'

But she knew, and her mother knew, that most of the women couldn't afford anything except basic lentils and wheat. Vegetables and meat were occasional treats.

'What's this?' her mother suddenly asked.

Simi turned to see Devi holding some snapshots. *Blast!* She had forgotten about the photos taken at Sunehri Begum's home. She had tucked them away in the cookbook.

'Who's this, Sam? Looks familiar – the doctor, isn't it? The one who came to your birthday?'

Simi nodded, turning her face away.

'This woman's familiar too.'

'That's Meena Kumari, your favourite dancer.'

'*Meena Kumari?* Where did you meet her?'

'At her home.'

'I don't understand, Sam.'

Simi's cheeks were flushed. 'She's nice, you'll like her, Mama.'

Her mother studied the photographs again. 'I didn't know you knew the doctor so well.'

'He's a … friend.'

'A *friend?* Since when?'

Simi avoided her mother's eyes. Instead she punished her scarf, twisting its ends between her fingers.

'Well, he's working for the slums, isn't he? He's the one who tells us what to do, you know with hygiene and all – him and Dr Nina.'

She hadn't seen Nina in weeks, but threw in her name as an alibi. It was hard to believe she had once imagined her to be a rival.

'He's so very nice, Mama, and the women adore him. He and Meena Kumari are great friends and I jumped at the chance to meet her.'

'Oh no, Sam! Don't tell me he's your boyfriend? A Muslim!'

Simi was afraid and denied it but her colour betrayed her.

'Tell me the truth!' her mother demanded.

She was unable to lie outright to her mother so she kept quiet, hanging her head. Her wet hair came loose, tumbling down her back.

Devi was furious. 'How could you, Sam? How could you do this? I trusted you. You've no idea of the flak I've taken for letting you run about in the slums – you know how your Dadi objected. Were you just going there to meet *him*? Is that it? I could slap you!'

'That's unfair, Mama. I'm doing good work – and he's never there. I mean, he holds a medical camp there sometimes but I'm never there when he is. In any case, he's so busy he doesn't even have time to scratch his head.'

'Then where have you met him?'

'At his surgery if I have something to discuss – about Nawabganj, I mean. Stop this, Mama, for Chrissake! I'm *twenty-five*. For once I feel I'm doing something meaningful. I wish you'd come with me just once to see for yourself.'

Devi ignored the last bit. 'Listen, Sam, stop it, you hear me? None of this boyfriend-shoyfriend nonsense, or I'll have to tell your father – and once your Dadi finds out you'll not be allowed to step foot outside.' She tore the photographs into little shreds.

Simi was appalled. Had her parents not raised her to respect all faiths? She had even toyed with the idea that they might be proud of her for living by their secular principles. She had certainly never anticipated such a strong reaction from her mother.

Christl! Part of her wanted to blurt out '*We're engaged, Imran and I!*' But another part trembled before her mother's disapproval. The enormity of her situation was beginning to dawn.

'You're not to see him again, understand? Perhaps I *have* spoilt you, like your Dadi says.' Devi stormed out of the room, taking away the shredded photographs. Did her mother think she would Sellotape them together again?

Later, Devi told Gogu what had happened. She was so angry that he kept quiet. Afterwards, he went and spoke to Simi.

'Your Ma's told me. Don't know what to say, Sam. Wish things were different, by golly, but they aren't. Don't want you to suffer, my girl. Think about it, that's all I say.'

Simi nodded sadly.

CHAPTER 20

The scene with her mother that morning upset Simi and her mind wandered all afternoon. She soon abandoned any pretence of teaching nutrition to the slum women. Instead, she asked them to talk about themselves so that she could make notes in her copybook. At least their stories distracted her from her own troubles.

Next she went to Imran's surgery. The receptionist threw her an occasional censorious glance while she waited. Simi cringed. To avoid the receptionist's glare, Simi kept her eyes fixed on the framed wall prints dotted around the room. She knew that Imran's American girlfriend had introduced him to art. They had visited SoHo's galleries at weekends. Simi almost wished he hadn't told her about Jenny. She was jealous of the freedom they had together. Freedom to spend their days together as a *couple*. For the first time in her life, Simi wanted to be somewhere other than Atmapuri. What bliss it would be to live alone in a studio apartment in a big city with no 'aunties' and 'uncles' to notice where she went or with whom.

Imran emerged from his consulting room and held the door open.

'Remember Mrs Malhotra, small meals at regular intervals. It'll help your acidity,' he said over his shoulder. Simi knew the woman slightly and slid down in her seat, holding an open magazine before her face, but it was impossible to hide in the otherwise empty surgery. *Atmapuri really is watching me*, she thought.

Finally the receptionist left and they were alone. '*Khuda*, I'm tired,' Imran said, taking Simi in his arms. 'You smell so nice, *jaan*.' He nuzzled her hair.

She had longed for this moment all day and his embrace was reassuring. She stroked his long fingers with hers.

'Missed you,' she said. Just being with him dispelled her fears.

Later, she told him of the row with her mother but omitted what Devi had said about his religion.

'I'm shocked. I expected something different from my parents I suppose – but we are a conservative family. I never thought of that before. There's been no divorce in the family ever and no marriages outside our caste.'

'I see. What else did she say, your mother?'

'She wants me to stop seeing you,' she added dolefully.

'You told her everything?'

'Of course not, but she guessed. My mother's sharp – and she knows me.'

'And you? What will you do?'

'How can you even ask?!'

'Listen, *jaan*, it won't be easy. You're still very young – in experience, I mean. Perhaps you should quit now before it hurts too much.' He turned away.

She threw her arms around him, her cheek resting against his back. 'I'll die if I have to leave you.'

The doorbell rang. He answered her surprised look: 'Heck! I'd forgotten. Just one last patient, *jaan*, then we can leave. Dinner?'

She had no time to answer because he strode away to open the door, but she couldn't have dinner with him tonight. Not after this morning.

In walked a thickset man with a round face and heavy moustache dividing it in half, like a child's drawing. He seemed vaguely familiar, but Simi couldn't place him. He was accompanied by two burly bodyguards.

'*Adaab!*' Imran greeted the man, who sized up Simi before he and Imran disappeared into the consulting room, its door clicking shut behind them.

Karimbhai! She suddenly remembered – he was the Don of the underworld! She knew about him. Everybody did. She was left alone with his men, who were dressed in polyester *khaki* safari suits that looked deceptively like police uniforms.

Simi was stunned. Imran knew this criminal? Well enough to give him a special out-of-hours appointment? Karimbhai resembled a yuppie on holiday in Lee jeans and a Lacoste T-shirt, but the list of his alleged crimes was chilling, including smuggling, larceny and murder. She wanted to flee but forced herself to sit still on the sofa, her gaze averted from the two bodyguards.

At last, Imran emerged and the Don left with an airy wave. Imran shut the door and walked back to her, tiredly cracking his knuckles together.

'That's that!' he declared. 'Two ticks, then we can be out of here.'

'Why was that awful man here?' she fumed.

Imran was turning off the lights. 'For a check-up,' he said casually.

'He's a criminal!'

'And I'm a doctor,' he said quietly.

'But can't you refuse to see him? Karimbhai! A Muslim crook!'

He stiffened and the muscles twitched in his jaw. 'I'm a doctor, Sim, not a judge. He's Muslim, as you point out, but what's that got to do with anything?'

'There are other doctors in the city. Why you? Why should *you* have to treat him?'

'Because he came to me. And because my family did many favours for his father.'

'Funny to repay favours by taking more favours!'

'*Khuda*, Sim, you don't mean to run my surgery, do you?'

It had been an awful day and Simi was overcome by fear. Why did Imran know the Don so well? How could she cope with that? They already faced an avalanche of objections and she'd have to sacrifice a lot for him – but suppose he let her down after that? Where could she go after burning her bridges with her family, her clan? Girls like Anjora could count on the support of their families, who wouldn't let the marriage break up. She suddenly wanted to be alone, to cry … a mountain began to crumble in her head.

Imran grabbed her by the upper arms so hard that his fingers dug into her flesh.

'Just cool it, will you? Just let it be,' he said.

They glared at each other before he let go abruptly and turned to look out of the window, his back arched in an angry curve.

'The Don! For Chrissakes, Imi, haven't we got enough problems? My family, your religion, my religion – and now this! Can we pile on any more?'

He turned to face her. 'Don't interfere with my work, Sim. What's your objection? That he's a criminal? Or that he's … ' the M-word hung between them like a dirty shirt.

She picked up her handbag from the sofa and headed out, but he barred her path.

'No! Let's talk about this … I thought it didn't matter, I thought you were like me and didn't give a toss about religion, but perhaps I'm wrong. It seems to come up all the time. Do you regret it, Sim? Us, I mean?'

She was confused. 'Perhaps it's best if we don't see each other for a while,' she said in a tiny voice.

'Cool!' he retorted sarcastically. 'Go back, Simi. Go back to your family, your safe world, your nice Punjabi life. I'm not good enough for them, am I? Go! They'll find you some nice Hindu man to marry.'

She ran out and the heavy fireproofed door of the surgery slammed behind her. She continued running down four flights of dark stairs that swam in her tears. Part of her wished she would fall and break her neck. She listened for the sound of his steps following her, but heard only the clatter of her own feet.

CHAPTER 21

Simi had thought she knew her mother, and Imran, but now that became hazy, like a windscreen in a storm. Recent events had confused her. Imran rang her a few times over the days following their argument, but she was confused, cold and agitated by turn. When she slept, she dreamt that he held another girl in his arms. She knew it was Imran without seeing his face. On another poisoned night, a red monster leapt out of a train and struck her in the thigh with a dagger. She awoke with a cry. Oddly, her right thigh was sore and painful for days after that. By mid-August, her dream diary was filling up nicely, but it left her very tired.

Dusty days spent in Nawabganj brought no solace. The soporific heat was deadening. The women's faces shone with sweat, their eyelids drooping. It was hard for them to concentrate on anything. Simi even stopped making notes about their stories.

Only the baba offered comfort. She went to him one morning, braving the hot wind which blew that day. The baba was standing in front of his blue door when she arrived. He greeted her with an enigmatic smile and she settled down on a cushion nearby, placing her offering of watermelon and mangoes on the floor before asking her question.

'Baba, what will I do with my life?'

He scratched his ear as he thought. 'Live as though you are immortal, but know that death is only one breath away.'

'And my family? What if they don't like what I do?'

He chuckled. '*My* family! *Whose* family? *He's* your family. He has made a map for your life. Find that map!'

He closed his eyes after this. Simi knew from experience that his silences were often long. She too shut her eyes but her mind buzzed like a bazaar, a hundred thoughts all shouting at once. She soon had the added discomfort of pins and needles in her legs, so she rose quietly and left.

The bad dreams continued. Simi lost her appetite. It felt like she was having a nervous breakdown. Her skin was stretched tautly over her jaw and the hollows in her neck were like grottos. She refused to meet Imran even after he apologised over the phone. She was confused and frightened about their relationship. She loved him – but did she love him enough to risk the wrath of almost everyone she knew? So she ignored him and stayed in to lick her wounds.

One day she told her parents: 'I want to go away. I need a break.' Her voice quivered. She was alone with her parents upstairs, on the landing outside their bedroom.

Her father shook his head in dismay. 'I say, I say, I say … what's wrong, darling?'

'Sam, you're moping all over the place,' her mother said, worried.

Simi gave her mother a reproachful look. *Isn't this what you wanted?* she thought. *Didn't you say I should go away?*

Devi sighed. 'OK, darling, why not go to Nimma *massi* in Delhi for a few days?'

Devi's sister, Nirmala, lived with her businessman husband in one of the capital's posh colonies. But Nimma *massi* was built like a tank and had the voice of a sergeant-major. Simi couldn't face the thought of her bracing aunt, not when she was so disturbed.

'Not Delhi,' she said.

'But there's a lots to do there – and you enjoy the shops, the galleries.'

Simi was adamant. 'I might go see Sunita,' she replied. 'She's asked me many times – maybe I can stay with her in Agra for a few days.'

Sunita Sharma, née Tripathi, was an old school friend.

'Are you still in touch?' her mother asked.

'Agra?' Gogu said. 'We haven't been there since you were a little titch.' He indicated about a foot above the ground.

'Rubbish! She was at least five!' Devi said.

Her mother was right and found the photographs to prove it: Simi in a frock with a ribbon perched on her head, running about with a young Marriam chasing after her.

'I'd like to see the Taj Mahal,' Simi said, spotting it in the background of one of the photos. 'I don't remember it at all.'

'Jolly good idea!' her father endorsed.

Devi was more cautious, worried that Sunita and her husband wouldn't want Simi bothering them. But Simi was confident and convinced her mother, who reluctantly agreed.

'I'll run you down to Agra!' Gogu offered. 'Say, Dee, we could make a little trip of it, how about it?'

Devi shook her head. 'I've got the studio booked for a new recording.'

Gogu looked crestfallen. But he soon left to struggle with his chronic constipation.

A sudden thought struck Devi. 'Is the doctor going with you?' she asked.

'Tch, Mama. What gave you the idea?'

'Is he? I want the truth, Sam. Regrets make poor companions in old age.'

'*He's not*. Promise. I'm not seeing him. Isn't that enough for you?'

Devi's face softened and she bit her lip sympathetically, but Simi didn't notice as she ran off to call Sunita.

In the end, Devi did join them on the drive to Agra, determined to keep an eye on Simi. After an early breakfast they set off on the three-hour drive: Devi and Gogu up front, Simi and Marriam in the back. It started out as a warm August day, but they got caught in a monsoon downpour almost immediately after leaving Atmapuri. It was like driving through a wall of water. Marriam was afraid of thunder and lay back against the seat with her eyes closed. But Gogu remained chipper and they reached Agra in good time, leaving Simi with Sunita and making it back to Atmapuri before evening.

Back at the White House, the sight of Simi's empty bedroom upset Devi. Sam had looked so young when they dropped her off, like a schoolgirl. Devi had longed to hold her tight and wished she would come back with them. But instead she talked charmingly to Sunita's in-laws, even though they were not her type.

She remembered the downy feel of the tiny babe they had handed her in hospital as though it were yesterday. Simi was her '*Chiriya*' – Sam had always been small, like a sparrow – but the fledgling had grown up and fallen *in love*. Much as she disliked the thought, Devi had to acknowledge it. Perhaps it was just infatuation. Agra would help. The one thing Dadi was right about was that Simi should find a husband soon; then she'd be too busy for anything else.

CHAPTER 22

Simi had come to Agra to forget about Imran, so it was vexing that everything there conspired to remind her of him. The brown monkeys cavorting in Sunita's garden reminded her of the monkeys in *his* garden. Even the *biryani* the family ate for dinner on her first night reminded her of *him* – although theirs was vegetarian and Imran ate only lamb *biryani*. Sunita, her skinny classmate, had turned into a plump mother-of-two. Her husband was a doctor with a practice at one end of their ancestral home, which he shared with his parents. Sunita lived with her family upstairs. A tall, shy man, Sunita's husband said little to Simi. Sunita, on the other hand, had always been a chatterbox and marriage had not silenced her.

Simi had a good view of the unkempt garden from her upstairs window. The high-ceilinged room was old-fashioned and Simi's two pairs of sandals looked lonely on the two-tiered blue shoe rack in the corner, which could have held twenty. Sunita sat cross-legged on the bed with a tea-tray in front of her and Simi was soon acquainted with the minutiae of her life. Sunita's mother-in-law, a roly-poly woman, rose at five for morning prayers. In the first year of marriage, Sunita had been required to join her. Pregnancy had solved that problem; when the baby came and kept her up nights, she was excused from the dawn service.

'She's thawed a lot!' Sunita concluded. 'Even likes the way I make *rasgullas* now!'

Simi, who needed a compass to find her way to the White House kitchen, was astonished at her friend's culinary prowess.

'I didn't know *anyone* made *rasgullas* at home!'

'My father-in-law doesn't like to eat anything from the bazaar. Everything has to be homemade: pickles, ghee, sweets, everything!'

They chatted if they were still schoolgirls, catching up on old times and new.

Eventually, Simi asked, 'Tell me, how far is the Taj Mahal from here?'

Sunita pulled a face. 'Not far. But my mother-in-law would say that the Taj looks like a pile of white butter!'

'Stop it! Or you'll spoil it for me.'

The one thing Simi had not mentioned so far was Imran. But before the day was done, she had confided everything to her friend.

Sunita was all ears and smiles. 'Romeo and Juliet! You remember Miss Wesley?' she trilled.

'Remember? Who can forget Miss Wesley? Hardly a Juliet though, more like one of Macbeth's witches!' Their English teacher had always used too much black kohl, but taught them Shakespeare with great aplomb. They reminisced more about school some more, enjoying in hindsight what they had resented at the time. It was good to forget their troubles for a while.

Finally though, Sunita asked, 'What *are* you going to do, Simi?'

'I'm going to the Taj Mahal tomorrow.'

'That's not what I meant.'

Simi knew that, but was not in the mood to answer. 'Goodnight,' she said, then turned in for the night.

In the morning, Simi dressed for the heat in her thinnest cotton salwar-kameez. Sunita wanted to accompany her to the Taj, but was prevented by her mother-in-law; a second cousin's husband's father had died in the night and they had to pay a condolence visit to the family.

'I can't even remember the man,' Sunita grumbled, but there was no help for it.

Sunita arranged for the Sharma driver to drop Simi at the Taj, but Simi insisted on taking a rickshaw back. She was glad to be alone. After all, she was going to the palace of love – and death – and wanted time to reflect. She was grateful to Sunita for giving her a bolthole, but having the Taj in her backyard meant Sunita didn't value it the way Simi did.

After the driver dropped her off, Simi took in her surroundings. Massive stone walls enclosed the Taj Mahal, like a pearl within an oyster. An outer courtyard, then an inner enclosure – and there it was! It looked so fragile from this distance, framed by the heavy stone archway. Simi sat down on the steps to savour it, her face cupped in her hands and knees drawn up. It was forty-two degrees in the shade and a streak of sweat trickled down her back like a drunken fly, but she didn't even notice.

Simi loved history and fragments of stories – phrases and details – floated through her mind. Empress Mumtaz Mahal had died giving birth to her fourteenth child. It was said that Emperor Shahjahan's hair had turned white overnight from grief. The Taj Mahal, begun in 1632, had taken over twenty years to build. Then the Emperor cut off the thumbs of the chief builders so that it could never be duplicated.

A voice interrupted her reverie. 'Picture?'

She looked up into the grinning face of a young man brandishing a camera. Without waiting, he clicked a snap and handed her a Polaroid image. She paid him and tucked it away in her handbag before making an escape. She passed the dry garden fountains that would have sparkled with water in Shahjahan's day, eventually reaching the base of the plinth on which the Taj was built.

It towered over her, despite having looked fragile from a distance. An attendant offered her foot gloves but she chose instead to go barefoot, as the Emperor would have done. The flowers and leaves that had been etched in gold above the main entrance had long since been stolen, but the inlay of cornelian, agate, jade and lapis lazuli had clung on tenaciously through the centuries. *The Mughals built like giants and finished like jewellers.* A visitor, Bishop Hebber, had written those words, long ago.

Inside it was hushed, even gloomy. Apart from Simi, there was a small group of Japanese tourists. Simi knelt beside Mumtaz's grave, which was covered with Arabic engravings. What had she been like, this beautiful Empress who had been mourned so spectacularly? She had accompanied her husband on his military campaigns, living out of tents — royal tents, admittedly, hung with carpets and silk, but tents all the same. Simi compared herself to Mumtaz. Could she, did she, love Imran as much as the empress had loved the Emperor? The baba spoke of love. Above all else, he valued love. Love was the secret heart of the world, even if obscured by lies. Yes, she realised, she truly did love Imran. A tear ran down her face as she thought about him. Simi thanked the empress silently and got up to leave.

Outside, the river curved like a lover's arm around the back of the Taj. Simi gazed pensively across the water at the empty space where the Black Taj should have stood. She knew the legend. Emperor Shahjahan had meant to build a mausoleum for himself in black marble to complement his wife's white tomb. But his son, Aurangzeb, thwarted him by usurping the throne and keeping his father prisoner for the last eight years of his life. She felt sad for what might have been.

Imran remained in her thoughts all the way back to Sunita's house. She considered calling him but wanted to see him in person, not discuss it on the phone. She hailed a rickshaw and it carried her through the crowded Agra bazaar. Her grandmother would never speak to her again if she married Imran. She knew that. Next, the rickshaw passed a shanty town that reminded Simi of Nawabganj, the acrid smell of burning cowpat filling her nostrils. *There'll be hell to pay*, she thought. The Bhandaris were one of the oldest Hindu families in town. And she was a Bhandari. An angry pulse throbbed at her temple, bringing on a headache. Simi sat quietly for the rest of the rickshaw ride, trying to ignore her doubts.

The hours in Agra seemed longer than back home. Simi ate downstairs with three generations of Sharmas and had to admit that 'homemade' was *delicious*. The two-year old mango pickle was outstanding, the fresh milk desserts even better. Mrs Sharma talked almost as much as Sunita, all the time keeping an eye on the kitchen, a sacred space where outsiders weren't welcome. Silver bells on her ankles and the key ring tucked into her waist jingled with every move.

That evening, Sunita took Simi for a drive past mango groves and on to the bazaar. Sunita was a compulsive shopper and did her best to tempt Simi. It was ages since she had gone loafing with a girlfriend and it was fun. They ate street food and sipped cokes while a shopkeeper unfurled sari after sari before them, then left without buying anything. When Simi told Sunita that she wanted to return to Atmapuri, Sunita protested and made her promise to stay a little longer.

Simi had an unexpected visitor the next day: Marriam. It was late morning and she was alone upstairs when the servant ushered her in. Simi jumped up in alarm. *Marriam? Here?* Her mind started racing for an explanation.

'Did Mama send you? What's wrong?' To Simi's dismay, the maid's eyes brimmed with tears. *What had happened? Was it* Dadi? 'Did someone die?' she asked, dreading the answer.

Marriam shook her head and sank down on the carpet. She sobbed as though grieving. It took time for Simi to coax the story out of her: Marriam had been dismissed from the White House!

'What rubbish! That's impossible,' Simi cried.

But Marriam explained. The previous evening Old Mrs Bhandari had discovered an expensive bracelet missing and straightaway accused her of theft.

'*Burri memsahib* said she knows I'm the thief. It's in her mind ever since the wedding. She says I am behind the robbery of the necklace – how do you call it? Some *rani*.'

'The Jaipur Queen,' Simi replied, absently. '*You* had nothing to do with that.' *It was Ahmed*, she wanted to say. *Your son*. But how could she break her old ayah's heart by accusing her son of theft? She still had no proof.

'Cut off my hands, Simi*baby*, if I'm a thief! Put ash in my hair, squeeze my throat, bury me in the rubbish heap – may I have a dog's death if I've stolen.'

Simi grasped Marriam's calloused hands in hers and said, '*Nobody* thinks you're a thief, Marriam. We all know what Dadi's like, so don't let her upset you. But why are you *here*?'

Marriam had gone home to Nawabganj a broken woman after Old Mrs Bhandari had told her to never show her face at the White House again. Unable to conceal her distress, Marriam told her son everything.

'He was angry, my Ahmudi, so angry. *Allah!* He's young and his blood is hot. And life's not been good to him. Last night I was afraid he'd do something *bad*, so I kept an eye on him.'

Ahmed had cursed the Bhandaris and told his mother she must never see them again. In the morning, Ahmed had rushed Marriam out of her home to catch the early bus for Agra.

'He wants me to go to our village, Kadamgaon, so he brought me here to catch another bus. Then Ahmudi went to see someone – *bizness*, he said – so I slipped away to see you.'

Christ! How could this happen? Marriam was part of their family, not just a servant. At that moment she hated her grandmother.

'I'll sort it out, Marriam. I promise. Which blasted bracelet did Dadi mean? And Mama? Didn't she do anything?'

Devi had managed to stop the old lady from ringing the police but failed to prevent her sacking Marriam. Gogu was out when the storm broke, just after tea, and Marriam had left by the time he returned.

'The house was turned upside down. Such a noise she made, I can't even begin to tell you, Simi*baby*! *Allah* cut off my hand if I'm a thief, cut out my tongue if I lie. Thank *Allah* Ahmudi's father didn't live to see this day. The shame of it!'

'The bracelet, Marriam,' Simi insisted. 'What bracelet was it?'

A horrible feeling was dawning on Simi. Tucked away at the bottom of her small suitcase was a thick gold bracelet with a tiger's head at either end, joined nose-to-nose. She had packed it with some smart clothes she thought she might need at Sunita's place, forgetting to tell her mother.

Marriam described the exact same bracelet, adding, 'You used to wear it sometimes, Simi*baby*, remember?'

Simi was mortified. Her carelessness had had terrible consequences for someone she loved.

'*You* don't have the bracelet because *I* have it. It's here with me in Agra, Marriam. Come, I'll show you!' She took Marriam by the hand and led her into her bedroom.

Marriam's tears streamed down her leathery cheeks as she held it in her hands. She gave it back and covered her face with her hands.

'Stop blaming yourself, Marriam. It was an accident.' Simi wondered how she could make amends. 'Everything will be alright. I'll tell Dadi and sort it out.'

Marriam soon departed, eager to hurry back before Ahmed discovered she had gone to meet Simi, who was left feeling depressed. She should ring her mother and clear up the misunderstanding, she thought, but Sunita called her to lunch so she didn't get the chance. She considered it again later, even picking up the phone, but put it down again because she thought her mother might be taking an afternoon nap.

Later the same day, in the early afternoon, Simi was again interrupted when Sunita burst into her room while she was trying to read. Sunita's eyes were sparkling and her lips were tightly clamped, as though to prevent something from popping out.

'*What?*' Simi asked.

'*Someone's* come to see you!'

'I don't know *anybody* in Agra,' Simi said irritably.

'Who said he's from *Agra?*

His name? '*Tchch!* Don't tease me.'

Sunita threw her hands up in mock surrender. 'OK, OK! It's your doctor. You never told me he's so handsome.'

'Imran?'

Sunita nodded. 'Right here, in the next room.'

A sense of relief swept through Simi as she jumped up, but Sunita stopped her.

'At least tidy up! Here,' she picked up a comb and made Simi stand still while she undid her plait and combed out her long hair. Simi could hardly breathe with excitement. 'Now go and put on some makeup.'

Simi laughed and ran into the bathroom to apply kohl to her eyes. Sunita held Simi back for a quick inspection, then nodded and let her pass.

Imran stood in the half-light of the sitting room, the curtains drawn against the blinding summer sun. He smiled, blowing her a kiss with rounded lips. Simi bit her lower lip and paused just inside the door, suddenly shy. He looked so confident and calm. Sunita was just behind her.

Imran spoke first. 'Hi Simi. Your mother asked me to stop by to tell you that she wants you back. Since I was visiting an old patient in Agra, I offered to drive you back myself.'

'*My mother?*' Simi asked in confusion. 'What's *wrong?* Why didn't she phone?' Her earlier fears at the sight of Marriam were reignited.

He winked a quick denial and she realised it was only a ruse.

'How nice of you to take so much trouble,' she said, joining in. 'But I can't go back just yet! I've only been here for two days. By the way, Sunita *knows*. I've told her everything.'

Without a blush, he turned to her friend and said, 'Oh! In that case, I'll be frank with you, Sunita. I have no patient in Agra – but I *am* a doctor. Simi's mother didn't send me but I *have* come to fetch her back. You see, I mean to marry her.'

Sunita clapped her hands. 'Of course she'll go back with you!' she declared. 'Now sit and I'll get some tea. Then we can talk.'

Imran raised his right hand to his forehead in a gesture of thanks. 'I know we're going to be good friends!' Sunita smiled and went out, tactfully closing the door behind her.

'Hang on a minute!' Simi protested. 'How come this has been settled between you and Sunita? I am not going back with you!'

'Sensible girl, Sunita,' he said, pulling her into his arms. His moustache tickled her nose when he kissed her.

'How did you find me?'

'You really thought you could lose me, *jaan*? I was desperate. I missed you. I couldn't even speak to you.'

'But how come you're here in Agra? How did you find me?'

'I rang your home, God knows how many times, but your dear grandmama was always at the other end. I'm not a coward but … I hung up. When your mother answered she was civil. Unhelpful, but civil. But she did say that you were out of town.'

Eventually he had got the truth out of Anjora, in whom Simi had confided before leaving.

'Anjora's the traitor!' Simi beamed.

'How could you just disappear? *Khuda!* Don't ever do this to me again.'

Instantly contrite, she kissed his hand.

'I'll never leave you again.' She stroked his cheek. Then her hand slipped down to his open collar, tracing the hollow between his collarbones and, light as a butterfly, the curve of his firm biceps under his sleeve.

Sunita was charmed, Simi could tell, and that made her proud. When he recited Urdu poetry Sunita drank in every word. She relished the conspiracy and refrained from summoning her husband to meet Imran. When it was time to leave, Sunita accompanied Simi to her bedroom and helped her pack her suitcase.

'I'll miss you! It's been such fun,' Sunita said wistfully. 'When's the wedding?'

Simi rolled her eyes, thinking of her family. 'You'll be the first to know!'

As Simi and Imran drove off, she settled down into the car seat with a contented sigh. The sun-scented air carried traces of red gulmohar and yellow laburnum. Life was good again.

'What next?' he asked. 'Where do we go from here?'

The future was suddenly upon her. All her life Simi had dealt in certitudes. She had belonged to her family, her home, and to Atmapuri. But in Agra the lady of the Taj had spoken to her. 'Yes,' she said.

He gave her a puzzled look. She laughed and flung her arms around him, making the car swerve.

'Yes, I'll marry you. Any day, any time. That's if you still want me.'

He pulled up under a vast tamarind tree and turned to her, wearing an intense look on his face. He held her as though she was made of eggshells.

'You know I want nothing more – but are you sure?' he asked. 'And your family? I know how close you are.' Now it was his turn to point out the obstacles.

'It's not going to be easy,' she admitted. 'But I can't bear to lose you.' Being away from home had helped to clear her head. 'And I have a life of my own – perhaps it's time. The baba told me that there's a map for everyone and I must find my own.'

She couldn't bear to lose her mother and desperately hoped that she would accept their decision. Dadi? Well, Dadi was Dadi and unlikely to change. Simi was tired of thinking, of trying to second-guess everyone.

'It's too late for worrying about anyone else. Now it boils down to us.' *Oh let us be married, too long we have tarried*, as the Pussycat said to the Owl. The poem whirled around in her head and wouldn't stop. *The Owl and the Pussycat went to sea* – now, how did it go? – *they took some honey and plenty of money. Pussy said to the Owl, 'Oh let us be married, too long we have tarried.* Having made the decision, she felt quite light-headed. 'Let's get married, Imi. Here. Now. Today.'

'What!'

'Don't you see? If we return to Atmapuri as a married couple, *they* can't do *anything*. Hindu, Muslim, what difference does it make? So let's get married. *But what shall we do for a ring, a ring?*'

Imran laughed as she sang.

'This is real life, *jaan*, not poetry. When people find out that we eloped – and that's what they'll think – well! Would you really do this for *me*?'

'I'd do more for you, much more!' she replied passionately. 'I went to the Taj and Mumtaz Mahal told me, I swear she did, that love matters.'

Love had many faces. But now there was only Imran. There would be conflict if they opted for a religious marriage. The thought dismayed her. She didn't really want to convert to Islam for the *nikaah*; she didn't believe in conversions. And Imran – would he be comfortable being married the Hindu Vedic way?

'In Hindu weddings, the groom arrives on a white horse. My grandmother would probably ask whether the horse was a Hindu too.' No matter what compromises they made, her grandmother would not attend. It was all so difficult.

They talked until it became too hot to linger any longer. They still had not come up with a solution, so they drove to Agra's air-conditioned Oberoi Hotel and ordered lime sodas.

Simi had been unusually quiet as they sat together, but suddenly she sat bolt upright.

'We could have a *gandhara-vivah!*'

Imran had never heard of it, so she explained. She remembered from history lessons that in ancient India, a boy and girl could go to a temple, exchange garlands, and that was a marriage.

'It's not common today, I admit,' Simi concluded.

'*Common?* No one's ever heard of it!'

'But it's valid! At least, it used to be.' She sounded uncertain.

He groaned. 'You know what'll happen? Your granny will chase me with a gun!'

'Dadi doesn't even have a gun,' she replied facetiously. 'Now let's go buy the garlands. But what do we do for a ring? Maybe we can find a pig with a ring at the end of his nose!' she joked.

He hesitated. 'Look, *jaan*, you know how much I want this – but we must do this properly. We should be married with your family present. What'll they think of me otherwise? A civil marriage, that's the answer. That way we'll cut out the religious crap.'

She clicked her tongue. 'But I can't go back as if nothing happened – and don't tell me you want me to!'

They argued back and forth like a ping-pong match before agreeing they would do it *her* way in Agra, and *his* way in Atmapuri.

He was adamant she should convince her family before they could marry, no matter how long it took. He did not wish her family to view him as irresponsible or having encouraged her to elope.

'People will punish us for falling in love,' he explained. 'As my old tutor would have said *sitaron ke age jahan aur bhi hain; abhi ishq ke inteham aur bhi hain.*'

'Iqbal!' Simi said, pleased to recognise the poet. 'My mother loves Iqbal. *There are stars beyond these stars; there are many trials of love to come.* How's that for a translation?'

He congratulated her on getting is *almost* right.

Simi wanted to visit the bazaar to buy garlands and a sari.

'Then we'll go to the Taj. It'll be spectacular at this time of day, all golden and syrupy.'

They resolved to drive back to Atmapuri the next day. But in her excitement, Simi forgot all about Marriam, the bracelet and ringing her mother.

CHAPTER 23

Simi and Imran went to the Agra bazaar at about three-thirty in the afternoon, braving the summer heat. Simi couldn't remember exactly where to find the sari emporium that she had visited with Sunita and stopped to ask. Once they found the right place, somnolent shopkeepers heavy with lunch attended to Simi. She wanted a bridal sari in traditional red, but Benaras brocades were too heavy for the heat and too ostentatious for a gathering of two. She finally settled for a sari in magenta georgette, the colour of wild roses, with a silver border. An armload of glass bangles completed her outfit. No Bhandari wedding had ever cost so little.

Simi then selected two fresh garlands, thick as a man's wrist, from a shack selling flowers. One last purchase – a kilo of milk sweets with pistachio – and they were done. Imran, who loathed shopping, happily followed her with bundles in his arms, quipping that he had become her 'coolie'.

They went back to the hotel and checked in as Dr and Mrs Chaudhry. He refused to write 'Mr & Mrs Misra' as she suggested, that being the commonest name here. They had spent over an hour in the bazaar and Simi was anxious to get to the Taj. First though, she decided to take a shower; when Imran teased that he might soap her back, she grinned and locked the bathroom door behind her. Afterwards, while adding the finishing touches to her toilette, she thrust her hand into her bag and found the bracelet. She pulled it out and the two tiger heads seemed to growl at her, so she quickly thrust it back inside.

'*Christ!* I forgot. How could I?' She told Imran about Marriam's visit. 'And I think Ahmed's the one who stole Anjora's necklace.'

'*Ahmed?* Ahmed's not like that surely. C'mon, *jaan*, just because he's rough.'

She was reminded that Imran liked Ahmed. But the lead burglar had been the same build and height as Ahmed, whose unique physique made him easily recognisable.

'I'm convinced, no matter what you say, but I have no proof.' She didn't want to hurt Marriam, especially after what had happened. 'You're the only one I've told. Poor Marriam.'

She did not ring her mother.

They stepped out again, Simi in her sari and Imran in a linen shirt and slacks, then drove to the Taj Mahal. It was exactly as Simi had imagined, with a patina of eighteen-carat-gold laid on by the setting sun.

'See the Golden Taj?' she said, excitedly squeezing Imran's hand. '*My* Taj is of many hues – white, black, gold – take your pick. Depends on its mood.'

He laughed. 'Yes, *jaan!*'

The photographer from her earlier visit spotted her and came running. 'Honeymoon? Photograph?' he asked with a pointed look at her sari and flowers.

Simi nodded and put her arm through Imran's. The photographer clicked away. He took snaps of them seated on a marble bench with the Taj as a backdrop, her sari a splash of rose against the white marble. He even followed them as they strolled past the dry fountains to the main monument.

They climbed up the plinth and stopped at the base of one of the minarets which stood at each of the four corners, turning to face each other. A cooling breeze came off the river. They asked the photographer to take pictures but keep out of earshot.

Looking into her eyes, Imran said, 'With this garland I take you as my wife. I will love you, protect you and stand by you always.' He placed it around her neck.

Simi said softly, 'And with this garland I make you my husband, my true husband. I love you, I'll look after you and we'll share everything always. No one will part us again.'

She reached up but Imran was too tall for her, which made them laugh. She tried again and he playfully ducked away, until finally relenting.

'Remind me to get you a step-ladder as a wedding present!' he quipped.

She placed the garland around his neck, her eyes moist with emotion. She was unable to stop her tears. He wiped them away gently.

'Darling, we are one, you and I,' he said tenderly.

And so, on Friday the twentieth of August, Simi and Imran were married, even though neither had expected it that morning. They gazed at each other, as if under a spell, but the camera flash going off in their faces brought them back to reality. Unable to contain his excitement, the photographer bounded up to congratulate them. They fed each other one of the sweets they had bought. The photographer ate two.

The saffron sun was now enjoying its final hurrah before disappearing to the other side of the world. The photographer took shots of Simi leaning against Imran and watching the sunset. They walked arm-in-arm around the monument, looking across the Yamuna River at the open stretch of land beyond.

'There,' Simi pointed. 'That's probably where the Black Taj would have been. Shahjahan's black marble tomb, like Mumtaz's white. That's love, Imi. That's how well we'll love each other too.'

Imran knew the legend. As a boy he had picnicked at the Taj many times with his mother, aunts and other palace ladies. He had also been there with his diligent tutor, who had told him fascinating tales of the Taj, making him read the Arabic calligraphy.

'I could tell you legends you've never heard of, *jaan*, but to me the Black Taj means something else. Shahjahan, I was told, would have built it had his son not overthrown him – but who knows? Instead, here's my theory – the Black Taj is nothing but a fantasy. A dream. We've all heard about it, so it's become part of our dreams too. It's my dream, your dream. It can be whatever we dream.'

She listened contentedly as he added, 'You should talk to Sunehri Begum about the Taj. She has terrific stories about the time my grandfather had a party for her here. He cordoned off the whole place. She probably hoped he'd build her a Taj Mahal too. But he's gone. And India changed. Only an emperor could have built like that. Or Donald Trump. Perhaps Sunehri Begum should go to New York.' Simi laughed and squeezed his arm.

'Do you see?' he continued, 'The Black Taj is a magic box, a kaleidoscope. You move it around and see something different each time.'

Simi did understand. *Her* Black Taj was a happy life with Imran. They strolled about until closing time, when an official chivvied them along. Simi paused for a last look at the Taj before they left. From a distance it looked again like a miniature of itself, a white swan on the river, except that it was now grey. The dim finger of night encircled it.

In the twilight, the Taj seemed to expand and fill the horizon. Its base was inked out and it floated above Earth. Simi watched, entranced. In the solemn darkness the Taj disappeared: speeding off to heaven and Mumtaz, its mistress.

They dined at the hotel restaurant on ambrosia and *amrit* elixir, though they had ordered only biryani and lentils.

'*Mrs Chaudhry!*' Imran teased, toasting her with his glass of beer.

Later, alone at last, he played with her hair, wrapping it around his finger, drawing in its perfume. 'You're so beautiful, Sim. Both outside and in your heart, your soul.'

No one had ever called her beautiful except him. *The Owl and the Pussycat danced by the light of the moon, the moon, the moon.*

He continued emotionally, 'Why *does* a man love a woman? Because she fills a hole in him that's been there for *Khuda* knows how long. She makes him complete.'

She caressed his face, running her hand over his brow and down his right cheek. 'You'll never be alone again, darling.'

He caught her hand and kissed it. '*Jaan*, I've come home now.' The arid hours of their separation, the weeks of doubt and despair, were swept away.

There was a sudden drumbeat of thunder outside, then the rain was knocking on their windowpane. But the outside world seemed very far away.

They drove back to Atmapuri in the morning, ready to face the music. Simi brimmed with the effervescence of new brides, seeing diamonds in dewdrops and angels lighting up avenues. But the city remained its old jumbled self.

First, they went to Imran's apartment. When his Nepalese cook opened the door and saw his master, his face lit up like a thousand candles. Nine hundred and ninety nine of them were then extinguished when he caught sight of Simi. She guiltily tried to withdraw her hand from Imran's, but he grasped it firmly and they entered. At least Hudson gave her a warm welcome, jumping up and licking her face.

'I'd better ring Mama and say I'm on my way back,' Simi sighed, noticing the time.

'Not just yet,' Imran pleaded. 'It's only one, must you go now?'

There was no hurry. She phoned her mother to say she would return by tea-time.

'*No, I don't need to be fetched. I'm taking a ride with a friend of Sunita's* … ' Well, that was true: Sunita had been very friendly towards Imran! And she would tell her mother about the bracelet when she got home.

They agreed that he would not tell his foster-parents about their marriage until she had told her family. Imran had to fly to Bombay the next morning for a medical conference and would be gone five days, giving Simi plenty of time to break the news.

For an hour or two, Simi clung to Imran in the privacy of his sitting room, but it was soon time to leave.

CHAPTER 24

Old Mrs Bhandari glowered when her granddaughter arrived home. 'Is this a hostel where people come and go as they see fit?' she commented.

Simi beamed at her, too happy to be annoyed. Everything at home looked different to her now, more tired and staid. The White House suddenly seemed old-fashioned and her grandmother more religious. The old lady now celebrated everything: the big festivals of course, Janamashtami, Ram Naumi, but also Ekadashi.

'I don't know what she's trying to do,' Devi confided to Simi, 'She's even *fasting!* Dadi had never been known to pass up on mutton chops or chicken curry. Her mother continued, a concerned look coming over her.

'About Marriam. I didn't want to tell you on the phone, Sam. I knew how upset you'd be, but something awful happened.'

'I know.'

'You know? But *how?*'

Simi told her about Marriam's visit to Agra.

Devi shook her head sadly. 'I'm not surprised. Marriam always treated you as one of her own.'

The moment had come to confess. It was hard, but Simi said it plain and simple.

Devi was appalled. 'I never believed for a moment that Marriam took that bracelet, she's not a thief – never! But your Dadi … you know how adamant she is. I'm so ashamed, I should have tried harder to protect her. Did Marriam say when she's coming back?'

'She'll never come back to us, Mama. Even if she forgives us, Ahmed won't let her. God, I feel so awful. But I'll clear her name if it's the last thing I do.'

Simi marched to her grandmother's room before she lost her nerve, banging the gold bracelet down on the table next to the old lady.

'Here it is!' she announced. 'It was with me all the time. Marriam had nothing to do with it.'

The old lady picked it up calmly and examined it. '*You* stole it? But why?'

'For Chrissake, Dadi, I didn't *steal* it! I *took* it to wear but forgot to tell Mama. I just *forgot.*'

'You can't just *take* it. It's not yours,' her grandmother said sternly.

'It is *ours,* isn't it? Family jewellery. It's terrible what you did to Marriam, throwing her out like that.'

Her grandmother peered over the rim of her reading glasses. 'Something *I did? You* took the bracelet, Simi. And tell me, why should we keep Ms in the house?'

'But Marriam is *family.*'

'Family, hunh! We're Hindu, she's an M! How can we be family? *And* she's a servant.' The old lady put the bracelet away in a drawer. 'You'll get *your* share of jewellery when you get married, not a day before.'

Simi found it hard to settle down after that, despite her parents' happiness at having her back. Throughout the evening, her grandmother could not lay eyes on her without finding fault. She also nagged Simi about finding a suitable boy to marry. Simi didn't mention Imran.

Impatient to give the baba her news, Simi went to see him the next day in a monsoon breeze that was spreading the clouds like wisps of cotton wool around an azure bowl. The baba's door was propped open with bricks but the wind kept trying to claw it shut. The baba was there alone, seated on the threshold, just inside the door. His cotton kurta flapped in the wind as he gazed at the river with unseeing eyes, unaffected by the turbulence of nature. She sat quietly nearby and waited. When he opened his eyes she spoke quickly, afraid he might slip back into meditation.

'Baba, I'm married!'

He looked at her calmly. 'It was a strong destiny.'

There were a million questions on the tip of her tongue, but the baba continued.

'First, there's the baby, helpless milk-sucking little thing. But that infant could grow to become a king. See how a little cub becomes a ferocious tiger? That's what the world is, an arena of growth. Why be afraid? Fear is only of loss. But in the divine there's no loss. His is the presence that contains no absence.'

As usual, the message was obscure. She listened to him quietly.

'And have you seen His face? *Bah!* You've wasted precious years, traded them for gold no more real than sunshine. Seek Him now! Seek Him when you're young and strong, seek him as the fish seeks water, as if you cannot live without it.'

> *The wind etches it in the sky*
> *The ocean traces it in its depths*
> *The sun and moon are His two eyes,*
> *It's the Face of God*

BLACK TAJ

In dark mountain caves did I seek Him
And in the desert's burning sands
Until my soul whispered: He is here! He is here!
He is the breath of your breath
The soul of your life
For He was never lost
We were never parted
The search is over for
There's no seeker left any more
All is bliss, all is bliss

The baba spoke of fear of loss. Was Simi afraid? Honestly, yes. Afraid of her grandmother, even of her parents and society. Her mother could be fierce at times. And society did not easily forgive transgressions. It was a sobering thought.

As she left, Simi was seized by a sense of foreboding, as if the baba was suddenly out of her reach. She tried to ignore it, but the niggling thought remained.

Two days later, Old Mrs Bhandari was in the thick of preparations for the Ganesh Chaturthi festival, the festival of the elephant-headed deity, the god of beginnings, wisdom and good fortune. She had dispatched Joseph to buy a clay image of Lord Ganesh and he returned with a large statue with a pendulous belly, painted a vivid blue.

'Oof! Just look at that colour!' the old lady carped to her neighbour, Mrs Puri. 'Still, what does Joseph know? He's Christian, after all.'

After being worshipped at home for ten days, her Lord Ganesh would be immersed in the river on the festival day, along with thousands of others. In previous years, the old lady had merely lit a token lamp before being driven to the club for her usual whisky-soda and bridge. How things change. Now, no ritual was left undone. She was a guardian of the faith. But too many evenings missed at the club made her bad tempered, creating a sour atmosphere at home.

Devi and Gogu, accustomed to having the house to themselves in the evenings, were put out when Old Mrs Bhandari tried to turn the sitting room into a temple backroom for making oil lamps and garlands.

'Dammit, Ma,' Gogu objected, 'How can I enjoy my drink in the middle of all this? It's bad enough you're not having one now.' She had chosen to eschew alcohol in the run up to the festival.

Simi had rarely seen her father oppose his mother and watched Dadi's reaction. To her surprise Dadi, despite her protests, moved the operation to her own bedroom. Gogu caught Simi's eye and winked. She burst out laughing. Devi too seemed less cowed. It was as if the old lady had been waiting for them to assert themselves.

Later, when Simi peeked into her grandmother's room, she overheard her grumbling to Mrs Puri.

'Those wretched Ms, all that trouble they caused on Janamashtami. *Chee-chee*, spoiling our festival like that! Who threw bones into the holy fire? Demons! That's who! Now they want their own street procession. For Mohammad's birthday. The Prophet.'

She went on to blame the Ms for everything from failed monsoons to the tacky quality of modern tailors. Three weeks separated the Hindu festival of Ganesh Chaturthi from the Prophet's birthday. Would that be enough to avoid a conflict? Simi's agitation grew tenfold. And what would her grandmother do when she found out about Imran?

Mrs Puri replied placidly, 'No worries, Tillotamaji. Our procession for our dear Lord Ganeshbapaji will be bigger and better than *theirs*, you can be sure of that.'

The day of Imran's return from Bombay dawned with Simi still not having broken the news to her parents. Apprehension had kept her awake all night and the morning found her pacing on the terrace. Her stomach heaved as she fretted about how she should couch her confession.

In the end, she made the announcement at the breakfast table when she was alone with her mother. Dadi had taken her breakfast in her room on a tray and Gogu was on the golf course.

'Mama, I'm ... I married Imran in Agra.' She could hear her heart thumping over the ticking of the grandfather clock.

Devi looked at her blankly, so Simi repeated herself.

'Mama? Did you hear me? I married Imran!'

This time Devi reacted. *'Married?! To the doctor?* You promised your Agra trip wasn't with him!'

Simi looked down at her plate. 'I went alone, but he followed ... '

'How? Who married you?'

'We ... we exchanged garlands, a *gandharva-vivaha*, at the Taj Mahal and ... ' her voice disappeared like a tail down a mouse hole.

Her mother stood up and Simi flinched, afraid she would strike her.

'You're *not* married at all!' Devi exclaimed. 'Have you lost your mind? Have you no shame? Have you ... have you been with him as husband and wife?'

Simi hung her head and clenched her clammy hands.

'You're as bad as Pia,' Devi hissed. 'Living with a man and pretending you're married. Your Dadi was right after all. You *are* wayward and spoilt. A selfish brat! First you walk off with that wretched bracelet and Marriam is sacked. And now ... you exchange cheap two-pice garlands and ... Oh, your poor father. I'm stunned! You've let me down, Sam. You've let me down badly.'

Simi hugged herself defensively. 'But I love him, Mama.'

'Love!' Devi scoffed. 'Your generation thinks it invented love, as if *we* know nothing about it!' She paced up and down, before stopping and leaning across the table, her hands on the polished surface. 'Listen to me, Sam. Dr Chaudhry's not the man for you. Look around you! Forget the others – just look at your own grandmother. *She's* never forgotten the partition.'

'I am sick of the partition!' Simi raised her voice. 'We're *still* being partitioned every way, every day.' In Simi's mind the partition had become a living thing, a monster gobbling up land while dividing families, homes and minds. Even today, everything was partitioned according to caste, community and religion. Politicians saw to that and newspapers were full of it.

Devi sat down heavily, like a sack of potatoes. 'And *his* family? Where are they?'

Simi explained that Imran was an orphan, the son of a Muslim Nawab, with Hindu foster parents.

Her mother struck her forehead with her right palm. 'What a cock'n'bull story! The trouble with you is you think you can get away with anything. You're a *Bhandari!* Intelligent and pretty. You could have anyone you want.' Devi fiddled with the sugar bowl, distractedly spooning sugar. 'Perhaps it's not too late even now. Perhaps we can forget it ever happened. It wasn't a *real* marriage, after all. Nobody need know.'

The thought of leaving Imran was like a knife in Simi's stomach. Devi saw her face and howled, 'Enough!'

Devi went upstairs feeling cheated. Hurt, humiliated, she was also furious at being cast aside by the person whom she loved most, to whom she had devoted twenty-five years. She was proud of Sam, had fought for her freedom – and look where that had led. Marriage was a difficult business. Sam and her doctor would face opprobrium, their love like a drop of dew pitting itself against the sun. A Muslim son-in-law? Devi did not relish the thought.

She broke the news to Gogu as soon as he returned from golf. His reaction was a confused cocktail of emotions.

'Good lord! Sam married? What tommy-rot! Can't be! Are you OK, Dee? Thought you looked a bit peaky.'

When he insisted that she drink some soda bicarbonate, Devi snapped, 'For God's sake, Gogu, it isn't my stomach. Sam says she's *married* that Dr Chaudhry.'

'Bless my soul! Some girls get hysterical, I've heard that, but I wouldn't have said Sam's the type. We don't even know him, dash it! Bit of an odour about him too. Wrangling with the municipality, dabbling in their affairs … dammit Dee, what's going on?'

Devi burst into tears. That flummoxed Gogu, because his wife rarely cried. He clumsily patted her head and proffered the edge of her sari to wipe her face. She ignored him.

'Who knows,' she wailed, 'perhaps she's on drugs too? It's like I don't know her any more. Why's she doing this to us?'

Gogu muttered something soothing to no effect, so he said drolly, 'At least Chaudhry's a good doctor, I hear. Doesn't appear to be killing off the old biddies! So there's that, I suppose.'

'Oh for God's sake, Gogu!' But Devi wiped her face with the end of her sari and stopped crying.

'Don't bite my head off, Dee.'

She grasped his hand, pleading, 'What are we going to do, Gogu? Where did I go wrong?'

'Dammit, you've done nothing wrong, Dee. Just talk to Sam.'

'*Tsk! You* try talking to her.'

She scolded him, but in that moment Devi loved her husband more than ever. There was no guile in him, nor a duplicitous bone in his body. Not once did he raise the question of Imran's religion.

'And you don't mind that he's ... Muslim?' she asked.

'Bless my soul, so he is, so he is.' He reflected upon the matter awhile. Gogu had long ago stopped saying his prayers or believing in 'someone up there.' A gruff, kindly man, he believed that if you meant no harm, no harm would come to you.

'That's damned awkward, Dee. Mummy will turn the house upside down! She'll point the finger at us, don't you know. Especially you.'

'You'll have to tell her.'

'*Me?* Dammit, that's not cricket. You'd better do it!'

She wagged a finger at him. 'In any case, Sam will never get *my* consent.'

'Your *consent?* But I thought you said she's already married? Dash it, what *do* you mean?'

'You think I'll let her throw away her life just like that? You only have to read the papers to know what madness this is.'

The papers today were full of a story of a five-year old girl in the old city who had witnessed her young father being beaten in another Hindu-Muslim gang fight. The man was critically ill in hospital.

Later, when they were alone, Gogu spoke with his daughter in his own inimitable way.

'Your mother told me, Sam. Great snakes! I could hardly believe that you've found a chappie to marry. But she won't hear of it, your mother I mean. As for your Dadi, by George, the fur will fly when she finds out. What *are* we going to do, Sam?'

We? Simi threw her arms around him. '*Papa!*' she cried.

Gogu stroked her head, saying gruffly, 'Bless you, my child. Be happy, that's all I ask. I'd have liked to see you marry differently but … '

In the evening, once Imran was back, Simi slipped away to his surgery. It felt as though he had been away for years, not days. The reunion was ecstatic. Relief flooded through her as she breathed in his scent and hugged him around his waist, her face resting on his chest. Despite his busy trip, he'd found time to buy gifts in Bombay – a box of mangoes, an expensive silk sari in emerald green, and a large conch shell. She was proud of his taste.

He also informed her that Marriam had come to the surgery in his absence, looking for her.

'Marriam's *back?*' Simi yelped. 'I didn't know she was back. She hasn't come to us.'

'Terrified of your granny, I expect!'

Sensing something was wrong, he asked, 'Are you OK? Did you talk to your family? What did your parents say?'

How could she tell him the truth? That her mother abhorred the idea?

'What's wrong?'

She couldn't meet his eyes. 'It'll take time. They need time to get used to the idea.' She heard his sharp intake of breath.

'Meaning?'

'Mama's very upset. She's angry that I went behind her back. She doesn't want to lose me. We've always been close.' She loyally attempted to cover for her mother, but Simi, like her father, had always found it hard to dissemble. Imran was worldly enough to read between the lines.

'Have you told me everything?' He turned away and she heard a match flare as he lit a cigarette. 'And granny? What did your grandmother say?'

Simi stared miserably out of the window.

'The old lady doesn't even know, does she?' Imran grasped her by the shoulder and turned her round to face him. 'Darling, be honest. What exactly happened?'

She continued to look at him mutely, afraid to speak.

'I'm Muslim, is that it? That's your mother's objection, isn't it? *Khuda!* I thought your folks were different.'

'They *are* but ... '

'But what? Am I a Martian? What *do* they want? Any other man under the sun would do for you, as long as it's not me?'

'They've not said a word against your religion, Imi!'

'What hypocrites!' He thought again of the Hindu families in Atmapuri who never invited him home. 'What happens now?' he asked.

She gestured helplessly. 'Let's wait a bit.'

He hurled a matchbox furiously against the wall. 'Grow up, Simi. Sooner or later you've got to choose. Life is about the choices we make.'

She repeated, 'Let's wait a bit.' They shared a wretched silence.

'OK. I'll wait for you,' he said finally. 'But you must come to me with your head held high. I don't want you to be ashamed of me. You've said yourself that your mother never had the courage – but do you, Simi? Can you stand up for yourself?'

She nodded.

'And I won't hold you to it. If you change your mind, if you can't level with your family, then we'll forget it ever happened. I'll disappear, I promise.'

'That's what my mother said,' she admitted.

'Does she hate me so much?'

Simi wished she hadn't said it. She wanted to wipe away the hurt from his eyes. 'They'll come round, Imi. Just give them time.' He had his back to her. 'I have to leave,' she said. Her heart was wailing silently as she spoke.

He didn't reply and made no effort to detain her, though she could see the sinews tensing in his arms. She walked out dejectedly, clutching her new sari but forgetting the box of mangoes.

CHAPTER 25

Ahmed returned to Atmapuri a day after Simi, glad to escape the dusty village. He'd enjoyed living there as a lad, with his grandfather, who these days hobbled about with a bamboo staff. Now Ahmed hated the village's post-twilight gloom, accustomed as he was to Atmapuri's electrified half-nights. Nor was he keen on the buffalo-smell of animals bedding indoors for the night. The village of Kadamgaon had electricity for roughly two hours a day, when the villagers would rush to play their music cassettes and watch the communal TV. His miserly grandfather only permitted 'the current' to be used sparingly, as though lightbulbs leaked liquid gold. Ahmed hoped his mother was OK there. She hadn't looked happy when he left. He felt a pang of guilt, but didn't want her back in Atmapuri, since he had decided to quit the city for good. It only remained for him to collect the debts owed to him and at last he'd be able to open his garage. But Ahmed's debtors proved elusive. No matter, he'd wait a day or two.

During that time, he received another summons from Kalludada, who was pleased with his successful disruption of the procession on Janamashtami. There had, however, been consequences. A couple of days afterwards, the bearded priest of a mosque not far from the Krishna Temple had stumbled upon the body of a pig. The swine's throat had been slit and its blood had trickled down the mosque steps.

A pig! That despised animal. Word had spread quickly and a crowd materialised out of nowhere. Muslim, of course: regular worshippers, irregular worshippers, idlers, the righteous and the furious. They said it was a Hindu plot. What else? *'An eye for an eye,'* the crowd had brayed. *'Revenge!'*

There had been trouble on the streets at the time, mainly young men stoning buses and burning empty vehicles. But the police cracked down and by evening things were quiet. Kalludada had been happy to bide his time though. Now he sought revenge.

'We know who did it, *salle*. We'll show them!' Kalludada roared.

Ahmed no longer felt part of all this, but Kalludada told him what needed to be done: a dead cow must be deposited at a temple in retaliation. Ahmed just wanted them to leave him alone. He was meant for bigger things, like Bentleys and Ferraris, but he could not refuse Kalludada.

Having been told to await further orders, Ahmed returned home dejected. He was even more worried when he found his front door open. Had he not locked it? He crept up warily and was only slightly relieved when he found his mother inside.

'Ammi!' he cried.

Marriam's face lit up. *'Ahmudi*, my son. How are you, *beta*? Did you get my letter?'

He shook his head.

'Tchch! I sent a postcard. Nobody has responsibility these days, not even the postman!'

Marriam was still learning the alphabet, so she had paid the village scribe to write to Ahmed informing him of her return.

'I'm sorry, *beta*, but don't make me go back to the village.'

'You came alone all the way? But you like the village!'

Marriam shook her head. 'Can't go back, Ahmudi, can't go back. What's finished is finished. It's long ago that I lived there, as a girl, a bride'

'But, Ammi ... there's trouble here.' He told her that a court notice had arrived threatening them with eviction.

Marriam already knew from her friends. 'It's Allah's will. What'll happen will happen. But the village, Ahmudi – why, I can't even digest buffalo milk. I've got used to city milk that's more water than milk. Pure buffalo milk ... ' she shuddered. 'I was belching all night.'

Ahmed was dismayed and confused. He wanted to yell at her for returning so soon. Her sudden appearance put paid to any thought he had of leaving the city. Agra could wait. He would persuade her to move with him, but that would take time.

Marriam continued, 'And Ahmudi, they don't eat like we eat. No vegetables! In our city we get everything! Vegetables all year!'

Ahmed left and went to the *akhada*, expending his rage on unsuspecting wrestling partners. Once finished, he wiped himself dry and was just leaving when a car drew up alongside him.

Sanjay Sethi leaned out of the driver's seat, 'I've been looking for you. Hop in, will you? I want to talk.'

Ahmed hesitated. He didn't trust Hindus but Sanjay was Dr Chaudhry's friend, so this was different. Ahmed couldn't believe his ears when Sanjay also suggested causing a disturbance at a temple. He, a Hindu, wanted – a *diversion*, he called it. Ahmed had no compunction about slaughtering cows or eating beef – but Sanjay*babu* was Hindu! He almost laughed aloud when he was offered money; Kalludada had expected him to do the same thing for nothing. The coincidence struck him as a good omen.

Marriam thanked Allah as she lay in her own bed that night. She relished the charivari of the city, the cacophony of horns and din of traffic. She had left the village on the pretext that Ahmed was alone and couldn't cook for himself. The family let her go without protest. She had known they would. They were too poor for sentiment and she was merely Behram's widow. Nor could she return to her father's old home: her younger brother, with whom she was still not speaking, had inherited the smallholding.

Besides, the village held too many memories of life with her in-laws. Their mud house had no toilet, so every day she had risen at four in the morning to accompany her mother- and sisters-in-law to the fields for their ablutions. Then they would cook breakfast in the dark over smoky wood fires, with the men leaving at dawn to work the land. That life was no longer for her.

Marriam had felt reassured after meeting Simi in Agra and seeing the bracelet. Everything would turn out right. She felt it in her bones. But she would never return to the White House to face that old witch.

Simi felt guilty about neglecting her friends in Nawabganj and went there the day after she learned Marriam was back. She found her at home, sitting on the threshold, cooling herself with a straw fan. Marriam's face lit up when she saw Simi and she clasped her to her thin bosom. Simi reassured Marriam that the family had been told about the bracelet and the path was clear for her return. But Marriam demurred.

'No Simi*baby*, not after big *memsahib* kick me out as if I was a stray dog. Such insults! Bad Luck Face she called me, and low caste. Allah! My Ahmudi will never let me go back.'

Try as she might, Simi could not convince Marriam otherwise. So instead she told her about Imran, though she used the word 'betrothed' rather than 'married', feeling unsure about their exact status. Marriam was beside herself with joy at the news and called down Allah's blessings on the couple. She loved the doctor, who had done so much for them, and called him 'a prince among men' with no trace of irony.

'But you mustn't tell anyone, Marriam. Not until I say so.' Simi explained the situation with her grandmother. Marriam understood, having endured the old lady for twenty years.

Ahmed's sudden arrival interrupted them. He stood with his powerful arms akimbo, demanding to know what Simi was doing there. Marriam objected to his rudeness, covering Simi defensively with her body.

'Haven't these people done enough harm?' he yelled. He had never before been so outright hostile.

'Simi*baby* wasn't even there. She was in Agra,' Marriam protested, concealing the fact that Simi had caused the entire incident.

Not wishing to hear any more, Simi ran next door to Marriam's neighbour, Zubeida, who was astonished to see Simi. Marriam followed moments later. Within minutes, the other slum women came hurrying across.

Zubeida said, 'Thank Allah you've come! We have big big trouble. What to do, we are poor, our kismet's poor too.'

They told Simi about the court notice ordering them to vacate their homes. With all that had gone on lately, Simi had almost forgotten that the women's homes were under threat. She knew that Nawabganj was an unauthorised colony, but it had existed for over thirty years. They had electricity meters and ration cards now; they had built *pukka* homes of brick in place of earlier tin shacks. Originally the land had been worth a pittance, but three decades later it was like gold. The fact that people lived there was not going to dissuade greedy developers.

Simi was deeply distressed by the news. It was people like her grandmother who had petitioned against the slum. The women handed her the court papers, which cited disease – cholera, typhoid, gastroenteritis, meningitis – as the reason to have them moved. Such diseases, they said, spread because of a lack of toilets and taps, along with a surfeit of overflowing garbage heaps.

'They want to us to go far away to Govindpuri.' Marriam said.

It seemed particularly unfair to Simi. Just as these women were beginning to understand hygiene, changing their lives, they would be sent where she could not reach them. Besides, like Marriam, they all worked nearby and wouldn't be able to earn a living out in Govindpuri.

The court date was fast approaching, set for the thirteenth of September, which didn't leave much time, but they arranged to meet again soon to organise something. Simi left them with heavy heart, wondering if someone with money was pushing the case through quickly. Once home, she rang Imran and told him the situation. He put her in touch with a lawyer, Ravi Chopra, who agreed to help.

CHAPTER 26

Simi was out on the terrace in the silent dawn the following morning. Her internal clock had gone haywire and a fretful night had left her tired. She tried to recall the euphoria of Agra, but it was like trying to remember the touch of ice in torrid heat. She was deeply worried and the day only brought more bad news.

A gang of smugglers had been ambushed at the river by police, caught trying to land contraband in the night. Simi overheard the news on TV when she went inside for breakfast. *I wish someone would smuggle some sense into* Dadi, she thought. Two of the smugglers had been shot dead, but the big fish got away. Since the two dead men could no longer talk, the nature of the contraband and the name of their boss remained a matter of speculation. There were plenty of rumours though. Most people, including Simi, assumed that the Don was responsible – he had reputedly begun his career as a smuggler. That suspicion seemed to be confirmed when a second rumour swirled round the city that the Don had been wounded by a bullet the same night.

'A bullet's too good for him,' Simi muttered to herself.

The real shock came when the man on TV claimed that Dr Chaudhry was being questioned by the police. He was said to have tended the Don's wounds in the night.

Simi's parents stopped eating to watch.

'Well!' her mother said coldly with a scathing glance at Simi.

On the TV, the picture cut to a journalist waiting outside Imran's home. The camera captured the doctor emerging freshly showered, water droplets clinging to his hair. He brushed past the reporter and drove off in his car. The journalist decided to chat to Imran's Nepalese cook instead. Simi was angry to see Bahadur state that his master had gone out at night with his medical bag. He added that this wasn't unusual, that the doctor's patients sometimes called him at unearthly hours. But the damage was done.

'The Don! What next, Sam?' her mother cried.

'He's a *doctor*, Mama! A patient must have called him out – people don't wait for the morning to fall ill.'

'Enough! Who're you fooling? Me? Or yourself?' Devi snapped.

Her father added, 'Jolly rum do, eh, mixing with hoodlums? Still, Sam you seem convinced there's nothing in it. Suppose she's right, Dee? Perhaps we give the chappie a chance to explain?'

'Explain, my toe! In any case, it makes no difference to me if he's guilty or not!' Devi said angrily. 'He's not acceptable. A foul reputation *and* a Muslim to boot.'

At last, it had been said.

'*Mama!* You sound just like Dadi!' Thankfully the old lady was taking breakfast in her room again, so was not present to make matters worse.

'Don't change the subject!' scolded her mother.

'What does his religion have to do with anything?'

'Grow up, Sam. Don't bury your head in the mud! You need to start living a decent life.'

'I say, that's a bit thick, Dee!' Gogu protested.

'You don't understand! What sort of a life will she have if we encourage this madness? Over my dead body!' Devi muttered. 'Hoodlums and smugglers. What company he keeps!'

Simi tried frantically to call Imran all morning but got no response. Desperate, she went to his clinic in the afternoon when she knew he would be there. His surgery was packed with patients, but she gave the receptionist a note and asked her to give it to him. A few moments later, Simi was ushered into his consulting room.

'Why didn't you phone me?' she demanded when they were alone. 'I've been worried about you.'

He looked very tired. '*Khuda!* This damned city! They can't catch the smugglers, so they catch me instead!'

'Hush! It'll be alright, Imi, you'll see. It's all a big mistake.'

He exhaled deeply and relaxed a little, reaching out to squeeze her hand. 'What must your family think of me now? I'm so sorry, *jaan*. This city is a snake pit of rumours.'

'You'll have to fire Bahadur, Imi. How dare he talk to the press?'

Imran ran his fingers distractedly through his hair. 'Bahadur's the last thing on my mind. I've so much work and there's that court date coming up for Nawabganj. The days are too short.'

She consoled him with soothing words. 'I just wanted to make sure you were OK,' she said. 'By the way, where *were* you last night?'

His expression changed.

'Mama's furious. I told her you couldn't possibly have been with that criminal but I'd like to reassure them.'

He shook his head. 'Can't tell you. Privacy of my patients.'

'Surely you can tell *me*?'

'No. Confidentiality.'

'Are you hiding something?'

'You just have to trust me.'

'*Christ!* I was worried to death about you, but you're keeping secrets from me. It's *you* who don't trust *me*.' She glared at him. 'You *were* with *him*, weren't you? Please don't lie.'

'Sim, please. Don't make an issue of it.'

'You'd better see to your patients,' Simi said, before stalking out with her head held high.

Simi didn't speak to Imran for a week after that, angry that he didn't trust her. In the interim, the parade for the Prophet's birth anniversary, on the thirtieth of August, passed without incident, perhaps because the authorities had placed extra policemen on the streets. The next day, things were normal too. Simi took some comfort from this.

Two days later, Pandit Mahesh was opening the doors of the Ganesh temple at dawn and shivered as his bare feet touched the cold stone floor.

'Ram, Ram, Ram … ' the rotund monk chanted, pulling his cotton shawl tight around his bare chest. He ran through a list of the day's jobs in his mind as he opened up the temple. He had already arranged the oil lamp, flowers and sacred *kusha* grass in preparation for the first *aarti* prayer at six.

He paused on the verandah to cast an appreciative look at the sky. The goddess Ushas was unveiling the dawn and the jackal of the night fled at her approach. Pandit Mahesh checked his watch and the big bronze bell hanging overhead, which would soon speak in its dull metallic voice. September had brought with it cooler mornings, so the hair on his exposed legs stood on end. He pulled his white dhoti closer. He would be glad to be inside again.

'Ram, Ram, Ram, Ram … ' he muttered, inspecting the steps at the edge of the verandah to see whether his apprentice had washed them. Young Mohan was a thief of time, stealing away to play cricket instead of attending to his temple duties.

'Ram, Ram, Ram … ' He peered over the edge and a ghastly sight met his eyes. 'Hai Ram!' he exclaimed, jumping back to the safety of the verandah.

Next to his own mother, a cow was the most sacred thing to a Brahmin. But now a dead cow lay at Pandit Mahesh's door. Loose folds of its dirty white skin cascaded down the steps like the careless sari of a wanton woman. Its slack udders flopped across the road. The carcass was speckled with wilted marigold petals, rotting mango peel and decaying black bits that had started life as vegetables.

'Hai Ram!' Mahesh Pandit touched his earlobes with his fingertips to purify them. He forgot to ring the bell.

Two early worshippers who were already at the gate rushed in. Others soon followed. Everyone talked all at once. Mother Cow murdered! The One who helped to begin and end the cycle of life: a baby's first feed included ghee and a good Hindu could not be cremated without it.

Pandit Mahesh was close to tears. For such a heinous crime to happen on the steps of his temple! Was this bad karma on his part? Perhaps from a previous life? He'd always encouraged his clients to do *go-daan* and give gifts of cows. Calves, generally. *Go-daan* could even wipe out sin that persisted over many lifetimes. And now this!

He moaned, 'Forgive me, Bhagwan, for sleeping when this terrible crime was committed.' *It must be the clash of Mars and the Sun in my horoscope*, he thought. His astrology chart had foretold a difficult six months.

People argued about what to do. At the city's edge were tanneries and they were always on the lookout for leather – perhaps they did this? Pandit Mahesh didn't know. No matter. The crowd already *knew* who it must have been. The Muslims. Who else?

Gogu heard about the incident at the Ganesh Temple on the radio while he was shaving. The heads of all twenty-one big temples in town had spoken out condemning it. But Hindu youths were trickling out onto the streets. Both sides, Hindus and Muslims, would have secret weapons stashed away: pistols, knives, daggers and various household items that could be put to lethal use.

Upon learning what had happened, Simi's spirits plummeted beyond despair. The world had suddenly gone mad and she was helpless. She quietly sipped her tea but couldn't eat a thing; instead, she watched her father pile thick-cut marmalade onto his third round of burnt toast.

'How can you eat, Papa? At a time like this?' she grumbled. He gave her a surprised look but continued munching.

They were still at breakfast when news came that gangs had clashed violently on the streets. A cycle-rickshaw-wallah named Mohammad had been the first casualty. The TV carried images of his smouldering rickshaw, overturned and crab-like. He was bruised but had no broken bones, so at least he would recover.

Simi's grandmother, who was present this time, glowered at the TV, saying, 'Next time, they'll think before fouling our temples!' She had little sympathy for the beaten man.

'Dadi! He's poor. And now he's lost his rickshaw, he'll starve!' Simi remonstrated.

'Hunh! *His* people are dirty, used to living in filth. He'll manage.'

Devi said softly, 'I wonder what Mahatma Gandhi would say today?'

'Old Gandhi?' Old Mrs Bhandari sneered. 'Gandhi sided with the Ms or he wouldn't have given them Pakistan.'

'It wasn't his to *give!* Simi cried. 'He tried hard to stop it but nobody listened.'

Soon they heard that a Muslim gang had retaliated by attacking a Hindu business. The shop was looted before being set alight, but no one was hurt. The TV cameras could not get anywhere near the scene, relying instead on reports from people on the street.

'I hate religion!' Simi howled.

Surprisingly, her father contradicted her. 'I say, Sam, people still seem to care about such bally things, religion and so forth.'

Old Mrs Bhandari gave him an angry look.

'Not that I'm an atheist, Ma,' he corrected himself. 'But, by George, when I see those loons out there – and for what? A dead cow and a porky that copped it ... '

Simi dreaded that a full-blown riot would turn the streets into killing fields, causing a rift between communities that would take months or years to heal. But the police came out in numbers and laid into the crowd with bamboo staffs, scattering them. By midday, life in the city had begun to return to normal.

Feeling dejected after the troubled morning, Simi decided to leave the house. 'They're waiting for me at Nawabganj,' she muttered to her parents as she got ready.

'Waiting for you, Sam?' Devi replied. 'You've no idea. They'll be worrying about their sons and husbands, not you. They don't expect you to turn up. You're not going anywhere.'

Simi was now unsure about everything – even Imran. Her life had turned turtle. She went up to her room and read for a bit, but dozed off and dreamt of a dark desert. She could feel the sand between her toes. It was night, a theatre of shadows. She saw herself standing on a railway track facing an old-fashioned steam engine. Less than a foot behind her, an abyss dropped away into nothingness. The train chugged forward and would have pushed her into the abyss, but she quickly side-stepped to safety. Then two men accosted her, shapeless forms in the dark. One grabbed her elbow. Quickly, she freed herself and ran. The men simply melted away. She awoke with a crick in her neck, unsure of what the dream meant.

CHAPTER 27

Despite the chaos created by the trouble at the temple, Imran kept to his schedule. He had been working in the heat and dust all morning in Nawabganj, assisted by his colleague Dr Gupta, but the queue of patients was as long as ever. It was the worst time of year from a health perspective. The monsoon brought dysentery, cholera, malaria and dengue fever in its wake, all of which spread rapidly through the over-crowded slum. But Simi's hard work had resulted in some noticeable improvements. The slum women were more confident, more articulate, and there were fewer fevers to report this year. He had missed Simi since their argument but she simply refused to speak to him. The thought of her made him feel slightly giddy; for a moment, while attending to one of the slum women, he imagined he was listening to Simi's heartbeat through his stethoscope. He pulled himself sharply back to the present.

At about four in the afternoon, Imran began packing up. Stretching and yawning, he thought longingly of the cold beer in his fridge at home.

'Thanks Ahmed,' he said with a friendly back-slap for the young man who had helped out all day.

Ahmed offered him tea at his home nearby, but Imran answered apologetically, 'Next time, *yaar*? I'm dirty and sweaty, so right now I need a shower.'

After Ahmed had helped to load Imran's things into his four-wheel drive, he casually mentioned that he had recently assisted Mr Sanjay Sethi. Imran turned in surprise.

'*Sanjay?* What sort of help?' Both spoke in Urdu.

Ahmed replied artlessly, muttering something about politics and the temple.

'What *are you saying?*' Imran demanded.

'It was … nothing really,' Ahmed faltered. 'Just to make people sit up. It was only a cow.' Vagrant cows were plentiful in Atmapuri. Ahmed had found one slumbering in the street at night.

Imran was appalled. He made Ahmed get into the Jeep and they spoke while he drove so they would not be overheard.

'Tell me again,' he commanded.

'It was only a Hindu cow.'

'You mean the one at the temple?'

Ahmed was quiet. Imran pulled over to the side of the road.

'Have you gone mad, Ahmed? Is this true?'

'Sanjay*babu*'s your friend, isn't he? I've seen you together. I wouldn't even talk to a Hindu otherwise!'

'What are you s*aying?* That you did this to please *me?*' Imran thought of the violence the act had provoked. 'People almost *died!* There could have been a terrible riot! *Khuda!* I could whip you for this!'

Ahmed looked chastised. 'But no one died, sar. Sanjay*babu* assured me there would be no tempest. I swear.'

'I don't believe you.'

'I swear on my Ammi's life.'

Imran was reeling with shock. His old school friend had the power to control a riot?

Ahmed continued, 'Believe me, sar, I hate the tempest.'

'Then why do this?' Imran yelled. He remembered Simi's suspicion that Ahmed was the dacoit at the wedding. 'Are you a thief too? Did you steal Anjora's jewellery?'

Ahmed was so startled at the accusation that he leapt out of the Jeep. Standing back, he pleaded with outstretched hands, 'No! No sar! I did nothing like that, believe me!'

Imran leaned and shouted, 'You want a better world, don't you? More justice? You think by stealing and rioting you'll get it?'

Ahmed turned on his heels and fled.

Imran drove off furiously, his tyres screeching. He had tried so hard to encourage Ahmed and could scarcely believe what he had done. Suppose he *was* a thief too? And what about Sanjay? What was Sanjay's excuse?

Back at home, Imran shut himself in his bedroom and rang his friend.

'Sanjay? It's Imran. I've just seen Ahmed.'

'Ahmed?' replied Sanjay, innocently.

'*He* knows you well. Seems he's almost your employee!'

'What rubbish! I'm famous, everyone knows me. You don't expect me to remember every two-bit man I meet, do you?'

'*Sanjay!* Less than an hour ago Ahmed told me about the temple. Do you deny it?'

'I don't know what you're talking about!'

'Remember who you're talking to. Your oldest friend.'

'Oh *Ahmed!* You mean the mechanic? What lies has he been spreading?'

'Is it a lie? Why should he make this up?'

Sanjay lost his cool, giving up any pretence of ignorance.

'Did the bugger also tell you he took 10,000 rupees from me? I offered five but he haggled. *Pucca* little businessman! And what about you and the Don? Look in the mirror, Imran, before you accuse me.'

Imran was so angry after hanging up that he went for a jog, pounding the hard earth furiously as Hudson panted alongside him. *Ahmed took money for a dangerous and shameful act – and my oldest friend paid him.* All his life he had loved Sanjay like a brother – but could he really trust him? New York had changed Imran. He had lived in a bigger world and sometimes wondered why he had returned to his parochial home town. His mind drifted to thoughts of meeting friends in Greenwich Village and going to Broadway, instead of worrying about dead cows and riots. They didn't have to contend with power cuts or polluted ground water in New York.

CHAPTER 28

Mornings were the worst. Pia retched and vomited and felt utterly wretched every time. And the tardy monsoon had turned the city into a humid *hammam* bath, leaving unsightly damp patches under her armpits that made her feel ugly. To top it off, Sanjay had started turning up the TV so he wouldn't have to discuss the baby. The time wasn't right, he said, to introduce her to his family. Pia knew his mother's reputation – a society dragon – and despaired that the time would never be right. After all, she was just a hill girl.

Suddenly, out of the blue, her own mother arrived to pile on further pressure. Mrs Pandey descended from Nainital primed with moral outrage, slivers of gossip having reached her ears. The sight of the shrunken provincial widow depressed Pia, but she secured a room for her at the Young Women Christian Association (YWCA) and parried her anxious questioning: '*What's this I hear? Who's the man? Will you marry him? See what you've done? Because of you I've had to bow my head in shame!*'

Mrs Pandey then issued an ultimatum: Pia must marry or else return to Nainital forthwith. She added, 'I can't have my daughter running round like a shameless loose woman. If your father was alive, he'd beat you.'

Pia felt a qualm at the thought of her father – but shameless? Loose? That infuriated her. She restrained herself and assured her mother that she would introduce her to her special friend.

'He's a very important man, Ma. And of course we're going to marry!'

'Has he asked you already?'

Pia hesitated before saying, 'Yes!'

The word stuck in her gullet. The only thing Sanjay had suggested lately was an abortion. She had screamed and thrown him out of the room when he did. And she would do it again.

Sanjay was very reluctant to meet Mrs Pandey – it was all becoming too real for him – but Pia was persuasive. She arranged to meet at a restaurant not far from the YWCA and went ahead to escort her mother. Sanjay came late. Sick with anxiety, Pia fretted throughout the awkward meal and her stabs at conversation failed in the face of Mrs Pandey's silent disapproval. Sanjay fidgeted with his cutlery, his laughter forced and too loud.

Two days later, Pia was caught in a sudden squall on her way back from seeing her mother. She arrived home wet and furious. Without changing out of her damp clothes, she lit a cigarette and sat down to think. She had given up smoking, but the situation merited an exception. Why did her mother have to spoil everything? Pia still believed in Sanjay. He could no more leave her than she could him. She longed to discuss things with Simi, but because of Imran they hadn't spoken in weeks. Once again, she found herself alone.

Pia savoured every drag of the cigarette, smoking four in a row before making herself stop. She decided she had been too complacent with Sanjay, too eager to please. What had she not done for him? From running his election campaign to dealing with the postman, she had taken care of everything. She had discarded her shapeless garments and dressed more feminine. She even cooked and kept their room tidy! And now she would give him a son. Despite not having any tests to check, Pia knew it would be a boy and had secretly chosen a name. A boy would mean a lot to Sanjay. And to his snooty family! Not that she cared two figs for them.

Sanjay, she felt, took her for granted. Some of her mother's warnings about men had begun to haunt her. *Men are different. Men want only one thing. Men aren't sentimental like women.* But Pia wanted to marry and have a home of her own. Her son deserved security. How could she make Sanjay see that? Pia decided to threaten to leave him. The thought made her nervous, but she knew what she must do.

Pia scrubbed herself in the shower and dressed in a flattering tie-dye sari. Its deep shade of turmeric made her dark skin glow like burnished copper. She was also pleased that her bare arms looked good in her sleeveless blouse. Finally, she fixed a tiny gold dot in the middle of her forehead – the third eye with which she would conquer Sanjay!

Sanjay whistled appreciatively when he entered. 'Going out?'

Pia smiled. '*We* are going out *together*. To eat and have some fun! Why did we stop having fun, Sunju? All I do now is stick envelopes and lick stamps!'

She had posted ninety-thousand of his leaflets for the election – endless licking, sticking and mailing, followed by even more licking, sticking and mailing.

'That's not *all* we did together,' he teased with a meaningful glance at her midriff.

She gave him a sultry look. Delighted, Sanjay bent to cuddle her, but she slapped his hand away, telling him to hurry and dress.

'Yes memsahib!' he grinned.

They dined at their favourite café. She fed him morsels of butter chicken and tandoori fish as they exchanged words of endearment. Afterwards, they drove to the river. He headed automatically for Scandal Point, where they had spent many enchanted hours of courtship. Pia inhaled the smell of damp earth deeply, the ground still wet from the rain earlier in the day. Pia savoured the brief moment of peace and soaked her feet in the river. Sanjay lay beside her on the bank, gazing at the cloudy, starless sky. He played idly with the loose end of her sari. As the clouds parted a star shone through to be reflected in the water, until a fish jumped up and swallowed it. *A perfect night*, thought Pia, *if only* …

Her train of thought was interrupted when Sanjay caught her hand and kissed her fingertips one by one, playfully biting her little finger.

'My Pi! What would I do without you? You're my best friend, sweetie.'

They kissed lying side by side, fanned by the gentle breeze. Soon they were sitting up again and discussing the Students' Union election. It was never far from their minds. Sanjay was favourite to win, but feared that many who had promised to vote for him could be lured away by Albert Pinto, who was flush with funds.

'*Tch!* Forget Pinto,' Pia reassured. 'You'll win, Sunju. Our campaign's been good. We've reached many people. So don't worry, sweetie.' She rummaged in her bag and took out a cigarette, lighting up while staring out over the river.

He smiled. 'You're right, of course *we'll win!* And it'll be *our* victory. Thank God *you're* not standing against me! There's a sharp political mind behind all that smoke!' He paused. 'But I thought you'd given up smoking?'

Pia had more important things on her mind. 'We should talk,' she said.

'Speak, empress!' Sanjay replied, flinging out his arms.

'The baby,' she said and felt him stiffen. 'When the bump starts showing everyone will know.' She stopped, flicking the rest of her cigarette into the river and looking towards him. 'Say something, Sunju! Why pretend the baby has nothing to do with you? Your son needs a father.'

'A *son*? How do you know?'

'*I know*. Call it mother's instinct, but I *know*. Your *son*, Sanjay Sethi. And I'll name him Abhimanyu.' A great hero from mythology, a great warrior. Like Maharana Pratap.

'Abhimanyu?' he repeated the name, as if testing it out.

'Manu for short. And he needs you. He needs your name.'

'My name?! Why couldn't you have had an abortion?' he asked again, despairingly.

She wanted to hit him but held herself back. 'Stop it! I'll have the baby alone if I have to. But I don't want to. Why can't we bring up our child together? We should marry. You've so much to teach him, sweetie.'

'*Marry*?' he sounded appalled.

'But things are different now!' Pia cried. Her hand shook as she pulled out another cigarette and lit it.

'You shouldn't smoke,' he chided.

'Shut up!' She blew smoke into his face.

'I can't marry just yet,' he said in a more conciliatory tone. 'I need to establish myself first. Politics is my life, *you* know that.'

'Where does that leave me?'

'I don't know.'

Her heart felt darker than the night. 'Is it your family? You're afraid of what they'll say?'

'Leave my family out of it, for God's sake!'

'Am I not good enough for them?' she screamed.

She thought again of Pia's Law, that if anything could go wrong, it would. But the strength of the goddess was in her tonight, as it had been when she won her man.

'Sunju, I'm leaving!' she announced.

He sat bolt upright. 'Leaving? You mean a holiday?'

'No, I'm leaving you. I love you. I've demonstrated that in every way, short of cutting my throat and laying my head at your feet! If you haven't the guts to tell your family then I'm sorry.' She explained that she intended to return to Nainital with her mother, take up a teaching job and raise her son alone.

Sanjay threw back his head and laughed. 'You can't do that.'

That was the last straw. 'You don't take me seriously at all, do you?!' she screamed.

'Pi-' he reached out for her but she pushed him away and hit him with her sandals.

'Don't you Pi me! Don't you ever touch me again! You selfish old … *pig! Your* mother, *your* name, *your* elections, that's all you ever think of. You you you!'

She ran away, her bare feet slithering on the wet ground. She was waiting in the car when he got there. Pia was gambling on her belief that he needed her as much as she needed him. He would come round in the end, she knew he would. And they would marry. She would win this game. She had to.

A chastened Sanjay watched her sleep that night with her back to him. He lay awake reflecting on what it would be like to not share his bed with her, to not be able to rely upon her in his work. He would miss her terribly if she went. *But marriage? Silly old cow.* He would talk to her in the morning.

CHAPTER 29

On the Monday of the court ruling on Nawabganj, Simi sat in the sweltering courtroom with her anxious friends, awaiting the judgment. She leaned forward to catch Imran's eye and felt concerned about how tired he looked. They still hadn't spoken since she had confronted him about the Don, other than briefly on the phone to discuss Nawabganj. Now Imran was sitting across the courtroom with the lawyer Ravi Chopra. She noted with satisfaction that Ahmed was several rows behind. She had not forgiven him for his rudeness at Marriam's home.

Simi had spent many long hours with the women and Ravi Chopra over the previous fortnight, preparing for this day. It had taken over their lives. Guided by the lawyer, they had kept vigils outside the court, staged a march and engaged in political activism, though this had left little time for the women to work at their normal jobs. Now the public knew who they were and what the issue was, but their purses were light and they could not eat newspaper columns.

They huddled closely together in court, Simi clutching Marriam's hand. On her other side, Jaddan Bai held her wrist so tightly that her fingers left bloodless marks.

After prolonged preliminaries, the Judge finally spoke. 'There has been an avalanche of newspaper reports on this issue but that cannot be allowed to influence the Law.'

That sounded ominous to Simi. She heard him utter other phrases: 'The Law is not a blunt instrument' and 'the Law will be applied fairly to all, no less to the rich than to the poor.' None of it sounded hopeful.

Ravi Chopra had called upon Imran to testify during the hearing. His first-hand knowledge of the improvements made in the slum in recent months was convincing. He spoke optimistically about their future if they were permitted to remain in their homes. Simi was proud of him. But Imran's old enemies in the municipal government did their best to discredit him.

In the end, the Judge ruled that the illegal settlement should be cleared, giving the residents ninety days to pack up and leave. Then the bulldozers would roll in.

Marriam burst into tears. Jaddan Bai closed her eyes. The courtroom erupted. Simi heard Imran shout, *'It won't do! It won't do!'*

They were ordered to clear the courtroom.

Incandescent with rage, Imran gave a long interview to the press outside. Ravi Chopra announced they would appeal against the judgment. Flashguns popped. The photograph of Imran made the front page of *The Puri Times* the next day, along with some of his more controversial statements.

Despite the hubbub, Simi managed to exchange a quick word with Imran outside the courthouse. Simi felt relieved to be close to him, but they were surrounded and it was impossible to find any privacy, so eventually Imran returned to his surgery.

Simi accompanied the women back to Jaddan Bai's home. Depressed, they barely talked, but collectively their sighs could have created a hurricane. The lawyer said they should protest with another street march and that everyone should turn out. But they were sick and tired of protesting.

'What's the use?' they asked, *'Who will listen to us? We're poor.'*

Simi felt equally glum but urged them not to give up. Finally, they agreed they would try one last time, arranging a march for the Thursday that same week.

When alone with Marriam, Simi impulsively suggested that the maid should move into the White House. She would sort it out with Dadi, Simi said, adding, 'only until I have my own home. Then you can live there.'

But Marriam shook her head. 'And my Ahmudi? What'll happen to him? He's a good boy, my son, but fate didn't smile on him. When you have a child, Simi*baby*, then you will understand the pain of a mother's heart.'

Simi had no intention of allowing Ahmed to live with her.

Later, Simi learnt that the Judge was a golfing acquaintance of her father. The man was nearing retirement and knew he would soon get a seat on the board of a construction company. *Outrageous!* She quietly decided she would join her friends on their protest march. Something had to be done to highlight the corruption and unfairness of it all. She rang Imran to tell him.

'*Khuda!*' he sighed. 'That's lousy news. Of course we must appeal in the Supreme Court. But I don't agree with Ravi Chopra about the street protest on Thursday. It's got us nowhere so far.'

'At least people will know how unfair all this is! And this time, I'm going with them!' declared Simi.

'*You can't go with them!*' Imran sounded panicked. 'Anything could happen! The city's like a powder keg. The police are edgy. Please, Sim, don't go.'

Simi hesitated for a heartbeat before saying, 'I have to do *something*. I can't just sit here.'

'What does your mother say?'

'They don't know yet.'

'Listen to me. Don't go. Please.'

She wanted to give in to him, but this was too important.

'Don't you see, Imi? Marriam's shattered. They're all shattered.' She had never been threatened with homelessness, but finally realised how devastating it would be.

After a slight pause he said, coldly, 'Have it your own way.' Then he hung up.

On Thursday, to prepare for the march, Simi got up before dawn. She threw open her bedroom windows and watched from the terrace as the sun slid up the horizon. The windless morning presaged another stifling day.

She dressed quickly, downed a glass of cold milk and shouted to her mother on her way out, 'I'll be out for the day. In Nawabganj.'

'What? Why?' Devi asked, but Simi didn't stop.

Everyone was busy getting ready when she arrived at Marriam's. To her surprise, Ahmed seemed to be in charge. It had been organised at short-notice, but Ravi Chopra had worked out a route for them past the courthouse and other government buildings.

Ahmed led the men. Simi could see him swell with pride. It was his finest hour. The women followed behind. They had a police escort, a thin line of khaki on either side, who were there more to control than protect them. Reporters and photographers joined in from time to time then loped off.

Jaddan Bai joined for about half an hour. Weakened by her tuberculosis, she couldn't manage more. Her grandson Munna, his hair slicked down with brahmi oil and eyes lined with kohl, insisted on accompanying her, saying he would help when she was tired.

'He wants to protect his grandmother!' Jaddan Bai told them proudly.

After Jaddan Bai left in an auto-rickshaw, Munna tagged along with Ahmed instead, jauntily singing a song about the many names of God: *Ishwar, Allah, Waheguru* … '

Simi found this poignant but ironic.

They entered Wellington Extension, an old British colony with bougainvillea flowers clinging to the grey walls like crimson butterflies. Next they passed Model Town, a new colony with manicured lawns and pedigree dogs, turning into the broad Akbar Mall and its hundred-year-old gulmohar trees. The hot sun slowed them down, but they reached the river just before lunchtime and stopped for a break.

Most of the protestors had brought chappatis and dry vegetable curry or pickle for lunch. Simi had forgotten to bring anything, but Marriam was so used to taking care of her that she had enough for two. After eating, Marriam curled up to rest, her dupatta covering her face against flies and mosquitoes. The others stretched out too. It was a bucolic scene, as if a bunch of carefree people were out on a picnic. Once again, Simi felt the irony strongly.

The mood had altered when they set off again. Men fretted about missing work; women worried about getting home before dark. It was a relief to reach the old city at the end of their long walk. The last few yards had taken half an hour, as by then it was almost four and the usual crush of cycles, rickshaws, cars and pedestrians choked the narrow streets. They finally stopped next to the old Church of St Mary and dispersed.

Simi took Marriam, Sangita, Munna and two other women into a small café nearby for tea before the bus journey home. Ahmed refused to join them but told his mother he would be back for her in an hour. The women's feet ached, their spirits were low and nothing Simi said could cheer them up. After they drank tea, Simi paid the bill. Ahmed returned when they were preparing to leave, but just then they heard a scuffle outside. Ahmed ran out with Munna at his heels. The women too rushed out, crowding the café door.

A fight raged in the street and the air was thick with the thud of heavy blows. They heard from the café owner that the altercation had started with two small boys playing marbles in the dust. They had quarrelled and used the marbles as missiles against each other. One boy was struck in the eye and his mother came running, cursing the other mother for raising a junglee. Then the fathers joined in and one punched the other. Friends came running to help and soon things escalated to a full-blown brawl.

Simi saw Ahmed leap down the verandah steps of the café and disappear. As Munna made to follow, she grabbed him by the collar and held him as he struggled to escape. It took all her strength to hold on to him.

The café owner urged them back inside. 'Quick! You must leave through the back.'

They followed his advice and found themselves in a dark service lane. The café proprietor had instantly locked the door behind them, so now they were on their own. Simi and her miserable companions flattened themselves against a brick wall, fearful of the destruction they could hear from the main road. But the lane was deserted. Simi caught her breath when something moved in the dark, but it was only a lank mongrel.

'Marriam! Where *are* we are?' hissed Simi. The old maid didn't answer, lost in prayer that Allah should protect her son. Simi felt totally lost. '*Marriam!*' she cried more loudly, her voice sharp with fear. 'You've got to help, Marriam. Ahmed will be fine. But only *you* can get us out of here.'

There was still no response from her old ayah, but Munna piped up. 'I'll take you home. I know the way!' Of course! He lived here with Jaddan Bai.

They walked in single-file through the hot lanes, their baggy salwar-kameez flapping noisily in the rising breeze. Simi was terrified. Her tight-lipped companions understood the peril too – all except Munna, who relished the adventure.

The boy led them through a series of narrow alleys that looked identical to Simi. It was early evening and the light was fading quickly, making everything indistinct. The streets, normally teeming with life, were eerily deserted and front doors were shut tight. If they heard a muffled cough, it was hastily choked off. The residents of the old city could read death in the eyes of a man from a mile off and knew when to take shelter. No one here was about to offer them sanctuary.

On they walked, more warily than lambs in a lion's cage. The din receded as they penetrated deeper into the old city. Fear had turned Simi's knees to liquid and her clothes were drenched with sweat. She would never again complain *about anything*, she swore to herself, if she escaped this. Imran had been right to warn her. In the future, she would heed his advice and they would live in perfect concord. For a little while Simi escaped into a rosy fantasy of life with Imran.

The labyrinthine lanes seemingly went on forever. Simi wondered if they were lost. She grasped Marriam's hand but it was hard to tell who gave courage to whom. One of the women needed to pee, so they stopped and she relieved herself in an open gutter. The others did likewise while Simi kept a nervous watch. Would this nightmare never end?

Suddenly, Munna darted ahead and banged at a closed door. 'Ammi, Ammi! Open up!'

Marriam too called out to Jaddan Bai and Farid, Munna's father. The door opened a crack, letting out the dim light of a hurricane lantern. Munna's mother, a slight women called Samina, pulled the boy inside, crying and kissing his head. They all followed and the door was swiftly bolted behind them.

Jaddan Bai squatted on the floor next to the lantern. 'Allah! Sister Marriam, I thought you'd be safely home on this night of the Shaitan!'

Marriam burst into tears, crying softly into her dupatta. 'Don't ask! My Ahmudi's out there.'

The tears welled in Jaddan Bai's eyes as well. 'My Farid too. Allah go with the boys.'

Simi's legs finally gave way and she slumped, crumpling like a rag doll against the wall. The sudden cessation of tension was too much to bear. She felt safe here. It almost had the appearance of a cosy domestic scene: Jaddan Bai with her grandson, Marriam and the women, as if they were waiting for her to talk about hygiene or literacy. Simi quelled the urge to laugh hysterically and instead tried to breathe deeply, as Imran had taught her: in, out, in, out.

Slowly she regained her composure and began to take stock. Her parents would be worrying. She had expected to be back by tea-time. Her watch now showed it was almost seven. She needed to ring home, but Jaddan Bai didn't have a phone. Her companions squatted silently around the flickering lantern, casting grotesque shadows on the wall.

Simi said softly, 'I must go—', only to be silenced by a hammering on the door. Frightened eyes turned towards the noise and Jaddan Bai quickly threw a blanket over the lantern, plunging them into darkness. Her grandson whimpered and she clamped her hand over his mouth. Male voices shouted obscenities outside, but the door was strong and they moved on.

Inside, they stayed still for what seemed an eternity. Eventually, Jaddan Bai cautiously uncovered the lantern. Simi's heart was racing and she reminded herself to breathe.

Half an hour later, since it was still quiet outside, Simi risked speaking again. 'I need to go home,' she said, getting up to signal her determination. The other women looked at her anxiously.

'But it's not safe!' Jaddan Bai squeaked, trying to whisper. 'Why not wait? Farid will be home soon. *Inshallah.* He'll take you.'

Simi was tempted to stay, for she was afraid to go out again, but she couldn't. 'No. I must go,' she insisted.

Marriam stood up too. She wouldn't dream of letting Simi go alone. Nobody else volunteered. The others were too afraid.

So Simi and Marriam, hand-in-hand, slipped out of the door like shadows.

Outside it was dark. Marriam led and Simi followed, her heart thumping. They walked close to the walls. The stench of garbage rotting in open drains nauseated Simi, so she covered her nose with her free hand. At one point they were startled by a ghostly white shape lumbering out of the gloom. They stood stock still until the apparition got close enough for them to see – it was a cow. Simi laughed before hastily swallowing her amusement. The beast squeezed past them, its bulging flanks pressing them against the wall. A posse of stray dogs followed. Simi had always been afraid of street dogs and tried to sink further backwards, but her foot slipped into the drain. Slimy sewage wrapped itself around her ankle and it took an effort not to puke.

At last they emerged onto a road that Simi recognised, the ring road encircling Atmapuri. She had driven down it many times in the daytime, but now shocking scenes of devastation met her eyes. A white delivery van had been set alight and was still smouldering, which meant the mob had not been gone long. Now though, the road was empty, so they kept walking in the direction of home.

They must have covered two miles before Simi heard an engine and tried to dive into the bushes at the side of the road, dragging Marriam by the hand. But the vehicle approached so fast that they got caught in its headlights. Horrific images of murder and rape flashed through Simi's mind as her grandmother's tales of the partition suddenly became real. This couldn't be happening. *Please God, don't let this happen.*

The vehicle stopped with a screech of brakes. Simi unfroze and crashed on blindly through the undergrowth, pulling Marriam behind her. She heard someone running behind her. *Christ! Are we going to die?*

'Simi?' a voice called out. 'Is that you, Simi? Stop! It's me, Sanjay!'

She didn't stop. Someone could be faking it, luring her back only to … but they had called her name, so it had to be someone who knew her. Utterly confused, she stumbled onwards. But Marriam, sobbing, fell face down and wouldn't get up. Simi turned round.

'Simi, for God's sake, it's me *Sanjay Sethi*.'

It *was* him, not some rapist or ghost of the partition. Sanjay caught up with her.

'Oh my God, Simi! What *are* you doing here?'

Her teeth chattered like castanets. Holding her by the arm, he pulled her back to the road and bundled her into his Jeep, instructing one of his men to bring the maid. He then reversed, turned and drove off fast.

'My God!' he exclaimed, keeping his eyes on the road. 'I can't believe this. What the hell are you doing here?'

Simi stared dazedly at the charred debris and broken glass picked out by his headlamps. Rickshaws and tongas had been overturned; a cloth merchant's shop had been set alight and his produce burned steadily. God was absent, death was present. She wept.

'What ... what're *you* doing here?' she sobbed.

'Don't you know what's happening? I couldn't believe my eyes when I saw you run off the road with your servant.' He scolded her roundly before adding, 'What can Imran be thinking, letting you out like this?'

Imran ... Imran had tried to protect her but she hadn't listened. How did Sanjay know about her and Imran? Pia. Of course.

'Lucky for you that I came along. I'm taking you home,' he said.

'I went with Marriam on the street march,' Simi tried to explain, but her words were lost amidst sobs. Making an effort to control herself, she asked, 'How's Pia?'

'Fine, fine. She's fine,' Sanjay said, but she heard his unhappy sigh. She was tempted to ask more questions but could hardly press such an intimate issue in front of his companions. She was saddened by the thought of so many shattered friendships. Who would have believed in May that a bunch of friends doing a play together would have fallen out by September? Tomorrow, when the nightmare was over, she resolved to bring them together again.

Sanjay drove the rest of the way in silence. When they reached the White House, he parked his Jeep outside and helped Simi down, followed by Marriam. As the maid was guided inside by the man on the gate, Sanjay took Simi aside to pass on a message.

'Tell Imran to keep a low profile until it has all blown over,' he said. 'One more incident and the police will have him. They'll lock him up.'

'*Why?* He's done nothing wrong!' Simi protested.

'Trust me. I've been tipped off by someone high up. Imran's midnight attentions to the Don—'

'That's never been proved!'

'*Tch!* The *police* believe it. Listen, Simi, *I'm* not the one judging him. But if they catch him, they'll book him for inciting a riot.'

'*Imran?* What's he got to do with the riot?'

'They'll make up a case, believe me. He's ruffled too many feathers. What with his speeches, his contempt for our dear *babus* at the AMC … well, just tell him I warned him.'

'He's only tried to help at Nawabganj – people like Marriam. Is it a crime to help the poor?'

'Simi, you don't understand!' Sanjay said impatiently. 'They say Imran instigated the riot because of his speech outside the court.'

'*You* don't think that, do you?'

'Does it matter what *I* think? I have to go now.'

'You saved my life today, Sanjay,' Simi spoke fervently. 'How can I thank you?'

'What are friends for?' Sanjay replied gruffly before racing off.

CHAPTER 30

From the café verandah, Ahmed had caught a glimpse of his cousin Farid. Instinctively, he jumped into the fray and found himself swimming through bodies. Ahmed knew the terrifying speed with which violence could grow and wanted to get out as soon as possible. Seeing his cousin ahead, he made a desperate push forward, managing to grab Farid's shoulder from behind.

Farid turned and shouted in surprise, '*Bhai?!*'

'Let's get out,' Ahmed yelled.

They stood back to back, fending off blows. Ordinary men and women had suddenly become a mob.

In the chaos, Ahmed and Farid were separated. Ahmed saw his cousin and frantically tried to reach him, but was flung in the opposite direction. Then he lost sight of Farid.

Men had begun to loot the shops nearby. They smashed their way into a furniture shop, the door falling with a crash like a cannon shot. Within seconds the looters were passing desks overhead and smashing chairs against walls. Two men fought over a heavy table fan, abusing each other. Soon the fan lay forgotten in the dust and knives had been drawn.

Ahmed was scared. This madness would spread like wildfire. He knew he had to escape and looked round desperately for a way out. A wall of humanity blocked him from the nearest lane. The two men with knives were still circling each other as Ahmed turned and fought his way through the crowd. He hoped his mother was safe.

Then Ahmed heard the dreaded taunt, '*Ay, mian!* Where d'ye think you're off to?'

He froze, breaking out in cold sweat. *Mian*, pejorative for Muslim, sometimes spoken in jest, was here uttered with angry contempt. He turned and saw a gang of Hindu youths, his neighbours from Nawabganj. But they had not seen him! They had their backs to him and had cornered another acquaintance of his, a youth named Iqbal.

For a split-second, Ahmed considered going to the cornered man's aid. He knew the aggressors. On the Hindu festival of Holi they had all delighted in drenching each other with purple and red water. On the Muslim Eid they had all eaten the delicious *sewiyan kheer* that Marriam cooked. But things were different now.

Ahmed dropped out of sight behind a large water tank, listening for signs that the mob had moved on. He crouched there until the pins and needles in his legs became unbearable, but as soon as he straightened up the gang spotted him. They ran towards him, yelling.

He was hemmed in. There was no escape to the left or right. He looked up and saw an electric cable dangling limply from a pole. It was his only chance. He reached up and grabbed it, praying it was not live. Fear lent him wings and he hoisted himself up the cable, up and up. The cable swung wildly and he slammed into the electric pole, taking his breath away, but at least he was out of reach. Even his pursuers had stopped to admire his feat of athleticism.

With a quick look, Ahmed spotted a gap on the far side. He pushed hard with his feet against the pole, swung over the mob and dropped down so quickly that the metal cable scorched his palms. He fled down a dark lane, his steps ringing on the hard surface. But they were still on his tail.

They shouted, 'We'll get you! We know where you live!'

Soon though, their voices were receding. Ahmed did not slow down until he was sure he had lost them. Still, his instinct was to hide. He selected a large open drum painted black, overflowing with rotting garbage, and crouched behind it, staying there for almost half an hour before risking a peek. The place was deserted. He slowly straightened up, stretching with relief.

He needed to find his mother. Would she still be at the café? Perhaps she has gone with that Simi in a taxi? But where would they get a taxi in the confusion? Ahmed was at a loss.

Jaddan Bai lived fairly close so he decided to check there first. He crept along with his back to the wall, freezing at the slightest flicker in the shadows. Where the lanes criss-crossed he stopped, all senses straining.

He was getting close to Jaddan Bai's home when he saw an unnatural glow in the night sky. *Are the police out with searchlights?* He crept up warily. Fire! *Allah!* Only a mob could burn down houses, set fire to entire warehouses!

A burning house! He could see the street it was on now. Ahmed felt gutted. Was it Farid's home? Was his family inside? Jaddan Bai? And his mother … he trembled, his tongue cleaving to the roof of his mouth. His legs seemed rooted to the ground but he forced himself forward, step by accursed step, almost shouting with relief when he turned the corner into Farid's lane. It was the house at the far end that burned, while Farid's was in the middle. *Allah be praised!* Neighbours with buckets and pots full of water battled against the flames, which leapt and roared like golden lions.

Ahmed ran towards Farid's home instead. Its front door was open, flapping on its hinges in the wind, banging against the doorframe. Once again he was seized with dread and stopped a couple of yards away. Tonight of all nights, Jaddan Bai would have bolted the door. *Allah! Let them be safe!*

He forced himself to go in and saw Jaddan Bai first, lying spread-eagled on the floor with her head thrown back. Her throat had been slit. The gash in her neck seemed to smile at him, like a ghastly mouth with thick red lips.

And there were others, their bloody wounds like grisly flowers in bloom. He took it all in with one blurred glance before running out again, retching and puking. He clung to the wall until there was nothing left in his stomach. It was worse, far worse, than he could have imagined. He could not comprehend it. Was his mother in there? He hadn't seen her but … he didn't know. Ammi, Ammi, Ammi … his heart wept but no tears came. *Allah, let her be safe. Preserve her. I'll do anything, I'll change, I'll … just let her not be in there.*

Ahmed spat out the last of the rancid vomit and wiped his mouth with the back of his hand. He knew he had to go back inside but … he hugged himself tight. He couldn't think of anything but his mother. He shut his eyes against the scalding tears that now bubbled up. The world was spinning. He could see Jaddan Bai, and himself, almost as if he were looking down on the gruesome scene from a distance. As if the creaking door, the fire, the bodies, had nothing to do with him.

He heard people running towards him. The neighbours had been defeated by the conflagration and were running. Someone had rung the fire brigade but no one seriously expected them to turn up on a night like this. An elderly man paused near Ahmed and urged him to get away.

Ahmed grabbed him by the elbow, pleading. 'Come with me inside. My Ammi ... '

The man looked at the house and touched his earlobes. *'Hei Bhagwan!'*

'Come inside with me,' Ahmed repeated, refusing to let the man go.

Without a word, the man complied. But he recoiled at the terrible sight inside, shielding his eyes with his hand. Others followed them into the charnel house and were similarly struck dumb by what they saw.

Jaddan Bai had been lucky – her loose kurta and tight *churidar* pyjama were intact. The three younger women had been raped before being stabbed to death. Ahmed saw Farid's wife among them, along with Sushila and Rampyari, the two young Hindu women who lived near him and Marriam in Nawabganj. Farid's little son and daughter also lay with their throats slit, near their grandmother. Hindu, Muslim, young, old, their bodies had been left lying around like garbage.

Ahmed retched again but his stomach was empty and the spasm passed. His mother was not inside, so he frantically searched for her in the tiny courtyard out back. Ahmed heard a tiny sound, barely perceptible. The hair on the nape of his neck bristled. He listened intently. Nothing. He was about to turn away when he heard it again. In one corner of the courtyard there was a primitive shelter that served as the family toilet. Its door was slightly ajar. If one of the murderers was hiding there ... Ahmed clenched his fists.

Ahmed yanked open the door. Empty. He examined every inch but found nothing. He punch the door in frustration, smashing right through. He looked behind the door instead. Nothing. Then he examined the cluster of dilapidated flowerpots opposite. He found a boy curled up in a tight ball, hidden. Ahmed recognised him.

'Munna!' he cried, bending to scoop him up. Munna remained curled up, his knees drawn up under his chin.

'Munna! What happened?' Ahmed asked, holding the boy effortlessly in one arm while he tried to elicit some reaction. But Munna stared blankly past his shoulder, even when Ahmed shook him. There was a lump in Ahmed's throat as he carried the boy back through the main room and out the front door, hugging him to his chest and shielding the boy's eyes with his hand. The neighbours were covering the bodies. But Munna had clearly seen too much already.

Ahmed left. All he could think about was Marriam. The lane glowed as if bathed in sunlight. The fire was spreading fast, fanned by the wind. At the corner, Ahmed turned for one last look. The fire was closing in on Farid's home. The dead women would be cremated by the blaze soon enough, Hindu and Muslim alike.

Ahmed called out softly, '*Khuda hafiz! Khuda hafiz Khala Jaddan Bai, khuda hafiz Khala …* '

He tried to name them all but choked. He stood and watched until the door caught fire, then turned and walked away with wet cheeks, pursued by demons. He would hunt their killers down one by one and tear them apart with his bare hands! He stumbled on through a haze of rage and grief, quite forgetting that he held Munna in his arms. *Farid's little children! Allah! Khala Jaddan Bai, Khala Jaddan … why them?* Sordid deaths. Undeserved. God-fearing women who had done *namaz* five times a day and observed all the days of *Ramzan*. The sight of their mutilated bodies swam before his eyes. *And* Ammi? Had *they* carried her off? *No, Allah, no!*

Munna whimpered briefly like a distressed puppy. Ahmed kept on walking for over an hour, pausing several times, wary of ambush. Slowly, gingerly, he made his way back to Nawabganj. The door of his home was locked and his mother was nowhere to be seen. Ahmed's heart sank. When he put Munna down the boy burst into tears, huge sobs racking his body. Ahmed gave him a drink of water, then told him that he would be back soon and left him inside, locking the door. He had to attend to business that could not wait.

CHAPTER 31

Back at the White House, Simi's parents rushed out to meet her, alerted by the watchman. They demanded to know where she had been, but the terror had left Simi drained. All she could mutter was, 'I'm fine, I'm fine.'

Devi hugged Marriam impulsively, glad to see her for the first time since her ignominious departure, which made the maid cry. Devi's eyes were wet too.

They went into the sitting room and Dadi joined them. Marriam, who had to be dragged inside, shrank back at the sight of her old adversary.

The old lady saw her too. '*You?* What are you doing here?'

But before anyone else could speak, Gogu said, 'For Pete's sake, Mummy. Let's hear what Sam has to say.'

Old Mrs Bhandari sat down in her usual chair to glare at them, and was quiet for the moment.

Simi didn't have the energy left to fear her family. She told them the truth about the march and everything that happened afterwards.

Devi, who had worried herself sick, suddenly flared up. 'Who do you think you are, Sam? *Nehru?* Street processions, indeed! Have you any idea what's going on out there?'

Simi wanted to shout '*I know! I was there!*', but thought better of it.

Marriam chipped in, '*Toba, toba, Bibi.* Trapped we were. If Sanjay*babu* hadn't rescued us, I don't know what would have happened!' She compelled Simi to explain.

Simi attempted to make light of the dangers, omitting mention of her own panic, but her mother turned white. Gogu looked grave too.

'You're staying indoors, Sam, by George! Let the dust settle. Nawabganj be jiggered! You're far too precious to us, your mother and me, and your Dadi.'

'And don't give me that hogwash that you're all grown up!' Devi added. 'Until you're married and in your own home, you're *our* responsibility!'

'At last, you've said something sensible, Devi,' Old Mrs Bhandari said, drily.

Gogu ordered the night watchman to double lock the iron gates. Then the windows and doors were re-checked, so that not even a mouse could have crept in. That only left the question of Marriam, who agitated to go home, worried that Ahmed would return and find her missing.

'How will you get there?' Simi asked. 'I'd drive you myself but-' she glanced at her parents. Her mother quelled her with a stern look.

In any case, Simi had no wish to be out on the streets again. 'Go in the morning, Marriam. Can you phone Ahmed? Where might he be?'

Marriam shook her head. She didn't know where to find him or whom to call. That left the maid with little choice but to bed down for the night in Simi's room, curled up on a cotton mattress on the floor. Despite her anxiety, Marriam was soon fast asleep. Simi smiled as she looked at her snoring ayah, resolving to drive her to Nawabganj in the morning, whatever her parents might say.

Leaving the sleeping Marriam upstairs, Simi crept down to use the phone in the sitting room. The others had all gone to bed and she needed to talk to Imran alone. He was horrified to hear of her adventures and scolded her for being foolhardy, but they ended the conversation with endearments. She went upstairs again feeling happier than she had all day, but still found it difficult to sleep. Her mind worked incessantly, re-playing the day's stressful events. She finally fell asleep near dawn. But then the nightmares started again, with red monsters, a desert, and a blue glass triangle which Simi felt offered salvation but which remained permanently beyond reach.

Simi woke at seven with the sun already up. Marriam's bed was empty; presumably she was down in the kitchen making tea. Simi wandered out onto the small terrace outside her bedroom, yawning and stretching. She was about to turn back when she spotted a knot of people at the far end of the road. They might well have just been a religious band strolling about in the early morning, singing *bhajans*. But somehow Simi had the feeling they were not minstrels. Unconsciously tightening the belt of her dressing gown, she dashed back into the house.

From across the hallway she heard her mother's voice saying, '*Gogu!* Come quick!'

Simi joined them in their bedroom. They were all still in their crumpled night clothes.

'What's happened, Dee? Is it Mummy?' Gogu asked, alarmed.

'They're coming to kill us!' wailed his wife.

'Have you had a nightmare?'

'It's on the news, Gogu! All night there's been trouble. And about ten dead! Now they're on their way here, the night watchman—'

Simi interjected. 'I saw a crowd, Mama, but—'

'The night watchman told me they've attacked the Mishra house.'

They all ran out to the terrace. A thin plume of smoke was visible at the street corner.

'*See?* Purnima and Rajan must be inside, it's so early—'

Devi suddenly broke down. Simi was stunned. Gogu put his arm around his wife, patting her shoulder clumsily.

Devi controlled herself and went back inside, saying, 'Gogu, get your gun.'

'Hang on, dash it! It hasn't come to that, has it?'

In his youth Gogu had gone camping with his boisterous cousins in the Terai jungles, hunting for chital deer, antelope and even tigers. But he had long ago given it up, partly because Devi disapproved. His rifle now lay locked in its case inside a steel *almirah* in his study.

'Papa, *do* get your gun,' Simi urged,

'OK, I'll get it, but it's a jolly rum do. Those poor beggars, the Mishras. I'll change in a jiffy and ring the police chief.' He pulled some corduroy trousers over his pyjamas and put on a polo shirt. 'And the fire brigade, telling them to get over here pronto before the damn fire spreads.' With that Gogu went down to his study for his gun.

Devi changed into day clothes and hurried down to check on her mother-in-law.

Simi was shaking. Nothing like this had ever happened before; street disturbances happened a great distance away, not right in front of the White House. *Imran, I must tell Imran,* she thought. But she would have to wait until her father finished using the phone. She went to join her mother in Dadi's room.

Devi was saying, 'No, no, Mummy, this isn't the *partition*—'

'It's the partition all over again, I tell you! *Papaji* lost everything!'

'Oh! What's the use?' Devi cried, summoning her mother-in-law's maid with a gesture. She instructed Ganga to rub her mistress's hands but the old lady tetchily waved her away.

'Pull yourself together, Dadi!' Simi said.

'Come, let's go sit in the main room,' Devi coaxed.

Old Mrs Bhandari allowed herself be led out, leaning heavily on her stick. On the way through she spotted Marriam, who had been in the kitchen. 'What's *she* still doing here?'

Simi lost her temper. 'Dadi for *Chrissake*. Marriam spent the night here – and does it *matter*? We could all be dead in a minute but you're still worrying about Ms and whatnots … Hs *Hindus*, I suppose!'

Dadi sailed past her, muttering 'she's got ten tongues now!', then disappeared into the sitting room.

The night watchman told them that the Mishra family had escaped to their neighbours through a service lane at the back. The news was greeted with a collective sigh of relief.

Simi collected Marriam, along with the cook and his family. She made them sit in the lobby under the small chandelier in the stairwell, opposite a big oil portrait of the late judge. Then she raced back upstairs to join her father on the roof.

Gogu squinted down the road, pointing his rifle. The gang had smashed open the Mishra's doors and strewn their possession on the grass. At least Simi could assure her father that the family was safe. But now the mob was making its way to the White House.

'Did you get the police chief, Papa?' Simi asked without taking her eyes off the road.

'He's not in town. But they told me he's on his way back. High time too! Nero's away and Atmapuri burns!'

Simi's heart sank. She had been expecting the police chief to send his men round immediately with sirens blazing. *Oh Lord, what now?*

'You go in, Sam. I'll pick off those bastards better from here.'

Simi flew downstairs again and made for the phone in the lobby to ring Imran, not caring who overheard her. *Oh come on, come on,* she fretted, waiting for a response. He had still not answered after six rings. When he did pick up, she choked at the familiar sound of his voice.

'Hullo! Hullo! Who's there?' he said irritably.

'It's me, Imi,' she squeaked. Her mother heard every word, as did the cluster of frightened servants in the lobby.

'*Sim!* Is everything OK?'

'No! They're burning the Mishras' house down the road and now they're coming for us! What are we going to do?' she wailed.

'*Khuda!* Why didn't you ring me at once?'

'It happened so suddenly! Do something! Papa's on the roof with his gun but the police chief's not in town-'

'Karimbhai,' exclaimed Imran, interrupting her. 'I'll call him.'

'The Don?!'

'Stop it, Sim. I'm hanging up, but I'll call you right back.' He hung up.

'*The Don?* So it's true after all,' Devi said, looking sadly at her daughter.

Simi tried to come up with a retort but failed. Instead, she ran upstairs again to her father, stopping by her bedroom to jump into jeans and a cotton kurta.

A short distance away, Ahmed roamed the streets. He had been out all night but had failed to trace either his mother or the killers of his aunt. Desperate, he drifted, joining up with youths he knew from his life of petty crime, all of them spoiling for a fight. Morning found them close to the richer neighbourhoods and it occurred to Ahmed to steer his group towards the White

House, goaded on by the memory of his mother's humiliation at the hands of the insolent Old Mrs Bhandari. They deserved to pay for that. He would make them pay. The mob followed him eagerly, their appetite whetted by looting the Misra house.

'That's the one!' Ahmed pointed to the White House. 'They possess treasures you can only dream of! Gold, silver, cut glass – you could feed your family for a whole year! *Arre*, those bastards live off our sweat.'

He painted such an extravagant picture of Bhandari wealth that his companions bayed like mating walruses. They could barely wait to get there.

Gogu saw them coming down the road and fired a volley of warning shots, which scattered them in confusion. Sheltering behind trees, they peered out hesitantly until Ahmed pointed to the roof.

'He's up there!' he shouted 'Up there! There's only one of him! What are you waiting for?'

They abused Gogu, waving their fists. One of them had a country-made pistol and took a pot shot. Luckily for Gogu, the crude weapon was not accurate, but the shot caught him by surprise and nicked his left arm. Gogu staggered back, dropping his rifle.

'*Papa!*' Simi ran to support him, clutching his unhurt arm. She almost fainted at the sight of her father bleeding and unsteady on his feet. Hearing the shots, Devi too rushed up. Seeing Gogu's blood-stained clothes, she faltered.

'Oh God! Are you hurt, Gogu? Say something!'

Of course he's hurt! Simi wanted to answer but was convulsed with nausea. She buried her face in her father's good shoulder.

Gogu attempted a smile but grimaced with pain. 'Just a scratch, Dee. By Jove, I thought it was curtains for me for a moment there.'

'Are you sure? You're not just putting on a brace face?'

'Cross my heart! It's a flesh wound. Spot of luck, by George!'

Sick with relief, Simi wept into the back of her father's shirt.

Recovering her poise, Devi picked up Gogu's abandoned rifle. Simi locked the terrace door behind them and they descended, the two women supporting the injured Gogu.

Old Mrs Bhandari had also heard the shots and was making her way slowly upstairs when they appeared at the top. Gogu was a terrible sight in his blood-soaked shirt. Devi's clothes were bloody now too, stained from helping Gogu back inside. The old lady took one look at them, recoiled in horror and lost her footing, sliding down the stairs.

'Mummy!' Gogu and Devi cried in unison.

Old Mrs Bhandari lay in a heap at the bottom of the stairwell. Simi left her father's side and ran to her grandmother, kneeling to cradle her head in her lap. The old lady's face was screwed up in pain. Gogu followed slowly, supported by Devi, who helped him into a chair and put his rifle on the floor before going to help her mother-in-law. Old Mrs Bhandari was in such pain that they made no attempt to move her, afraid she might have broken a bone. All they could do was try to make her comfortable with cushions.

Old Mrs Bhandari was more worried about her son. 'Have they shot him? My poor Gogu!' Devi explained that it was only a flesh wound.

'I'm fit and fine, Mummy,' Gogu added. He picked up the phone from the table next to where he was seated, intending to try the fire brigade again, only to find the line had been cut. They fell silent. It seemed like a prelude to worse things and they could do nothing but wait. The cook's family huddled abjectly on the floor.

Then someone banged on the front door. Gogu snatched up the rifle with his uninjured right arm. Now that the crisis was upon them, Devi was calm. She put her arm around Simi and gestured to the servants to form a knot around the old lady. Except for their petrified expressions, they might have been a family posing for a photograph.

Gogu's arm was steady as he pointed the rifle, despite not having the use of his other hand. Devi looked at him proudly. Then she glanced at Simi and felt sad at their recent rift. Now that death was beating at her door, it all seemed much less important.

Simi simply wondered if she was destined to die before she had even lived. Life wouldn't cheat her like that, would it?

Angry blows rained down on the door. They expected it to crash open at any moment, but the sturdy old teak held fast. Then they heard glass breaking round the back. The kitchen! Gogu swung around and pointed his gun at the kitchen door. Devi shut her eyes. Simi wondered where Imran was. It would be too late if he didn't come soon.

After getting past the gate Ahmed ran through the garden of the White House to the front door, trampling on flowers and flattening herbaceous borders. Revenge was his at last! It filled him with savage delight to think that the Bhandaris would soon be at his mercy. But the front door was reinforced with iron bands, while iron grills and bars on the windows prevented him from entering that way. So he left his companions and searched for another point of ingress.

One of the other men shinned up a drainpipe to the terrace and climbed over the balustrade. Another youth ran round to the backyard, hurling a brick at the kitchen window and smashing the glass.

Then a Jeep drew up outside with a screech of brakes. Out jumped Kalludada. His usual coterie accompanied him.

'Oi!' Kalludada shouted from the road. Ahmed saw him. Kalludada was summoning him, gesticulating with a crooked finger. He approached.

Kalludada shouted, 'Bhai says you stop this NOW, you hear?' A sudden hush descended on the frenetic scene.

'B-Bhai's orders?' Ahmed stammered in confusion.

Kalludada nodded. 'Karimbhai says this house is not be touched. This family is not be touched. Not one hair of their head to be harmed. Those are his orders. Understand?'

Just in case Ahmed harboured any doubts, Kalludada drew a line in the air with the tip of his fingers and made a horrible clacking noise in his throat. His message delivered, he got back in his Jeep and drove off with his men.

Ahmed was stunned. *The Don* had sent a message? How? Why? To have come within a whisker of his purpose – then this! The blood rushed to his head. He would defy the Don and get his revenge! But the others had all begun to drift away.

'Stop!' Ahmed shouted. His companions stopped and looked at him.

'Are you deaf? You heard Kalludada,' one of them shouted.

'Don't go now. Think of the money!' Ahmed pleaded.

The man snarled, 'He questions Karimbhai's orders! *Arre*, don't you love your life?' They laughed.

Ahmed shouted abuse at them as they disappeared. Seething with rage, he turned away, cursing, and followed them. Why would Karimbhai want to protect *the Bhandaris?!*

Inside the house, the family wondered what had happened. The commotion had abated before abruptly ceasing altogether. Devi opened her eyes and realised she had been praying. When they heard nothing more, they began to stir and ease their cramped limbs.

Gogu lowered his gun. 'What's going on, dammit?' he asked.

'Do you think they've left?' Devi asked softly. She noticed she was whispering and cleared her throat. But the nightmare was not over. They heard the sound of a car pull up outside, followed by footsteps running down the driveway. Gogu cocked his gun and grimly took aim at the door.

CHAPTER 32

'Open the door! It's me – Imran Chaudhry,' a voice called out as someone knocked. Simi could scarcely believe her ears and flew to the door, yanking it open. He stood there like a miracle and she threw herself at him with such force that he staggered back.

Holding her close, he asked, 'Are you OK, *jaan*? Are you hurt?'

She shook her head. 'I'm sorry. I'm so sorry. They could have killed us. *Christ!*

The ordeal of the past twenty-four hours was taking its toll. The others watched the two of them in dazed silence.

'*Shh!* It's going to be alright, I promise.' He moved her aside gently, spotting her blood-stained father. 'Where are you hurt, sir?' he asked.

'I'm OK, bless you,' chirped Gogu. 'Just a flesh wound. But Mummy there needs attention.'

Imran gently probed Gogu's arm to check that it was just a superficial wound. He instructed Marriam to fetch hot water before turning to Devi, whose shirt was also blood-spattered. But she pointed to the old lady.

Imran, who knew how hostile Simi's mother could be, was courteous but professional. The other servants began to drift away from the lobby.

As Imran knelt by his old nemesis, Old Mrs Bhandari turned her face away. She had watched the scene between her granddaughter and Imran in disbelief. She gritted her teeth when Imran enquired about her injury and, despite the intense pain, beat him back with her hands.

'Don't touch me!' she snapped. 'Gogu, send this man away. As for Simi, lock her up in her room. Did you see what she just did? Disgraceful! And with an M!'

Imran stiffened and sat back on his heels. Simi cried, 'Dadi! Imran's an excellent doctor. Let him help you!'

'Good doctor-phood doctor! Don't try and cover up for your behaviour!'

Simi was furious. 'Stop it! Why won't you let him look at your leg?'

'Over my dead body!'

'It almost came to that!' Simi shouted. Her grandmother's intransigence was suddenly too much to bear. 'Leave her alone, Imran! There's nothing we can do.'

Gogu, woozy from blood loss, replied tetchily, 'Stop fussing will you, Ma? This ain't no tea party. We're jolly lucky those thugs didn't make mincemeat of us! Now be a good girl and let the doctor look at your leg.'

Old Mrs Bhandari bit her lip in pain. 'I want my family doctor!'

'I *am* your *family* doctor now,' Imran said impatiently.

'What nonsense!' the old lady barked. 'Our family doctor is Dr Roy.'

Imran whistled noiselessly in frustration, but his professional training militated against ignoring anyone who so patently needed his attention.

'I'm a doctor too and it's my duty to look after my grandmother,' he said gently.

Her eyes widened. 'What cheek! Don't you go calling me *grandmother!* Just because my hair's grey doesn't mean I've become the whole world's *grandmother!*'

He grinned. 'Of course not! But since you're Simi's grandmother, that makes you mine too. Now let me look at your leg. Can you move it at all?'

Old Mrs Bhandari turned to her son. 'Gogu! What is he on about? He looks mad to me!'

'Look! We're family now,' Imran said, exasperated. 'Now that Simi and I are married … '

He stopped, suddenly remembering she had not been told yet. The old lady was speechless. But only for an instant.

'Simi's *married?* To *him??*' She averted her eyes from Imran. 'Gogu, what's this man saying? Get him out of my house!' Gogu and Devi both looked away.

'*Khuda!*' A look of consternation came over Imran's face. He threw up his hands. 'This is too much for me. I'm sorry – perhaps I should leave.'

Simi covered her eyes in shame at her grandmother's rudeness. Gogu stood up but was unsteady on his feet, so Devi went to support him.

'Nonsense!' declared Gogu. 'You're not going anywhere Dr Chaudhry – Imran, I mean. I need a drink and I'd like you to join me. Welcome to this family. Course you might not wish to sign up after all this – but if you still do, by Jove, I'll be the first to shake you by the hand. Sam seems to like you and after what I've seen this morning – I'm sure I speak on behalf of my wife too when I say we're delighted to have you on board. Jolly happy.' Everyone stared at Gogu. 'By the way, do you play golf?' he added.

Imran said that he did play golf and Simi could see that he would get on well with her father. But her mother looked uncomfortable.

'It's true, Ma,' Devi said to the old lady. 'Sam and Dr Chaudhry … well, they're … they wish to marry.'

Old Mrs Bhandari looked as though she had been struck in the face with a dead fish.

'You're all against me!' she said furiously. 'Gogu! Are you going to let them do this to me?'

The servants heard the family quarrel and crept back to watch. No one noticed or thought to dismiss them.

'Sam's always had a mind of her own, dash it!' Gogu said.

'And whose fault is that?' Old Mrs Bhandari aimed a pointed look at Devi.

Simi could tolerate it no longer. 'Dadi! I've done nothing to *you!* And it has nothing to do with Mama. I am doing this for *myself!* Imran and I are married whether you like it or not.'

Simi explained about Agra. Dadi asked the same questions as Devi had and scoffed at the notion that exchanging garlands meant a solemn marriage. But Gogu gallantly supported his daughter.

'Attagirl Sam! I'm with you. These religious types are getting up my nose. Dr Chaudhry – I mean Imran – seems a damned fine fellow to me. You have my blessings and we'll have a jolly good knees-up when the time comes.'

Devi kept her eyes to the floor. Simi hugged her father.

'Thank you, sir,' Imran said.

'Bless you, my boy. Now, how about that drink? Unless Mummy's changed her mind and wants to keep her leg.'

But the old lady would not be vanquished without a struggle.

'If it's true that Simi wants to be married to that' – the M-word scorched the air – 'she's not to set foot in my house ever again, you hear!'

Her attempt to domineer while sprawled on the floor with an injured leg was both pathetic and comical.

There was a short, terse silence. Then Gogu spoke firmly to his mother, surprisingly them all by taking charge. 'We *all* live here, Ma. And don't forget my father built this house. The family house.'

Imran moved to defuse the situation. 'Mrs Bhandari, if you don't get that leg checked soon there might be complications. At your age you can't afford that – not that you're old. Far from it – I can see where Simi gets her good looks! But you don't want to limp for the rest of your life, do you?'

Devi suppressed a smile at his awkward attempt at flattery. But at least he had stopped addressing her as 'grandmother'.

Imran added, 'If I can't take care of my family, Mrs Bhandari, what's the use of being a doctor? My parents died when I was a child. All my life I have longed for a family – but even if you don't accept that, at least let me help you.'

Old Mrs Bhandari said to Gogu. 'But he's an M!'

Gogu shook his head in despair. It was Imran who replied, 'You mean Muslim?'

She looked him in the face. 'Yes! Do you know what your people did to my family? We don't give our daughters in marriage to Ms!'

'She means the partition, Imi,' Simi quietly explained. 'Her father lost everything. For *Chrissake*, Dadi–'

'My *people?*' Imran said with a bitter laugh. 'That happened *fifty* years ago, long before I was born.'

'Us Bhandaris? Forget the past? No sirree! By George we don't!' Gogu chimed in sarcastically.

Imran leaned in to Simi and muttered, 'I may be an M, but your grandmother is an M-U-L-E! I know she's *your* grandmother – but still, there's a limit.' Simi held his hand, squeezing it with a defiant look at Dadi.

Imran attended to Gogu, washing and dressing his wound. He refused the offer of a drink because, after the previous night's violence, there were plenty of injured people who needed him.

'I'll take a rain check for now,' he told Gogu. 'Is it OK if I return this evening?'

'Jolly good!' said Gogu, before practically ordering his mother to allow Imran to treat her. Her agony finally compelled her to give in, but she did so with bad grace.

'Only as a doctor!' she said churlishly. 'As long as he understands there's none of this family-shamly, marriage-sharriage nonsense!'

Imran pursed his lips and knelt beside the curmudgeonly old woman. Her left leg was heavily swollen. Only an X-ray would reveal if there was a fracture, as Imran suspected. The streets were still unsafe though, so they decided not to risk driving to the hospital. Instead he improvised a splint for her leg and got the servants to help her to her bedroom, leaving instructions not to use the injured leg until he could arrange further tests.

'Thank you – Imran,' said Devi, once the doctor had finished treating her mother-in-law. She even gave him a half-smile, which he acknowledged with a grin.

Suddenly, Simi remembered that she had a message from Sanjay and pulled Imran aside to speak with him in private.

Leaving Simi and Imran alone, Devi assisted her husband upstairs to their bedroom. He took a shower, which was difficult because his bandaged shoulder had to be kept dry. Devi held it out of the way while Gogu rubbed himself down with his left hand, the water running pink with his blood. His wife helped to towel him dry, powdered his back and did up his pyjamas. He got into bed and Ganga brought them a tray of hot, sweet tea.

'So how about it, Dee?' Gogu asked, looking at his wife over the rim of his cup. 'The doctor's a good looking chap. And I don't want to be the one to try and change Sam's mind!'

'Will they be happy though?' Devi was more possessive of Simi than Gogu. 'Look around you … take last night, for example.'

He shook his head. 'We can't pretend to see the future, darling. Did you know yesterday that today would be like this? Let's not make the gel unhappy. You don't want to lose her.'

'But a marriage like *that* in a city like *this*? *They* won't let them live! Why can't she be more like Anjora?' Devi sighed. But Gogu smiled.

'Because she's *our* daughter, Dee! Dammit, we brought her up this way – and I'm proud. Thank the Lord she's the way she is.'

It was true. They had raised Simi to be blind to religious differences and caste hierarchies. But Devi feared for her daughter and didn't want her to waste years in unhappiness.

'What about your mother?' she asked. The old lady was now in her room being sponged down by the faithful Ganga, perhaps washing away the touch of Imran's hands.

'Ma? Piece of cake! Leave her to me!' Gogu said airily. 'But you, Dee, it's you that worry me. Sam needs you.' He then yawned and closed his eyes, exhausted from the hectic morning.

Devi couldn't imagine life without Simi. She sipped her tea while Gogu dozed.

When he opened his eyes, he found her still there. 'So, what's the verdict?' he asked.

'Sam phoned him in the morning and he said something about the Don?' Devi pointed out. 'The Don! What sort of man is friends with a criminal?'

Gogu pondered on that. 'We'll have to ask Sam,' he said eventually. 'But, dammit, I like the man. Imran, that is. And I'm going to build bridges if it makes Sam happy. She has to marry *someone*; why not let her follow her heart? Like I did when I set eyes upon you.'

She laughed. '*You?* You sat there without a tongue in your head while your father did all the talking! Don't you bamboozle me after all these years!'

'He talked – but I looked! By George, I looked and liked what I saw!' He patted her hand. 'It's not been easy for you, darling, I know. But I'm glad you stuck round. What would I do without you?'

She stroked his head. It had been difficult. But Devi believed in karma. Nothing happened without a reason.

'Let go, Dee. Let Sam find her own life.' Gogu stretched, yawned and lay down on his good arm. 'Good lord, feels like I've been mauled by a tiger! Be a good girl, Dee, draw the curtains. And how about a little massage? Whatever happened to wives rubbing their husbands' feet, eh?!'

She chuckled, closed the curtains, picked up the tea tray and left. He was already fast asleep.

CHAPTER 33

Along with the crowd of party workers, youth wing activists and other loyalists who gathered daily at Rajababu Mahajan's home-cum-office, Sanjay was spending much of his time with his political mentor. The incidents Sanjay had masterminded at the temple and the mosque had won him a spot at Rajababu's right hand. In return, the politician's team worked ever harder for Sanjay's university union elections. He was now confident of winning by a comfortable margin.

One evening, Sanjay was considering going home early, perhaps taking Pia out to dinner. He was relieved she had not left him as threatened and wanted to prove that he was serious about their relationship. But then news reached them of rioting in the old city. So Sanjay and the rest of Rajababu Mahajan's team re-grouped, waiting anxiously for further details.

Rumour and conjecture were as abundant as flies, but there was little first-hand information. Sanjay volunteered to drive to the old city, accompanied by a couple of trusty men. Before he left, Rajababu casually told Sanjay that he had information: the police had made a case against that Dr Chaudhry. This astonished Sanjay but he was careful to remain po-faced. He had to warn his old friend but could not ring him in front of his companions, so he drove off and tried to come up with a plan. He was glad to be able to pass the message through

Simi, even if he was stunned to find her out on the road with her maid.

After dropping them off at the White House, Sanjay had intended to do a quick reconnaissance of the city. Unfettered violence raged on the streets, making progress slow. The scale of it shocked Sanjay and it was past midnight when he arrived back at Rajababu's home, where he reported back to his mentor. A picture of desolation was steadily building up. Gangs roamed the streets, maiming and looting. Sanjay's rage turned to numb horror as fresh reports of mayhem poured in. It was morning before he was finally able to leave for home, setting off alone in his Jeep, eager to get back to Pia.

At that moment, Ahmed was returning from the White House. Being thwarted within a whisker of exacting revenge on the hated Bhandaris had enraged him. He was completely mystified by the Don's intervention, but now the sun was up, there was no choice but to return home. He and the other men had drifted for about a mile when they spotted the Jeep approaching from the opposite end of the narrow road.

Sanjay saw the crowd ahead of him from a distance and hurriedly reversed. They were too far away to identify, but gangs of young men spelt trouble. A car behind him cut off his retreat. Suddenly the gang started to race towards him. Sanjay panicked, abandoned his Jeep and ran. The driver of the car did the same.

Soon the youths were upon the vehicles. One of them smashed the Jeep's windscreen and ripped the seats. Someone else set fire to the soft top. They smashed the glass of the car too, then slashed the seats with a knife.

Ignoring the vehicles, Ahmed recognised Sanjay. *Isn't that the bastard who used me?* Now his pent-up frustration found a focus.

He blamed Sanjay for causing the rift between him and his hero, Dr Chaudhry. Ahmed blamed Sanjay, and all Hindus, for the wrongs done to him. He yelled to his companions, 'He's mine. He owes me.'

Sanjay was in a tight spot and heavily outnumbered. He was therefore greatly relieved to spot Ahmed. 'It's you, Ahmed, brother!' he called out.

'Yes, it's me!' Ahmed snarled.

Ahmed's tone should have warned Sanjay, but he blustered on. 'I am glad it's you! What a bad night, *yaar*!'

'Don't *yaar* me! You're not my friend.' He walked slowly towards Sanjay, clenching his fists so tight that his knuckles turned white.

Sanjay backed away with outstretched hands. 'Ahmed, my brother, like you, I've been caught up in this madness all night.'

Ahmed lunged forward and slapped Sanjay hard across his face. The blow made Sanjay stagger. 'And don't call me brother!' Ahmed yelled. 'Hindu dog! People like you *use* poor people like me!'

Sanjay began to panic. 'Ahmed, what's the matter? I'm on *your* side, don't you know that?'

'Liar! Cheater! I am sick of being duped! I am sick of being your coolie!'

Sanjay saw this was no time for talk. He backed off slowly, afraid that running away might trigger a violent reaction. Ahmed was young and strong and would catch him in a trice. He regretted leaving the safety of the Jeep, but it was now a blazing wreck. In an effort to placate the advancing man, Sanjay raked up the name of the one person he and Ahmed had in common.

'Have you seen Imran, Dr Chaudhry? I've been looking for him.'

That was the last straw for Ahmed, who let fly a stream of expletives. Sanjay turned and ran for it. Ahmed leapt forward, grabbed him by the scruff of his neck, swung him round and punched him savagely on the nose, crushing the cartilage.

Sanjay fell over, clutching his face in agony, blood streaking his shirt like a crimson tie. Ahmed boxed him in the stomach, landing a succession of quick blows. His fists were like iron. The pain was unbearable and tears clouded Sanjay's vision. He knew he was in grave danger. Ahmed rained punches on him like a man possessed. Sanjay desperately defended himself, pummelling Ahmed in the chest and stomach. His opponent, caught off-guard, momentarily lost his balance.

Sanjay turned and fled. Ahmed quickly regained his feet and lunged at his target, the tackle sending them both sprawling. Sanjay kicked Ahmed in the shins and managed to free himself by landing a blow on his jaw. He stood up shakily, but Ahmed grabbed his legs and felled him. Again they grappled with each other, rolling over, now one on top, then the other, both tired after a traumatic night.

Sanjay eventually managed to get free and staggered back to his feet. Quick as lightning, Ahmed jumped up too, grabbing the disoriented Sanjay and placing his hands around the man's throat. Grisly memories of death crossed Ahmed's mind as he squeezed, Jaddan Bai and Munna's mother had to be accounted for. His fingers gripped like steel cords. Women who were like family had died without cause. Ahmed squeezed harder. *Their bodies had been desecrated!* Ahmed didn't hear the death rattle in Sanjay's throat or see his eyes protruding from their sockets. *Had Farid's tiny mites deserved to die!?* Within seconds, it was all over for Sanjay.

Ahmed blinked and let go, watching the body slide to the ground. Then he whipped out the knife strapped to his calf and buried it in Sanjay's throat, severing the windpipe. The other men formed a shocked semi-circle around them. Ahmed saw their faces and slowly stepped back from Sanjay. He had only intended to teach him a lesson. But rage had taken over.

They heard the sound of running feet. A gang of Hindu youths came towards them. Ahmed stared at them uncomprehendingly for a moment. The youths stopped too, shocked by the sight of Sanjay on the ground, blood flowing from his neck. Ahmed turned and fled in the opposite direction.

Some of the Hindu youths had recognised Sanjay and were overcome with shock. They knelt by the body and wept. Eventually one of them took charge, improvising a stretcher using a rear seat salvaged from the smouldering Jeep and some bamboo poles from a nearby building site. They laid him on it and carried the body away.

The rest of the mob chased Ahmed, who was now running for his life. Behind him, Ahmed could hear his pursuers closing the gap. He spotted a wall to his left and ran to it, hoisting himself up and cutting his hands on the shards of glass embedded on top. They bled profusely but he did not notice. Leaping down into the courtyard behind the wall, he sprinted across and over another wall to escape into a service lane. He ran as fast as he could. But Ahmed was built for strength, not speed.

Meanwhile, back at the White House, Simi gave Imran Sanjay's message. 'Why not go away for a few days?' she suggested. 'If Sanjay is right, the police will be looking for you.'

'*Khuda!* Hide like a rat?' Imran replied, rejecting the idea out of hand. '*Jaan*, when you called, I went to a place beyond death. I'm not going anywhere without you.'

Simi shivered. 'Another minute and the mob would have broken in! What made them leave?'

'They were told to leave,' said Imran. 'There's only one man who could have saved you – and he did.'

Simi looked shocked. '*Not*—'

He nodded. 'Karimbhai. No one else could have turned them back – not the police, not the chief minister.'

Imran had implored the Don to save his wife. It was the first time he had asked for a favour. Karimbhai had listened quietly as Imran explained, giving him the name and address. Then Imran heard him dispatch his men before returning to the phone.

'He scolded me for not telling him I was married and made me promise to bring you round to dinner. Our first dinner party as a couple might be with the Don!'

So now she owed her life and those of her family to the Don!? This was not what Simi had expected.

'OK, OK,' she conceded. 'I can't pretend to like him, but I'll thank him.'

Despite everything, Simi was relieved that her relationship with Imran was now out in the open. She smiled at him. 'Papa already loves you, and Mama will too.'

'And your granny?'

'Oh she … she'll just *adore* you!' They both laughed.

After checking once more on Old Mrs Bhandari, Imran offered to drive Simi and Marriam to the maid's home. Devi resisted at first, but the streets seemed quieter now and Simi convinced her mother they would be safe. Marriam was desperate for news of Ahmed, so they left as soon as they could.

On their way they passed the charred remains of burnt-out vehicles. The scene was unsettling, but eventually they arrived safely at Nawabganj, where all doors were shut and the silence was deafening. Simi could scarcely believe that just yesterday the place had rung with excited voices and people preparing for the march.

Today it was as though a man-eater prowled outside. The three of them proceeded quickly to Marriam's home. The lock was still in place, which meant that Ahmed was not at home. Marriam's face fell. But they heard a whimper as Marriam unlocked the door. It came from behind the door, where Munna was curled up with his cheek against the floor. Imran bent down and scooped up the boy in his arms, placing him gently on the bed.

'Are you hurt?' he asked, running professional fingers down Munna's thin body. Marriam gave the boy a quick hug then went into the other room to check for Ahmed.

Simi's heart went out to Munna. He seemed a completely different lad to the jaunty boy she had marched with yesterday. But how did he get here from Jaddan Bai's home? Where was his family? His shoulders drooped and his chin dropped down to his chest.

Marriam's second room was also empty and she quickly returned. 'Munna, where's your dadi? Where's Jaddan Bai? And my Ahmudi?' she enquired. Receiving no response, she ran next door to ask there instead.

Simi knelt down to Munna, lifting his chin and looking him in the eye. 'Why are you here, Munna?' she asked. 'Where's your family?' He stared at her blankly. It was like looking into a dark, empty house.

'Shock,' Imran explained to Simi and slapped Munna. It made no difference. Marriam returned to say that her friend's door was padlocked, exactly as it had been the previous morning, before the march. That frightened Simi even more.

Marriam gathered Munna to her bosom. 'For Allah's sake speak!'

'Where's Sangita? Where are the others?' Simi asked.

The tears poured down Marriam's face and she shook her head.

'Let's go and look,' Imran suggested.

The women Simi had left at Jaddan Bai's home were nowhere to be found.

Finally, Imran said, 'I really must go now. I need to get back to the hospital.'

Marriam would not budge and kept Munna with her, but Imran refused to leave Simi behind, so she reluctantly followed him.

Inside Marriam's small home, she cradled Munna, rocking him gently as he snuggled at her breast like a baby monkey. The warm September sun filtered through the open door and struck the nape of his neck, which he scratched. Apart from that he gave no sign of animation. A shadow fell across them and Marriam looked up fearfully, but it was only Ahmed.

'Ahmudi, son!' she jumped up, dropping Munna. 'Allah be thanked, you're safe.'

'Ammi!' he cried. There was anguish in his voice and he hastily bolted the door behind him. Ahmed had taken short cuts through familiar lanes on his way home, so he had temporarily lost his pursuers. But he knew they could not be far behind.

'What's wrong, son?' Marriam asked.

'You mustn't stay here, Ammi. It's not safe!'

'Not safe? Why? Where's sister Jaddan Bai?'

Ahmed shook his head.

'In hospital?' Marriam asked fearfully.

He shook his head again.

'And Samina?' she whispered, not wanting Munna to overhear them talking about his mother.

He looked down.

Marriam's face crumpled. She mouthed the word, 'Dead?'

He nodded.

'*Allah!*' she shrieked, covering her face with her dupatta.

Someone banged on the door and shouted, 'Ahmed! Run! They're coming!'

Ahmed started, unbolted the door, lifted his mother and Munna in his arms and almost threw them outside. 'Run, Ammi! Quick!'

Marriam stood there dazed. For a split second Ahmed hesitated, not knowing which way to go. Then he plunged blindly to the right, dragging his mother along with him and half-carrying Munna. Together they hurried through Nawabganj's maze of lanes.

They almost made it out to the main road when they heard someone shout. 'Oi, stop! Stop *mianbhai!*'

They whirled round. Three armed youths confronted them. Ahmed threw himself in front of his mother. His enemies laughed.

Their laughter chilled Marriam. Over Ahmed's shoulder, she recognised two of the Hindu youths and wanted to call out '*beta*', son, because they were about the same age as her Ahmed. But she couldn't find her voice.

There are only three of them, Ahmed calculated desperately. I can hold them here … but Ammi must get away.

Out of the corner of his mouth he spat the words, 'Ammi, go, *go!*' Marriam wanted to defend her cub and tried to nudge Ahmed aside, but he pushed her away. 'Go, Ammi, for my sake. I'll catch up with you.'

She obeyed blindly, grasping Munna by the hand.

Ahmed's lip curled as he faced his tormentors. Without losing sight of them, he quickly retrieved the two knives he still had strapped to his calves. Crouching with a blade in each hand, he silently dared them to attack. His strength was legendary and he was known as a tough street fighter. But he was outnumbered.

The pack circled him, wielding knives and iron rods. The leader launched himself at Ahmed with a terrible cry, landing a blow on his left shoulder with a heavy metal bar. The pain was agonising, but Ahmed swung his right arm through the air and buried one of his blades deep in his assailant's stomach. He twisted the knife and the man crumpled to the ground.

A second man was now upon Ahmed, who transferred the other knife into his right hand and thrust it up under his enemy's ribcage, puncturing a lung. But the man had thrust his own dagger as he collapsed, embedding it in Ahmed's chest even as a fountain of blood erupted from his mouth.

As the knife sank deeper into Ahmed's flesh, he stared up at the blue sky, fragments of memory flashing through his mind: happy childhood days spent with his grandfather; his smiling father holding out a set of new clothes for Eid; his mother crooning a lullaby. Ammi! Who would look after her if something happened to him? Not a thought of his carefully accumulated money crossed Ahmed's mind.

Marriam looked back and saw her son caught in a soundless scream before he toppled over backwards, hitting the brick lane with a thud. With a piercing cry, she ran to him.

Simi and Imran had been delayed on their way back to his car by a Nawabganj local, who stopped the doctor to ask about a locked knee. As she waited, Simi heard Marriam scream and turned round immediately.

'Imi!' she cried, grabbing his elbow. 'That's Marriam screaming! Something's happened. Oh God!' She ran off, he followed.

'*Ahhhmudddiii!*' Marriam wailed.

Simi spotted Marriam and stopped, shocked by the sight of three bodies on the ground in a pool of blood. Imran caught up to her and she grabbed his arm for support, feeling sick to her stomach. She saw that Marriam was cradling Ahmed on her lap. There was a knife sticking out of his chest. Was he dead? She had never seen anyone die before. But he must be. She saw it in his mother's face.

One youth had survived. He too was staring at the bloody scene. Simi looked at him and lost her head.

'Murderer!' she screamed. 'Murderer! I'll see you hang for this!' She ran full pelt at him, shouting in English that he couldn't understand. With her long black hair streaming behind her, she looked like an avenging goddess.

'*Simi!*' Imran chased her, but she was already upon the man, slapping him and kicking him in the legs.

'The police will hang you for this! I'll make sure they do! I know the Police Commissioner and General Kapur. From the army! You WILL hang!'

The youth, stunned by the deaths he had witnessed and confused by her English, stared stupidly. But he understood the words 'police commissioner' and 'army'.

Imran reached them and pulled her back. The youth fled.

'*Sim!* Stop it, stop it!' Imran put an arm around her and walked her back to Marriam. Simi went quiet.

Marriam was stroking Ahmed's hair, caressing his cheek and promising him the Earth if only he would speak. She wiped the blood off his face with her white dupatta.

Imran felt for a pulse but there was none. He shook his head in answer to Simi's unspoken query, but Ahmed's ripped and bloody chest told its own story.

'Marriam,' Simi said timidly. 'He's gone, Marriam.'

Marriam ignored her. Simi repeated herself. Marriam looked up at her.

'Dead? No, no, Simi*baby*, can't be. He's too young. The hospital! Doctor*saab* will make him alright.'

'Doctor*saab* is right here,' Simi pointed out. 'But his heart — Ahmed's heart is broken.'

Marriam looked again at the fatal wound and swooned, hitting her head against the wall. Simi swooped to lift her up. The maid opened her eyes and recollection flooded back. She sat up abruptly, screaming, but the sharp movement made her dizzy. She crawled back to his body. Sitting in the prayer position, she raised her hands to the overcast sky.

'Allah, The Compassionate, The Merciful, Ahmudi is very young. Take me instead, I am ready to go. But spare him. Allah, his life has only just begun.'

'Poor Ahmed,' Imran shook his head, wiping away tears. 'He's only a teenager. He didn't deserve that.' He kneeled and gently closed Ahmed's eyes, then took Marriam's hand. 'I'm sorry,' he said. 'He would have grown up into a good man, but we must accept Allah's will.'

Munna crept up to Simi and slipped his hand into hers, reminding her of his presence. She turned and hugged him. The sight of Ahmed on the ground had disturbed the boy. Munna sobbed quietly, clinging to Simi and repeating over and over, 'Dadi's dead. Ammi's dead.'

It was too much for Simi to bear. Waves of nausea engulfed her and her legs buckled as she fainted, almost landing on Munna. Imran dashed over and grabbed her by her waist, calling out her name. She opened her eyes and snivelled, wiping her runny nose with the back of her sleeve.

'Hush, *jaan*, it's going to be OK,' Imran said. But he worried that the youth who had escaped might return with reinforcements. 'We can't stay here any longer,' he said.

Neither Simi nor Marriam seemed to be listening; Marriam was oblivious to everything and continued praying, while Simi stood by her old ayah's side, one hand on her shoulder.

'Ahmed died to protect you, his mother,' Simi told Marriam, 'You should be proud of him.'

Imran added, 'Ahmed made the supreme sacrifice. He will surely go to paradise.'

The words brought a measure of consolation. Marriam stroked her son's face gently, as if to comfort him, like she had done when he was little. The intimate gesture brought tears to her eyes again.

With a deafening thunderclap and a boastful display of lightning, the monsoon arrived, heavy raindrops falling like silver coins. They were quickly drenched.

Simi knelt beside Marriam and put her arms around her. 'Come, we need to leave. I'll be your child now, your son. I'll look after you, you'll live with me.' It was as though Marriam had been orphaned.

But Marriam would not leave her son unattended. Imran agreed that they shouldn't leave him and hefted Ahmed's muscular body onto the rear seat of his car. Marriam crouched next to it, holding his limp hand. Munna sat on Simi's lap up front.

They drove to the city morgue, where Imran knew the attendant, which helped to conclude matters swiftly without the police having further reason to regard Imran with suspicion. Afterwards, they went to Imran's apartment and changed into dry clothes. Marriam sat quietly, not talking to anyone. Simi tried to draw her out, but she was deep in her own world.

She drew Imran aside. 'I'm worried about her, Imi. I've told her she can live with us. Is that OK?'

'She's your old ayah, *jaan*. It's right we should care for her.'

'And Munna?' she asked, drawing a deep breath. 'What if he has nowhere else to go?'

'What about his father?' Imran protested. 'Farid? And taking on a young boy is a big responsibility.'

'We can't shoo him out though, can we?' replied Simi. 'We'll try to find Farid as soon as we can. But if we can't … . I thought … in time … we might even adopt him.'

'Adopt him?! Oh *Khuda!*'

Her impetuousness tried Imran's patience. The boy should be with his family. Even if they couldn't find his father, adopting a ten-year old boy seemed like madness … but then Imran recalled that he had been adopted – fostered, at least. They dropped the subject. The important thing for now was to make sure the child was safe.

They agreed Imran would drive Simi, Marriam and Munna back to the White House before he went to the hospital.

Just before they left, Simi insisted that Imran should come clean about his whereabouts on the night the smugglers had been shot. He hesitated.

'You're asking me to betray a professional confidence,' he protested.

'We *have* to clear this up,' she said. She could not live with her suspicions.

Imran sighed. 'OK. I was with the Don that night.'

While annoyed, Simi could hardly object after the Don had saved her life.

'Well, what was it? A bullet, as the papers said?'

'A bullet? No!' he chuckled. 'It was a baby.'

She stared. 'You're pulling my leg.'

He shook his head. 'What do the papers know? Karimbhai was nowhere near the smugglers that night. His wife went into labour and he called me. Of course, the gynaecologist was there for the delivery, but-'

'Nina Singh?' Simi interrupted, jealousy getting the better of her.

'*Not* Nina.'

She was glad to hear that.

'And? Was it a boy or a girl?'

CHAPTER 34

Sanjay's political work meant he had been home late every night recently, but Pia always waited up for him. He would often appear with a peace offering, which pleased Pia, even when it was only a ten-rupee string of scented jasmine.

One night, Sanjay did not come home at all. After a few hours of restless half-sleep, Pia found herself still alone at dawn. She rose wearily, heated a cup of milk and drank it for the sake of the baby.

Sanjay was still missing when the torrential rain came down later, by which point Pia was frantic with worry. When the knock on the door came she flew to open it, ready with a reproach for causing her such anxiety. But it was not Sanjay she found standing there. Instead, four men carried him on a stretcher. Pia froze.

The men walked past her silently, bringing in small puddles of water with their feet. They placed the stretcher gently on the ground and lifted Sanjay, laying him down on the bed. His eyes were closed. He could have been asleep, but for the bloody bandages around his neck.

Pia took in the dreadful scene. She simply could not comprehend it.

'Is he ill? Was Sunju in an accident?' she asked, but could see no shadow of pain on his peaceful countenance. Why were his companions so solemn? She had no idea who they were. One of the men approached her.

'I'm sorry, sister,' he said. 'We did our best but we were too late.'

Another added, 'No one could have done anything for him. Sanjay*bhai* was gone. He must have died instantly.'

Sunju dead? She felt as though she were in a dream, or a nightmare, from which she would soon wake. '*Liars!* You're liars!' she screamed.

Pia ran to the bed and threw herself down on Sanjay, crying out his name. His body was warm to the touch, but his eyes remained shut. Pia picked him up by the shoulders, watching his head loll back as she did so. She massaged his hand, thumped his chest and cursed him for not speaking to her.

The men looked down at their feet, comprehending her relationship to the dead man.

He can't be dead, not Sunju, who's so brimming with life. Pia refused to accept that her beloved would leave her like this. He neither moved nor uttered a word. Bitter tears coursed down Pia's cheeks. Grief hit her like a tidal wave and she could scarcely withstand the weight of her sorrow. When the spasm passed, she became conscious of the men watching her. Steeling herself, Pia gently placed Sanjay's head back on the pillow. Her legs trembled as she stumbled back, wondering, *am I going mad?*

Pia sat down next to the bed, staring helplessly at the body. Within an hour the room had filled up with people, news of Sanjay's death quickly spreading across town. His life had been lived in the public and the crowd grew steadily, soon spilling over onto the verandah. Others stood in the rain, with or without umbrellas.

Eventually, Sanjay's family arrived too. Pia caught a glimpse of a dignified man who must have been his father.

Sanjay's mother accompanied him, her pinched face lined with fear. Was this woman really so terrible she would not have accepted Pia? She was clever and would have tried hard to fit in; she wanted to tell Mrs Sethi, but it was no use now. Time had run out. She longed to cry out, *here I am, his … wife, and his child too!*

But it was all over. She could see that now. Pia got up, struggling through a miasma of grief and steadying herself against a chair. There was no reason left to stay here. Her dreams lay dead on the bed. So she took one last look at Sanjay, memorising his features. *If only he hadn't gone out last night …*

Tormented by thoughts of how she could have saved him, Pia walked out into the storm. She trudged through the city, howling into wind and weeping into the rain, hoping she would catch pneumonia and die. It took her almost an hour to cover the two miles to the YWCA.

At the White House, Simi found her parents in the sitting room and told them about Ahmed's death. She also told them about Jaddan Bai and the other women, Marriam again breaking down as she counted her lost family and friends.

Gogu stayed quiet, nursing a gin and tonic. But Devi wept inconsolably, feeling Marriam's loss deeply. She insisted Marriam would stay with them, in an outhouse, along with Munna. Old Mrs Bhandari objected, but her protests fell on deaf ears. Devi was adamant and her husband supported her decision.

Simi had other plans. 'Marriam will live with me when I'm settled. Munna too, if we can't find Farid.' They still had no idea where the boy's father might be. 'But they can stay here with you for the time being, Mama.'

Devi agreed.

Imran was devastated when he learnt about Sanjay's death. He had received a phone call at the hospital and immediately left to go to his friend's house. He was overwhelmed by grief when he saw the body. He looked for Pia there too, but she had gone.

'How could this happen?' he asked Simi over and over when he saw her later that day.

Unable to work during the days which followed, he spent most of his time with Sanjay's parents, as much for his own comfort as theirs. When not with them, he sat alone at home, brooding over the death of a friend who had been like a brother. His surgery remained shut for an entire week and his receptionist cancelled all appointments, explaining that the doctor was unwell.

Simi too was shocked by Sanjay's death, even though they had not been friends very long. The Sethis and the Bhandaris were acquainted, like all the old families of Atmapuri. She went with her grandmother and parents to the cremation and religious ceremonies on the fourth and thirteenth days after his death. Large crowds filled the crematorium and his parents' home. But Pia was not amongst them.

Simi eventually traced Pia to the YWCA and rushed to see her. She was unable to persuade Pia to move in with her or even to stay in Atmapuri. Instead, she helped Pia make arrangements with the university to complete her studies from Nainital. When the time came, Simi drove Pia to the train station and wept as she bade goodbye to her dearest friend. They clung to each other until the last moment. Simi waved to Pia through her tears as her friend boarded the train. She kept waving until she could see her no more.

For days afterwards Simi moped, missing Pia terribly. Along with the strain of Sanjay's death, witnessing Ahmed's violent end, supporting Imran through his grief, and taking care of Marriam and Munna, Simi felt exhausted and depressed. She was alone with her parents in the sitting room when her father urged her to have a drink. He had now recovered from his injury and kept trying to cheer Simi up.

'Sherry, Sam? Don't know about you, by Jove, but I feel like I've got a new lease of life!'

His jovial remark simply reminded Simi that she could have lost her father, and she burst into tears. Gogu patted her on the head.

'Tricky time, tricky time. But your doctor chappie took splendid care of us. I'm tickety-boo now, Sam, so don't cry, baby.' He covered up his emotions by gulping some gin.

Devi met her husband's eyes and silently gave thanks that death had spared them. She wondered how she would have coped in Marriam's shoes, hastily pushing away the unbearable thought. She knew they were lucky to get off so lightly, but Simi's choice of husband was a hard pill to swallow.

'I won't pretend it will be easy, Sam, about the doctor, but I will accept it. Just give me a little time.'

That was a big step for Devi. But Simi was in no mood to be understanding.

'Mama! Imran saved our lives! What more do you want?' She told her parents about Karimbhai's intervention. Devi had the grace to look embarrassed.

'I'm sorry, Sam. All the same, this has to be done properly. We must mind our reputation. After all, the Bhandari family stands for something and I've been part of it for thirty years. Exchanging garlands at the Taj Mahal and calling it a marriage is humbug. You and Imran must have a proper wedding.'

Simi was so relieved to hear those words from her mother that she drained her glass of sherry in one big gulp and choked.

When Imran came round for a drink in the evening, Simi could tell that her mother was trying to be friendly. The effort showed. At least, it did until Imran recited some Urdu poetry. Devi completed the verse under her breath.

Turning to Simi, she said, 'You never told me he likes Urdu poetry!'

After that, it was difficult to interrupt them as they conversed at length about long-dead poets. Devi was thrilled to hear about Imran's father's patronage of court poets. And when he spoke about Sunehri Begum, aka Meena Kumari, Devi could scarcely wait to meet her.

It was a lot longer before the old lady could bring herself to mention Dr Chaudhry by name. She lectured Simi on the importance of religious compatibility, of being able to worship together. On the morning of Ganesh Chaturthi, she made a point of saying it would have been nice to celebrate the festival with another Hindu family. The festival day passed uneventfully in the end, despite the long procession and assortment of temporary street shrines. Not a single stone was thrown, as if there was tacit agreement that, after the violence of the preceding days, Atmapuri needed the fresh start that Ganesh — the elephant-headed god of beginnings — promised.

Eventually, however, Old Mrs Bhandari discovered that her disapproval of Imran carried little weight any more; her power was shrinking and Gogu had quietly become the master of the house. With her grip on the household failing, Old Mrs Bhandari's anger gave way to sorrow that the world had changed beyond recognition. She lamented that the old gentry had given way to jumped-up shopkeepers, that family antecedents no longer seemed to count, and that girls were pig-headed. While she permitted Imran to examine her, strictly on a professional basis, she refused to address him. She had escaped a fracture, but her leg was swollen and painful.

After witnessing a fortnight of her grandmother's frosty attitude towards Imran, Simi could stand it no longer.

'For God's sake, Dadi, Imran saved your life.' Under her breath she added, 'you ungrateful so-and-so.'

But Devi understood that the real trauma for her mother-in-law lay back in 1947. Crouching next to the old lady, she spoke to her softly.

'Mummy, poor Marriam lost her son, her only child – just think of her sorrow. And we could have died! Do you think others didn't suffer in the partition? Your father lost money, but at least he lived. Millions lost their lives, their husbands, wives and children.'

The stern matriarch had ruled the family for decades, but now she paused. Something about what Devi said rang true. She was carrying restless ghosts she had never laid to rest and suddenly felt the full weight of her seventy-seven years.

'I'm tired. And old. Maybe you are right. Thank God we're safe! Your generation has no idea what we suffered.' She shook her head. 'I was bitter.'

Mollified, Devi smiled at the woman with whom she had shared three difficult decades. 'You mustn't fret, Mummy. Just lie still and get well.'

Simi's heart went out to her Dadi, who suddenly looked vulnerable.

'I'm sorry, Dadi. I didn't mean it to happen like this.'

Her grandmother shot her a wistful look.

'Child. I know you think I was harsh with you, but I didn't want to see you ruin your life. It's our grandchildren whom we love most of all.'

With tears in her eyes, Simi hugged Old Mrs Bhandari, pressing her smooth cheek against her grandmother's wrinkled skin. The old lady felt comforted that her family would live on long after she had faded from memory.

'It's not easy for me,' Old Mrs Bhandari said, 'to accept an M.' The word stuck in her gullet. 'But I'll get used to it, I suppose. I've been wrong about things in the past. I'll have to be more ... more ... '

'Flexible?' Simi suggested.

'Perhaps.'

It wasn't a lot, but it was a start.

Later, Simi repeated the conversation to Imran. The next time he came by the house he startled Simi by grasping both of Old Mrs Bhandari's hands; what's more, the old lady allowed him to keep hold of them! He even kissed each hand in turn before replacing them in her lap. Simi held her breath. Old Mrs Bhandari frowned but Simi could tell she was secretly amused, so she relaxed. Imran stayed a while, chatting, cajoling and charming Simi and her grandmother.

After Imran had left, Dadi told her, 'I like him, Child. He's a rogue, flirting with an old woman like me! He reminds me of somebody.' She did not bother to elaborate.

The next day, still restless after the traumatic events, Simi decided to visit the baba. Imran and Marriam went with her. Surprisingly, Imran had never met the holy man. Simi had wanted to take him there on a sunny day, but the monsoon had not let up and they arrived to find water swilling around the empty courtyard.

A young man opened the baba's blue door. Simi recognised him as an acolyte. He recognised her too, silently stepping aside to let them enter. The baba was unhurt and seated on the floor, still as a statue. His eyes were shut. Simi prostrated herself before him and motioned to Imran to sit beside her. Marriam sat behind them, silent tears pouring down her face at the sight of the holy man whose prayers had once given her the gift of a son.

They sat quietly and Imran studied the man who meant so much to Simi. After a while he nudged her, whispering, 'How long do we stay?'

'Just a little longer.' She hoped the baba would open his eyes soon.

The acolyte who had met them at the door meditated alongside the baba. Simi slid across the floor to him and whispered, 'Is the baba likely to come out of meditation soon? Shall we wait?'

The acolyte rose and beckoned them to follow him. Just inside the door, he stopped and whispered, 'The baba speaks no more. Five days ago, at dawn, he had a vision. After that, he stopped speaking. He said that the world was in pain and that he must be silent.'

Simi was confused. 'Is that all? Did he say anything else?'

The disciple nodded. 'I wrote down his last words. Here, you can read them.'

He handed her an exercise book. In it was written:

> *The world burns in the night*
> *Without warmth*
> *My bed is made of tears*

Simi read the words over and over before reluctantly handing back the book. His vision had already come true. They left, thanking the acolyte as he quietly closed the door behind them.

Simi clutched Imran's arm on the way back to the car, trying to explain what the baba had meant to her. But how do you describe the taste of a mango to someone who has never eaten one?

Unable to fathom the depth of her sorrow, Imran said, 'We can still visit him, *jaan*.'

She felt indescribably sad at the thought of never hearing the holy man's voice again. So much loss, so much grief ... how would she bear it without the baba? She recalled her sense of foreboding when she had last visited him. How she wished she had written down the baba's words when she had the chance.

CHAPTER 35

At the end of September, when the intense summer heat had abated and the nights were growing cooler, Imran took Simi to visit Sunehri Begum again. The begum's obsequious servant Kader ushered them inside, informing them that his mistress was taking a siesta. He left them in the main room and they heard his timorous knock somewhere in the depths of the apartment. It was a while before Sunehri Begum appeared, freshly bathed and shampooed, her long wet tresses trailing down to her hips. She floated in on a cloud of perfume and greeted them warmly.

'You are like the cool waters of the Zamzam well, Imran*saab!* And dear, dear Simi.'

The begum stretched out on a divan piled high with Urdu magazines, and they talked like old friends. When Imran told her he had married Simi in Agra, she shrieked with joy. But she also protested.

'And you didn't invite me to the wedding? *Jao,* I'm not talking to you!'

Simi laughed. She explained that they would be formally married in Atmapuri and that Sunehri Begum would be their honoured guest. The dancer was delighted.

'That's alright then!' she exclaimed before demanding to be told everything about the arrangements. 'And I shall dance at your wedding!' she added.

'How lovely! Thank you!' Simi cried.

'The day Imran*saab* brought you here, I knew you were *special* to him. I saw it in his eyes. And if he's anything like his grandfather, he knows how to treat a woman.'

Imran acknowledged the compliment by touching his forehead with his right hand.

'And I want you to meet my mother, Sunehri*aapa*,' Simi said. 'She admires your work. She's an artiste too. She sings.' Following Imran's suggestion, Simi addressed the dancer as *aapa* or 'older sister'.

The begum smiled. 'Call me Soni,' she said. 'Your mother and I will be good friends, I already know it.'

The begum beckoned to Simi, patting the seat next to her, eager to hear more about their time in Agra. Simi was happy to relive the memories and told her all about Imran's unexpected arrival and exchanging garlands at the Taj Mahal.

'The Taj!' the begum sighed. 'Did you know that, for my eighteenth birthday, the Nawab*saab* threw a party for me at the Taj Mahal? A white picnic in the moonlight! We all wore white clothes and the food was all white. We even drank white drinks! We sat on white mattresses looking up at the full moon, and we sang and danced. The Taj Mahal shone like a pearl in the moonlight and I was the happiest girl in the world!'

Turning to Simi, Imran said, 'I told you, didn't I, *jaan*, that the begum has amazing stories to tell about the Taj?'

Sunehri Begum smiled at him. 'I even saw the Black Taj.'

'*What?*' yelped Simi, turning to stare at the begum.

The dancer nodded. 'There it was, not a phantom, not a ghost, but a rare gift. Call it fate, call it what you will, but I saw it alright. They say it's lucky to see the Black Taj. And only very, very few do. I did.'

EPILOGUE

It was settled that Simi and Imran's wedding reception would be held on the twentieth of November and the invitations were sent out. After a tussle over the wording of the card, it was agreed that it would include all titles:

Mrs Tillotama Bhandari w/o Late Rai Bahadur Justice Bhandari, requests the pleasure of the company of _____ at the marriage reception of her granddaughter SIMI, daughter of Devi and Gautam Bhandari, and IMRAN, son of the Late His Highness Nawabsaab of Akbarabad and Her Highness Begum Nargis Bano, and nephew of Dr and Mrs Manu Chaudhry, on Saturday the 20th of November, 1993, at ...

Old Mrs Bhandari had insisted that her name should appear at the top of the invitation, despite her previous misgivings about Imran's religion. When Gogu had diplomatically suggested using his and Devi's names instead, the old lady harrumphed, saying that nobody should try and sideline her at her granddaughter's wedding. Simi was the only child of her only son, she was the head of family, and it was fitting that the invitation be issued in her name. The presence of Imran's Hindu foster parents, Dr and Mrs Chaudhry, went a long way to placate her. And with Old Mrs Bhandari's name on the card, nobody declined the invitation, not even those who privately disapproved.

Secretly, the old lady was quietly delighted that both of her granddaughters would be married in the same year.

In mid-October, Simi travelled up to Nainital with Marriam to invite Pia to the wedding. Munna came too, as the boy was now under Marriam's care. Munna had lost his entire family in one stroke: his grandmother, his mother, two younger siblings, and his father, Farid, who had never reappeared, presumed dead in the chaos. Marriam, who had been drowning in an ocean of sorrow, slowly realised that Munna needed her, so she took charge of the boy, scolding him to bathe and eat on time. It turn, he became the balm for the terrible ache in her heart. In teaching him to live again, Marriam slowly healed herself.

In Nainital, however, Simi found Pia in subdued mood. Her friend had gone to live with her mother and the bump of her pregnancy was showing. She told people that she had secretly married Major Sethi, a brave soldier who had fallen to a sniper's bullet on the Siachen glacier. If people were sceptical, no one questioned her. Simi pleaded with her to attend her wedding, but Pia obdurately refused to return to Atmapuri, the crucible of her love and loss. And when Simi tentatively suggested Pia should tell the Sethis about the child, Pia raged so much that Simi was sorry she had raised the subject. She left Nainital with a sense of failure.

By the first of November, the White House had been freshly painted inside and out. Strands of pink fairy lights covered the house like a delicate web and a kitchen tent went up in the rear courtyard to cater for the many relatives who would be attending. Old Mrs Bhandari kept the servants on their toes, ensuring there was enough food for thirty people at all times. Devi placed fresh flowers everywhere, humming as she arranged them in tall vases and low bowls. She was secretly working on a composition that she intended to sing, either at the reception or one of the many pre-nuptial celebratory dinners.

A few days before the reception, with a delicate sense of propriety, Sunehri Begum arranged to visit Simi at the White House. It was early evening and the begum charmed Devi instantly. At the begum's insistence, Devi sang a *ghazal* for her and found herself talking about her composition for Simi's reception, humming snatches of it. The begum said that she would dance to it and they arranged to meet up again to rehearse. Imran, who arrived later, was delighted to see them get on so well.

With Imran now present the moment had come for Sunehri Begum to present them with a gift. With a flourish she produced a long blue velvet jewellery box from her bag. Simi instantly recognised it and her heart began to race. She gasped when she looked inside, for there lay the Jaipur Queen! She and Devi were speechless, even if it meant nothing to Imran, who had never seen it before. The begum beamed at them, pleased that her gift had rendered them speechless. They never told her why.

At Gogu's insistence, the reception was held at one of Atmapuri's newest hotels. The guests included Mr Arora and the other mandarins from the AMC who had for so long opposed Imran bitterly, but were now appeased by the doctor's marriage to a Hindu girl from one of the old families. On an impulse, Gogu had invited them to the wedding, thus neutralising them altogether.

Sunehri Begum put her heart into her performance that evening, mesmerising the guests. Devi sang with her. Old Mrs Bhandari watched with pride, satisfied that the cream of Atmapuri society had arrived to pay their respects.

Simi glowed with Imran standing next to her, handsome in his dark *achkan* coat with his father's jewelled buttons. Imran held her hand firmly throughout the long ceremony and the hours of greeting guests. It was two o'clock in the morning before Simi and Imran escaped to their honeymoon suite to begin their married life together.

Acknowledgements

I thank all the guides and mentors who have helped me along the way, to create, edit, and complete this novel: Ms Liane Aukin, Dr Shomit Mitter, Lord Professor Bhikhu Parekh, and David Standen. I thank Rosemarie Hudson, my publisher, for her faith and patience, and Amit Roy for introducing us.

I am a reader first and foremost, and I thank all the literary giants whose books opened up worlds beyond imaginable worlds for me, from childrens' authors to the great novels of the world, the Sufi and Haiku poets, the writings of visionaries and mystics. The power of the word is immense.

Black Taj is a story of love and hope, for as Sri Aurobindo writes: 'Do not belong to the past dawns, but to the noons of future.'